⟨THE⟩ MARRIAGE CODE

amazon publishing

⟨THE⟩ MARRIAGE CODE

A Novel

BROOKE BURROUGHS

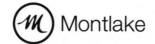 Montlake

Text copyright © 2021 by Brooke Burroughs
All rights reserved.

Published by Montlake, Seattle

www.apub.com

Amazon, the Amazon logo, and Montlake are trademarks of Amazon.com, Inc., or its affiliates.

ISBN-13: 9781542025072
ISBN-10: 1542025079

Cover design and illustration by Micaela Alcaino

Printed in the United States of America

For Prabhu, my real-life Rishi

CHAPTER 1

Emma Delaney woke up, a silk pillowcase under her cheek, a modern midcentury lamp beside the bed, and some kind of framed squiggle on the wall that had been explained to her twice, but she still couldn't remember what it meant. No comfortable, haphazard clutter of books and random clothes she hadn't put away yet or the Goodwill bedside table she'd carried with her since she was an undergrad. And most of all, there was a distinct missing aroma of coffee coming from the kitchen.

She groaned as the memories of last night rushed at her while she reminded herself why she'd stayed the night at her best friend's house. Followed by the question, Why didn't Jordana drink coffee? She needed a good, strong cup to wake her out of the nightmare of the past twelve hours.

A patter of slippered feet came down the hall. "There's my girl! I was just coming to wake you up."

Jordana sat gently on the side of the bed, and Emma wheezed out a weak "Hi."

"How are you feeling?"

Emma was feeling like she wanted to hide under Jordana's five-hundred-thread-count sheets and sink into her silk pillowcase for the rest of the day, if not eternity. She was feeling like she might have made a huge mistake last night by listening to her gut and not her brain, which measured everything out in logic and reason. Because logic and reason said she and Jeremy were perfect together. They both worked in IT, they watched the same movies, they had a weekly rhythm of dinners and coffee and friends that was practically scheduled in their calendars, and they fit in well to each other's long hours and busy work lives.

But when he'd asked her to marry him, she couldn't do it. Even though the fifty people around them were staring at her, making her feel like she was the unfortunate star in the final episode of a TV series. All of them holding their breaths for the big yes.

"I've been better," Emma said, and then her nose detected the faint smell of coffee. Could it be? "But I'm hallucinating a coffee smell, so that is probably a weird sign of something."

"Oh!" Jordana whisked her right hand around. "I brought you this. Double latte, no sugar."

"You're the best. I'm like fifty percent better already." She sat up and cradled the to-go cup like it was a chalice and gave a big smile to her friend. Jordana knew her. She knew that Emma needed a double latte every morning to wake up. She had to wonder if Jeremy did.

In the past two years she and Jeremy had been together, Jordana was always the one to make sure no one was planning a surprise party for Emma's birthday and that there was no public fanfare when she did well at work or had a successful project. But as Jeremy had sunk down on one knee last night with all those people watching, she'd wanted to slide under the table and disappear. He'd been oblivious to the torment inside her and had grinned at the people sitting at the neighboring tables as they gave him knowing smiles. Like it wasn't even about her. Like he had no idea that for her, this type of public spotlight was nothing less than a nightmare.

He doesn't know you. And you don't even love him. That's what Jordana had said last night when Emma had run over to her apartment after Jeremy had abandoned her at the restaurant. And maybe she was right. Maybe love wasn't an easy life of cohabitation. Sunday: walk to get coffee and read the paper day. Friday: happy hour with friends day. Wednesday: midweek sex night.

When she looked at it like that, it was exactly what Jordana had said. She'd organized her and Jeremy's relationship like something for work.

"God, what have I been doing for the past two years?" Emma asked as she took a big sip of her coffee, the warmth flooding her body. "If love isn't that easy feeling that fades into the background and stitches itself into your life, what else is it?"

"You make it sound like a quilt your grandmother gave you. Love should be more like an electric blanket. If you mishandle it, you could get shocked. Or, if you're lucky, it's like being electrocuted." Jordana shook her head at Emma like *she* was the crazy one.

As if on cue, Charlie, Jordana's fiancé, appeared in the doorway. "How's our little Emma doing?"

Jordana smiled at him with a look that beamed all the electricity she'd spoken to Emma about, and Emma had to wonder if she'd ever looked at Jeremy that way. "Aww, she's going to make it through." She joined him at his side, and his hand just naturally slid around her waist like they were two lost puzzle pieces who had found their interlocking mates.

Emma was certain she and Jeremy had never looked as comfortable as these two.

Take their proposal. They just knew. They sort of mutually proposed to one another while they were at IKEA one night. Charlie didn't have an elaborate proposal planned because they'd talked about their future and had decided together that they'd get married. So perfectly them.

"Well, *Dad*, *Mom* got me this delicious latte, since you weirdos are tea drinkers, so I'm going to at least survive the morning." Emma took a big sip and smirked at Charlie. They joked about how he and Jordana were like Emma's parents sometimes because *someone* had to take care of her, but secretly Emma relished the idea, especially as she lay in their spare bedroom with their fancy sheets and coordinating furniture. Although Jordana and Charlie were nothing like Emma's parents. Or at least what she remembered of them. When they'd been alive, and Emma was a little kid, everything in their small house had been mismatched and randomly eclectic, and Emma, maybe subconsciously, had embraced their theme of organized chaos into her own decorating.

"Well, how nice, you taking care of the kiddo," Charlie joked. He looked back at Emma. "Have you heard from Jeremy at all?"

"I texted him again before I went to bed, and he said he's not ready to talk to me." A fact that made Emma feel a little glum. It wasn't her fault that she couldn't say yes to him, and yet he'd treated her like she was a stranger who'd done the unspeakable, like run over his childhood dog. But maybe she'd just run over his heart. She'd tried to explain that she wasn't ready, that she'd been taken off guard, that she was horrified by the public spectacle he'd made of their relationship, but he wouldn't let her get a word out. "Last night, before he left the restaurant, he said he couldn't even look at me."

"I'm sorry, Emma. I'm sure he's just hurt," Charlie said.

Jordana added, "I know he's hurt, but that's not fair to you." She went to sit next to Emma on the bed, and Charlie took his cue that it was girl time and disappeared back into their bedroom with a little wave.

"You two never talked about marriage. You've never gone ring shopping. I don't know why he just surprised you with it. No wonder you were blindsided. Before launching into a big public marriage proposal, you should be pretty damn sure your partner is going to say yes."

Emma sat up straighter, but she wasn't quite ready to get out of bed. "And now I feel like the bad guy. I was so embarrassed last night I wished I had the power to evaporate. Plus, I thought everyone in the restaurant was going to hold a public stoning if I didn't run out of there."

"Poor Emmie." Jordana hugged her. "But maybe it's for the best. It sort of feels like you and Jeremy have run your course."

Maybe they had. She couldn't imagine getting married to him, and he'd already gotten down on one knee. That probably wasn't going to change. It was just unfortunate that it had taken a proposal to find this out.

"I have to get ready for work. Didn't you say you had a meeting to get to?" Jordana said, brushing out the long dark hair Emma had always been envious of.

Emma grabbed her phone. It was seven o'clock. "Shit. Yes."

"Can't you call in sick or something?"

"No, it's my postmortem for my Helix project." Emma scrambled out of bed and grabbed her clothes, which Jordana had meticulously folded on the dresser, apparently while she was asleep. "I need to get all the feedback from the team so I can request budget for phase two of the project. Besides, it will be good to get my mind off Jeremy and what happened. I could use the distraction."

"Okay. Well, good luck! I know how much this project means to you."

She hugged Jordana. "Thanks for taking care of me last night. And say a prayer I don't run into Jeremy when I go grab my laptop."

{ /** *. // }

She clutched the remnants of her latte on the way into the office and hoped that it would power her through her postmortem. At least someone had said they were bringing Top Pot doughnuts: in her opinion, the best in Seattle. She'd go to war with those Krispy Kreme people all day over their cake doughnuts. Besides, why did the name have *K*s where there should have been *C*s? It conjured up too many visions of the E-Z Mart she'd had to shop at as a kid. That had been anything but "easy."

By the time she'd walked in to work, she was feeling better, and it wasn't just the promise of good doughnuts. It was one of those beautiful spring days with only freckles of clouds in the sky, a miracle after two weeks of not seeing the sun. It made her think it must have been a sign, a sign that things were looking up. That if they were changing, maybe they were changing for the better.

She paused in front of the room and checked her face in her phone's camera. No blotchy patches: check. No red eyes: check. Her team needed her. They needed more funding. They needed to find out exactly which updates to make and how to get them done so the five of them could keep working on Helix for the next year. She'd be strong for them. So she took a deep breath, cleared all nonwork thoughts out of her head, and walked in the room.

Her first vision was of that glorious cardboard Top Pot box on the table and of her project team perched around the room chatting. "Hey, guys! Whoever brought these, you are the best!"

She grabbed a chocolate cake doughnut with chocolate frosting out of the box and took a bite. Dessert disguised as breakfast was just what she needed. These were her people, her project, her safe space, her postmortem mecca. One hour of happiness would push away all the feelings of the past twelve hours.

"Okay, let's get this show on the road. Seems like everyone is here."

Stephanie, her project manager, looked at her watch. "Actually, there's one more . . ."

"Really? Who else is coming? Maria?" Emma asked her, trying to think of who outside the project team would want to attend their postmortem.

But Stephanie just did some kind of weird gesturing at her face in response. "Uh, Emma?" Her words were interrupted by the door opening.

A man with a messy flop of wavy hair met her eyes. Emma blinked. His eyes were actually gray. A color that she hadn't known existed in the eye palette. "Hello," she said, more like a question than a statement. And then she realized why Stephanie was gesturing. Emma's hand came up to her lip; she had a giant glob of chocolate frosting on it.

"Hi. Is this the Helix postmortem?" He stepped forward and stuck out his hand to Emma. "I'm Rishi. I got the invite forwarded to me."

The fingers of Emma's right hand were now smeared with chocolate, so she stuck out her left one, and they did the most awkward handshake in history—when his right hand cupped her left one, it was as if she were expecting him to kiss the back of her hand. "Hi, I'm Emma. Nice to meet you?" Apparently every sentence was coming out like a question this morning to this mysterious stranger at her meeting.

She studied his face, trying to conjure up her diagnostic superpowers. His eyes were lit up. His hand was tapping at his side. He looked at the rest of the team and smiled a little, then back at her. He had a nice smile. One of those sort of crooked ones that seemed like it was winking at you.

Evidence of a little nervous excitement, perhaps? Maybe rumor had gotten out about how well Helix had gone from ideation to product in record time, and this guy wanted to hear all about it. Of course, Emma thought her software was amazing. It had been proved to accelerate literacy rates for all their users—from children with challenges like dyslexia to refugees who didn't speak English when they moved to the US. Naturally Emma and the team were proud, but did that mean other people were intrigued? Did Helix have fanboys? That's what she needed. Someone to actually be all aflutter at something she'd helped create, as opposed to acting like she was a terrible person because of one simple word she couldn't say to Jeremy. They had T-shirts left from the launch, right? She'd totally give him one, just to thank him for making her feel better about life.

"So, Rishi, are you interested in the Helix project?" She settled on his face again, trying to place him. Her stomach was doing something a little squirmy—likely calling out *Doughnuts, please!*—and it was making her restless. Her body seemed to be extra alert at this fanboy prospect. Probably latching on to any potential good news she could get today. Anything that wouldn't make her feel like a monster who'd stomped on her boyfriend's heart.

She pushed herself back on the conference table to sit on it, crossing her legs oh so demurely, channeling the kind of woman who didn't smear chocolate all over her face like she was two. "I haven't seen you around the office."

"Oh, I'm here for a few weeks wrapping up a project for our customer-relationship app. I'm based out of Bangalore." He looked at the floor and then back up at her. Those eyes were an assault on the senses when they flashed at someone like that. She leaned back on the table, like she needed some distance from them.

"So, I guess our little project has been making waves over in the Bangalore office? And with the app developers, no less?" She smiled at her team. They should have been proud that all their work was being heralded around the company, globally and cross-functionally. The developers in the app division were their own breed, while the leadership in the desktop division still clung to their laptops as the source of truth. Everything was merging, but so far Helix had proved successful as it was.

The fact that an app-developing stranger had come to learn more must have meant Helix was making waves across the company. And that was what she needed today. To know that all the hours, sweat, frustration, joy, and pain and the extreme amounts of caffeine that her body had absorbed over the past two years had been for something good. For something that would make her parents and grandmother proud. That they could look down on her and see exactly how far she'd come from the tiny town she'd grown up in. That all the hardships her grandmother had struggled through were worth it. Emma was on the path to success. She'd done it for them. She'd done it for herself. And if things with Jeremy were coming to an end, then it would still be okay, because at least she'd have this.

Rishi grinned, the right side of his cheek pulling harder than his left, and looked at her team with his eyebrows raised. Was that nervousness? Around her? Too sweet. She could've hugged this guy. "Oh, um . . . no. Actually, I'd never heard of the project, but they're developing an app for it. I think it—"

"Wait, what?" The *Pomp and Circumstance* playing in her head abruptly halted its fanfare and wheezed out. "I'm sorry, an app for Helix?" She didn't mean for her voice to make that choking sound that mirrored a pubescent fifteen-year-old boy's. But if they were going to be building an app for her project, then she would have been told. Her manager, Maria, would have asked her to help with it.

"Yeah, I think the adoption was lower than expected, or something, so they wanted to see if an app would be better, since the audience worldwide is moving more toward tablets."

"The adoption was *low*?" Emma almost choked on nothing but the air around her. God help her if he'd just mansplained the data she'd been analyzing for months. "We've had great adoption! There are more people using it in the US than any other literacy-software programs."

He shrugged at her. "Maybe outside the US it's not so great. I'm not sure." He reached for the last vanilla cake doughnut with chocolate frosting. "Doughnuts! Don't mind if I do."

Emma hooked her finger in the corner of the box and boomeranged it behind her, out of his reach. No way was he getting one of their Top Pots. She was still fuming over his comment about low adoption. Who was he, anyway?

"Hold on a sec. How would you know about this app that is apparently being developed and not us?" She looked at her team, who all wore varying expressions on the shock-and-awe spectrum.

This traitor-disguised-as-fanboy still had his mouth hanging open, and his eyes studied her with what she thought might be absolute disbelief as he looked from her to the doughnut box. She didn't really care at this point. All she needed was for this morning to be a salvation from the night before, and this Rishi guy was morphing from pretty boy into giant finger poking her very open, and freshly sore, wound. And he was not getting a doughnut.

"Look, I was just asked to join your postmortem so I could learn more about your project." He said the words like they knew each other, like he could explain how her project was being taken away and whisked off into the app world. Well, he didn't know her, or them, or how much this work meant. Like the fact that it was all she had going for her at the moment.

"You mean to *steal* it away from us?" She glanced at her team again in solidarity. They sat silently beside her and Rishi at the table with wide eyes, munching on their breakfast like a herd of cats watching a Ping-Pong match.

"What?" He laughed uncomfortably. "No. I just want to learn about it. Help with the transition so we keep what's valuable and discard what needs changing."

She'd sacrificed and sweated over this project for so long that to just hand it over to another team, to this guy who didn't know her or

Helix, sounded insane. Emma hopped off the table, and Rishi took a step back.

She imagined the team's collective disappointment as they watched the series of intricate literacy games flattened into a tiny screen once Rishi and his team had smooshed it into an app. That all the cool things about it, from the richly detailed story-based characters to the carefully articulated messages they'd developed, would lose what had made them great. How could all that still work when shrunk down to fit a two-by-four-inch screen?

She'd seen what the app developers had done to her email. And what they'd done to the group-collaboration app she relied on to work with her team. Both were barely usable on her phone, while on her laptop they were the software tools she used the most. What had Rishi said? "Discard what needs changing." He was going to throw away the precious hours, days, and months the team had spent on Helix to make it the amazing literacy software that it was today.

She couldn't let them strip it bare like they'd done everything else.

She pulled the box around, set it next to her, and analyzed the contents. She plucked out the one Rishi had reached for.

"You want this doughnut?" she asked, holding it out.

"Well, yeah, I mean . . ."

She took a bite of it when his hand was an inch away from grabbing it. "Now you know what it feels like to have someone steal something from you." When she heard the team's collective gasp beside her, she hoped they knew that she'd done it for them. For Helix.

But then the gasp turned to whispers. A snicker. A barely covered-up groan that seeped into her, hitting what must have been some kind of shame organ. What was she doing, swiping doughnuts from people as retaliation? Clearly yesterday's events were affecting her logic more than she realized.

Rishi raised his eyebrows at her, an annoyed look on his face. She was acting like a child, but damn if she was going to let another guy make her feel bad about herself or her work today. Especially if work was all she had left.

But she wouldn't have anything left if she kept acting this way. She clearly owed him an apology, but at this point she had no idea how to recover from the great doughnut debacle. She grabbed her laptop and scurried to the door. "Meeting's canceled!" she called out over her shoulder.

CHAPTER 2

Emma made a beeline for Maria's office, hoping she wouldn't come off as a demented squirrel as she scurried down the hall. She'd put everything she had into her job. And now they were just going to toss her hard work aside? And not even tell her? That couldn't happen.

But maybe Maria didn't know. Maybe this whole thing was ridiculous, and they weren't moving her beloved project to an app, which would be in a whole different department. Maria had taken Emma with her to lead this project when she took this position; otherwise Emma might not have had the chance. With Helix it felt like she was doing something that mattered, because she was developing software for people who struggled with literacy. And it was cool and fun. If it was being morphed into an app, that couldn't be good news for her job. Or her team.

She knocked as she opened Maria's door and wedged her head in, completely aware that she must look like Jack Nicholson in the poster for *The Shining*, crazy eyes and all. Maria was on a call and gave her a look.

She slunk around the corner, pulled the door tight, and waited outside. What was she doing? More importantly, what had she done? Had she actually eaten Rishi's doughnut? There was no excuse other than her clearly fragile emotional state had taken over. People in their late twenties should have had better coping skills than they did in kindergarten.

Just because she was having a rough patch in her personal life, and her career, apparently, she didn't need to lash out at strangers. Even if they were trying to take away her job. Or maybe it was the company's doing. It probably wasn't even Rishi's fault. She'd committed a fatal flaw at work and had then shot the messenger by eating his doughnut. She needed to track him down and apologize once she regained control of her rational disposition. And send her team an explanatory email to reassure them that she wasn't losing her mind and was just having a personal crisis that she'd allowed to get in the way of logic and reason.

The door opened, and Maria stood there with raised eyebrows. "Hi, Emma, what's up?" She walked back to her desk and rocked side to side on her inflatable ball, the poster child for office ergonomics in action. "To what do I owe the pleasure?"

Maria wasn't just her boss; she was also her friend. Surely if she knew about the app, she would have told Emma.

"I have a question for you. Have you heard about the Helix app?"

Maria took a sip of her coffee oh so casually. Oh thank God, it was all a ruse. Emma's shoulders relaxed, and her face unfroze from its ready-to-freak-out-at-any-moment stoniness.

"How did you hear about that? I was told it was on the hush-hush."

"What? It's for real?" This couldn't be happening. The balloon of hope that had briefly filled her deflated with a wheeze. Maria, her trusted colleague, manager, and friend, had kept this information from her, whereas some stranger from another division had seemed intimately familiar with the project. A groan thumped out of her as her back hit the metal chair.

"It's very new, very in the works, so to speak. Nothing's happened on it yet, but I heard mumblings of it and spoke with the app-division director, Jas, on Thursday. But nothing's been started on it. Nothing's been confirmed. And no one is supposed to know about it," she whispered.

"I just had a guy show up in my postmortem who mentioned it."

"Really?" Maria looked confused.

"Yeah, his name is Rishi, and he's from the Bangalore office." She didn't add that it had ended . . . not well.

Maria squinted and nodded, looking toward the ceiling. "Oh, yeah. Actually I met him on Wednesday. But we didn't talk about the app." She leaned in toward Emma. "And you're not really an app developer. We have to focus on you. Get you ready for what's next."

Emma sighed. "I thought Helix 2.0 was next. But it seems like that's now going to be an app, and all my ideas I was going to pitch for the next phase are useless. I was going to run them by the team today and then talk to you about them. See if we could get some budget for the updates . . ."

"Budget, hmm?" Maria lowered her voice and leaned in farther across her desk. "I don't know if technically I should be telling you what I'm about to tell you. So, if I tell you, you can't say anything."

"Promise! Scout's honor." Emma held up two crossed fingers and then uncrossed them, unsure what that honor looked like. She'd never actually been in Scouts. "But you can't say things like that and then not tell me." She gave Maria a smile of encouragement. At least she was willing to tell her *something*, since apparently *telling Emma important things* was not high among her priorities.

Maybe the company was imploding. Or Maria had some kind of super gossip she wanted to share to make her feel better—she wouldn't be surprised if salacious, drunken antics resulting from the office beer tap had been caught on camera and released on some web TV show called *Nerds Gone Wild*.

Maria looked around her, like she was checking the walls for some forgotten person hiding in the corners who could hear them. "Well, it's not a hundred percent sure yet, but I think they might be shutting down our desktop division." She issued the missive and then rolled back on her ball as the news sank into Emma's psyche.

Helix as she knew it. Gone. Her job as she knew it. Gone. Her future, a black hole of emptiness.

The questions rose up in her throat, accompanied by the acid burn of her coffee and maybe bile. "But what about the existing version of Helix? Like, that's not even going to exist?" She shook her head in disbelief.

"I think the management of it will be absorbed into the rest of the company. You know, until they have the app version."

"Okay . . ." She took a deep breath. "So, what about me? And what about you?" She swallowed, knowing that if the division was closing, then it was probably time to start looking for another job.

"Emma, don't worry about me. And I'm not going to let you go anywhere. You're one of our most valued employees. You've done amazing work on this project."

She hadn't realized she'd been so tense, holding all her muscles tight as she waited for her answer. "Okay, that's good." She let herself relax and trust Maria. Having a job she loved was great and all, but a life of canned vegetables and playing Russian roulette with rent money was not something she could survive alone. Or again. A paycheck was the most important thing you could have. Her upbringing had taught that well.

"But it will likely be in another group. Like, one of our business applications—customer-relationship management, office tools, or maybe back into machine learning. Your old group, maybe? Hmm?" She said this like she was trying to reassure a hospital patient of something joyful even as they were confined to a bed with only a tiny window to see the world through. Like, *Look, it's Jell-O. You love lime. And neon green. Mmm, Jell-O.*

"My old group?" Her previous boss had been super political and had made her work long hours just to look good for the VP. And the work was years behind what she was doing now. There had to be something else. She didn't want to leave the company. She appreciated their dedication to underdogs. How they donated so much of their profits to charity. She didn't want to build applications for salespeople or companies who just wanted to document their customers' every move. The business world needed those things and all, but how could she be proud of that kind of work the way she'd been blissfully happy the past few years with Helix?

"Just an idea." Maria shrugged. "Everything is moving more to app-focused projects, so . . ."

The app! A heavenly soundtrack with a glow beaming down from above started playing. She had spearheaded the whole Helix project, the code, everything. No one cared more about Helix's success. She could lead the app development and still get her updates in, and then she could work on something cool after that. "Maria, what about that app? Why can't I work on that?"

"You're not an app developer."

Such a tiny detail. "But I know enough to lead the project. It will be like a stretch project. The app devs can do the code work. Knowing what I know about Helix, I can make sure we roll this app out flawlessly with my new, improved vision. I'll work my ass off to do it."

"Is that really what you want to do? Instead of moving on and working on something else?"

"Yes, a thousand times yes." Even as she said the words, she realized it might be a bit much. But it was true.

Maria raised her eyebrows at Emma. "Okay, if that's *really* what you want, I'll bring it up to our leadership team next time we meet."

"Okay, thanks, Maria. You're the best!" She knew it must have been hard for her too. They'd celebrated when they'd gotten this project, gotten drunk together when the first testing had failed miserably, yelled at each other in frustration when the bugs were overwhelming. She paused at the door. "Hey, regardless of what happens, I want you to know I still hope we'll work together again. We're a great team."

That got a grin out of her. Emma had been so flustered that she was just noticing how stressed Maria seemed as well. "Thanks, Emma. I'll see what I can do."

CHAPTER 3

Rishi settled into the sofa in the company housing. Thankfully, the other two guys visiting the Seattle office weren't home, and he was able to stretch out without anyone flipping through the never-ending TV channels or being subjected to someone's bad music playing. It was like university all over again.

The days he'd been in Seattle had raced by, back to back, busier than ever, as he'd run to one meeting and then the next. But he loved it. He loved the cool weather outside, so different from what he was used to. The occasional sound of seagulls squawking near the lake by the office. Saturday and Sunday he'd spent just walking around the city, drifting from one neighborhood to the next. He'd drunk coffee, so much coffee. While the cappuccinos were good, they lacked something that was in South Indian coffee. Something he craved with a swelling at the back of his throat.

He'd compensated for his alimentary homesickness by sampling from the vendors at the market downtown, watching the fish get flung over people's heads with expert targeting, and trying a Vietnamese sandwich, Mexican tacos, and American doughnuts. Well, he was pretty sure he was over doughnuts now. The idea of eating one was now soured after his experience with a certain redheaded vexation in the office.

Not that he would have expected much from someone like Emma. Someone oblivious to the trajectory of the company, unable to sacrifice her own ego for the greater good of the business. No one had said anything after their interaction in the conference room. No *Sorry, man* or *Don't take it personally.* Maybe Emma had created a little brainwashed dominion over the project team in the room, who had all given him that *How dare you* look as they'd filed past him after she'd marched out the door.

If he were to move here and take over the app development for Helix, he wondered how many more of these toxic Helix team encounters he'd have to endure. The company was moving toward apps for everything. But he'd seen this behavior before. Some people couldn't let their egos go.

He picked up his laptop and called his parents. It was nine in the morning at home, so he knew they should be finishing breakfast. Dosas, idli, sambar, chutney . . .

He stared at the leftover pizza that awaited him for dinner. At least his mouth could vicariously live through theirs.

The video screen came to life with a way-too-intimate, up-close-and-personal view of his dad's nostrils. "Rishi, can you hear us?" he said too loudly.

"Yes, Appa. I can also see up your nose." He'd shown them how to use video calling on their computer before he'd left. He was pleasantly surprised to see that they'd actually turned it on successfully.

His dad laughed and stepped back to settle on the chair in front of the computer. It was a plastic chair, the kind Rishi had seen on a few people's balconies as he'd walked around Seattle that weekend. His mother then came into the camera's view from the dining area and swooped down too close to the camera. "Hi, Rishi!" She waved.

"Hi, Amma!" He waved back. Rishi looked around at his parents' sitting room area. They hadn't needed to sell anything yet, but everything was starting to look a little faded. A little worse for wear. When he'd gone home a few weeks ago before leaving for Seattle, he'd noticed a rip in the fabric of the chair where his dad sat to watch TV. The buckets they'd used for washing had duct tape on them to seal up the cracks, and even the plastic wrap covering the posters of gods they had perched around the living room had rips in it, dust gathering at the corners and clouding the tops. It was these little things that Rishi noticed. Things that were a constant reminder of what had happened.

"How is the US? Is it cold?" his father asked.

"No, not too cold." Although if his parents were visiting here, they'd be wearing woolen hats, scarves, and jackets everywhere they went. "It's spring, so it's warming up."

"Are you eating?" His mom's brow was lined with worry, the chief concern of mothers everywhere. "Rice? You can find rice and vegetables and dal?"

"Yes, of course." He tried not to laugh. Rice and vegetables and dal were all she knew. His mother rarely ate outside the home. Technically, in their community, you weren't supposed to eat anything cooked by someone outside your caste, and those restaurants were rare. And even when she did eat out at those places, she complained that the food wasn't good enough. They put baking soda in the rice, or too much chili in the rasam. It was easier for her to just cook three super-complex meals a day, taking up eight hours in the day with just cooking. Something Rishi would never understand, since he ate takeout for pretty much every meal. And meat. Oh my God, how he loved a good lamb biryani. Cue the drool. He cleared his throat. "How is everything there?"

His parents looked at each other, and after apparently exchanging some kind of secret message sent over parental ESP, his father said, "We've received an email."

As if email were an ominous thing that bewitched you with some kind of sorcery once opened. "Okay . . . what was in the email?"

His mother looked uncomfortable, her gaze drifting to the other side of the room. His father whispered, "It was from Sudhar."

"Don't say his name in this house!" his mom said, muttering something else under her breath.

Oh, so that was it. "How is he?" Rishi asked, curious but at the same time unsure if that was the right question to be asking.

"They have a baby." His father turned around, like he was worried that Dharini, Rishi's sister, might be nearby, listening. So they were keeping it a secret.

A baby? Was it a girl or a boy? He couldn't ask. His mom would throw up her hands, storm out of the room, and spend the day moping around, thinking about how her life had been thrown upside down by Sudhar and his bad decisions. "Did you reply to him?" Was there a chance in hell that they would?

"No, never!" His mom crossed her arms and stared off in the distance, not looking toward the camera, like she had to put her derision on display even for him.

His father shook his head. "We've been focusing on other things. Actually, there's something we wanted to discuss. Your sister is ready to start looking . . ."

Rishi squinted at the screen, waiting for the sentence to finish. But then it hit him. There was only one reason for his sister to look for anything. It wasn't a house, or a car, or a new job. It was a husband. He leaned against the cushions of the sofa and propped his legs on the coffee table. "Ah, okay . . ." He nodded. What else could he say? His little sister wanted to get married. That meant things. That meant things for *him*. Things he'd been avoiding. Like getting married himself.

They just stared at him from the screen, waiting for his sentence to finish. This was the way his family, maybe most families, approached this conversation. Rishi had to initiate the ask. They had been through enough, and Rishi had to be the good guy, the savior, the one who needed to suck it up and do his familial duty so his sister could get married. So his sister could find a good husband.

"I guess that means you want me to start looking, too, then?" he asked.

His mother nodded. "Yes, you know if you're not married, the boy's parents will ask questions. 'Why is this man not married? What's wrong with him? He's almost thirty.' Also, if you wait any longer, who will you find? Someone your sister's age? Those are the girls who are looking now. That is a big age difference. I don't like it. You need a good girl." His mom wrinkled up her nose and shook her head. As if there were only two types of girls—good and bad. And Rishi knew from experience that the size of the "good" population he'd be interested in rivaled the population of his current company apartment.

He'd heard the speech so many times on the kind of wife he should have. A *good* girl. Good meant someone from their state of Tamil Nadu; someone who was their caste (Brahmin); someone who was from their community (Iyengar); someone who would get along with his family; someone his parents liked; someone Rishi was in love with, or could at least see himself falling in love with. Good was the impossible dream.

Rishi had hoped he'd find someone naturally before marriage was forced down his throat. Like, he'd meet the perfect woman at work, at a bar, or having coffee. But he'd never found someone who fit all the parental criteria. Someone who'd had the qualities his sister's future in-laws would also be looking for. None of that stuff mattered to him as much as it did to his parents or to his sister. Dharini was sweet and as traditional as the rest of his family, while Rishi had pretty much broken every traditional vow he was supposed to have been upholding.

Girlfriends.

Meat eating.

Drinking.

Sex.

Surely there were a few others to add to the list—a list that his family would never know about.

Besides, he knew how much weddings cost, and his parents didn't have that kind of money. At least, not anymore. "Amma, how are you going to finance this wedding?"

She waved at the camera and looked away, getting up from the chair. "Nothing for you to worry about."

No eye contact. Leaving the conversation. His mother clearly didn't know how to answer him, which meant she also was going to get the money in a way that he shouldn't know about, like shady high-interest loans. Or else they didn't know how to get the money yet. "Where is Dharini?"

Dharini wasn't known for early-morning anything, which was part of playing the role of spoiled little sister. But, as if on cue, she came in from around the corner of the adjoining room. "Hi, big brother!"

Sometimes when Rishi saw his sister, it was like looking in a mirror. They had the same nose that sharpened in a downward V shape, the same almond-shaped eyes, the same angular jaw, but softened on Dharini, so her face was rounder and fuller. Today, she wore dangling gold earrings, and kajal rimmed her eyes. It was a change from the weekend he'd gone home just a few weeks ago, when she still looked young and kiddish. Now she was transitioning into work mode. Grown-up mode. Makeup mode. He'd never actually seen her in makeup before.

"I see you're finally waking up before noon." Rishi tried to clear his head of the realization that his sister was no longer a baby. He was still used to her being his kid sister, eight years younger, whom he'd always had to coo over and spoil.

Now she was squinting one eye at him and giving him a teasingly annoyed look. "Yes, well, I am a working girl now."

Rishi choked on a laugh that threatened to come up. He decided not to tell her what else that could mean as his parents bickered their way into the kitchen and Dharini settled in front of the computer, small steel cup in hand.

"Dharini, are you drinking coffee?"

She rolled her eyes. "Uh, yeah. Like you said, I can't get up at noon. I had to start drinking coffee."

"Where is my little sister who hates coffee and only drinks Bournvita? What have you done with her, and how did you get inside her body?" Was he that out of touch with her, or was this a recent change? The last time he'd seen her, he could have sworn she'd been guzzling glasses of her favorite vitamin-rich chocolaty drink with milk. A kid drink. Not coffee.

"Oh, ha ha. Very funny. And I still drink Bournvita." She picked up a glass of that awful concoction and gestured toward the computer.

"So, tell me about your job," he said. "How is it? Are you liking it?"

She shrugged. "You know, it's fine."

Rishi nodded. Dharini, like him, had essentially been forced onto a career path determined by their parents. They had three choices from which to decide their future: IT, economics, or medicine. "Those are the only jobs where you can make a decent living these days," his father had said when Rishi finished up secondary school. Deciding what you wanted to do for the rest of your life didn't seem to matter when you were sixteen anyway. Rishi didn't like the sight of blood, and economics sounded boring, so he was stuck with IT.

His sister, however, had been nurturing the fantasy of a career as a veterinarian for years. She hand-fed the peacocks that had infiltrated their neighborhood when the nearby forest was mowed down to build a housing development. She'd nursed a baby parrot that had been abandoned by its parents to adulthood. She lugged any leftover food at the end of the day to the street corner and fed it to the stray dogs that roamed the neighborhood. When they'd started following Dharini home, and their dad had forbidden her feeding them, she'd still found a way to sneak out on her bicycle and ride, crisscrossing through the neighborhood and dropping off food in random places.

So when she'd had to make the call about her career and what she would study, it was a much more dramatic conversation. She'd settled on IT because, like Rishi, it seemed the lesser of the three evils. If she became a doctor (for humans), she would be in school forever. And to get a good job as a doctor, she'd have to go abroad to study, and that was something she, unlike Rishi, had never wanted to do.

Rishi sighed. "Some of your university friends are also at your office, though, correct?"

"Yes, that is the nice thing." She looked off to the side. "Except now Priya is getting engaged, so . . . we'll see."

We'll see meant *We'll see if she comes back to the office*, or at least *How long will it take before she gets pregnant and starts a family and then maybe won't come back?*

"Is that why Amma and Appa said you are starting to look for someone?"

She shrugged. "My job is boring, so why not have something else to do too?"

Wow. Rishi was pretty sure his head had just completely retracted into his neck. So this was his sister—ready to embark on the new adventure of getting married and having a family, just because her job was boring. This was what happened when the optimistic, dreamy-eyed wannabe veterinarian was denied her career. *Thanks, Mom and Dad.* Not that he would have said any of that to her. She'd cry, tell him he was wrong and that she loved her parents. And it would all be true. She did love them and probably didn't regret her job. It was just that she hadn't had much of a choice, and they wanted the best for her. Besides, he was pretty sure his mother was grandchild hungry and would be pressuring Dharini, since her guilt trips hadn't worked on Rishi.

"You don't think it's too soon?" Rishi asked.

"No, why? I've thought about it. I think it's time." She looked down at the table, lashes bashfully sweeping her cheeks. "They've told you to get married, too, then, is it? You don't want to, and now they're asking you to?" She looked up, a gleam of worry in her eye.

"I just think it's funny," Rishi said, shaking his head but still smiling. "You start drinking coffee and getting up at eight in the morning, and now it's time to get married? I guess that's the order of the universe."

"Maybe . . . my universe, yes." She lifted the steel cup of coffee to her lips again and tilted her head back to get the last of it and then sighed. "I have to go to my boring office job now. Don't want them to wonder where I am."

"Bye, little sister! Tell Amma and Appa I said bye." Rishi tried to hide his own momentary melancholy as he waved to the laptop and watched her picture disappear. He closed the computer and took a deep breath. So it was true. His baby sis was ready to get married.

A few years ago, he had been ready to take the marriage plunge with his girlfriend, Sapna. He hadn't cared what his family would say because he was in love. And then she'd gone and left him to get married to someone her family thought was appropriate. She'd insisted they would have never spoken to her again if she'd married a South Indian guy. Like the north and south of the country were so different that they couldn't understand each other? An irritation burned in his chest as he still remembered the day she'd told him she was getting married—to someone who wasn't him. He could hear her superficial words even now. *Your mom doesn't even speak Hindi. I mean, how will they even talk to each other?* Like that was the most important factor in spending their lives together. He should have known better.

It was like a wound that still ached when he thought about getting married. But the time had finally come. He didn't want to let his sister down, because his mom was right, after all. How would it look if the older brother wasn't married already? Well, the one who was still acknowledged by the family. Especially with everything else that had happened.

But . . .

His manager, Jas, had essentially promised him a promotion to lead the new Helix app development. The week before he'd left Bangalore, they'd sat down for lunch, and Jas, in a hushed voice, had told him, "I've got something for you." Like he was going to do a drug deal instead of have a work conversation.

"What's that?" Rishi asked.

Jas looked around, like people could actually hear them talking over the cacophony of plates and trays and hundreds of voices in the open-air cafeteria. "There's a new app, and I think this opportunity will be the promotion we've been talking about. They're working on it in the Seattle office, and I think you'd be perfect."

Everyone wanted to go to the Seattle office. If you got a chance, you went. Because of the exposure, the money, the opportunities. Corporate headquarters was the dream if you wanted to be successful. It was a no-brainer, and the chances were few and far between. "I'm definitely interested. Tell me more."

Jas briefed him on the current desktop version and how they were planning on turning it into an app next year. "I'm putting your name in the hat, and I don't think anyone else would come close to being qualified. I've already talked to leadership about getting you the visa, and with your track record, I can practically guarantee it's yours. We've talked about how the next step for you is leading a team, and I think this might be it. My suggestion is to just pack everything you'd need for at least a year."

For at least a year in Seattle he could live life on his own terms and still give Dharini the giant wedding she deserved. He could send twice as much money back home as he could with what he earned in Bangalore. With that money, they would adorn Dharini with the requisite amount of gold so she'd shimmer like a queen. Give silk saris to everyone in the family. Have a wedding hall and food that would feed a thousand guests. And not need those shady high-interest loans that landed people in more debt, which was the last thing his parents needed right now.

And the gold crown plopped on top was an excuse to postpone his own marriage. His parents couldn't refuse him if he was financing his sister's wedding.

His new job could help all of that become a reality.

Because after everything they'd been through, if they wanted Dharini to find a good husband, one she deserved, then they wouldn't be able to afford a wedding on their own.

The Helix app meant salvation for him and his family. Now that his current project was nearing an end, that promotion couldn't have come fast enough.

CHAPTER 4

Can you come to my office for a quick chat when you get in?

Emma was picking up her morning latte extra early when she got the message from Maria. She was sleeping in the spare room she and Jeremy had previously used as an office, and she'd tried to leave the apartment before he emerged from the bedroom. Maria would be shocked to see she was in so early.

But this message was ambiguous. A "quick chat" could mean that in fifteen minutes' time she would be applying to one of the other ten thousand IT companies in Seattle, or she'd be celebrating her upcoming birth to a baby Helix that would soon sprout up on smartphones and tablets everywhere. If she ended up leading the app project, she would make sure they didn't swipe away any of the features she and the team had painstakingly implemented.

When she got to her office, she peeked through the inch of glass that wasn't frosted to try to gauge Maria's mood. Maria's face always crumpled up like a paper ball when she had to give someone bad news. And, if she was happy, she flipped through cat memes, laughing at even the cheesiest ones. Whoever stuck their cat's head through a piece of toast in their spare time had "cheery Maria" in mind.

But now, her face was stone. Serious. Blank. Lasered in on her monitor. Anything could happen. A promotion. A dismissal. The apocalypse. She knocked on the door. "Come in."

Diagnosis: not the worst she'd ever sounded.

"Hey, Maria." But she wasn't going to get too excited just yet.

"Guess what? I have some news for you. I talked to the leadership team . . . and, are you ready for this?" She did a little drumroll on her desk. "I convinced them you should oversee the app development. They had another candidate in mind, but when I explained how Helix was your brainchild, and how 'passionate' you were," she said with air quotes, which made Emma wonder if she should feel the teeniest bit insulted, "it was almost unanimous that you should lead the team."

"Seriously?" She hadn't realized how doubtful she was that they'd give her the job until now. Her face was stretching from the smile that was taking over.

"Well, you may not be an app developer, but you're closer to the project than anyone, you've synthesized all the data from the team, and you already have a vision for the next iteration. I don't think a little ol' app coding is going to stop you. Plus, it will be more like a leadership role, which will be a good experience for you. We've been talking about getting you promoted to the next level."

A flock of pastel cartoon birds twittered around Maria's head. Sunlight streamed in from invisible windows. Rainbows and unicorns gamboled about on her desk. Was this actually happening?

"This is just so amazing. Thank you for supporting me and believing in me and trusting that I will help lead this app to excellence!" She resisted jumping over the desk to hug her. This faith in Emma was exactly what she needed. Not just for her career but also as a sign that at least someone could still remember that she wasn't a bad person whose boyfriend still wouldn't talk to her. "You will not regret this, Maria."

"Well, hold on. I'm not done." Maria's smile shifted. Emma sensed something ominous, like the rainbows and birds over Maria's head were being blown westward by rain and sizzling cracks of lightning. "In the meeting I had with leadership, they announced that not only are they indeed closing down our division, but they're also making some budget cuts this upcoming year. They want to work on it somewhere that's cheaper than Seattle, so the project will be moved over to the India office."

"Bangalore? Okay, so I have to work nights then or something?" Emma tried to envision this new schedule. She'd been waiting for the inevitable, dreadful breakup conversation she knew she and Jeremy were heading for, but maybe this way she could finish out their lease in her beloved apartment. She and Jeremy could coexist in silence for months with minimal awkwardness, because they'd have completely different schedules. Mimosas would be swapped for happy hour. Done. Totally fine with it.

"Not exactly. How do you feel about the idea of moving to India for a while?"

Move to India? Emma, conjuring up what she knew of India, tried to picture what that would be like: stories she'd heard from coworkers about traffic a hundred times worse than Seattle's or festivals that involved throwing colored powder on strangers until the streets became stained like a giant rainbow.

Then that was overtaken by visions of her weekly takeout dancing in her head. Butter chicken. Garlic naan. Saag paneer. Chana masala. How did she feel? She felt hungry about it. India seemed like a place populated by her kind of people (programmers) and her kind of food (she ordered from India Palace twice a week for a reason). They collaborated with teams in the Bangalore office all the time, but she'd never had a chance to visit. Leaving Seattle. Her friends. Her team. Jeremy. Jordana. Hmmm.

"I wasn't sure, because of Jeremy, if you'd still be interested," Maria added.

"How long is it for?"

"Probably a year."

A year was nothing. Helix had taken two years to develop, and that seemed like it had just started yesterday. She'd be gone and back just like that. Besides, when would she ever get another offer to move continents and live in another country?

"How are you feeling?" Maria asked.

She wondered if she could be excited and terrified all at once. She had never been out of the country before and could count on her hands the number of times she'd been on a plane. It wasn't like she could afford vacations when she was younger. And for the past five years, she'd been working off her loans, paying rent, and supporting her financially disastrous and decadent restaurant habit.

Maybe this opportunity and Jeremy's proposal were a sign from the universe that this was the chance for Emma to get her life back on track.

"I'm in."

"Really? I mean, you don't want to talk to Jeremy first?"

"I'll tell him tonight." Or, if he still wouldn't talk to her, she'd send him an email and leave a note on the microwave with some India Palace takeout.

Maria rolled on her ball, arms crossed, her eyes asking a question that Emma wasn't ready to answer. "Okay, then. I'm going to send you an email with all the details, and I'll tell Jas and connect you two. He'll be your new manager."

Jas was Maria's counterpart in the Bangalore office. Emma had talked to him on calls before, and he didn't check the boxes for sociopath, VP suck-up, or egomaniac, which made Emma breathe a sigh of relief.

"Don't worry, though: I won't let you stay," Maria called as Emma tried not to skip toward the door.

"Ha! You can't get rid of me that easily." She could adjust for a year without her favorite coffee shop across the street, her beloved rainy Seattle weather, and her mint-green Linus bicycle, but for all her excitement, there was no way she'd stay.

"Also, remember Rishi, who you said was at your postmortem?" Maria asked, and she froze. Rishi. The guy she owed an apology to and hadn't run into again. Who also knew about Helix and the app. This couldn't be good.

She spun around on her heel. "Yes?" she croaked out.

"He's on Jas's team, and since he's here for a while, you should talk to him. He's supposed to be amazing at app dev, like the *best*, and I know you like working with the best. Since this one might be a stretch project for you, I would say to start talking to him now, figure out the lay of the land, and make sure he'll be on your project team. I think you'll need his support, and he's in a great position to help you ramp up. Plus he's here right now, so it's the perfect opportunity to start building that connection."

Rishi, who she needed to be on *her* project team now, and against whom she'd committed unabashed doughnut robbery. That shaggy-haired, gray-eyed guy she'd first met with chocolate smeared on her chin. To whom she still owed an apology, and who was going to laugh in her face when she not only asked for his help on the project but also said that she needed him on her team.

"Roger that." She couldn't let Maria see how terrified she was, after she'd stuck out her neck for Emma. She made a little salute and headed for the solace of her desk, groaning. Her temper and overall acrimony over Jeremy were launching with a nosedive into enemy territory something that should have been happy, happy news.

She slid down in her chair and read through the email that had just come in. Furnished corporate housing in Bangalore . . . one-year relocation . . . new position starting in two weeks. She was going to have to act fast to apologize to Rishi, scrape together some kind of explanation for her behavior, convince him they would work great together, and then give Jeremy the news.

Two weeks?

Could she get Rishi not to hate her in that time?

And Jeremy . . . what would he say?

But if the same happened to him—a chance to work overseas, to save his position in a company that he was passionate about—she would be happy for him. And maybe that was exactly Jeremy's point: that Emma could actually be happy for him if he left. Whereas he was ready to spend the rest of his life with her.

A sigh blew out of her, ruffling the papers on her desk. It was clear she needed to be the one to initiate the painful breakup conversation. She hadn't been able to talk about all the craziness that had happened this week since she'd been downgraded to resident ghost in their apartment. She pulled out her phone and texted him.

> Jeremy, I really need to talk to you tonight. Can you please make some time for me?

She could do this. Just pack up her life and move halfway across the world in two weeks. She basically just needed to take some clothes. Everything else would wait in Seattle for her. It would all be just fine.

Her phone buzzed.

> Okay. Maybe I have been a little harsh. We can talk.

> Great thanks. I'll grab us a pizza. My treat :)

If Jeremy thought he'd been harsh, how would he feel about her news that she'd just accepted a job on another continent?

But she couldn't focus on that now. Now she had to think about the other complicated relationship, which wasn't even a relationship. Rishi.

CHAPTER 5

Emma scanned the rows of cubes, looking for Rishi, and thought about her strategy. If she was going to somehow simultaneously apologize, convince him that she would be a great team lead, and persuade him that she didn't have an impulse-control disorder, she needed an approach. She needed to befriend him. She'd made a mistake and now needed to repair it. She needed to approach this situation like she would her software, like a bug fix.

Rishi was a developer, and developers were the same the world over. Logical, practical, and quietly egotistical, if they were good at their jobs, which he was famed to be. She needed to appease his logical side by explaining the situation and then flatter him. That had usually worked in the past, and hopefully it would work on Rishi.

She just needed to find him.

His hair would be easiest to spot. From what she remembered, it was like an overgrown shag carpet. Black as night, longish and wavy, like he needed a haircut but refused to get one. She saw numerous heads peeping over the partitions in the cube farm in front of her, but not his. As she rounded the corner by the kitchen, who was standing in front of the coffee machine but the very owner of the hair she was looking for?

He was taller than she'd remembered. When she examined his profile, she saw that his nose deepened into almost a hook, his gaze intent on the coffee machine, his lips pushed down into a frown. That frown she remembered very well. Along with his eyes as they'd stared those impenetrable cement blocks into her.

"What's wrong?" she asked.

He looked up from the machine, eyes narrowed. "What do *you* want?"

She held up her hands. "Look, I come in peace. I just wanted to apologize." She tried to smile sweetly at him. The same sweet smile she'd given Maria a half dozen times after she'd dropped the f-bomb on her code at a volume that echoed across the freakishly efficient office acoustics.

He peered at her suspiciously and then set a cup under the machine and pressed the start button.

"I'm really sorry about my behavior toward you." Even as she said the words, her eyes fluttered and closed. She still couldn't believe she had actually committed an act of Top Pot barbarity. She took a deep breath. "I was not myself that day, and I'd been going through a lot, and I want to apologize. I'm also sending my team a note to explain the same and to state that in no way did you deserve the retribution I bestowed upon you." There it was: logical, straightforward, and practical.

"Hmmm." Rishi nodded at her, like he was thinking this over. She just needed to now initiate Operation Flattery, and they'd be set. "Actually, it's interesting, the word choice you used. *Retribution*. Retribution seems to imply that I did something to provoke this behavior you're apologizing for."

Emma tried not to roll her eyes. When had developers gotten all selective about word choice? "Well, I was upset, obviously, and I just meant that my harsh words and doughnut hoarding were a result of that emotion that had been drawn out."

"Drawn out . . ." Once the coffee had finished percolating, he took a drink and made a face that looked like he'd just taken a sip of toxic waste instead. "It's like you're still not taking ownership of it."

"Well, to be fair, I did feel a bit surprised by the update you'd delivered to us. I think we all were."

"But not everyone verbally attacked me because I'd simply attended the meeting I'd been forwarded and had a little more information than you did."

"No, but they probably were, in their minds." The words just popped out of Emma's mouth, and her hand flew up to cover her lips, like that could hide the evidence. But it was too late. Her racing heart, rather than her brain, was controlling the rapid fire of her words. Rishi's eyes got big, like full-on revolving drums agitating the concrete within. "Wait," she said, trying to salvage what she could. This was not what she was supposed to be doing. "That's not true. They're much more civilized and mature than that."

"So you're saying you're uncivilized."

She could see the look in his eye: so pleased with himself at getting her to say this. Because there was no way out of admitting that she was an uncivilized heathen who couldn't deal with confrontation or surprise proposals, or maybe human relationships at all. Her hands formed fists at her sides, and she tried to crack a smile. "Yes, I suppose in that meeting, in that moment, I was."

"Would you put that in writing? To your team? And maybe you could cc me?"

"What?" She'd admitted it to him. That should have been enough. She opened her mouth to tell him exactly what he could do with that email but then closed her eyes. Took a breath. Reset. She'd gotten so caught up in defending herself that she'd forgotten to get this guy on her side to help her. This was never going to work. She might as well have kissed her little Helix app goodbye right then.

"Okay, sure. I will email that and cc you." She held out her hand to shake, and he looked at it, thinking for a minute, and then took it in a firm shake.

Then he poured the coffee down the drain.

"Did you make that coffee as a defense mechanism?" she had to ask. "I can't drink this sludge."

Emma laughed. A weak laugh, but still. "That's because it's shitty coffee." An idea lit her up. Perfect segue into the rest of what they needed to discuss. "Hey, do you have like thirty minutes? I wanted to talk to you about something, and there's a great coffee shop across the street. My treat. I definitely owe you."

He seemed to examine her face for what felt like a full minute before pulling out his phone and looking at his calendar. "I don't have any meetings. What's this about? I need to know if I need to inform my defense squad."

"Do you *have* a defense squad?" She looked back at the cubes.

"It wouldn't be a defense squad if you knew what to look for."

Briefly, she wondered if he had some kind of underground app-developer mafia at his beck and call. Maybe ninja warriors who would pop up out of the shadows when one of their own kind was threatened. "I promise you don't need them. I mean, what can happen over coffee?"

CHAPTER 6

Emma was acting like they were old friends walking down the sidewalk as she pointed out the coffee shops they passed, which were way too numerous for one block. "That's a chain over there. That place sucks." The only reason he was letting her give him this coffee tour was because yes, she did owe him, and also one coffee was five more dollars he could save up for the Dharini wedding fund.

He texted his coworker Ramesh as they walked.

If I'm not back in an hour, send out a search party to the coffee shops on the street. Look for a red haired she-demon and you'll find me.

Emma stopped in the middle of the sidewalk, and he almost tripped as he tried to keep from running into her. "But this place. This!" she exclaimed, holding up her arms at a coffee shop on the corner. "This is just the best. They roast their beans in the back, and sometimes it smells a little funky, but the coffee is awesome."

Speaking of funky, Emma's actions were at the top of the list.

His phone buzzed. Ramesh. **Dude, that's awesome!** Followed by a string of dirty vegetable emojis.

Rishi resisted explaining over text that "she-demon" in this case was most definitely *not* a good thing. He opened the door and took a whiff. "I know this smell. My grandmother used to roast her own beans."

Emma stopped, her eyes wide, like he'd just told her that Krishna himself had roasted the beans, danced a little jig, and blessed their family's coffee consumption. "Like at home?" she said, her voice almost a whisper.

"Yeah." Was that unheard of in the US?

"Oh my God. That must be some amazing coffee."

"Yeah, it was pretty good. We mix the coffee with chicory at home, though—"

"And adulterate the most sacred beverage of programmers everywhere? Blasphemy!" Emma said.

Rishi couldn't tell if she was joking.

The inside of the coffee shop was plain. White walls. Light wood tables. Metal chairs. It looked like any of the countless coffee shops he'd visited in Seattle. But it recalled childhood summers in his grandmother's home with that sour, smoky smell hanging in the air.

"What would you like?" Emma asked.

The menu on the wall behind the baristas listed out the regulars, plus a few of those unnecessarily ostentatious drinks Rishi didn't bother trying to decode. As if microbubbles were really a thing. "Just a cappuccino."

Emma ordered, and they waited for their coffees at a bar set against the wall.

"So how much longer are you in Seattle for?"

Rishi studied her, wondering how to answer. Her eyes were too bright, a glittering green color. He'd noticed the one purple curl that hung down her face in the middle of all that red hair, but he was getting a much more intimate view of it now. It reminded him of the syphilis bacteria he'd once seen through a microscope in college. Magnified, it had been a bright-purple curlicue, almost cute for something so diabolical. He could make a similar comparison to her. But the smell of her hair was more like oranges and honey than whatever syphilis smelled like.

He cleared his throat. "Oh, a few more weeks, and then we'll see."

"You're going back to Bangalore, then?"

The barista called out Emma's name, and she hopped up to get their coffees. Rishi watched her walk to the counter, still confused about why this was happening and what she wanted from him. She couldn't have just had a change of heart and wanted to buy him a coffee to apologize. Could she?

"Okay, cheers." She held up her cup to his.

He'd heard that the whole "cheers" thing was invented by a king who wanted to make sure his drink wasn't poisoned and so heartily hit his goblet against his dinner guests'. In the same spirit, Rishi clunked his mug hard against hers, although the foam was too resilient to splash anything out. She gave him a look and muttered "Geez" under her breath. He dumped in some sugar and took a sip. It was good. Rich and strong. Not South Indian coffee, but a thousand times better than what had emerged from the office machine, which looked like it had an oil slick swimming on top of it.

"I can tell you like it. Way better than the office coffee, right?"

He nodded. He'd give her that. Anything was better than the office coffee.

"So what's the Bangalore office like?" she asked.

"It's like the Seattle office but not as big. Looks pretty much the same on the inside. Is that what you mean?" Discussing the architecture of the office could not possibly be why she'd invited him out.

"Yeah, I was just wondering about it. I've worked on a few projects virtually with some people there."

"It's pretty much the same, but we have free breakfast and lunch. And the coffee is better."

"Don't tell me." Emma held up her palms. "Someone hand roasts the beans."

Rishi tried not to laugh. "What? No." He didn't add that his grandmother did that mostly because she didn't trust anyone from outside their caste to touch anything she put in her mouth. Super old school.

She actually looked a little disappointed. "Oh. Well, anyway, I wanted to talk to you about something. I heard you're the best of the best app developers at TechLogic."

Now Rishi was on full preservation mode and cycling up his mental ammunition. An apology, an offering of coffee, and now flattery? "That's interesting you say that." He would not give in to her honeyed words. The phrase "sickly sweet" existed for a reason.

"Come on!" She elbowed him in the side, which made him tip over and almost take the barstool with him. "You don't have to be shy with me."

"I'm not being shy—I'm being cautious."

"Rishi, I told you I was sorry. I wasn't myself that day."

He sighed and turned to face her. She did look a little hurt, but was that the real Emma, or was the doughnut-hoarding bully the real one? "Okay, but that day and this day are all the Emma I know."

"That's fair." She pressed her lips together and nodded. "But the good news is that we'll get to know each other a lot more. And I promise you: you'll see that I'm not that other person."

"What do you mean, we'll get to know each other more? A *lot* more?"

"Well, you know the Helix app, of course . . ."

Rishi opened his mouth to say, *Yes, that's my project,* but she overran him before he could get a word out.

"I'm going to be leading the team!" She smiled big, like it was his birthday and she'd just given him a giant piece of shit wrapped up in a lovely box and topped with a sparkly bow.

"What?" he asked, but it came out like a roar.

"The app-dev team for Helix. And I want you to be my star dev!"

A sick feeling twisted its way up his sternum. "What are you talking about?"

She smiled brightly at him. "Well, I'm going to move to Bangalore for a year to lead the Helix app project, and I heard you're a rock star app dev, and I'm hoping we can make it awesome. Together."

Rishi blinked at her, at a loss for words and wondering if the clouds in his mind would clear. Was she crazy? Was this some trick? That project was his to run. Not hers.

"Are you already dedicated to another project? I really want you to be on my team. I can talk to Jas . . ."

He coughed a little to clear his throat. "You know Jas?" His apparently traitorous boss.

"Sort of. We've been on the same conference calls before. This all happened suddenly."

"What do you mean, *suddenly*?" Rishi tried to stay calm, tried to maintain a cool watery surface while sharks and killer whales fought it out in his chest. His sister had told him how vicious those killer whales could be. They lived in the waters near Seattle, didn't they? Maybe Emma was one of their spawn.

"My manager, Maria, just assigned me the new project, and I'm moving to Bangalore in a few weeks to launch it." She took a sip of her coffee, like this was just ordinary news.

"Bangalore? Whoa, wait." He had to pause. Did he just travel through one of those alternate-reality wormholes? "I think you're confused. Jas is *my* boss. I'm leading this project. And in Seattle." Was his world just flipping on his head? None of this could be real.

Her eyes narrowed, and the woman from the other day emerged. "Me, confused? Uh, no."

"That project is mine. That's been the plan all along. I'm here to finish my current project, and then I'm transitioning to lead the Helix app development. That's why I came to your meeting. There must be some misunderstanding." He had to talk to Jas. He chugged the coffee, which burned his throat as it coasted down. But that burn was nothing to the one he'd just received from Emma. Or Jas. Or the company. Wherever this story of hers had originated. He just hoped it was wrong wrong wrong.

"I don't understand how it can be your project if they gave me the assignment yesterday. I've got a letter and everything . . ."

Rishi jerked his gaze to hers. When he'd mentioned the app in her meeting, she hadn't even known about it. Did she run to her boss and tell her she wanted it, stealing it from under his nose and ruining his plans? His family's chance at happiness? Fuck! He wanted to scream.

"I have to go." He slammed his cup down and raced back to the office without turning around, ignoring Emma calling out to him. He had to talk to Jas and figure out what the hell was going on.

{ /** *. // }

The small conference room was the closest thing Rishi could find to a sanctuary in the zoo-like cubicle layout of the office. He needed to be alone, he needed a phone, and he needed to stay hidden away from Emma. He looked up Jas on the company's instant messenger. Did he care that it was ten at night in India? No, not really. At this point, any faith he had in his manager or the company or his job had been corrupted like some badly written code, and Rishi was more than ready to hit delete.

Jas wasn't online, so he punched his cell number into the office phone. He answered immediately, as Rishi expected he would at seeing the corporate number pop up.

"Hello? Jas here."

Rishi was ready to let his voice pounce out of his mouth and attack, but he needed to stay calm. After all, maybe Emma was crazy. "Hey, Jas, it's Rishi."

"Rishi, hi. How are you?" But Jas's voice wasn't cheerful, happy to talk. He sounded guarded, cautious, like he knew some bad news was on the horizon. He hadn't asked why Rishi was calling him so late at night. All of this said something. Any sliver of hope he'd been harboring vanished.

Best to just come right out with it. "I'm not great. I just had someone ask me to be on the team *she* is leading for the Helix app. As in, the project I was supposed to lead. And that the team was in Bangalore, not Seattle. And *you* were her manager."

Silence.

"Jas?"

"Rishi . . ." Jas's voice was a little creaky. Rishi could imagine him hesitating, trying to select the right words to soften the blow.

He just closed his eyes and readied himself.

"I don't know what to say. It just happened. The higher-ups made the decision, and I just found out. I wasn't on the call when the decision was made. I emailed them to reverse the decision, but they said that they'd already told the new project lead . . ."

"Emma Delaney?" Rishi asked, hoping Jas would say *No, that's not it.*

"Yes, Emma. And moving the project to India—that was new. That decision came from the CEO."

How could this be? Everything that he'd pegged his hopes on for himself, for his family, just gone in a second. With just a few words.

"I'm sorry, Rishi. But you can still work on the project. She's just overseeing it since she worked on the desktop version. And you can come home!"

How could he work with her on this? How could he look at Emma every day and work side by side with her—clarification, *under* her. She wasn't even in his division, she wasn't an app expert, and she had clearly run to her manager to beg for the job as soon as he'd opened his mouth about it.

And there was the money he would've made had he been able to stay in Seattle. This whole situation was thwarting the plan he'd so carefully crafted in his head to help his family. How could he give up on that so easily? How could he disappoint his sister and not try to postpone his own fate of finally having to settle down?

"Jas, do you think there's any way I could still find something at corp? Do you know of any other project where they need someone?" His only hope to stay in the US was by transferring within the company. He had to at least know if it was a possibility.

Jas sighed. "I don't know, Rishi. You know it's near impossible to just get transferred."

"What about some other promotion? Maybe some other app project I could apply to that's not this one." There had to be some way he could still get a raise.

"We just had those three big launches in the app space. I don't think we have any new projects coming up—just updates and stuff. But I'll let you know if I hear anything."

"Okay." Rishi groaned, picturing the next year of his life. Constantly looking over his shoulder, making sure she wasn't trying to swipe something else from him. Trying to escape her eyes, which he was convinced doubled as laser pointers that could blind him if he stared too long into their depths. "Jas, I just can't work under her. I can't do it."

Jas sighed, causing it to sound like he was on his phone in a wind tunnel. "Rishi . . . I tried to fix it, but it was too late. I'm sorry that I wasn't there to defend our plans."

"Just to clarify, I don't blame *you*. But I just can't do this. We don't get along."

"What are you talking about? You get along with everyone. And I've met Emma. She seems nice, and she has a great reputation."

Rishi grunted at that. Maybe he'd only had two interactions with her, but he'd seen how childish she could be, regardless of how smart she was. He couldn't work under someone like that.

"We need you on this project, Rishi. I know you're upset, but please hang in there. We don't want to lose you. *I* don't want to lose you. I'll try to figure out how to make it up to you, okay? I promise I'll try my best."

Rishi had no idea what else to say. "I'll let you go; I know it's like your bedtime."

Jas gave a half-hearted laugh because they both knew neither one of them slept until after midnight. As soon as Rishi hung up the phone, he pulled up the internal company job portal and searched. Jas was right: there was nothing. With the Helix app, the argument had been strong. But everyone wanted to move to the US. Everyone wanted a bigger salary. But not everyone needed it like he did.

Not everyone had an older brother whose by-product of marriage had depleted his family of their money. When Sudhar had made the decision to marry a girl from another state, another region, and another caste, Rishi had thought it was harmless. His parents, of course, hadn't agreed with this at all; he was the only person from his family who had actually attended the wedding. But with everything that happened afterward, that wedding had not only left a stain on his family that couldn't be rubbed out but also forced him down a carefully paved path that he couldn't stray from.

He ran his hands through his hair and just plunked his forehead on the table a few times. This was a disaster on many levels. If he couldn't find another job, he'd have to slog under Emma for a year. And moving back to India would mean he couldn't provide his family with the extra money they needed. He also wouldn't have a solid reason to postpone his marriage any longer.

Maybe he should just embrace Dharini's philosophy about it. Work was clearly going to suck for the next year. He could devote his energy to a new relationship.

He couldn't rely on the marriage profiles his parents sent over, though. They were in a desperate state to find someone for him. Even before he'd left, the matches that his parents had found and that filled his inbox weren't the kind of life partners he was looking for. Now that Dharini was ready to settle down, they were going to be turning over rocks in the futile hope that a unicorn was hiding under one.

It was once again time to take matters into his own hands. Now that he was out of alternatives, it was time to find a bride. He had to get ahead of his parents' ineffectual searches and find a wife who interested him before they spent too much time and heartache trying to find "the one." He owed that to his family. They'd been disappointed too much already.

This time, he hoped the results of his handcrafted algorithm would surface the kind of girl he could fall in love with.

CHAPTER 7

Jeremy was on a conference call in their bedroom. Correction, *his* bedroom. The pizza had just arrived and was warming in the oven, and Emma wasn't even sure if she could eat it. The smell of garlic and onions and truffle—all the beauty that was the smell of a good pizza—had filled the house, but all she could focus on was how her stomach was revolting. Staging a full-on protest, nay, an assault, on her desire for delicious pizza. Her stomach had conspired with her nervous energy against her taste buds and now demanded only wine to ease its suffering.

She had a feeling that after her conversation with Rishi and the impending one with Jeremy, it was going to be Emma: 0; all the other people she'd let down around her: 2.

Rishi was upset when he'd left the coffee shop. By the time she'd followed him out the door, he was jogging down the block toward the office, and she couldn't catch him. She wanted to know what had happened. Maria hadn't said anything about Rishi initially having the job—just that he was on Jas's team. Initially, she'd dismissed Rishi as another guy trying to take over her work, but something about his eyes seemed sad. Maybe tomorrow she could talk to him again. She had to fight each battle one at a time.

She'd been texting Jordana about her decision to go. The messages had started with Noooooooooooo! Don't leave me!

Just think about my new Instagram food stories, Emma wrote.

Food and stories without me : (

Or the fact that you could have a free place to stay if you visit.

You know my vacation time is shit.

Textiles, then? I can bring you fabric and rugs and pillows and all that stuff you like.

Emma could play dirty and appeal to interior designer Jordana instead of best friend Jordana.

Ok, if you are abandoning me regardless, I will take textiles as a consolation prize.

Well, it may not matter because there is a 60% probability that Jeremy may kill and/or maim me after I drop this bomb on him. Wish me luck.

Emma looked at the pizza she couldn't imagine eating, even though this new place had rave reviews and an even more amazing list of ingredients. She hadn't spoken to Jeremy in a week, and somehow this morning she thought a really good pizza would be the perfect peace offering. Something to soften the blow as she casually mentioned she was leaving the country for a year and that it would be a good idea to go their separate ways. In retrospect, an absolutely ridiculous idea.

Jeremy's footsteps tapped on the hardwood, and the creaking floorboards let her know his call was done. He would come into the kitchen, lured by pizza smells, and what? Now that the moment was here, she didn't even know where to start, and this wine was not helping at all. She just felt more confused, like she was enveloped in a fog of weird indecision and doubt.

You need more than luck. Duct tape, thread and needle, a balaclava and some post it notes.

As Emma tried to decode the weird list Jordana had just texted, a thud on the counter made her jump. Jeremy had set his laptop down and was taking his earbuds out. "Pizza smells good."

She nodded and held the bottle toward him. "Want some wine?"

He bent down to look at it, his eyes examining the bottle through his horn-rimmed glasses. "If you saved some for me." He laughed. An actual laugh. Somehow, she'd forgotten he had a dimple in his right cheek. It was like in the past week of avoidance tactics, she couldn't even remember the details about his appearance.

"I was thirsty. But I saved the best half for you." She smiled, feeling the awkwardness of a difficult conversation stifling the words that needed to come out. This morning she'd been confident that it was time to break up. But now? He'd laughed *and* made a joke. Not telltale signs of someone who was still so angry at her he couldn't even look at her.

She took the pizza out and cut a few pieces before setting them onto a plate, which she placed on the dining table. They never sat at the dining table. He gave her a look as he sat down that said the same thing.

"Jeremy, I have something I want to talk to you about."

He took a bite and nodded. "Yeah, this has been going on for too long. I should have been able to talk about it earlier, but . . . I don't know . . ."

"I get it, and I'm sorry I wasn't able to make a commitment to you like that. But it just took me by surprise."

He nodded, looking at the space in front of him. "I should have discussed it with you first. I just didn't realize we were on such different wavelengths."

When she looked into his face, there was affection there. She cared about him, but it was also kind of how she felt about Jordana. Not about a lover, a boyfriend, a fiancé. Maybe the ease of their relationship was just another piece that had been conveniently slotted into her life so her work could be the centerpiece. Now, doubt about whether she had ever loved him filled her mind. It very possibly had always just been affection and admiration.

She sighed as she tried to figure out the words she needed to say. "It's okay. This week, while we've been on a hiatus, a lot has happened at work, which is what I wanted to talk about." How could she say this so he'd understand? "Basically, there have been budget cuts, and my Helix project, as I know it, is ending."

"Really? That sucks. What about your job?"

"Well, I have an opportunity to take a job as a project lead for a year, and I'd be switching to app development, so I'm going to take it." Deep breath. "But it's in India."

"Wait, what?" Jeremy's neck jutted forward, the veins popping in a way she hadn't known was possible. He looked at her like she was a stranger. A stranger who'd done something unspeakable.

"It's the only way for me to continue working on my project. Otherwise, I don't know what I'd do. Plus, it's a great opportunity for me."

"You could get a job at my company, I'm sure. You don't have to leave the country—there are a thousand tech companies here."

"Jeremy, I think this might have come at a good time." Emma shrank into her chair more than she had at his proposal, because she had to get the words out. In her heart, she knew it was over, and this was never easy. "Don't you think we're in very different places in our lives?"

His hand ran through his hair, leaving it looking crazy, though not as crazy as his eyes, which were bulging wildly. "I thought you wanted to try. I thought my proposal just came too soon, and you wanted to tell me you still loved me tonight, that you were sorry."

"Sorry?" He wanted an apology? Maybe nothing had changed.

"Yeah! You totally embarrassed me."

"I was also embarrassed. I had no idea you were going to propose. And in public. Those people looked at me like I was a terrible person."

"I mean, if you loved me, I don't think it would have been a problem. You've always been obsessed with your work. Even this is about your work. You care more about your job than you do me."

He was right. Something inside of her sagged at hearing this. The fear of losing the sacred recognition as a star employee had always plagued her. Since junior high, she'd had this deep-seated desire to be needed, wanted, recognized. When she was a child, her grandmother had told her that Emma had a gift and that she needed to use it. To not make the same mistakes she had. Too many times she'd heard how her grandmother had never had the opportunity to make anything of herself and that, when her husband had died, she'd had nothing.

And now Emma also had nothing. Without her grandmother, parents, or any family she was close to, all she had to rely on was her work.

It was so easy with Jeremy because he allowed it, but she shouldn't have let things go this far. Now they'd found themselves here, at this juncture, with her leaving and him still upset with her.

She reached for his hand, unable to keep the tears at bay any longer. "Jeremy . . . I am sorry. I should have realized earlier on that we looked at things so differently." She grappled with words, anything that would help him understand. "Like two incongruent angles. Similar but just not the same in terms of how we feel."

"What? Don't compare us to a triangle." He grimaced, slid his hand away, and stood up fast, knocking his chair over, and then awkwardly picked it back up. He met her eyes after a dramatic pause, and she almost had to look away. "I thought we were a circle." And with that, he grabbed the pizza box and wine and stormed out of the room.

She stood up to chase after him and then heard the door slam upstairs, and she sat back down. Her head collapsed on the table, her eyes following the path Jeremy had taken out of the room. And probably out of her life.

She texted Jordana as she wiped at her eyes. Well, that didn't go as planned. What was that list about?

So you could put him back together after you break his heart, and escape in the middle of the night.

Way too soon.

She slammed her phone down, only to hear it buzz again. She tilted it up on its side to peek at whatever snarky follow-up Jordana had written. But it wasn't Jordana; it was Maria.

Why did Jas just call me and say that there are issues with you and Rishi working together?

She sat up straight. What was this? Had Rishi contacted Jas before she'd even talked to her new boss?
I don't know. I bought him a coffee and tried to talk to him. Then he ran out and I haven't seen him since. It was sort of the truth.

Patch up whatever is going on. Otherwise, there might be a rationale for the new job arrangement to change. Just wanted to give you a heads-up.

Emma swallowed. She would fix this. She had to fix this. Her livelihood depended on this new job, a relocation, and a chance to save Helix.

Will do! Don't worry.

The worrying was going to all be on her. Tomorrow she would have to salvage whatever she'd done to Rishi and reverse her scoreboard so it was at least even.

CHAPTER 8

It was late, the cubes were mostly empty, and the hum from the army of vacuums that flooded the building each evening had already started down the hall. Emma had been busy, talking to Jas and trying to prove she wasn't a terrible person. She could only imagine what Rishi had said.

She hadn't confirmed whether or not Rishi had fabricated his "that's my team" declaration, but from Jas's behavior on the call, she could assume that maybe there was a bit of truth to it. The company was competitive, and yes, she felt bad, but it wasn't as if she'd asked to work on the project knowing she'd be taking it from him. She'd lost her fair share of opportunities, too, but none of those projects had she owned so completely as Helix. She was emotionally invested, but why did Rishi care so much?

They might have their differences, but this app needed to be the best it could be, and she needed Rishi on board. Maria had made that clear.

She walked toward the kitchen, and that's when she spotted him in the conference room at the end of the hall. Through the strip of clear glass that stretched at table height across the wall, he huddled over his laptop, staring at the projector screen. She'd recognize that messy head of hair anywhere, that nose like an eagle's beak. She strode toward him and, when she was ten feet away, rethought her strategy. She needed the right words to ask him to get on board. And explain how it had all happened. Surely he'd understand. It wasn't as if she was like some of her other spotlight-hungry colleagues, who weren't above stealing code or bad-mouthing others to get ahead.

His eyebrows were hunkered over those cement eyes of his. He was intent on something. His pupils scanned the screen, studying, analyzing. This was work, hard work from the look of it. But this late, hidden inside a corner conference room, it seemed like he was doing something secretive. Maybe even sneaky.

He did seem a bit odd. Crashing his mug into hers. Insisting she cc him on her team-apology email. A little crazy and a bit overly confident—his posture was something out of a chiropractic manual, very un-coder-like. In an odd way, he reminded her of that guy on the bus next to her last week who'd petted the air beside him and kept saying, "This is my dog, Precious. Do you want to pet her?" He'd seemed very confident as well.

Maybe Rishi was better looking and didn't smell like hay and stale beer with a slight tinge of urine. He smelled more like a dark forest with something spicy in the air. But if he truly thought she'd stolen his job and was out for revenge, he could be the kind of guy who would try to sabotage her.

This could be Robert all over again. Robert, who'd stolen her code and presented it to their VP as his own. But she'd been naive back when she'd first started at TechLogic, and she was excited about her first job. Her new career with coworkers who seemed as enthusiastic as she was about working for an innovative startup. Robert had been so kind in offering to review her code, since she was new. And then, in a day's time, he'd robbed Emma of all the recognition she'd deserved as he presented her work as his own. When she'd brought this up to her manager at the time, he'd said he believed her, but at this point it was just Robert's word versus hers. And now that asshole Robert was a freaking director already.

She should be over it now—it was years ago—but it wasn't fair. Even with Maria's coaching and counsel, rage still burned in Emma's stomach when she thought about it. Just because she had been young and trusting and didn't try to weave a web of bro talk, she couldn't claim credit for her work.

Well, she wasn't that trusting anymore; Robert had seen to that. She didn't know what was going on in that conference room. But she would find out.

No one else was around. Emma slunk over to the door of the room and slipped down to the floor. She crouched behind the wooden partition that rose two and a half feet from the ground. This way she could peer through the glass strip along the wall, and Rishi wouldn't notice her. If she had to get down on her knees and crawl like a baby to see the code projected on the screen, she'd do it. She had to be certain that this new job was not going to be swiped from her, like everything else in her life.

{ /** *. // }

The dim light and quiet hum of the projector screen provided the perfect setting for what Rishi had to do. The white noise was almost meditative, like the chanting of a priest in a temple. And this was Rishi's temple, his place to sit quietly with his thoughts, remember his purpose, and achieve clarity. One hundred percent fixated on his goal. He had to be.

It was almost 8:00 p.m., and he'd waited for most of his colleagues to trickle out of the office, which meant no one would interrupt him. He'd devoted a good portion of his twenties to the study of programming. Enough that he should have been able to create a simple web crawl. Just simple code that, with some precise word selection, would venture out into the depths of the internet and surface up the key contenders for the perfect wife—and, like magic, his ideal woman would appear.

The ideal woman for him *and* ideal woman for his parents, as if this unicorn lady existed. If she did, then he had to find her soon. His parents had already thrust one profile into his inbox that afternoon, and it had been one day since he'd told them he was coming back to Bangalore rather than staying in the US.

His two closest friends, John and Aamir, had already married and were now siloed off in their new married world, where they were getting to know their wives better in newly married bliss. Now they were busy, too busy for him, hanging out with their new wives' friends and their husbands. Rishi's evenings at the pub had been dramatically reduced now that they had other priorities. He'd been resigned to a pity case. John's wife had said more than once, with a "poor you" look, that she'd be on the lookout for him.

If only she knew what a task that was.

He pulled up the code he'd written the first time a few years ago, after Sapna had broken up with him and he'd told his parents he was ready. The candidates his parents had provided proved just how unready he was to settle down with anyone. No one could compare to her. But the code he'd written had failed beyond anything he could have imagined. Maybe he'd been too busy with work back then to devote enough time to its development. Web crawls weren't his strength, and it wasn't like he could ask his colleagues for help. He scanned it over. What had gone wrong?

He'd put in all the parameters he'd wanted in a wife, then for his parents some key words they would insist on. After all, this was a "marriage of families," as people liked to say. The caste, the community, his state—all the things his parents needed for the girl to be considered a good match. So how had the star contender ended up being a Russian prostitute living in Lucknow?

He shook his head.

Maybe he needed to wipe it clean and start over. Or give up on the whole idea altogether. Or just settle for the next woman his parents threw across his path and hope things would work out. Rely on fate to make his decision for him. After all, it seemed to be working for Sapna.

A bump on the glass wall behind him made him jump. He whipped around just as a pair of green eyes ducked away through a clear strip of glass between the frosted panes. "Emma?" The last person he expected to see, especially on the floor. And the last person he wanted to witness his vain attempt at a web crawl.

Her muffled voice came through the glass, but he couldn't understand what she was saying. "What?"

She straightened up, shuffled around the corner, and opened the door. "I dropped a pen, and then I couldn't find it. It just kept rolling . . . ," she said, shrugging a little too much, like a bad actor who'd hit the coffee a little hard that day.

He looked toward the hall. It couldn't have been that challenging to find a pen in an empty hall. How they'd picked *her* to lead the project over him was truly a mystery. "Okay . . ."

"What are you up to?" Emma's eyes jerked toward the screen.

Rishi wheeled around in his chair and unplugged the projector from his laptop as fast as possible. Emma had a reputation as an expert web crawl programmer. Yet another reason he was pissed she was leading the app. The last thing he needed her to see was his motley code, a sad copy/paste bypass toward marital bliss.

She glanced up at the now-blank-and-blinking projector screen, then back at him, studying him. Suspicion all over her face. If she saw the code on-screen, broken parts and all, he'd never hear the end of it. Even if he wasn't working on her team, she'd walk past him in the Bangalore office with her entourage, whispering, "Nice code," then snicker with her new team about how he'd run out of the coffee shop, so convinced the Helix app project was his. Or leave sticky notes on his monitor with little hearts drawn on them, striking him in the chest with their bared insults. *#BASIC4EVER.* He'd seen her embryonic maturity in action.

"Oh, you know . . . just trying to finish up some stuff." He tried to stay calm, but he was pretty sure his breath was rapid fire, in and out, out, out.

She hummed like she didn't believe him.

He looked at her hands. She didn't even have a pen. "Where's this elusive pen that kept rolling away from you?"

Instead of answering him, she leaned against the wall. "I wanted to resume our conversation, if you have a minute?" she asked, peering at his laptop screen.

Rishi leaned on the table, blocking her view. "Okay, but can we do it tomorrow morning? Maybe we can go to that coffee shop again?" He was sitting at an awkward angle, tilted toward her, propped up by his elbow. He just had to act totally normal. Like this wasn't cramping his back, and he sat like this all the time. He was hiding nothing. Nothing at all. "I'm kind of busy at the moment."

"It'll just take a few minutes." She sat down in a wheeled chair and pushed off the ground, propelling toward him. But when she reached him, one of the chair's wheels broke off. Emma tried to stand up, likely to keep from falling, but tripped and stumbled onto Rishi. She landed with one hand on the table and one hand on his chair arm and then hovered over him. And then she didn't move.

Well, this was awkward.

Heat radiated off her chest and into his, their breath mingling in the five inches between their faces. His heart thudded deep and low in his chest. The tension of her body so close to his made him feel strung on a rope, unable to move, vibrating with the fear of looking in her eyes for too long. Or what would happen if he moved. If he rolled back two inches, she'd fall on the floor. She would probably face-plant in his lap. He swallowed hard.

Her voice was just over a whisper. "Rishi, are you already doing something with the Helix app?"

"What?" He shook his head to empty his mind of whatever was happening to it, muddled by her proximity. Of all the things she was going to say, that was the last one he'd expected. "No, and can you move? You're stepping on my toe."

She adjusted her foot. "Oh, sorry." She pushed herself up to standing. "But Rishi, there is code on your screen, and you're obviously trying to hide it from me."

"This is. Not. The. App." Rishi seized his laptop and moved it out from in front of her, snapping it shut.

"Then why are you being so sneaky about it?"

A mix of frustration, anger, and humiliation rifled through his chest. "It's none of your business." He packed up his laptop.

She slumped on the conference table and sighed, muttering to herself, "What's wrong with me?"

He'd like to know what was wrong with her too.

Her foot was propped up on the broken chair, and she sank over her thighs, cradling her head in her hands. "You're right. It didn't look like Helix. It looked like a web crawl."

"Yeah. Exactly."

"Look, Rishi, I'm sorry if I interjected into another project or something; I'm just on edge. I've had a really rough week, and in the past I had a bad experience with someone taking credit for my work, and I'm a little paranoid about it. I know you're upset with me, and that's just where my mind went."

He spun around, his backpack almost flailing off his shoulder. With a deep breath that made his shoulders settle as he stared into the air in front of him, he spoke. "You know, you're not the only one who's having a rough week. You're not the only person in this office. And I'm betting no one barged in on you while you were working in a conference room after hours and interrupted something important you were doing. And that person was the last person you wanted to see because she *stole your job* from you."

"I'm really sorry. Seriously, I didn't know the job was supposed to be yours. I am not the kind of person who would do that. I swear." She peeked up through her hands.

She did look sorry. In fact, he was afraid she might cry. "Excuse me." He swept past her and toward the door before things could get any more awkward.

"Wait, I'll go with you. Can I make it up to you? Buy you a drink?" Emma hopped up and followed him out the door. No one was in the office at this point, except for the custodian vacuuming the carpet in a faraway, dimly lit corner while monitors flashed reminders that they were still on.

She took a turn behind him, and relief slowed his pace. She'd given up. He said a thank-you to whoever was listening. But after he reached the elevator, he heard a clattering noise in the distance, and she emerged around the corner of the hall, run-walking toward him while stuffing her laptop in her bag.

"Drink? Please?" she said breathlessly. "I want to prove to you that we can work together."

The elevator dinged its arrival. She was giving him this half-sorry, half-crazy expression as they stepped into the elevator together. This could be his future. Every day, watching as she held his job in her hands and struggled to do in a week what he could do in an hour. Since she wasn't an app coder, she'd just delegate to them all, bossing them around like a tiny coder dictator. The pressure built up in his chest like a balloon.

"Emma, I can't work on your team, and I think you understand why."

"But you can. I promise! Is this because of the doughnut thing at my postmortem? I told you I was sorry. I cc'd you on my email to the team, didn't I? Just like I promised." She was begging now, her voice two octaves higher than it had been when she was oh so confidently informing him about "her new team in Bangalore."

The door dinged on the ground floor, and he walked toward the dusk settling around the street outside the glass walls. He couldn't reach the street fast enough. The give of the door handle at his palm was one more step away from this office. One more step away from how everything had gone so wrong. The evening air brushed past his face with the promise of rain. The busy sounds of the dinner crowd on the sidewalk and the guitar strumming from inside a bar were a welcome escape from the white noise of his laptop as he struggled with his code. Behind him, though, Emma's voice pleaded. "Come on, Rishi, please? I really want you to work on my team."

My team. A silent scream inside him burst that bubble of pressure that was making him hold his breath in and just stew in his own frustration. He whipped around on the sidewalk, and she abruptly stopped right behind him, a few nose distances away. "Why on earth would I work on your team? A team that was supposed to be mine."

She pointed at the bar that was next to the office building. "Let's go here. They make a great manhattan. I'll tell you why."

Something in him softened with the word *manhattan*. Like it wasn't just his favorite cocktail but some magical beverage from a faraway land that could ease his worries. At least if she stole his job, he could get a drink out of her, right?

"I can tell you want one. Come on." She hooked her hand around his elbow as she dragged him toward the door.

He wasn't quite ready for her to lead him anywhere, but he would allow her to buy things for him, including overpriced cocktails he normally wouldn't splurge for on his own. He shook his arm out of her reach. "I'm coming. But I'm telling you now that it will require no less than two drinks."

CHAPTER 9

"I know we've had our differences, but I really want you to be my lead developer," Emma said, now that they were settled at the bar, twin martini glasses in front of them, ice crystals on the top like a skating rink falling apart in the summer.

He sipped on his cocktail. She was at least correct about this. A very delicious drink. But there were a lot of missing pieces in the story of how this job was once Rishi's and had somehow slipped and fallen into Emma's lap.

"Well, let's take a step back. Jas promised me that promotion when I was done with my current project. I was supposed to move to Seattle and lead the app. Now it's in Bangalore. Now you have it. Now none of it makes sense."

"I asked Maria about the app, and she told me that our desktop division was likely to shut down and that they were moving the project to Bangalore to save money. I'm leading it because my job will not exist now, and I've already led a successful implementation of the desktop version of the software."

So his little dream of staying in the US and making more money to send his family was nonexistent anyway. Great. And Emma was losing her job. That softened the blow for him a little. "Jas didn't tell me it was a cost-saving measure" was all he replied. And down went the first half of his manhattan.

"And I didn't know you were already supposed to lead the project." Her hand clutched onto his forearm. The heat from her palm was momentary before she picked it up and set it back on her lap. "I just told Maria I didn't want to let Helix go without a fight. I'd really like you to work on the team. Everyone says you're the best. And I have a vision of what we could do next with it. I want the app to be awesome, and I feel like you would be essential to making that happen."

"I don't know . . ." He tried to envision the next year or so. Trying to stay here and find something had proved impossible. But making "awesome" happen for Emma would also be impossible.

"What would you do instead?" she asked, taking a dainty sip that seemed very uncharacteristic of her. For some reason he'd expected her to swallow the whole glass in one gulp and then wipe her mouth off on her sleeve.

"That remains to be decided."

Her shoulders rolled forward, and she sulked at her glass. "I know you told Jas you didn't want to work with me."

"Well . . . can you blame me?"

She looked up at him from where her hand was tucked into the chaotic vines of red hair. "You should ask everyone else I work with. They'll say I'm lovely."

"Really? *Lovely?* Is that a verbatim description you've fed to them?"

She raised her eyebrows at him and said deadpan, "Yes, my team is actually a horde of robots who I've programmed to only say kind and generous things when my name is mentioned."

"I don't know what goes on in the corporate office." He laughed.

"Seriously, if you have doubts, you should ask them. Ask Maria, ask whoever. But I promise if you work on my team, I will make you look amazing, shine, sparkle, whatever you want. I just want to make this app great."

Her eyes had this genuine gleam to them when she talked about Helix. Very different from the look she'd had at the coffee shop the other day. She did seem to care about the work. "But why do you care so much about it? I'm sure you could get another job."

Emma's smile slipped away as her gaze shifted to the rows of bottles behind the bar. "Working on something that really helps people has been so fulfilling. It's not like it's just another money-generating engine for the company. Plus, my grandmother had to quit school to work on her father's farm and never had the reading skills she wanted. I guess Helix was like my tribute to her." She blew out a breath and looked back at him. "Sorry, that got a little heavy, huh?" She huffed out a laugh.

Rishi didn't know what to say. He was blindsided, and he knew it might take some time to redraw the picture of Emma in his mind. Before, she was a career-driven job thief. And now she was a thoughtful coder who built software in memory of her grandmother?

He said, "If you want to do something else, we can take good care of it, since you don't really work on apps."

"Well, you're an app specialist who works on web crawls. So why not the other way around?"

He choked on a laugh. "No, I'm not."

"Well, that's what it looked like you were working on in the office."

"Oh, I just was playing around with a search engine I made." He ordered drink number two from the bartender.

"You made your own search engine? Why?" she asked.

He laughed. *Because you took my job* was what he wanted to say, but did that even matter now, since they would have moved it back to India anyway? There was no way she could understand his situation. "You wouldn't understand."

"Why? Try me. If we're going to be working together for the next year, we should get to know one another."

He turned to look at her. "I haven't agreed to work on the app." His chest was tight, like the air inside him wanted to escape his lungs and be swallowed at the same time.

"Yet," she said.

He tried not to roll his eyes. "Well, since I'm going back to India now, it's time for me to get married, and I have to find a wife. Hence, the web crawl."

Maybe he shouldn't have said that. He felt her body stiffen beside him. Now things were even more awkward, and she still wouldn't get it. She was an American and likely didn't know a damn thing about his culture and traditions. "See, I told you you wouldn't understand."

Emma turned to him and scanned him up and down, apparently analyzing what kind of loser had to write his own code to find a wife. Her mouth opened like she was going to say something; then, with a slight shake of her head, she looked back down at her drink.

She cleared her throat. "No, I get it. But aren't there like a thousand sites out there to help with that already?"

"Yes. But none of them are good enough. I haven't found the right girl, and it's . . . time. My parents keep sending me all the wrong girls. It's just a search I made." He sighed. In a million years, this was not a conversation he'd ever imagined having with her.

"Has it worked then? Did you find someone? Maybe I could use it." She half groaned, half laughed.

"Well, as you said, I'm more of an app dev than a web crawl specialist, so I'm sure it's not anything like you would design."

Her eyes lit up. "Can I see it? My last job had me creating web crawls to mine data for the company. Just saying—I'm not that shabby." She elbowed him in the side with a big smile.

"I don't know . . ." He couldn't let her into this window of his personal life. They were strangers who just worked at the same company and who apparently both held their grandmothers in high esteem.

"Please!" she whined like a toddler. Her lack of maturity could also make her a bit more endearing than threatening. "It sounds fun."

Although maybe because they were strangers and not friends, it didn't matter. He could use someone with expertise to look at it. So now, at least if she took his job, he could get a drink *and* her opinion on whether his code would work.

"Fine."

He pulled out his laptop while she literally clapped beside him. Okay, so really like a toddler now. Like a toddler tipsy on bourbon, excited while watching the fireworks on Diwali. He laughed. How was this all happening?

He set it on the table, and Emma moved closer so they were both looking at the screen. Too close. He could feel heat coming off her again, though maybe it was just the fizzling of her childlike excitement. He could smell a faint mix of citrus and flowers and bourbon, which, to his surprise, was not an altogether unpleasant scent. He shifted a little to the right to create some distance.

"Hmm . . . there are quite a few things going on here." She scrolled through the code. "I mean, you used Python, so that's good. But the techniques are outdated. In the past few years, there have been a lot of advances in machine learning, and there are some new open-source bots that can help with a search like this."

"Okay . . . ," he said, trying to figure out what she was getting at. "So, it's basically useless?" Great. No surprise there. His little bourbon high was fading fast. He closed his laptop and shoved it in his bag. He was going to have to wade through the sea of matches his parents found for eternity. It was a full-time job—checking his email, reviewing every profile, and trying to find out if any of the girls could be "the one." And, when someone did seem promising, he'd look her up on social media to find out that she was one of those people who reposted obviously fake stories about celebrities with a stupid caption, like they were best friends. Or checked in everywhere she went, like she was begging someone to come stalk her. Or had an unhealthy cat-video obsession.

Maybe he was choosy, but he felt he had a right to be—this was his life.

Her hand stopped his as he pulled at the zipper on his bag. "Wait. I have an idea."

Panic buzzed inside him. He was sure her idea was that he quit the company for being an incompetent coder who couldn't draft a simple algorithm. Why had he let her see his code? This wasn't going to end well. "What could that be?"

"If you join the team, I'll write you a marriage code."

"What?" Rishi shook his head.

"Please? I need your skills to make this app successful. And it seems like you could use my help with your code." Emma crossed her arms and leaned back. "I could have it up and running for you fast. Like, super fast."

If she could see an issue with his flawed code in less than a minute, she could probably have the results in a few weeks. His parents could stop sending him less-than-ideal matches. The pestering calls from his mother would evaporate. "The one" had to be out there. He could find her. Was it possible?

But there was more at stake here. He'd have to be on *her* team, watching her try to lead a group of app developers who should be on *his* team.

"I don't know . . ." His stomach tangled.

"Did you try your search already?" she asked.

"Maybe." Rishi's phone buzzed, and he picked it up, trying to avoid further probing into his current algorithm. As if on cue, it was another email from his dad with another woman's profile attached to it. It was like all his spare time in Seattle was spent eating takeout and analyzing these potential matches. A hobby that was apparently going to continue for a while once he moved back home. Unless he accepted Emma's offer.

"And did it come up with any results?"

"Not really." Rishi wouldn't admit what it had found.

"Hmm. I'm not really sure what you have to lose then."

What did he have to lose? His dignity. His pride. His sense of self-worth. Any respect that his coworkers had for him if they found out. A groan stretched out of him as he rubbed at his temples with his palms.

"Rishi, you're thinking about this too much. I would love to help you with your search, and I really need you on the team. This app and my job are really important to me. I'll do anything it takes to make it work for you."

"Anything?" He immediately pictured Emma tied up. He'd set a cup of coffee and a box of doughnuts in front of her, just out of reach. With each doughnut, he'd hold it so close to her that her face would twitch with longing so that she'd think she'd get a bite. And just as her lips parted, her tongue rearing back, mouth opening wide, he'd jerk it away and stuff it all in his mouth.

She rolled her eyes. "I mean, you know, within reason. I was thinking along the lines of going above and beyond helping you with your web crawl and making you look awesome for leadership."

He slumped over on the bar, his head pretty much cradled by his hands. Finding a wife would at least mean one less worry for his family. One less worry for him. He peeked through his fingers at Emma, who was giving him this hopeful, starry-eyed look as she sipped her drink. She seemed fairly innocent at the moment. And then, in Bangalore, he at least had friends and a real defense squad if anything went awry.

He looked at his phone and clicked the attachment from his dad. He opened it, wondering if fate would grace him with an answer. Maybe it was a woman he could envision as his wife, or something in her CV that spoke to him about a potential future together. But he didn't feel anything as he looked at the photo. There was no bright spark of hope in the document either.

And he didn't really have another job out there that was calling to him.

So what other choice did he have?

He took a deep breath. "Okay, I'll do it."

"Really?" she asked, excitement evident in her voice. "We'll have a great team. Make a great app. Everything! You won't regret this."

He wasn't sure about all of that. But maybe, just maybe, it was possible that with her help, he'd finally find his future wife.

CHAPTER 10

Emma looked up toward the SeaTac airport, set against the sky, gray on gray, and tried to picture what her new Bangalore sky was going to look like. Funny how as her current life was crumbling around her, the shock of moving halfway across the world hadn't really hit until she was ready to get on the plane. Going to a land where she knew nothing and no one. Except Rishi.

"Any last words from Jeremy?" Jordana asked as she pulled into the departures lane.

"No, he had some fire drill at work the other day, and we've been communicating only over email. I've been trying to avoid him, honestly." Emma sighed. This was code for hiding in her office (now bedroom) with her white noise machine on whenever he came home.

"Well, it can't *not* be weird with the two of you living like that. You're like a brother and sister who are fighting but who have seen each other naked. Awkward," she sang.

Emma laughed weakly and looked out the window. They'd had a few more conversations after the night of the disastrous pizza, but it was mostly Jeremy confirming her decision and working out the logistics of getting a roommate to replace her half of the rent. She didn't feel any better than she had a few weeks ago about how they were leaving things, but she kept telling herself it was for the best.

"You'd take this job, right? I'm doing the right thing?" Emma asked.

"Look, it's going to be awesome. You are going to have an amazing time. What's not to like? Instagram every meal for me, okay?" They pulled to the curb, and Jordana got Emma's suitcase out of the trunk of her car, while Emma checked her carry-on for the seventh time, ensuring her laptop, phone, and passport were all inside. She dragged her body out of the car and wrapped her arms around Jordana.

"I'm going to miss you!"

"Maybe this will be a good, new start for you. Look at it like that." Jordana moved a piece of hair out of Emma's face as it blew in the wind. "Plus, there are like half a billion men there, and you'll forget all about Jeremy."

"Ha."

Uneasiness ballooned in her belly over being suspended in a hulk of metal over the earth for so long. But she'd looked up the statistics. It was safer than a car. She knew better than anyone how safe cars were. They said their goodbyes, and she walked into the airport.

After security, she took a deep breath and pulled out her phone. She'd harassed Rishi throughout the week to take the same flight as her and had even coaxed out his number.

She messaged him. Hi, at the airport. Where are you?

Getting coffee across from the gate.

He'd responded, so it couldn't be that bad. Besides, he'd be so busy finding a wife and making wedding arrangements that he'd forget all about their little ongoing altercation of the past few weeks. Judging by the way his clothes seemed tailored to his body, hugging at his thighs and snug on his biceps, with shoes that looked like they were hand-crafted in Italy, he clearly didn't have concerns with financial stability like she did. He probably hired a personal shopper, like Maria did.

Why a guy as objectively handsome as Rishi needed to create his own search engine to find a wife was beyond her.

"Hi," she said, clunking her backpack onto the table.

"Hey." That was it. He looked back down at his laptop.

"What's your seat?" Emma asked. Maybe she could distract herself by working on his code. What better plans did they have during the next two flights to get to India?

Rishi pulled out his phone. "34B."

"Hmm. I'm five rows away. I'll see if I can find someone to trade me seats."

Rishi's fingers froze on his keyboard, and he looked up at her. "You will?"

"Yeah, we'll work on your code during the flight. Why waste time, right? A promise is a promise."

{ /** *. // }

Rishi boarded the plane, recognizing that distinct smell of disinfectant and trapped air that he particularly hated. The last trip over, he'd sat by the bathroom, and he couldn't get the smell off his clothes even after disembarking. It clung to him like a coating made of synthetic summer days and fresh bacteria, and he'd ended up changing shirts in the airport bathroom.

Now he had something else he couldn't get off—a coat of Emma clinging to him.

She was going to force him to talk about work and the code, when he just wanted some peace before he had to face the reality that he was back home again and all his plans had failed. But he knew, somewhere deep down inside, maybe snuggled up inside his appendix, that the faster this web crawl was developed, the faster he'd find "the one." And the faster he could stop being nagged by his family. And the faster Dharini could find her partner too.

He put his carry-on in the bin and slid into his seat. He'd seen Emma's seat assignment, though. No one was going to give up their aisle seat to trade.

He browsed through the movies available and made a mental list of which ones he was going to watch. He had twelve hours to kill on this first flight. Three movies. One book. That should hold him for a while. He settled in and flipped through the in-flight magazine while the hordes of people jumbled and fumbled their way up the aisle.

Emma's red hair popped into his peripheral vision like a warning light flashing *Incoming! Incoming!* "Rishi, no one by me wants to trade seats." She made a little pouty sound and squeezed herself against the backrest of the seat, her breasts practically leering in his face.

"Well, you tried." He shrugged, thanking fate for the next twelve hours of peace.

The man next to Rishi volleyed his head back and forth like he was watching a ball go between them. Then he paused and shook his head. "Hell, I'll move so you can sit with your girlfriend. Airlines these days screw everyone over."

Rishi opened his mouth to protest. Girlfriend?

"Oh, sir, that is so nice of you!" Emma exclaimed to the man. They exchanged a brief complaint about seating as he moved, and Emma praised his kindness.

So much for the next twelve hours of movie watching and music listening he'd planned out.

"That was nice of him." Emma plopped down next to Rishi and stuffed her backpack under the seat. "I thought you'd want to start working on your code. It's the least I can do. Besides, we have to focus all our energy on the app when we're in Bangalore, so I don't see why we would waste any time. I would have done it last week, but things were a little crazy."

He turned to her. If she thought he was going to work nonstop on her app, she was wrong. He'd worked his ass off before, and what had it gotten him? Nothing but empty promises about a job she now had. No more of this all-nighter shit.

"What? Why are you looking at me like that?" she asked.

He shook his head. "I'm not looking at you in any way."

"Yes, you are. I've seen that look before." Her hands settled in her lap. "I'm trying to *help* you. That's what we agreed on, right?" She said it like she was explaining something to a child or someone who was hard of hearing.

Emma scrolled through her phone, probably reading the emails he should have been getting. The lights dimmed, the pilot and flight attendant spoke over the speakers, and the plane whooshed off into the sky.

She was quiet. Too quiet. All he wanted was a break from her, but he couldn't stop staring at her leg vibrating on the floor, like it had its own kind of nerve disorder. She leaned forward and seemed to be looking out the window that was an aisle and three people away. Then she sat back in her seat and started pressing the screen in front of her. Rishi wouldn't have called it exploring—more like methodical pressing. First the music. Then the TV. Then the movies. Then the games. It was maddening, and accompanied by that crazy leg shaking. It was like watching an accident. He couldn't look away and just waited for the aftermath to unfold.

She wiped off her forehead. Was she sweating?

"Are you okay?" Rishi asked.

Emma jumped a little in her seat. "Yeah, yeah, fine. Why?"

"You just seem a little, I don't know. Antsy?" Rishi didn't want to say *crazy*. He had a little more finesse than that.

She shook her head fast. "I just don't like flying. I mean, I know people do it all the time. But the thought of these two guys controlling this tube of metal that we've all put our trust in to get us a quarter of the way around the world? It's a bit much, don't you think? I don't know them, and I just put my life in their hands. And what if something happened? I mean, what can we do? Nothing."

So she was nervous. Rishi leaned back in his seat. This was the last thing he'd expected. "I don't have anything to calm you down, but they should bring the drink cart around soon, I think."

Emma nodded and spoke to the seat in front of her. "Yeah, I'm sure a few drinks will help."

Maybe she just needed a distraction. Since they were stuck next to each other anyway, he might as well go along with her plan to start this code development. The two other matches his parents had sent in the past week were flagged in his inbox, but he'd already decided neither were worth pursuing. He'd chatted with one woman, but she didn't seem to have any passion toward life. She'd gone to university but was now just staying at home. The other he'd messaged, but she complained about her job the entire conversation. He couldn't imagine marrying someone who didn't lead her own life or find joy in the life she had. His mom seemed to think that his moving back to India was a green light flashing in her face to get his marriage set up as soon as possible, with all and any options on the table. And he was trying, dammit. "Would it help if we started on the web crawl, as you suggested? I think we can get our laptops out now."

Her head pivoted to him so fast that he caught a whiff of her hair's flowery citrus smell. "Yes. Excellent idea. Let's get started."

They both reached under the seats in front of them at the same time and bumped heads. Her hair was a wild tangling vine that seemed to want to trail up Rishi's nostrils. He shot back up, rubbing at his nose, and reached around the other side. That hair. He shook his head. His mom would grab her head and douse it in a bottle of coconut oil.

They both pulled out their heavy, development-ready laptops and slung them on their pullout trays.

"So . . . ," Emma said as she opened her laptop up. "I usually like to start projects out with an analysis phase." She turned to him. They were so close. It was awkward having a work-type discussion with someone who was shoulder to shoulder with you, who you could smell, and with no escape in sight. "So, what do we need to find in the future Mrs. Iyengar?" She laughed a little, like this was funny to her. Like his life and his family's tradition were just hilarious.

He took a deep breath, reminding himself this should be expected. Emma would never understand what he was dealing with at home. But he had to push that aside. If she was that good at her job, which he knew she was from researching her, then he might have the algorithm set up by the time they landed.

"Well, we have to narrow the results down to my caste and community and state. The state I'm from is Tamil Nadu."

"All right. And caste?" She typed in the notepad on her screen. "What's your caste, and what's a community?" she asked.

This was going to be such a process. But it would hopefully be worth it. He had to keep reminding himself. "My caste is Brahmin. And community is like the subset of a caste. For me, it's Iyengar."

"Your last name?" Emma asked.

"Yeah, some people have it as their last name. Not everyone."

"Sounds good." She typed out some more notes and looked over at him, then back to her laptop. "Okay, Rishi, what are the keywords that will help find this lady of yours?"

He leaned back into his chair and tried to picture the woman he'd want to marry. There wasn't any reason to hold back on the fantasy of what he wanted, if this was the "ideal" search, customized just for him. And then, of course, there was what his family needed. If this algorithm was going to work, he might as well stuff it full of his dreams. And theirs. "I want someone smart. She should have a master's degree in something challenging and interesting, like medicine or IT. Training to be a doctor, professor, maybe be a manager at a software company, something like that." He couldn't have a wife who wasn't curious about the world around her. But he also didn't want an ugly, smart, aspirational nerd. "Good looking, though," he added.

Emma wrinkled up her nose as she noted it down. "Oh, of course." Was she seriously disapproving? No one ever put *looks don't matter* in an online profile. If he did, then the guy was probably a serial killer or wanted a free maid. Or both.

Maybe it did sound bad. He didn't even know Emma. He probably was coming off as a vain, superficial asshole.

"But not just pretty. I mean, pretty, smart, and I'd like her to have hobbies and interests, like a sport or travel. Maybe she takes acting classes or something." That made it sound better, right? He wanted a well-rounded wife. Someone who wouldn't rely on him for everything and would have her own life too.

"Acting lessons?" Emma asked, as if it was the craziest thing she'd ever heard.

"Some kind of hobby." He tried to think about what else was important to him. Food was important. He'd been spoiled, with a mom who was such an amazing cook. Whatever talents his mother had had not been passed on to him. His cooking talent consisted of decent omelets. He didn't want to be married to a slob either. "Also, she must be a good cook and like an orderly house."

Emma blew out a breath she must have been holding in for ten minutes and kept on typing. Her eyebrows rose as she clacked away on the keyboard.

Whatever. If she was judging him, then she should probably judge herself too. Everyone had an ideal. Why not reach for it? That was the whole point of his algorithm. Otherwise, he'd settle for the next pretty face his parents sent over, someone less than perfect.

So much went into a marriage pairing. His parents were über traditional, and he had to consider his sister as well. Since his family had a black sheep, maybe marrying an ideal woman would cancel Sudhar out. And that would definitely help with his sister's future in-laws.

"Okay. Another thing. It would be preferable if she could play an instrument or sing."

She rolled her eyes. "Wow. You're really looking for a Renaissance woman."

"Some of this is for my parents. What's important is that she's Brahmin, Iyengar, and Tamil. So, she's like a daughter to my mom. And from a family that is upper-middle class or well to do. That's usually a filter on the sites."

Emma's eyes slid over to look at him. The laser stare striking again.

"What?" he said, having to look away for a moment to evade its penetration. "I'm sure you have similar requirements."

"Actually, I was just thinking about what I would include in my search terms if I ever made a web crawl for a potential mate, and that they would be so absolutely different."

"Really? Like how?" Emma had no idea what his situation was like—or his family. And it was all about what his family wanted. Needed.

"I think mine would be less precise. More about the person's interests and belief systems. Like, their class wouldn't matter to me."

Rishi rolled his eyes. "You'd be okay with someone who didn't have a good job?"

"Yes."

"So if you were more educated or they were practically living on the streets, you wouldn't care?"

"No, I wouldn't."

"Bullshit. If you couldn't talk to them about your work, your latest code, or your team's work, that would be okay?"

"I mean, I would choose someone who could understand the concepts. But they don't need to be a coder. Or a beautiful doctor who is also an excellent maid." She smirked.

"Well, I think you're telling yourself that because it sounds good, but not because it would ever happen." The flight attendants were two rows away. That drink cart couldn't come fast enough.

"You don't know that. If someone had the same beliefs and principles as me, I don't see why it wouldn't work." Emma glared at him.

"There's more to a relationship than your beliefs." Like family, traditions, lifestyle. It was all so complicated. The temples you went to, the way you prayed, the festivals you celebrated—all those things were important to being a family.

"Is there? Really?" Emma stared at him, her clever eyes glimmering, expecting a rebuttal. But he couldn't take it anymore. She'd never have to find a husband in the way that he needed to find a wife. She had no idea. It was so hard to find someone you liked, someone you were really passionate about and who also fit your family's criteria. Especially after your family had already had those criteria flung in their faces once before in the name of love—and that had not only slapped them in the face but also stolen all their money.

"Family is super important. And then chemistry has to be there too," Rishi said.

Emma laughed. "What? How do you account for chemistry through an algorithm? I believe in technology, but there are just some things it can't do."

"The code just narrows down the acceptable candidates. Then I have to filter through them and find the chemistry. Then fate does the rest."

"Fate?" Emma blurted out, like he'd just told her he'd eaten a frog for breakfast. "Fate is not real."

Rishi shook his head. People in the West threw around the word *karma* all the time, but they didn't really embrace it. "Life is based on fate. Our world revolves around it. How can you say fate isn't real?"

"Well, then," Emma said as she lifted her head with a wicked smile spread across her face. "If fate is real, that means I got this job and this project all through fate's doing."

Rishi folded his arms and sat back in his seat.

"Can I get you two anything to drink?" the flight attendant asked, her smile beaming down on them like the drink-cart dream girl she was.

"Can I have two whiskies?" they both said at the same time. Emma turned to eye him, like it was his fault they wanted the same thing.

"Well, I'll give you both two, but don't go joining the mile-high club." She winked and handed them each two bottles of Jameson and little cups of ice.

Emma groaned and said thanks. Rishi gave the woman the weakest smile he'd surely ever given anyone.

"I think that's enough of project scoping for now." She poured the first whiskey into her glass and drank the tiny bottle in all of thirty seconds. Rishi was still stirring his around.

He was the one who really needed the drink. He was the one whose cultural values were being mocked. The urge to just tell her everything rose in his chest, but he pushed it back down. He put in his earbuds, started the first movie on his flight queue, and tried to forget that Emma was sitting beside him.

This was not how he'd wanted the next year of his life to start. Everything had gone wrong. The job. His trip to the US. His family situation. Having to find a wife to set things back in balance.

And this plane trip.

An hour and a half into the movie, he was fully into the climax of a car-chase scene when a weight pushed at his shoulder. He turned, and a curly tendril of hair sneaked into his nose. What was it with that hair? It was half octopus.

"Emma," he said, and he tried to nudge her off his shoulder.

Nothing.

He took his earbud out of his right ear. "Emma." A little louder this time. He tried to push her off, and she slumped back against him. So awkward. He was practically manhandling his colleague.

"Emma," he said a little louder, and the guy next to him shot him an annoyed look. But all it got out of her was a snort of a snore in response.

"Fuck," he muttered under his breath. He tried to nudge her again, but her head fell back a little, then rolled onto him like it was more comfortable, and she snuggled into this new, intimate position.

He stared at the screen in front of him. The car chase ending. A building blowing up. The hero's girlfriend dead in the wreckage. He shook his head.

If this wasn't as bad as it could get, then what was?

CHAPTER 11

Maybe Emma should have finished scoping out the web crawl with Rishi on the plane, because after they landed in Amsterdam, he made obvious excuses to escape her. Who really needed to search for a pair of nail clippers during a layover? But it was fine. Emma walked from coffee shop to pastry shop to cheese shop and ate and drank and sipped and chewed. It didn't matter that it was ten in the morning; she was in food heaven.

And she didn't insist they sit together on the flight to Bangalore. She needed time apart from him too.

Fate was the word that made Emma cringe over any other. More than *debug has failed* or *failure to initialize properly*. *Fate* was a word that justified why her parents were taken away from her when she was just a kid. Or why her smart, sassy grandmother had had to work multiple minimum-wage jobs to take care of her and never got any peace for herself while rich assholes in her hometown seemed to have gotten everything handed to them. The only people who used *fate* were people who'd never had anything bad happen to them. Who didn't know heartache. Who didn't understand what hurt down to the bone felt like.

Her breath was deep and aching against her ribs again. There were so many things she could have said to him. But if all of it had come out, her truths would have tumbled out as well. Her guard would be down. Vulnerabilities of who she was and where she came from would appear, ripe and ready for him to feast on. The fact of how alone she was, completely apparent. She didn't want a pitying eye from him. She couldn't take it. She needed to spend the second leg of the journey away from Rishi and his fate.

She'd finish up this web crawl in the next few days so she could keep their time together at a minimum. He could take his perfect wife and live happily ever after. Emma could picture her—she'd have shimmering straight black hair and that impossible gleam Emma drooled over in shampoo commercials. She'd wear more sequins than the eye could process and delicate ankle bells. Gold bangles, maybe three or four, just to show she could casually wear a few thousand dollars on her wrists. A doctor's coat on one arm while she sang to her pediatric patients, and in the other hand a dish of homemade, perfectly spiced paneer tikka masala. More arms sprouting from her waist like a spider-armed goddess. A mop in her third hand and a violin in her fourth. Perfection. Hitting each criterion.

No wonder their female deities sometimes had so many arms. Men were impossible with their demands.

But she shouldn't care about Rishi's future wife. If there was a woman out there who could accept his requirements for what they were, good for him. A woman who would look into his shiny concrete eyes and see love in them. Somewhere. The poor thing would have to take a jackhammer to that cement stare, but somehow she'd find it.

The plane dipped low, taking her out of her thoughts of Rishi and his perfect bride, and the attendant announced they were making their descent toward the Bangalore airport.

Knowing the seat belt sign would come on any minute, she jumped up to go brush her teeth. As she walked toward the bathroom, she eyed Rishi, who was a few rows back, his face illuminated pale blue by the TV screen.

The bathroom overpowered her senses with its disinfectant smell that tried, and failed, to cover up the germs. She had gray shadows under her eyes, and her face was unusually pale. Or was it these lights? She looked green. All she needed was some coffee and to stay awake until the evening, and she should be good to go for the office tomorrow.

The flight landed, and Emma waited for Rishi at the gate. She powered on her phone, and gloriously, her international plan worked. A flood of emails and text messages filled her screen. She glanced through them and clicked on the one from Jas with an important flag on it.

Emma/Rishi,

I wanted to come to the airport to meet you both but had a meeting come up this morning I have to attend. Rishi, can you bring Emma to the office from the airport, and we'll sort things out from there? She can meet the team and I'll give her keys to her housing, etc. Sending a company car to get you. Thanks, Jas

Emma looked down at herself. Not only was her dress wrinkled from twenty-four hours in the air, but a smell also wafted from her that could only be described as eau d'airplane bathroom. This would not do. This was definitely not how she wanted to meet her new team, her new boss, and show them that she was capable of leading the project to success. Maybe she could grab her makeup bag, which also housed her deodorant, out of her suitcase.

People were pouring around her from the flight like she was a boulder in a sea of humanity. In a moment, Rishi was standing before her, also looking at his phone.

"Jas wants us to go . . . ," they started to say at the same time.

Of course. Emma pressed her lips together. It should have been funny. She should've been laughing. But she felt stiff and her limbs unmovable, almost like she had no control over her body. Like his mere presence stressed her out.

"So I'll meet you at the baggage after customs?" he asked, sounding as excited as she was. The most reluctant welcome wagon.

"Sure." It felt like a moment when they should have been parting ways, but in reality they still had to walk together, down the long hallway to customs.

After a beat, Emma started and Rishi fell in beside her, looking through his phone and typing.

"Do you live near the office?" Emma asked.

"Uh, no. I'm not particularly excited about going there first. Traffic here is insane," he huffed out.

"Well, I can just go by myself, I'm sure. It's fine." He didn't need to act like it was such a major inconvenience to her. She would be fine if he left now.

"I'm not going to defy Jas by letting you go by yourself. He'll wonder what happened to me."

"I'll just tell him you wanted to go home."

"Emma, he asked me to take you."

She rolled her eyes. "Yeah, but it's not like you *need* to take me. I'm a big girl. I can take care of myself."

"I'm aware, trust me."

"What's that supposed to mean?" They'd reached the point where the lines parted. One for foreign nationals and one for Indian citizens.

He just smiled and walked into the Indian citizens line.

Fire breathed out of her nose. Or at least what felt like fire. Like he literally made her blood boil, and her lungs needed to filter it out before she exploded. She was still watching him walk away into his line when someone hit her backpack while walking behind her. She couldn't let Rishi distract her. She just needed him for his skills—that was all.

There were other people on the team. She didn't have to spend all her time with him.

She met him outside customs, and beside him were both her bag and his.

"Thanks for getting my bag," she said.

"Yeah, it's the only bright-blue one, so it was easy to spot." He rolled it over to her. "Ready?"

"Let's go." The glass doors slid open, revealing the outside world. Emma blinked as she stepped out into the sunlight, half-blinded and half-trying to welcome its vitamin D to her parched skin. But it wasn't just the sun that was dazzling. Diamonds and gold flashed on billboards. The glint of the airport's massive glass walls sliced through the light. Sifting dirt and construction in the distance even sparkled somehow. Saris in a kaleidoscope of silk occasionally swished past her.

And the honking. The honking was everywhere.

Her new world was intense, loud, colorful, glittering, and refusing to relent on even one of her senses.

A muggy heat seared her skin and forced her breath down into her throat. Her stomach turned on itself as she eyed her surroundings. A coffee shop across the parking lot lured her from a distance.

Coffee, the sweet nectar of the jet lag gods.

A wind blew, the smell of heat masking something earthy and pungent. Everyone around her was being greeted by drivers with official uniforms or family members excited to see their husbands, wives, and children. More uniformed men lined the inside and outside of the Bangalore airport, holding signs with names typed in a large font. She was examining them all, and apparently so was Rishi.

"Do you see our ride?" she asked Rishi.

"No, I'm calling." He already had his phone against his ear and then was talking to someone in not-English. "The driver is stuck in traffic." Rishi turned around and put his phone back in his pocket.

The coffee shop across the parking lot caught her eye again, glowing as if the heavens were beaming down on it; her mind was playing tricks on her, promising a taste of how good it would feel on her tongue. So good. Milky and dark and caffeinated. "Do you mind if I get a coffee?"

He looked behind him. "I can get you one."

"No, it's okay. I can pay for it—"

He swatted the air behind him as he walked toward the shop. "Just watch our stuff."

She searched her purse for a mirror. A crumbly old compact was still in there. She opened it and wiped the powder off the mirror.

Puffy and blotchy, her pale skin showed every emotion in varying hues of clown-cheek crimson. She took the bottle of water from the plane she'd been rationing off, sip by sip, and splashed some on her face.

A throat cleared behind her. She whipped around, water droplets still clinging to her cheeks.

"Your coffee?" Rishi held out a cup toward her.

"Thanks," she said as she took the two-inch-high cup from him. She held it at eye level, trying to hide her disappointment when she really wanted sixteen ounces of latte to jump-start her mind into catching up with her senses. Honking cars and masses of people streamed past, across, and alongside them. The language was mostly unfamiliar, some the same flavor of English she recognized from her colleagues at work. Her mind needed to process all of this, and it was on a thirty-second delay. She took a sip. The coffee tasted like it was 50 percent sugar.

"I got you our famous South Indian coffee, and you don't like it?" He sounded seriously offended.

Jordana always told her she could never hide her feelings—they just popped up on her face like an unwelcome visitor—and she could only guess at the kind of grimace that was gracing her face now. "It's fine. Just sweet. I don't drink sugar in my coffee."

"Just fine? I can't believe you don't like it." He took a drink, and a hungry kind of hum vibrated in his throat that she would almost have described as sexual. He must really have missed that coffee.

The dirty truth was that Emma was a creature of habit, of routine. She craved the predictability of her Sunday-morning latte being made the same way by her favorite barista, and of the Science section of the *New York Times* sitting on her doorstep every Tuesday. She loved taking the bus to work because it was on a punctual schedule that somehow defied Seattle traffic. Of course, she'd have to adapt to living in a new country with new kinds of coffee, noise, cars, language, and—if the billboards near the airport exit could be believed—people dripping with diamonds and silk. But she thought this would involve a gradual change and not hit her all at once. Not in the first ten minutes she stood outside the airport.

She threw the coffee back like a shot of whiskey. Her nerves buzzed, forced awake by newness and the excessively sweet coffee trying to jolt her senses to attention, when all they yearned for was a bed.

Rishi's phone rang. "Driver's here."

They got in the car, left the airport, and headed onto the highway. Emma gripped the bar above the window as the car surged into one lane and then back into the next. Outside the window was a blur of the fascinating and unfamiliar. The motorcycles and scooters wove in and out of the cars as if the riders were on a dare. One motorcycle carried a family of four. Black smoke from auto-rickshaw exhaust pipes puffed out like a hacking cough. The hem of the passenger's blue sari, the rich hue of a peacock's chest, fluttered out the side, sequins catching the light. Dust billowed along the sides of the road behind the vehicle. Bright-pink bougainvillea hung down the sides of a cement wall. Her eyes took it all in—the glorious contrast of an electric rainbow against a dull-beige background. This would be her new life.

"What do you think of Bangalore so far?" Rishi asked. So casually. Like landing in Bangalore had transformed him into a normal person.

"I'm really excited. I love Indian food." The car lunged around an auto-rickshaw, and the driver honked as he squeezed in between it and a motorcycle.

"You like spicy food?"

"I do. I always ask for three stars at Indian restaurants in the US."

"In India, restaurants don't ask how many stars you want to dumb down the spice. You should try Hyderabadi biryani. See if you can handle it," he said.

She could handle anything this guy threw at her. "Oh, I can handle it." She tried to sound as confident as possible, even through the driver's manic swerving around the traffic.

"Really? It's super hot. So, what do you actually know about India?" he asked. "You aren't scared about all the cobras and scorpions we have?" He bit down on his lip like he was trying to keep from laughing.

What game was Rishi playing? "I mean, it's not like they're all over the place, right?"

"Well, not *everywhere*," he said, looking out the window. "But they're there."

She rolled her eyes. What did he think he was going to do? Have her write his stupid marriage code for him and then scare her back to Seattle?

"And I've heard there's still bubonic plague." He waved his hand dismissively. "Somewhere. And leprosy. And malaria. I hope you're prepared."

It didn't say anything about cobras in Bangalore in her guidebook. Or did it? The other things she'd been assured weren't really issues. She couldn't worry about snakes when she had an entire new world to adapt to. The clogged-up, whiplash-inducing traffic seemed more dangerous than a cobra at this point.

"We're here," Rishi's voice piped up again as they slowed down.

Emma's gaze shifted to the other side of the street. The tech park in Bangalore jutted up stories above the other buildings, proclaiming, in glass and steel, its position of power in the world of technology. The power-supply tower was protected by barbed wire, and set back off the road were ten-story buildings with words like Dell, Microsoft, and Google plastered on the sides.

Several women with low-handled brooms swept the road with broad, bored strokes. The dust had no place to go, though, except back out to the street, to be swept again. Emma stared after them as the car descended into the parking garage, ferrying them away from the chaotic reality of the outside world.

The car pulled into an empty space in the garage. They both got out and walked to the trunk, which the driver popped open.

"Can I just get my bag out?" Rishi asked him, and then he turned to Emma. "You can leave your suitcase in here and get it when you leave." He tilted his head as he examined it. "It's really big."

The driver started to shut the trunk, and she stopped him. Deodorant. Makeup. Double standards. There was no way she could meet her team looking like she did now. "Wait, I need something first." They should be in a plastic zippered bag, easy to find. She'd stuck it on top, the last thing she'd packed.

Emma unzipped the side of the suitcase, which was squeezed in the small space the hatchback allowed for it to fit. She submerged her arm and couldn't feel for it. "I need to get the suitcase out."

She tried to heave the bag out. But it was stuck. The driver edged in, gripped the sides, and pulled hard, almost falling backward. As the suitcase dislodged, a few things spilled out on the parking garage floor from where she had opened the zipper—a shirt, underwear, and a book. She grabbed the underwear first, hoping he hadn't seen it, and stuffed it in her pocket. But Emma hadn't packed a book, besides her travel guide, and she definitely didn't recognize the art on the cover.

The Kama Sutra?

Rishi stifled a laugh at the cover lying on the ground mere inches from his feet, an illustration of two lovers intertwined in an embrace.

"That's not mine." Emma pointed at it like it was a dead rat on the floor. Was this some kind of jet-lagged nightmare? She couldn't imagine having a rougher start to a working relationship than what she and Rishi had already had, and now this? She looked like an American character out of a bad comedy who took this job to have her own *Eat, Pray, Love* experience with a side helping of stereotypical sex guide.

It couldn't get worse than this.

"That's not mine. I don't know how it got there." She somehow managed to get the words out, ignoring her heart as it threatened to lurch out of her chest. She snatched it off the ground and stuffed it back in the suitcase.

As she bent over, her body was seized with the sudden urge to stay squatting on the garage floor, to stay curled up like one of those roly-poly insects, feigning paralysis. She'd turn mute, and someone would rush her back to the airport. They'd want someone who didn't hallucinate the Kama Sutra emerging from her bag, like a curse from the breakup fairy telling her to *Get back out there, sport.*

She could hear Jordana's last words to her in her head. "Half a billion men . . ."

This had to have been her doing.

She glanced up at Rishi. He was biting his bottom lip to keep from laughing.

"Rishi, I swear, it's not mine." She replaced her shirt, grabbed her makeup bag, and zipped her suitcase closed before setting it upright. The driver awkwardly took it from her and put it back in the car.

"Sure." That stupid smirk on his face. Those concrete eyes about to crack with laughter.

"I swear," she insisted.

"Oh, and I totally believe you. The Kama Sutra often sneaks into my luggage when I'm least expecting it."

She couldn't even shoot him a look. Of course he didn't believe her, and why should he? The book had shot out of her bag like a big, hardcover sex cannonball.

She stood up, unable to even look at him. She'd have to ignore what happened and hope he'd just forget. "Where are we going?"

"Just follow me." He gave her the biggest smile she'd seen from him yet. And this time it was real, full of absolute glee, and completely directed at her.

CHAPTER 12

Rishi couldn't believe it. As he pressed the elevator button to go up, he chuckled to himself, shaking his head. The Kama Sutra? Was it supposed to be her guidebook?

He glanced over at her. She was fully immersed in her phone, her cheeks red, and she still refused to make eye contact.

The elevator dinged and opened. "Jas is hopefully in his office now. We'll check there first."

"Wait, can I go to the bathroom first?"

"Uh, yeah." He led her down the first hall and gestured to the bathroom doors. She disappeared inside. Maybe he could just leave her. Go find some coffee, his friends. She could figure out her way around the office. No one had given him a tour on his first day. He shouldn't have been stuck as her escort. *Not cool, Jas.* He should have let him mourn his lost promotion without sticking the person who'd gotten it right in his face.

Rishi looked at his watch. Ten minutes. She must have been taking a shower in there.

Now Rishi had to go. He might as well, if she wasn't coming out. He ran in and splashed water on his face. He looked like a zombie. He should have tried to sleep more on the plane. And the smell. It wasn't as bad as the bathroom stench that had woven itself into his clothes last time, but it wasn't pleasant either. He had a sink and soap. Might as well use them. He took his shirt off and washed his armpits. At least that was a little better. Now he just needed coffee. Coffee alternating with naps. As he dried off the water with a paper towel, the door cracked open.

"Rishi?" Emma's eyes locked with his, and then her mouth paused, half-open, as she stared at his shirtless torso.

Surprised, he grabbed his shirt and held it in front of him. "Emma, what are you doing? This is the men's bathroom!"

She cleared her throat. "Uh . . . I didn't know where you were, and my badge doesn't work here. I tried it. I thought you left me."

He rolled his eyes and threw his shirt on. Impossible. "I'm coming. You were taking forever."

"I didn't want to meet Jas and any other potential coworkers looking like I was subjected to twenty-four hours of air travel."

"But you *were* subjected to twenty-four hours of air travel." Why were they having this conversation in the doorway of the men's bathroom? "Go. Shut the door." He gestured toward the hall. Thankfully no one had seen them, or the rumor mill would be going wild. *Why was Rishi in the bathroom with Emma?* He could already hear the stories getting out of control.

"You shouldn't open the door to the guys' bathroom, by the way," he said as he badged them into the office.

"Well, it's not like I normally do, but you left me a little stuck out there."

Twenty feet in front of them, Jas was coming out of his office. "Jas!" Rishi called.

Jas pivoted. "Hey! There are my world travelers. My project lead and lead developer here at last."

Emma grabbed Jas's hand in a severe handshake that looked like she was going to yank his arm off. "Jas, it's so nice to meet you in person. Finally!"

Jas stepped back, and his eyes lit up in surprise at Rishi, as if they were mutually amused by this creature who was invading their space, running over Rishi, and sucking up to his boss. "I don't want to keep you too long, but I have your keys to your corporate housing."

"Hi, Jas." Rishi waved. Maybe he'd remember that he was standing there, too, and not merely the shadow of Emma, Jas's new star employee.

"Rishi, welcome back!" He shook his hand like they were old friends. Old friends who sometimes betrayed each other.

Jas looked back at Emma. "While you're here, let's meet the team. Then tomorrow we can have a normal day." He ushered them toward the cube farm. "I think they're all huddled over here."

Rishi saw Kaushik, Preeti, and Manuj, other app developers he knew from around the office, and gave them a small half wave as they all turned around when they heard the three of them coming.

"Team, meet Emma," Jas announced. "She's our new project lead for the literacy app. And you know Rishi."

"Hi, everyone. So excited to start working with you." Emma squeezed her hands together in front of her, clearly used to being the darling of the office. "We're going to make this app so awesome."

"I'm going to get a coffee," Rishi said. He didn't need to witness the horror show that was his new team finding Emma oh so amusing.

He exhaled and marched outside to the coffee station on the balcony. He made his coffee and decided to drink it out there, for a moment of peace, away from the reminder of what he'd be dealing with for the next year.

The door opened and Emma emerged, her hair blowing in all different directions from the vacuum-like effect of the air-conditioning. It was like one of those horror movies where the seductress monster emerged, wild and sexy, hair blowing in the wind as she traced her fingers up an unsuspecting dork's chest, right before she bit his head off. Except with Emma, she was trying to eat his soul with one of her glares.

What was he doing to deserve that? Nothing, just leaning against the balcony with his coffee, minding his own business. Her head pivoted to the coffee machine. She walked over to it and silently made a cup. Then she brought it over and stood directly in front of him, a blank look on her face.

They were the only two people on the balcony, except for a guy at the other end, completely absorbed in his laptop. If she decided to throw him over the rail, no one would be his witness.

"Rishi, are we cool? We need to be cool. We're partners, remember?"

"Partners?" The blasphemous word came out louder and more ridiculous than he'd expected. The guy at the end stopped typing and even looked up. He thought he had gotten over the turn of events that had led him back to Bangalore, but then the anger resurfaced. Jas treating her like she was the star pupil. The team he should be leading, nodding and smiling at her like she deserved her place as their collective lead, instead of him. They didn't know how she'd run to her manager and begged for the job after Rishi had told her. "Does one partner usually steal the other partner's job?"

She threw her hands up in the air, like *she* was the exasperated one. "I did not *steal* your job. We've been through this! And I want to make something clear . . ." She leaned forward, and the scent of citrus and flowers leaped toward him, trying to weave a web of perfumed confusion in his head via his nostrils. He resisted physically brushing off his shirt, afraid somehow that she would entwine herself with him and get in his head, her presence taunting him all day long about what could have been. "I love my work and this company and this product, and you need to get on board. I can't be worried all the time that you're out to get me. Like your stupid little immature taunts." Her voice was like urgent nails sliding along glass.

All his mounting irritation burst out in a laugh. "Me immature?" Emma was like an annoying fire ant stuck in his room that he couldn't get rid of. She might look small and cute, but then she kept biting and biting, her sting a motherfucker.

But she stuck her finger up, telling him to wait. It was mere centimeters from his lips. He could reach out and lick it if he wanted.

No, bite it.

"What about that stupid shit that you were saying to try and scare me? Cobras or whatever—it's not going to work. I'm here for the year. No little snake is going to freak me out."

She leaned back, her eyes steady on him. And then, apparently feeling proud of herself, she took a sip of her coffee, waiting for him to admit she was right.

Maybe she was a little right. Maybe he had been immature, but she had, too, Miss Queen of the Doughnuts. And he'd deserved the position as team lead. But Emma thought she deserved it too. They were both going to be working side by side for the next year. Essentially joined at the hip, surely, as Emma developed faulty code and Rishi corrected her tiny disasters. He'd just have to get over it. Possibly admit they were a little too similar in their perspectives to keep this up for months, or they'd never get anything done. He finished up his coffee and crumpled up the cup in his fist.

He should have told her what he thought. That he was a mature professional who was above those comments, and above her petty pastry thievery. Reassure her that they could work together and make the app successful. Or, he could just clear his throat and say . . .

"Emma, it's actually quite a big snake."

He stalked off toward the door, not sure if she'd follow him after that. A burning in his chest propelled him, a tightness that made him swallow hard. That was not dignified. It was not mature. It was the kind of thing that could get him an HR violation.

Would he regret what he'd just said? Maybe. But as he neared the door and saw Emma's reflection in the glass, her mouth still open, absolutely speechless, it was all worth it.

CHAPTER 13

This was not how Emma had imagined her start in India. In her head, she had seen marigold garlands, splashes of fuchsia and turquoise. A buffet of curries and pakoras. The saffron-hued sweets she'd only seen pictures of. Her new team, passionate and clinging to the potential of technology, would be united in the cause to fight illiteracy. And everything would be done up in a wildly vibrant Technicolor musical number. Clearly she'd watched one too many movies to prepare for her trip.

She walked down to the parking garage with Jas, who gave instructions to the company driver on how to go to her home.

As Emma settled into the back seat, she closed her eyes and groaned, trying to piece together the sandstorm that had blown over her in the past few hours. Like Rishi . . . all she could do was groan.

The driver looked in the rearview mirror. "Everything all right, madam?"

"Yes, sorry. It's nothing," she said. But it was something. On the plane ride over, she'd imagined kicking things off with her team after a full night of sleep, not spending the day fighting with the one person she should be collaborating with the most—her lead developer. She could envision him whispering doubts about her capabilities to the rest of the team as she rode home in the car.

She just needed them all to give her a chance, and she hoped it wasn't too late.

The car turned down a road and stopped in front of a brick house painted white with terra-cotta shingles. The garden and home were gated shut. Roses and bougainvillea sprouted up from behind the five-foot-high wall. A spiral staircase led to a second floor outside. This house was a thousand times nicer than her run-down apartment in Seattle.

The driver brought her luggage inside, and Emma followed. She stepped inside and thanked him, maybe a little too much, because it looked like he wanted to run away. Who could blame him for wanting to escape the tired, jet-lagged, sallow, groaning woman in the back seat? She surveyed her new home while her feet chilled on the cool tile. The creamy swirls in the flooring looked like marble.

She knew she should wait to sleep for just a few more hours to avoid waking up at two in the morning, ready for the day. It was almost a twelve-hour time difference. But the burgundy cushions on the sofa called to her like sirens of jet lag. *Just lie down for a minute, Emma. Don't we look comfy?* But she needed to unpack, connect to the Wi-Fi, and get acquainted with her home.

She unzipped her suitcase, and there, lying on top, was her new book. She pulled it out and rolled her eyes. The Kama Sutra of Vatsyayana. She thumbed through the beginning and found the inscription on the first page.

Emma, have a great trip and know I'll miss you like crazy. But I hope that you find some use for this while you're there. I recommend starting with Congress of the Cow.

XO

Jordana

Congress of the Cow? She flipped through the pages. A book on sexual positions wasn't at the top of her reading list. And she wasn't sure she wanted to know how a cow was involved. She zipped it back in the pocket of the suitcase, only because she couldn't bear to throw a book away. It had already caused her more embarrassment than she needed on her first day in India. Or really, for the year.

She frowned as she looked at the contents of her suitcase—a suit she was now certain she would never wear after visiting the office, button-up blouses for interviews that had each been worn once, and some linen pants she'd bought just for the trip. Everyone was so casual, just like at the Seattle office. She already missed the collection of vintage dresses and boots she had amassed over the years, the clothes that had formed her into quite the visual juxtaposition from her grubby neighbors in the Dev Lab. Maybe she could enlist her new coworkers to go shopping with her.

With her clothes put away, she walked into the kitchen to get some water. She flung open the fridge and kitchen cupboards, where she found bottled water, coffee, milk, sugar, rice, and a few prepackaged Indian meals. Tears sprang to her eyes at the generosity of it all—the beautiful home, the stocked fridge, a bed made and ready for her, and towels in the bathroom.

Suddenly, the whole day didn't seem so awful. Really, there was just one unbalanced variable in her equation for happiness and success here: $x =$ Rishi. But she was going to be here a year, and she hadn't come halfway around the world to fail. She'd show the rest of the team she was a lovely person, absolutely delightful, and that she'd been asked to come for good reason.

Two could play at this game. If Rishi thought he could mess with her, then she could mess with him right back.

En garde, Rishi Iyengar!

$$\{ \; /** \; *. \; // \; \}$$

Emma's sleep came in fits and starts. After passing out on her bed, still dressed, at 6:00 p.m., she woke up at 11:00 p.m.

Emma, it's actually quite a big snake.

Her eyes flew open in the dark, a ripple of irritation sliding down her abdomen. Ugh. If she could just sleep and put it behind her.

Then at 2:00 a.m., there was Rishi again in her thoughts, shooting darts in her eyes as he said "partners" to her like it was a curse when she'd tried to bring them together. She'd looked away from his eyes and settled on the tendons in his forearms straining against his skin. Proof of his heart racing. Maybe it would explode if she pissed him off enough. She turned on her side and tried to bury her face in the pillows.

At 5:00 a.m. she decided to give up. It was like he was haunting her in her jet-lagged sleep. She couldn't let him nag at her anymore. It was his problem anyway. He reminded her of someone from her old team—a guy who liked to mansplain basic code to her or shush her in meetings when she interjected something. She was done with it.

She threw off the covers and got out of bed.

Something about Rishi fueled a fire in her that she couldn't extinguish. She'd felt bad about what had happened, but he wouldn't put the past in the past. A simmering rage was taking the place of the guilt. It had her fantasizing about doing imperceptible, torturous things to him. Spreading that "grow anywhere" grass seed on his desk. Finding itching powder (was that a real thing?) and, somehow, subtly sprinkling it on his clothes. Putting salt in his coffee instead of sugar. She looked down at her hand, clenched in a fist. How could one person prick her like a thousand needles, irritating every pore?

It was 6:00 p.m. Pacific time and the perfect time to tell Jordana her gift had turned into more of a curse.

Hi, just wanted to tell you I got your little gift. Rishi actually saw it fall out of my suitcase. He's definitely amused that his new coworker packs sex guides as reading material.

OMG. Amused or intrigued? Maybe he'll ask if you want a partner to practice with.

Emma paused before responding, with Rishi materializing in her mind's eye: hovering over her as she picked up the book, biting his full bottom lip to keep from laughing, his shaggy hair hanging over one concrete eye. He'd crossed his arms in front of him, making the curves of his biceps apparent, and the indentation of his pecs through his shirt formed a deep line down the center of his chest.

A line that would be perfect for tracing with a sharp object. Like a shiv. A dinner knife. A freshly sharpened pencil.

Not possible.

I thought you'd just set it on your coffee table. Not advertise with it LOL

Of course Jordana would think in those terms. Not about what would happen if someone came over and saw the Kama Sutra lying as the pièce de résistance on her coffee table.

Got to get ready for work. Miss you!

Emma put her phone down, and a shiver subtly shook her again as she thought of how embarrassed she'd been yesterday. If there were a scoreboard for their interactions, it would say *Rishi 2, Emma 0.*

Somehow, some way, the score needed to be evened, if not tipped in her favor.

{ /** *. // }

Emma walked with Jas toward the cafeteria for breakfast. He spoke as fast as a bullet train, and she clung onto every dip in intonation as he talked about the general process of moving desktop software into an app.

The scent of the cafeteria wafted down the hall and filled her nose, which had a direct line of communication with her stomach.

They entered the cafeteria, and Emma stared down the line of food she didn't recognize. Jordana had been right. They kept all the good stuff here. This breakfast spread was like a buffet of secrets. So many times she'd eaten Indian food, yet all this was unfamiliar. Even the smells were different. An orange-hued stew, a milky-looking soup, something that looked like couscous, and small, fluffy white pancakes.

"This looks exciting!"

Jas smiled at her, and she followed him, mirroring his food selections. "You like South Indian breakfast?" he asked, picking up two of the fluffy-looking clouds.

"I don't know. I hope so." Emma laughed and followed him to one of the tables. She had no idea how to eat what she'd just put on her plate, but her powers of observation had never let her down. Well, until recently.

Jas broke off a piece of the white fluffy cloud and dipped it into some soup. "I thought you would have gone for the cereal."

"Cereal?" Emma followed Jas's nod and saw containers of cornflakes and milk, then turned around to face the enigma on her plate. "Oh no. I would much rather eat an authentic Indian breakfast."

Emma leaned over her plate and inhaled the aromas of cayenne and turmeric and cumin that wafted up toward her. "It smells good." An intense flavor profile for breakfast.

She broke off a piece of the spongy white circle and dipped it into the red-hued stew, as she'd watched Jas do. A symphony of flavors burst on her tongue—tart tamarind, savory onions, acidic tomatoes—and ended with a blast of heat. Emma drank half her glass of water, and her tongue was still burned raw. It was like she'd asked the waiter at her favorite Indian place in Seattle for a ten-star meal.

"What is that?" she asked Jas, pointing to the bowl on her plate.

"Sambar. It is a kind of lentil stew. The idli is made from rice. Is the sambar spicy?"

"My tongue is on fire." A parade of chili flakes marched on her tongue, celebrating the capture of their newest victim. She was excited at discovering the authentic flavor profile she was searching for, but also trying to hide the pain.

"Let me get you some chutney." Jas jogged off to the line and brought back a small dish. "It's made from coconut. It will soothe the burn."

Emma dipped the idli into the chutney, and the coolness of the coconut coated her tongue like a creamy poultice. It was so fresh, like sweet cream and water and a coconut flavor that was beyond anything shredded that came in a bag.

"This is amazing. I need to get used to the heat index on the food here, I think."

"We grow up eating this way, so we're used to it. That's why most foreigners who visit opt for the cereal or pasta or whatever we're serving that's not spicy."

"Nope. I love spice. I was excited about coming here for the food. I mean, obviously the project too," Emma added quickly, not wanting Jas to think she'd just come here to eat. "I'm really hoping we can really wow the company and make a dramatic impact on ROI with this app."

"Me too." Jas looked off in the distance. "Rishi, come join us!" he called.

Her cheeks and neck grew hot, and not from her breakfast. She turned back to Jas, who was talking about something, but all she could think about was how to get the flush from her cheeks. When Rishi came to the table, he would see the bright red in her cheeks and nose and know it was about him, Mr. It's Quite a Big Snake himself.

Breathe.

She was fully rested, logic had regained its ground, and she would not let Rishi stand in her way.

Breathe. And eat your idli.

Rishi's tray plunked down on the table, next to her forearm. She smiled at him, maybe a little too broadly, because he looked at her askance, as if she were an untrained dog with the potential to bite. The way he shifted his body away from her when he sat down told her he hadn't forgotten about yesterday.

"Rishi, glad we ran into you," said Jas. "I was just filling Emma in on some project details. I think the two of you should spend part of the day together discussing the back-end infrastructure. Give her a primer on the stages we take to develop apps."

Rishi took a bite of his idli after dipping it into the sambar and chutney. "Sure, boss."

Emma looked at her hands, the sambar and chutney muddled on her fingers like a grainy red oil slick. She wiped them off on her napkin, hoping Rishi hadn't noticed how dirty they were. Somehow his and Jas's fingers were clean, even though they'd been eating with their hands as well.

"I would love that. Are you free after breakfast, Rishi? Why wait to get started?" Emma asked. Jas needed to see she was a team player, a delightful employee, and that she and Rishi had no issues whatsoever. Besides, why wait to tackle the problem sitting beside her?

He seemed to hesitate as he examined her face. What was he thinking? If she'd read the book last night? How she was eating like a messy five-year-old?

She sat back in her chair and attempted to channel a sense of cool and calm. Shrugging, she said, "I mean, if you have other priorities, I have stuff to work on if you're too busy. No big deal. I could read a book about it."

His face suddenly came to life. "Oh, I saw you'd brought the one . . ." He furrowed his brow into a faux-pensive look as he rubbed at his chin. A smile teased at the corners of his lips.

She should have seen that coming. Rishi 3, Emma 0. "I've been studying it. That is, a book on app dev."

"Which one?" Jas asked.

Emma's eyes darted in a panic to Rishi, who seemed to find such amusement that he cracked the first full grin of the morning. "*App Coding for Dummies*, was it?" he asked.

Emma blew out a huge sigh and glanced sideways at Rishi, who was still smiling at her like they were sharing some kind of joke. Were they?

"Don't worry: we can meet when you're done." He picked up a piece of idli and stuffed a big, fluffy bite into his mouth.

"Perfect! Why read a book when you can do it together?" Jas said.

In simultaneous slow motion they both looked at him. Emma swallowed. If Jas only knew. He stood up and grabbed his tray. "I knew you'd be great together. And I love those Dummies books. I got one to train my dog."

As Jas strolled away, the awkwardness between her and Rishi simmered, as thick as the sambar that had burned her tongue.

"*App Coding for Dummies*? Seriously?" she whispered.

He just laughed and got up to get some water. Now what? There wasn't enough chutney in existence to cure this fiery tension between them.

CHAPTER 14

"I'm going to get a coffee first," she said. "Then do you want me to meet you at your desk?" Emma asked Rishi when he came back to the table.

"Yeah, that's fine."

"Do you want me to get you one too?"

"Yes?" It had definitely come out like a question as he thought of all the things she could put in his coffee for revenge—arsenic, spit, her finger. He was regretting it even as she shook her head at him, muttering something as she walked off.

Rishi sighed and walked toward his desk.

He settled into his seat and surveyed the mess on his desk. It was like a tornado had hit his desk as he'd rushed to Seattle, and he'd never cleaned up the wreckage.

"Ready?"

Rishi jumped in his seat, his heart a jackhammer in his chest. The voice to his left jerked his head and his thoughts straight into Emma's breasts. He whipped back around.

"Aw . . . did I scare you?" she said, an expression of mock sympathy teasing on her face.

"You didn't. I mean, it's fine." Why did he sound like an adolescent half the time when she was around? Like when he was twelve and he avoided asking questions because his voice was changing and always cracked at the end.

She made a small noise in the back of her throat that was a hint of a laugh but sounded like she'd swallowed a baby bird. He wouldn't have put it past her.

Rishi tried to straighten up his desk. His hands fumbled as he grabbed a stack of notes and papers and books. The entire stack slipped out of his hands, spreading even farther on his desk and knocking two half-empty coffee cups over in the process. He glanced at Emma, who sat down in a chair and pressed her lips together to suppress a laugh. He would have thought it was funny, too, if anyone but Emma had been laughing at him.

"Messy desks are one of the seven habits of highly effective coders, didn't you know?" she said.

"That makes sense," Rishi grumbled, scanning the room. "Looking around here, some of the others must be bad posture, carpal tunnel, and needing to get—"

He'd almost said *get laid* but had caught himself before he finished. He couldn't believe he had almost said that to Emma. To a woman. To a coworker he was on perilous terms with. That was the kind of language that slipped out of his mouth when he was hanging out with his friends, watching cricket and drinking beer.

"I mean. I guess there's just the two," he finished, and he opened up the bug list he'd been working on earlier.

"You clearly thought there was a third," Emma said.

"No."

"What was it?"

"Nothing." An exasperated sigh grunted out of him, like it was on autopilot-Emma mode.

"Hopefully at some point you can act like a professional, and we can just have a normal conversation." She shook her head and rolled her eyes at the same time.

Rishi couldn't believe her insistence. "It was nothing. Can we get started? Professionals and all?"

Her mouth parted as if she was going to say something, but then she slumped back against her chair. With a sigh, she opened her laptop. "Fine. Before we start talking about app dev 101, I've been thinking about how to make the app more gamified with the current content and wanted to see if you had any ideas."

Work. They had work to do. "Okay. Do you have some examples of mobile games you like or that you want to emulate?"

"Just a few. Let me know if you think we could design it like any of these screenshots." She turned her laptop toward him and clicked through the images. Rishi couldn't help but notice a name in one of the bottom tabs. *Marriage code.*

"Is that my algorithm you're working on?" He pointed at it.

"Yes, but I haven't had a chance to do much else with it since the plane. But don't worry. We had a deal. You were going to help me, and I will help you. That's still the plan, right?" She turned to him. "Are you on board?"

Rishi tried to lean back in his chair, but something about her presence made him unable to relax. More time with Emma. His body was weirdly stiff as he thought about it. If she was as good as he thought, it shouldn't be much longer before he'd have the results.

"Yes, that's what I want." His words reluctantly agreed with her.

"Okay, good. Let's schedule time to finish up your code, and we can get on with our lives and start focusing on this project." She pulled up her calendar.

"Sunday?" he asked.

"Sunday it is."

And just like that, as she created a meeting in her calendar, his fate was tied up with hers.

CHAPTER 15

Emma had in tow four new bags of clothes from her day out shopping. She'd gone with her new team member, Preeti, who'd graciously agreed to show her the best places to shop. As soon as they opened the door to the air-conditioned coffee shop, her body heaved a sigh of relief. Coffee and cool air. Two things she hadn't realized she desperately longed for that afternoon. "This is perfect. And my treat, since you're my unofficial stylist."

Preeti laughed. "Maybe that can be my job if coding doesn't work out."

Emma ordered two cappuccinos for them, and they sat at one of the small tables in the brightly lit shop.

"Well, I hate to break it to you, but I'm pretty sure it's going to work out for you." Emma laughed. Preeti was the most enthusiastic coder on the team. She was younger than Rishi and had less experience, but she made up for it in her willingness to do anything. "Did you always want to go into coding?"

"I don't know what else I would have done. I'm glad I had the opportunity. I mean, twenty years ago, I probably wouldn't have gone to college for engineering, and my parents would have married me off. My dad is living in another time." She laughed it off, waving the jab away with her hand.

Emma winced in sympathy. Working as a woman in IT was a struggle anywhere. Her quest to find a balance between pushing herself to excel and demanding the same of others had cost her. Cost her more than one unflattering nickname. Cost her free time. And cost her the ability to find men who could handle it. But she couldn't imagine getting married after college. And obviously, she couldn't imagine it now.

A week had gone by since she'd left, and Jeremy hadn't even emailed her. Not an instant message, not a social media like, nothing. But to be fair, she hadn't reached out to him either. In fact, she'd been so busy dealing with her new life in a new country that she hadn't even given much thought to what had happened. Or maybe she was trying to block it out of her memory.

The barista set two cups of perfect cappuccino in front of them. She inhaled hers and took a sip. "So are you planning to get married anytime soon, or are you waiting?"

"My parents are looking for someone, but I'm not in a hurry." Preeti grinned. "I can be a bit choosy."

"I hope your parents have good taste in men!"

"Me too. But they'll find someone good. They're like a search party. They bring back all the spoils from their journey, and I get to choose the one I like the most. They have my best interests in mind."

She could appreciate the approach. She was in no hurry to start dating, which, before Jeremy, had felt like a part-time job. Relentless nights on dates fueled by some pinprick of commonality on a dating app. Clinging to the idea of what could be rather than what actually was. In the past year, she'd heard more horror stories from her friends than hopes of potential relationships. Horror stories that she was likely to add to if she went down the same route.

At least with an arranged marriage, your family was involved, so no one could be too horrible without someone finding out or them vetting the person first. It begged the question of why Rishi wasn't using his parents and family to help with his search. He was going through all this trouble when he could have just taken Preeti's approach. In fact, if Emma could do the same, she would. "That sounds like a really good system. I wonder if I can make arranged marriages a trend back home."

"Well, of course there are love marriages, too, but it's difficult sometimes."

"Is it because of the caste and community and state you're from?" Emma asked. Maybe she could find out why Rishi hadn't found someone on his own yet.

"So you know about all that?" Preeti looked impressed. "Yes, mostly. Each of us has our own traditions and way of living, so it's difficult sometimes to bridge that gap. I mean, I don't even know all our traditions. When I have kids, I'll have to have my mom teach me half of them so they can continue to be passed down."

Emma tried to take stock of her family traditions. Or if they even had any. The traditions of her own family had been so generic they could fit into any random working-class household in America. And maybe hers were even weirder. Frozen meals on Thanksgiving. Shopping for Christmas presents the day after Christmas, since everything was on sale. And Velveeta seemed to take center stage like some on-screen narrator as she thought about her childhood.

She tried to fathom having so many traditions that you didn't even know half of them by the time you were in your twenties. Impossible.

"Like what kind of traditions, if you don't mind me asking?" Now Emma was just curious.

"Oh, I mean, there is the difference of language and religion and where you're from. But then there is how you pray and which festivals you celebrate and how you celebrate them. How you cook food and whether you're a vegetarian or not. And then there may be certain foods you don't eat on top of that. And there are things like what kind of clothes you wear or how you wear them. Oh, and what kinds of jobs are acceptable to your parents." She took a break to inhale. "I think that's it."

"So basically your entire life."

"Yeah, I guess it is. Our generation is more open minded about it, I think, but there are a lot of people out there, and a lot of parents haven't really come around to the idea."

"Maybe they don't want to lose all these traditions." The idea that she could have had so many traditions to remember her parents by, and really had none to cling onto, made melancholy sweep over her.

"I think so. I know my parents are already talking about their grandchildren, and I'm not even married yet!"

"I guess that's why it's hard to have a boyfriend. You never met anyone at work?" Emma asked, wondering how boyfriends and girlfriends fit into this world of arranged marriages.

"No," she said, looking down at her coffee. A smile emerged. "I mean, seriously, have you looked at those nerds?"

Emma laughed. Rishi popped into her head. With his polished shoes and tight jeans and messy flop of hair. She'd been too busy and, if she was being honest, concerned about him to take notice of anyone else at work.

{ /** *. // }

Tonight she had to meet Rishi to talk about the algorithm. At a pub. Her idea had been that beer would serve as the referee and keep them from killing each other. Her stomach felt a bit fluttery, though. Another new adventure in a series of weekly adventures.

She'd been sitting in traffic in the back of a Maruti Suzuki for a full thirty minutes. Cars packed together in the street, forming a solid mass of headlights, exhaust, and honking. Scooters, motorcycles, and bicycles emerged from the cracks, weaving through a labyrinth of exposed pavement. When a gap opened, engines surged, each vehicle inching its way down the crowded street. Emma sat in the unmoving car, watching the smoke billow around in the headlights. People walked through the traffic, and she wondered if it would be quicker to do the same, even if it did seem like a smog-saturated death trap.

The life of the city streets beyond the uneven sidewalks was darkened, set against the glaring abundance of headlights. Emma caught glimpses of buildings and sidewalk but couldn't see past the edges of the road. They were surrounded by people. There were countless couples on motorcycles, the women covering their faces with their dupattas or the hems of their saris to keep out the smog. A group of young women huddled together in an auto-rickshaw, laughing, looking at their phones. A man passed her, pedaling his bicycle in flip-flops and tired-looking khaki pants.

Emma stared into their lives and saw a glimpse of what they might be doing—a woman going home to wash the soot out of her hair, girls going out to a pub for the first time, a man cycling home to a small one-room house where his wife had cooked rice and lentils for dinner.

As they inched closer to MG Road, the main thoroughfare in Bangalore, hundreds of young people crowded the sidewalks, their bodies meshed together like the traffic, packed in and barely moving.

What had Preeti said about it being difficult to have a boyfriend? Emma couldn't imagine all these men waiting to touch a girl until they were married. She couldn't imagine Rishi waiting at all.

Emma, it's actually quite a big snake.

There it was again. Could she ever forget those words, or the way he'd said them? How his eyes had burned into hers, secret laughter boiling behind them, just waiting for her to say something, anything. Maybe he was just talking about cobras, but she couldn't deny that, on impulse, her eyes had flitted to his crotch. Then, afraid she'd been caught, she'd turned mute. Speechless. A rarity for her.

But Rishi would just have to lean over a girl, flash her those metallic eyes, the muscles in his forearm vibrating at her, and with one carefully crafted sentence she'd be his victim. Poor things. There was no way he was saving himself for marriage.

The driver stopped in front of a tall office building bordered by a coffee shop and a grocery store. "Thank you!" She shut the door and walked into a dark wooded bar with cricket games playing on four different TV screens in each corner. The Rolling Stones drifted softly out of the speakers. Her stomach was in knots. And there was Rishi at a table in the corner.

She sucked up any lingering anxiety, the origins of which she couldn't quite place, and walked over to him like she was auditioning for the role of cheerful, pleasant, yet dynamic coworker. "Hello."

"Hey, Emma." Rishi straightened up and put his phone down. "How's it going?" His voice was tentative. Almost wary. Maybe she wasn't the only person who was anxious over being together outside the office. Neutral ground, and yet not neutral at all. Wars had been started over similar circumstances, she was sure.

She squinted up at him and forgot what she wanted to say; the only thought was *Alone with Rishi. Alone with Rishi.*

"Well, it must be really complicated if it's taking that long for you to answer." Rishi laughed.

The last thing Emma wanted was to appear like a complete dolt. "I'm just dandy." Because, yeah, that was a totally normal thing to say.

"Do you want a drink?"

She looked at the bar. *Need* was the more appropriate word. She needed a drink. She needed to calm her nerves. She needed to think.

But what she really needed was to figure out Rishi. The one person who made her feel like she'd regressed to an awkward adolescent girl clad in hand-me-downs. And also, her best hope to make the Helix app successful.

Hopeless.

She took a deep breath. A drink could help lubricate their conversation. Ugh, *lubricate*? "Maybe a beer?"

"What do you like?"

She glanced at the menu on the table. "Kingfisher?" She'd seen the signs and commercials for the brand. "Is it good? I haven't had any Indian beer yet."

"Kingfisher's good if you prefer a lager. But if you're in an adventurous mood, try a Haywards 5000."

"It's not some kind of secret fiery, spicy beer that you're going to torture me with, is it?" Maybe she should verify, just in case . . .

A roar of a chuckle erupted out of Rishi as he tilted his head back, Adam's apple bobbing in his throat. She could see the silver in the back of his molars. Quite the intimate view. But this laughter was the contagious type, and she found herself smiling just watching him. "What?" she asked.

"Your face!"

Emma's hand came up to her cheek. "Why? What is it?"

"You look so scared. Geez, why are you so paranoid? You're the one who took my job, remember? And I'm putting my trust in you to find me a life partner."

She bit down on her lip. Okay, maybe she was being a tad paranoid, though she had good reason to be. But she wasn't about to regale him with *The Story of Emma*, the one subtitled *The Hardships of a Poor Orphan from the Trailer Park*, and below that, in parentheses: *Who had to struggle like hell to get where she is today.*

"Sorry." She smiled at Rishi. "Let's get two Haywards. I'm intrigued."

The server set down two 750 ml bottles of beer in front of them and poured them into pint glasses. Maybe they were intriguing because of their size. Emma took a sip of the bitter, thick beer and almost coughed. She picked up the bottle to read it. "This is almost eight percent alcohol. Now I know what you mean by 'adventurous.'" She drank up, easing her nerves into a dense Haywards-induced fog.

"It's good, though, right?" Rishi said, drinking his down smoothly like water, the smile still lighting up his face. "I like this place. My friends and I used to come here all the time and watch cricket." His smile glazed over with melancholy, a look that Emma had seen in the mirror when she remembered fleeting moments with her parents.

"Oh." She whispered, "Did something happen?"

Rishi leaned back in his chair and blew out a sigh. "Yeah, they all got married. Pub outings now are severely diminished."

"Ah." So he also needed to join his friends in their marital bliss. She asked, "You must be dying to finish your algorithm then?" at the same time Rishi asked, "So what do you think of Bangalore?"

She laughed, and Rishi smiled.

"Sorry, you first," they both said at the same time.

"No, you," she said, just as he said, "I insist," gesturing his hand toward her.

She shook her head, marveling in horror at how their brains seemed to be connected on some higher plane.

His thumb and forefinger pressed together, and he made a zipping gesture across his lips.

She chuckled. "Okay, I'll start. Why don't you tell me what you thought of Seattle?"

Rishi set his beer down with a thunk. "Well, first of all, the people there are sort of fake friendly. They'll stop if you try to ask a question but then try to escape from you as soon as possible, like you could potentially murder them after you got directions. It's kind of rude."

"Hold on!" Emma interrupted him, wanting to defend her precious city, but also, he was sort of right. "*Maybe* they take a while to open up."

"Maybe? Maybe they act like a stranger is trying to steal their first-born when you just want some pizza."

"It's the gloom. Everyone is just scurrying off for shelter in case of rain."

Rishi hiked up an eyebrow at her. Maybe she wasn't buying her own argument either. The Seattle Freeze was a thing, after all.

"Well, what about here? I get stared at all the time. That's kind of rude too."

"Well, you do have red hair. That's something to stare at." He paused, studying her face. "And that purple strand. And your eyes . . ."

When their eyes met, Emma realized concrete was maybe not the most accurate color to describe his. There was a luminescence about them that shone in even the bar lights. Too bad they were wasted on Rishi. She looked back at the table and pulled the beer to her lips, needing to avoid them.

Rishi continued. "The other thing that bothered me was all the homeless people. Asking for money, screaming at people."

"Wait a minute," Emma said, holding out her hand to stop him. "The homeless people? There's poverty here too. And the kids!" Emma sighed and took a drink. She hadn't been able to forget the kids who had surrounded her and Preeti's auto-rickshaw the other day, asking for money, for anything.

"I know. But in the US, you have so many resources. There's free food for poor people and places for them to sleep. Organizations dedicated to it. We have nothing compared to that here. And so many of them seem to have some kind of mental illness. Why isn't anyone helping them?"

Emma took a drink, thinking back to only a few months ago, when she'd had to jump in the street and had almost gotten run over to escape the flailing arms of a guy yelling at himself, or at imaginary people, or at her—she couldn't tell. "People help, but I think it's complicated." She swallowed. She had convinced her team to go with her and volunteer at the shelter once a month, and she tried to help people when she could. But as much as the city said they were working on helping these people, it just seemed to get worse.

"And another thing is that the food doesn't taste as good."

She almost spit out the mouthful of beer. The food? This, she could argue. Seattle had a phenomenal food scene. The best! Enough of this silly exchange. "What do you mean? You clearly didn't eat at the right places."

"Yes, but the Indian food doesn't taste like real Indian food. It's dumbed down, or something, for your weak American palates. You can't take the spice. You have no idea what you're missing!"

She felt like she had to jump to India Palace's defense, to champion her beloved takeout. "You're exaggerating. And at least there's variety," she said. "Italian, Spanish, Mexican, Vietnamese, Japanese . . . and that's just what my week looks like."

"You don't think there's variety in Indian food?" Rishi sat back in his chair, looking offended. "Oh my God! We have so much variety— Gujarati, Punjabi, Mysore, Chettinad, South Indian, Kerala, Hyderabadi, and the list goes on. You have no idea." He shook his head. "And that's just what my *day* looks like."

"Hmm. Well, looks like I need a tour guide of Indian food."

"We've started," Rishi said, holding up his beer. "First we're starting with Haywards; next stop, Kingfisher!" He clinked his glass against hers.

Emma picked up the menu. "Actually, I'm kind of starving. Do you want to eat anything?"

"Yes, pub food is the best." He scanned the menu. "We should get gobi manchurian, masala papad, and oh my God, they have kothu parotta. Done." He called the server over and then paused. "Wait, are those okay?"

"Yeah, I'm up for whatever." She almost said, *I trust you*, and then she realized that even if that statement was referring to the food, she was handing over the keys to her mental castle. Horrified, she drank the rest of her beer as he ordered. What was happening?

"Good call on the food," he said as the server hurried away.

"Which kind of Indian food is your favorite?"

Rishi scrunched up his face, apparently deep in thought. His mouth opened and closed, like he was on the verge of speaking but then changed his mind. He worried at his lip during this process.

"My mom's." He nodded to himself and took a drink of his beer.

"She must be an excellent cook then." Emma couldn't believe that, in a country of a billion people, twenty-nine states, and apparently just as many cuisines, his mother's cooking was still his favorite.

"Damn good. Our community's food is unique. We're vegetarian, don't eat garlic or onion or even paneer, really, but it's amazing how good the food can taste. I mean, I eat everything now, but I didn't even try a lot of things until college."

A life without garlic or onion? Or meat? She had friends who were vegetarian—that was one thing—but flavor was not something she could eagerly sacrifice. "I just can't imagine how the food can taste good. It's basically just vegetables and lentils then?"

"And pulses and rice and spices. There is so much taste; you can't even imagine."

"But why no garlic or onion? It's not meat."

Rishi laughed, and it sort of faded into a groan. "It's supposed to cause heat in the body, which, in turn, makes you . . . desirous." Was he blushing?

"What?" Emma laughed. "So you're telling me that garlic and onion breath has an amorous quality to it?"

"Something like that. Or that's what they think."

"Interesting. I'll have to try it sometime. I mean, the kind of food you're talking about—not using garlic and onion breath as a seduction technique." Oh my God, did those words just come out of her mouth?

Rishi didn't seem fazed, though. "There is one place that's okay, but it's not like my mom's. We can go next week for lunch."

Lunch plans with Rishi. The idea made her breathe deep, hoping that it was a real invitation and not some kind of deception. Because when food was concerned . . .

And just then their order was dropped on the table, bringing with it the smells of spice and tomato and cilantro. Cauliflower coated in some kind of salty, tangy sauce that wasn't quite Chinese or Indian. Like the two cuisines had mated and had a glorious red-tinged baby. She couldn't stop popping them in her mouth with the toothpicks embedded in each one.

"So good with beer," Rishi said, still chewing.

Emma moaned in response. It just came out of her. Like the food was turning her tongue into a helpless, sensory-starved organ that needed more. She crisped off a piece of the lentil-and-rice popadam sitting on her plate that was coated in chilies and onion and tomato. "Why is this so good?" She shook her head at it. It was so absolutely simple, and yet it was divine.

"It's like these mad chefs just know what food to serve with booze."

"Usually, at a pub at home, all we have are fries and chicken wings or some crap." Emma shook her head again at the dumbness of it.

"Try this one." He pushed over the dish of what looked like cut-up pieces of parathas with some kind of reddish-brown sauce flecked with cilantro. "It's from my state, and it's amazing."

She dug in with her fork. The flavor melted into her every pore, if that were possible. She actually felt like she was sinking deeper into her chair. The pleasure of such good food was weighing her down, carrying away the worry, leading her down a delicious saucy river.

"So good." She shook her head, and he laughed. It was like her vocabulary had been reduced to a four-year-old's and her body had been overtaken by flavor.

While they finished the bottles of Kingfisher they'd ordered, the barman announced last call.

Emma sucked in a breath. "We didn't even get to talk about your algorithm."

Rishi waved his hand in between them. "Ah, it's okay. When we go to lunch, we can talk about it."

"Okay, if you're sure. I started working on it, but I had some questions."

He nodded and downed the rest of his beer. They split the bill, and Emma pulled out her phone. "I'm going to call a car to go home."

"Alone?" Rishi asked.

"Uh, yeah." Who did he think was going to go with her?

"I'll go with you. Sometimes you have to be careful."

Emma studied his face. Maybe he was right. She couldn't speak the local language in Bangalore, Kannada. She didn't know her way around this city at all. And if she was honest, the only people she could call if she was in trouble were Rishi, Preeti, and Jas.

"Okay, thanks."

They walked outside, and Rishi studied the app on his phone. "It's like three times the price as usual." He looked around. "Let's just get an auto."

A procession of auto-rickshaws was down the street. He walked over to one, throwing up his hands after a brief discussion, and then another. Emma guessed he was trying to negotiate a price.

Was it the extra-large-size beers, or did Bangalore at the moment seem almost like Seattle? The bars were closed, and people were sprinkled together on the street corner, trying to get a ride to take them home. Maybe the two cities weren't so different.

He found a ride and they hopped in. As they drove toward her house, the cool night air twisted in her hair and around her face.

"One time"—Rishi leaned toward her, his breath skating her cheek—"I was coming home from the pub, and I convinced the auto driver to let me drive."

"What?" Emma laughed as the driver glanced up with a hard look in the rearview mirror. "I bet it's fun to drive one."

"Yeah, see how small that seat is? We were on it together, and this guy was not small."

Emma eyed the tiny bench seat in front of her and then glanced down at Rishi's thighs. Rishi wasn't small either. He had thick, muscular legs and probably went to the gym every day.

"Well, I'm sure you can be very persuasive when you need to be."

"You have no idea." The way he said it made Emma stiffen. Like his voice had dropped two octaves and purred. If men could purr.

"I'm sure," she said with a sneer, her hard shell sneaking up her spine. Manipulation and condescension could likely get a guy like him far.

They got to her house, and Rishi said something to the driver she couldn't understand, maybe in Kannada. He got out with her. "I can walk you to the door."

"That's okay. I'll be fine." She glanced around. A wave of nervousness caused every hair on her arm to tingle.

"I insist. There could be a cobra lurking nearby." His voice was playful.

Suggestive snake jokes flooded her mind. She swallowed the thoughts whole and cleared her throat. "Don't worry about it. Thanks for the ride. I'll see you tomorrow."

She walked as quickly to her house as she could without running and then locked the door behind her. Her chest was heaving. Why was she so out of breath? Why had she run away from the auto? She just needed some sleep to set her mind straight. It had been a long week.

And a brand-new week, full of work—and Rishi—was starting tomorrow.

CHAPTER 16

Rishi cringed, his thumb hovering over the call icon on his phone. His phone, his nemesis. His portal to another tirade of disappointment. He currently had three profiles of potential brides in his email that his parents had sent over.

Regardless of whether he was ready or not, he still had to call his mother back after replying to her every call over the weekend with a text message saying he couldn't talk. He was shopping. Work had come up. He had a whole pocket of innocent lies and feeble excuses in reserve. After all, what could he say to her this time? *Sorry I can't find anyone good enough for me* and *you*. *Sorry my own attempts at creating an optimized search have only turned up prostitutes.*

He hunched in a corner so no one at work could hear his conversation, steeled himself, and waited for her inevitable disappointment. He wasn't interested in the profiles they'd sent over, but he had a plan. He wasn't going to take the night train back to Madurai until his algorithm was ready and he had at least a few women who seemed like perfect matches. Perfect for him, perfect for his family, and perfect for any potential families who were interested in his sister.

"Hi, Ma."

Rishi got the words out just before his mother asked, "Why haven't you called? Are you okay?"

"Yes, Mom. Everything's fine."

"Did you see the email from your father? We haven't heard from you. What about this Pallavi? She seemed like a good match for you."

Pallavi was practically his sister's age. He didn't even know what his parents had been thinking. "She's too young."

"What do you expect, Rishi? You've waited until the last minute to get married." The exasperation in his mother's voice shredded him with guilt.

"Look, I have something in progress. Something that will help me find someone perfect. You and Appa are working too hard at it. Focus on Dharini, and I will try to find someone. Then, if it doesn't work out, you can search again."

"Rishi, you are one year from thirty," his mother responded in their native Tamil. "You're already so old. I'll die before I have grandchildren. How long will this take? Look at your schoolmates. Kumar down the street has been married for years and already has two babies."

Rishi rolled his eyes. Only because he was on the phone and his mother couldn't see. He'd heard this argument so many times that it played in his mind like an old record. The soundtrack of his life for the past few years. He knew what she would say next, even though he'd tune it out. *The relatives are asking why you aren't married. Most good boys are married by twenty-eight at the latest. Everyone is wondering what's wrong with you. All we want are grandchildren and someone to take care of you.*

Sometimes it was like she'd stepped out of one of those drama-filled soap operas she took a break every afternoon to watch. He wanted a partner in life, not just someone who checked all his parents' boxes.

"Your horoscope lines up with Pallavi's. She's from a good Iyengar family, just like you."

"I have to go to a meeting." There was no way he could consider marrying someone who was just out of college.

"Rishi . . ."

"How is Dharini?"

"She is fine. Going to work. Not as choosy as you when we look at potential matches."

"I said I'm working on it. I have to go. I'll call later." Rishi hung up the phone.

He looked out into the distance of the tech park with a sigh. His chest felt as if he'd been punched the day before, and an ache was spreading across his sternum. Guilt. The feeling had been present after every conversation with his parents about a potential marriage match over the past year.

His phone beeped. If this was his mom again . . .

He pulled out his phone. His stomach dropped when he saw the name. A name he hadn't seen in far too long.

Rishi, Are you still in Bangalore? I'll be there next week. Can we meet for lunch?

Sudhar. His brother. The man who had defied convention and married outside their caste and community. Even outside their state. The same person who was responsible for his parents' loss of their money.

But Rishi had a nephew or niece—he didn't know which yet, but he could find out soon. It wasn't the baby's fault that his brother had acted recklessly. Beyond recklessly. Had been an idiot. Thought with his heart, and likely other essential organs, over his head. Maybe he could meet him. At least see a picture. Maybe get the baby a present.

Lunch? Lunch he could do. It wasn't like he was making a blood pact with the one person whose name wasn't allowed to be uttered in his house.

Sure, let's do that.

He'd admired Sudhar so much growing up. He'd even admired him for breaking tradition and marrying for love. At the time he'd been dating Sapna and thought that this would be the path for all of them, and Sudhar was simply paving the way. Until Sudhar's marriage had destroyed the family. And just like that, the unraveling of their familial threads and the loss of their savings had proved their parents right about their über-traditional values.

And, of course, now he wasn't going to make a mistake by marrying the wrong woman. He'd find something like he'd had with Sapna, but this time with a woman who was appropriate in all ways possible. And who wouldn't leave him because her family wanted her to marry someone from her community in North India.

You've just made my year. Thank you.

He and Emma had to finish the algorithm, and soon.

Since last night, Rishi had thought of his time with Emma at the pub more than once. He hadn't imagined that the buttoned-up, closed-up ice queen would drink one of the giant beers, but she'd had two, and she hadn't even erupted in giggles and nonsense like a lot of women would have.

He trudged down the hall to her office and found her typing away, busy at her screen. "Emma?"

Her fingertips stopped dancing on the keys, and she looked up at him. The deep green of the salwar top electrified everything about her. The rhinestones plucked the controlled seriousness from her eyes, while the red and purple of her hair vibrated in contrast to the color. Her face was less pallid, almost bright.

"Yes?" she crooned out with a smile. It confused him but made him smile in return.

"You look nice today." The words just fell out of Rishi's mouth. "I didn't know you wore our traditional clothes."

"When in Rome . . . ," she said, running fingertips along the top. "I was thinking how it's like ninety degrees outside, and I'm covered head to toe in two layers of polyester and a scarf. A dress, pants, scarf—it's quite a lot. Although I like the freedom to just sit however I want, so there is definitely practicality in that. No risk of indecent exposure or anything." Her face, which had briefly laughed, abruptly closed off. "Sorry, TMI, huh? Did you need something?"

Rishi shook his head slowly. He was still caught up on the fact that Emma seemed to be talking to him about spreading her legs. "Since we didn't talk about the algorithm this weekend, I wanted to follow up. I need it. Like soon. Very soon."

"Oh. Yeah, crazy how we ran out of time, right? I had all these words pop up in my search, and I'm not sure what they mean, so I need to do some refining. Do you want to talk over lunch?"

"Sure."

Her eyes lit up again. "Hey, can we go to that place you were talking about that has your traditional food? I need to continue my tour of Indian cuisine."

"It's vegetarian. Is that okay?"

"Yes, I'm fully prepared to eat a wholesome meal of lentils and vegetables. It will be like medicine for my complete indulgence this past week. I've been stuffing myself full of kebabs and parathas and paneer butter masala."

"Okay. I'll come back at noon."

{ /** *. // }

A few hours later, Emma popped up behind him. "I'm starving. Can we eat a bit early? Please?" Amazing how Emma could morph from domineering project lead into a hungry toddler in the span of a few hours.

"Sure." He locked his laptop, and they started toward the elevator. "Do you want to catch an auto?" he asked. "It's like five minutes driving away."

"Is that how you get around everywhere?"

"No, I have a bike. It's in the garage."

"Motorcycle bike, not a bicycle, I'm assuming?" She hit the button on the elevator.

"Correct."

"Do you want to take it?"

"Do you want to ride on it?" Surely she wouldn't. What would people say if they saw the two of them together like that? Emma slung over his body, her arms around him, on the back seat of his Bullet?

"Yeah, why not? I've actually never ridden on a motorcycle before, and I figure this is the perfect place to do so, since the traffic travels at a snail's pace."

"Okay." He rubbed at his chin. He hit the garage button once they were inside, and his heart sped up. The thoughts in his head volleyed between wondering if Emma would wrap her arms around his waist and wondering what the drivers would say when they saw her on the back of his bike.

She followed him to his bike. Black and chrome reflected the garage lights along its curves. Its custom handlebar, muffler, and paint job made it uniquely his. He would have missed it for sure if he'd moved to Seattle.

"Ooh, it's so shiny. I like it."

"Thanks." He thumbed the helmet hanging off his handlebar. "I only have one helmet, though, and I have to wear it by law. Or else . . ." This wouldn't do. "Why don't we just take an auto?"

"Five minutes, right? Going maybe fifteen miles an hour? I'm pretty sure I could jump off before anything would hit us. Just don't wreck it, okay?"

He started his bike, and Emma scrambled on behind him, like she was mounting a wide horse instead of a medium-size motorcycle, her shoes searching for the footrests, the dress of her salwar getting tangled under her legs. He turned around, their faces too close, the fabric of her clothes sprawling everywhere like silky tentacles. He tried to scoot up in the seat. "Emma, wrap your dupatta around you so it doesn't get caught in the wheel." Number one cause of bike wrecks and unfortunate accidental choking of women riding on the back.

She wrapped the scarf around her body and tied it. "Okay, I'm ready."

"Just hold on to . . . something." He couldn't say *me*. "I don't want you to fly off." But she was right about the snail's pace. Traffic midday, in the same neighborhood: they weren't likely to go over forty kilometers an hour.

They shot up the parking ramp, and the sunshine of the day poured over them. As they hit a speed bump at the top, his shirt tightened across his chest, the pull of Emma's fist holding on to the fabric over the bump. His breath caught in his throat. Such an awkward sensation, feeling the tension looming in the inch between her chest and his back, his annoyance at her stretching out one of his favorite shirts. He wanted to say *Stop* and *Hold me instead*, but he couldn't get the words out. Like the letters were all scrambled and reversed in his head. Longing and distrust like two friends fighting it out.

But it was five minutes. He could deal with five minutes.

They pulled up to the Pure-Veg eatery. As he got off the bike, Emma stared up at the sign, her face pinched in confusion. Maybe this wasn't the best idea. She probably didn't eat at places like this, with stand-up tables for people who needed to eat fast and a separate AC room that charged more for the food so you didn't have to sweat and eat at the same time.

"Is this okay?" he asked.

"Yes. I'm excited to try it."

The bright lights lit up the plain, almost sterile interior. Rishi claimed one of the regular tables inside so they could sit down, and a server brought two menus. "Okay, what should I get?" Emma asked.

"Well, do you want a meal, like the little dishes with rice? See that guy's?" He nodded toward the table next to him, where a stout man was mixing rice and sambar on his metal tray. Emma stared at the guy's plate. He stared back, his eyes unflinching.

She whipped back around. "What's the other option?"

"Their dosas are really good. I like their chutney here."

"Sold! You said 'chutney.' Get me one of those."

The one and only thing that Emma didn't try to take over was the process of ordering with the waiter. Like food and Haywards 5000s were the two things that could coax her into submission. Or at least equal ground. He tried to get comfortable on the hard seat. "So you wanted to ask me some questions?"

"Yes, let me pull out all the phrases I've seen. I need to just pinpoint which are relevant and which aren't. Some of these things . . . I'm just not sure what they mean." She shook her head and looked at her phone. "Oh, but this one I do. I've been dying to ask you this all day."

His heart sped up. What could it be? Something humiliating, something she'd found out about him? He cleared his throat. "Okay, what is it?"

"Are you, Rishi Iyengar"—her face was so serious that the question made his stomach stir—"a mama's boy?"

"What?"

Emma exploded in laughter. The tables around them all turned to the red-haired foreigner slapping the table like he'd told her the funniest joke she'd ever heard.

"No, I am not a mama's boy." He lowered his voice. "Why on earth would you ask me that?"

"Because I saw it in the web crawl results and just needed to know if I should include it in your profile." Her smile was wicked, so pleased with herself. "You did say that your favorite food was your mom's."

"That doesn't mean I'm a mama's boy. I have a healthy respect for my mother's cooking."

"Well, whatever. I'm sure most guys who are don't think they actually are. Next question." She looked back down at the notes on her phone. "Okay, this word—*homely*. I have a feeling it doesn't mean the same thing as in the US."

"What does it mean there?" he asked.

"Like a plain-looking, below-average girl. It's definitely not something you *want* to be described as. I'm imagining it stems from a girl who looks like she's never been out of the house or something."

Rishi almost coughed up his water. "What?" Now it was his turn to laugh, although not as loudly as she had. "No, that's not what it means here. It just means a girl is good in the home, like she cooks and cleans and has an orderly house, like that."

"Ah, so you *want* a homely girl?"

"Yeah, sure."

"That was a box I definitely didn't think I would be checking. Okay, also 'no dowry'—how does this apply to you? Are we thinking about a dowry?" She squinted at him as she tapped her nails on the table, toying with him.

"No, we are *not* thinking about a dowry." But in reality, the family of the woman he married would surely pass on some gold to their daughter. Some people gave houses or cars. Something would come out of it. "Next question."

"I just love all this medieval dowry stuff mixed in with this super-tech-fueled world we live in."

"I know. Change is hard. Tradition still reigns, et cetera. Dowry is technically illegal, by the way." For the next generation, he was convinced things would be different, but for his parents, they were unflinching in their beliefs.

"Dowry is so illegal that they only post about it if they're *not* interested?" Emma's eyebrows rose up to contradict him. He was getting ready to explain how nuanced their society was, but she was already moving on to the next question.

"Okay, let's talk about your values. Would you say you have moderate, liberal, or conservative religious values? Tell me about the values of the Iyengar family."

Rishi's values were ten steps ahead of his parents' on the progressive scale, but the marriage was for him *and* them. The girl would be his wife but his parents' daughter-in-law. "I would say my values are modern, liberal, and traditional."

"Don't modern and traditional contradict one another?"

"Not necessarily. Like I think it's important for her to do whatever she wants and be who she wants to be, but it's important she knows about the festivals and traditions and all that stuff. I mean, it's more important to my mother than me. I just care that she wants to light up firecrackers during Diwali—that's my tradition."

"Okay, so it's not your matrimonial ad I read online that said 'Modern and traditional—you can wear jeans at home, but wear traditional clothes to show respect outside.'" Emma's smile was somehow both sarcastic and amused at the same time.

"No, that's not mine," he said, deadpan, and with perfect timing, their food arrived. The waiter set down a dosa in front of each of them, the rolled-up lentil-rice batter cooked so thin it was like a paper scroll.

Emma leaned over her plate as she usually did and took a big sniff. He laughed. "Do you do that every time?"

"What?" She glanced up at him, still bent over her plate.

"Smell your food?"

"I want to savor it all." Then she took a picture of it.

"And you always take a picture too?"

"I have to document it all. I post my photos of each meal. Kind of like a journal for myself, but I have followers. And my best friend and I promised to share all our food experiences while we're apart."

This was not what he'd expected to hear. He'd expected her to say she took pictures to conduct some kind of comparative quality analysis online, where she wrote an algorithm to pull all dosa photos and compare the size and shape of her meal with others' meals to determine if hers was the best. And if it wasn't, she'd come back and complain.

"Okay, what are these?" She pointed to the three different chutneys on her plate.

"That one is coconut chutney. This one is tomato—it's the best, in my opinion—and then that one is peanut."

"Yum!"

Rishi grabbed a bite of dosa and dipped it in the tomato chutney. His fingers paused in front of his mouth as he realized Emma was watching him. "What?" Was she judging him?

"I'm just watching you to know how to eat it."

"Oh. Well, you just take a bite." Why did he need to explain how to eat her food?

Her lips pressed together, and she seemed to wiggle in her seat. Her right hand pinched off a small piece of the crispy dosa edge and dipped it in the chutney like a chip in salsa at a Mexican restaurant.

"If you eat bites that small, we're going to be here for five hours."

She sighed and took a bigger piece, probably too big to fit in her mouth, and pinched the chutney around it. That was more like it. She stuffed it in her mouth. Her eyes fluttered closed, and her chewing was slow and calculated. A moan growled in her throat.

Rishi had to look away. Why did it seem like every time they ate she was having an erotic experience? It unsettled him. It was intriguing and uncomfortable at the same time. He tried to focus on his food.

"Oh my God, what is in this? Why does it taste like butter, and there's something rich and thick about it. It's so good." She pointed at the tomato chutney.

"Thick?" The weirdest way to describe a taste.

"Yeah, like it seems as if it's just tomato or something, right? But it's so much more. And this." Her finger slid along the dosa. "How do they get it so thin? It's like a work of art."

"I mean, I told you they make a pretty good dosa."

"So good." She took another fingerful of dosa and savored it just as before.

He was clearly missing something. He loved food, but Emma's reactions made him feel like he didn't appreciate it as much as he should. He took another bite and tried to focus on what she sensed. He smelled ghee and mustard seeds and the almost charred scent of something roasted. In his mouth, the tang of tomato. There was an earthiness from the fermented batter he didn't usually recognize, the textures soft and hard on his tongue. The tamarind and cumin added dimension to the tomato. Was that what made it taste "thick"?

"I can tell you like it," she said, smiling at him.

"Well, yeah, I like it." He cleared his throat, hoping he didn't look like he was on the verge of orgasm like Emma did. "I eat here all the time. I'm just trying to see what you see in it."

"I'm just showing my appreciation, my respect for this thing I can absolutely not do. I can't cook, and my family wasn't really into cooking either. You're lucky to have been raised on food this good. I grew up on cans of vegetables and hot dogs."

Rishi nodded. "I'm sure some people would say that the food is lucky to have someone getting so much pleasure out of it."

She paused her chewing and gave him a blank look. Maybe it was surprise. It was so brief Rishi didn't know what it meant. "I love the balance of everything. How the chutneys calm the heat of the sambar. The liquid against the hard crust of the dosa." She swallowed another bite.

"We have to have everything in balance. That should be most things. Hot and cold in equal measures. Soft and hard. They are principles in a lot of cultures."

Emma nodded. "I agree with it all. Although I'm tempted to go into excess from wanting to eat too much of the balance."

Maybe that was the trick with her. He needed to find what balanced her out. What thawed the ice queen's frosty exterior? What kind of unique heat did she need to relax and enjoy and be calm?

"Can I ask you something?" she said as she finished her dosa and sat up in her chair.

"Yes?" But it came out as a question. Rishi was poised for potential disaster.

"Do you still resent me for getting the job instead of you?"

"I don't resent you." These words came out, and Rishi realized they were true now, even though a week ago he couldn't have said the same.

She gave him a doubtful look, her eyebrows up and demanding a real response.

He leaned back in his chair and fiddled with the napkin that lay untouched beside his plate. "Look, I was upset because Jas had essentially promised me that job, and I wanted to work in Seattle—well, in the US." He looked up and met her gaze. The demanding stare had evaporated, and her lips were parted and her eyebrows nestled over her eyes.

"Why? You're like Indian food's number one fan, and you told me you didn't like Seattle."

While Rishi hadn't planned on telling her any of this, a weight felt like it was lifting off him. "There are some family things going on, which is part of the reason I need to get married." He took a deep breath. He didn't have to tell her the whole story, but at least she could know how much he needed that algorithm to work. "My sister wants to get married. She's younger, and weddings are expensive. So, I was hoping to have a bigger salary by working in the US and send the money back to my parents to help. But then things changed. That's why I need to find a wife. It looks bad that I'm not married yet, and I need to make sure my sister doesn't have yet something else stacked against her in her search for a husband."

"I didn't know it was for your family, and especially your sister." She shook her head, looking down at the space between their two plates. Her lips pressed together again, and she looked up at him, a steely seriousness falling over her face. "I'll finish your code this week."

CHAPTER 17

Rishi pulled up in front of the South Indian place his brother had suggested and killed the engine. The week that had passed since Sudhar had contacted him hadn't really prepared him to see his brother. It had been two years since the marriage. Not that he was expecting him to look completely different, but it wouldn't be the worst thing if he looked a little bedraggled, some bags under his eyes, maybe like he'd lost some sleep over what he'd done to their family.

Or they could be bags from waking up with a crying baby. It was hard to imagine Sudhar, the brother who had once pulled Rishi's pants down in the middle of the street, as a father.

His hands trembled slightly. His breath was heavy. For God's sake, this was lunch with his brother, not the first time he was meeting his hope-to-be-future wife. They'd eaten countless meals together. They'd gotten in fights, made up, and then fought again. That's all this was. Except Sudhar was married to a woman who was responsible for stealing his family's money, and he didn't care. He hadn't left her, and they had a baby. There was no real explanation for it.

He walked inside and scanned the tables, wondering if he'd be able to recognize Sudhar after two years. Or if there was some brotherly pull that would just bring them together like a long-lost magnet and a hunk of iron.

"Rishi!" a voice called from behind him.

He turned around. There was a bearded man at a booth, his arm raised in a hesitant wave. A beard? No one in their family had a beard. No one in their community had a beard. Just having this hair on his face made him a different person now. Like he was saying a big *fuck you* to their traditions and customs and heritage. Maybe it was just facial hair, but they both knew how odd it was for him to have it.

Rishi swallowed and walked toward Sudhar as his brother stood, a little wobbly as he leaned on the table. Sudhar had a bit of a belly now, that was all. Otherwise he was pretty much the same old Sudhar who had tortured him growing up. The same Sudhar he'd always admired.

Until a year ago, when everything had fallen apart. It was absolute irony that the steps his brother had taken to bring the two families together after his marriage were the breaking point that would split them apart for good.

Rishi was at first afraid Sudhar would try to hug him, but he just stuck out his hand like they were meeting each other for a business lunch. Rishi shook his hand back formally. What a strange sensation.

He sat across from him in the booth. "You have a beard."

Sudhar rubbed his cheeks with the broad expanse of one hand. "Yeah. I just got lazy. I thought about shaving it before we met, but . . . I kind of like it." He huffed a laugh.

"So, what are you in town for?" Rishi asked. He had to know if it was some additional shady business with Sona's shady family.

He gripped the metal water tumbler and tapped it gently on the table. "I'm here for business. I work for an IT company in Delhi, doing sales. I have a meeting here this week, and I'm just in town for a few days."

Rishi nodded. Delhi. So that's where he was living. "Sales? No more accounting?" His brother had been an accountant, like their dad, at a company in Madurai.

"Well, when you have to move, you have to find a new job. Turns out I'm good at sales." He shrugged.

"I knew you must still be living up north if you requested we come here." Rishi shook his head, grinning, but not because anything was particularly funny. It was just comforting that he still knew something about his brother.

"I miss good, spicy Andhra food."

The server came by, and they both ordered meals. When the server asked "Veg or nonveg?" the two brothers looked at each other. Sudhar said "Veg" and Rishi said "Nonveg," and they both laughed.

"You're nonveg now?" Sudhar asked. He shook his head, laughing. "Does Amma know?"

"No way, man. Are you kidding? I figured you'd gone to the dark side as well."

He shook his head. "I didn't leave my beliefs behind. I just married outside the community."

And your wife's family stole our family's money. Why don't you care, again? Rishi wanted to say it, but he wanted to know about his new family member before getting so pissed off at Sudhar that he walked out the door.

"So, tell me about your kid," Rishi said.

Sudhar's face lit up. Maybe he did have moon-shaped puffs below his eyes. He pulled out his phone and held it in the middle of the table so they could both look. "Her name is Sejal, and she is now two months old. She is beautiful and she cries all the time."

The first photo was of a wrinkly red-hued baby just slightly bigger than Sudhar's hand. Then the next, a less red, cuter baby with chubby cheeks and eyes squeezed tight. He moved on, scrolling through the photos. "These were just taken last week," Sudhar said as he showed a few pictures of a baby who was beautiful, with almond-shaped eyes and grayish irises.

"Wow, she's got eyes like mine." Rishi shook his head. He couldn't believe it. Like staring at a baby version of himself.

"I know, dude! That's what I said. I wanted to ask Mom for your baby pictures to see what you looked like when you were just born, but you know . . ." His voice trailed off.

Something hit at Rishi's chest. Here was this baby, who was a part of him, a part of his family. All the way in Delhi. He'd probably never meet her. But how could he not? It wasn't the baby's fault that his brother had fucked up.

"So, she has a Punjabi name?" Rishi asked.

"Yeah, well, it's like the only family Sona and I have, so . . ."

The server came back, dishing out rice on their plates with sambar and vegetables and some lamb and goat for Rishi. Sudhar took the spicy dal powder from the table and sprinkled it over his rice.

"Wow, you really missed the spice, huh?" Rishi asked. A niece. A niece who looked like him. He still couldn't believe it. "I'm going home soon, so I'll see if I can find the old photos and send them to you."

"Really?" Sudhar's eyes beamed with . . . what? Hope?

"Yeah, I'll text you some pictures of them."

"Anything is better than nothing."

Sudhar was right. Any relationship with his niece would be better than no relationship. Same with his brother. But how could that happen? How could he get over what had happened, when Sudhar didn't even seem to be remorseful over it? He eyed his brother, examined his face. How could that face, the one Rishi thought he'd known so well, betray his family?

Sudhar met his gaze, and like he could follow the train of thoughts rushing through Rishi's head, his shoulders fell, and his head weakly rolled down to his chest. "Rishi, look. What happened with the bank account . . . I want you to know that Sona and I had no idea. She didn't know her uncle was making a bad investment. Her family lost money too. It was bad for everyone. I just want you to know it wasn't like some kind of targeted attack on Mom and Dad."

Rishi looked up at him. "But you told Appa that the money was a done deal, that it was good, and that Sona's family wanted to make amends with our family."

"Yeah, but I didn't know. All I heard them say was what a great investment this land would be. They were building some big shopping-complex, apartment-building thing, and the land was going to sky-rocket in price. But it had already been bought. Her uncle's buy was bogus. He was told it was a sure thing, but it was like one of those real estate scams you see in a movie or something. After buying it, he went to the land, and a construction company had already started building on it. He showed the company his deed, and the lawyers said it was a fake. He spent all our money on a piece of paper that didn't mean anything."

"And her family didn't research it? I mean, our parents trusted you, and you—" Rishi shook his head, amazed at the idiocy of all of it. "I mean, you're an accountant. All you do, well, all you did, was deal with money. How could you let her uncle make a bad buy like that? How could you get conned and then in turn let your whole family get conned?"

"I know, it sucks. Trust me. I have felt terrible. Sona's felt terrible, I've tried to explain to our parents, but they won't listen. I swear to you: it wasn't like Sona or her parents were out to get our family. It was just unfortunate."

"Unfortunate?"

Sudhar shook his head. "It was horrible. But I can't turn back time and make it unhappen. I can only ask forgiveness, which they've denied me. Now I'll probably never see Dharini again, or our parents. My daughter will be denied half her family. They just blame Sona and Sona's family because they're not one of us."

Rishi had heard it so many times. *This is why you always marry within the community. People don't treat their own kind this way. This is why we never agreed for him to marry this girl. Her family is not like ours. They don't respect us, and now they've stolen from us.* This was only one version of what his mother had said after everything had happened. Before she'd banned their names from being spoken in the house. *If Sudhar had agreed to one of the matches we'd found for him, these good Iyengar girls from families we know, who are like us, then none of this would have happened. We'd still have money, and we'd have our son. He's left us.*

It was always Sudhar abandoning his family, rather than Rishi's parents putting down a decree to never speak to him again. But to them it was the same thing. If you went against the family, then you were not part of the family.

"Rishi, the only thing I can do now is get the money back. I'm trying to save up so I can at least pay Mom and Dad back the money they lost."

Hopefully Sudhar was a really good salesperson. "How's Sona doing with all of this?" Rishi asked. She seemed like a nice girl, but he hadn't had a chance to get to know her. Now she didn't seem so much like the evil temptress their mother had made her out to be, knowing that her family had also lost a lot of money. If what Sudhar said was true.

But why would he lie about it?

"Well, we have her family to help out, so that's why we're in Delhi now. But she's good. She'd like to get to know you, if you're interested."

Rishi sighed. All he'd heard from his parents was how evil Sona's family was. It had all seemed far fetched to Rishi, but it wasn't like a hundred movies hadn't been made about this very scenario.

"Okay, I'll think about it. Right now I have to focus on my own marriage. Dharini wants to get married, so . . ."

"She's a baby!" Sudhar said.

"I know, trust me. She drinks coffee now, has a programming job . . ." Rishi shook his head. At least Sudhar understood what it was like to see his little sister growing up.

"Well, Sona has a very pretty younger sister, if you're interested." He laughed, like it was a hilarious idea.

Rishi just glared at him. How could he even start joking about that?

Sudhar gritted his teeth in an apologetic smile and raised his hands in surrender. "Sorry, I know. Too soon."

{ /** *. // }

Ding. Ding. Ding.

Rishi rubbed at his eyes. A yawn escaped his mouth as he reached over to see what the emergency was on his phone.

These stupid bugs are driving me crazy. I need master app dev skills. That means you.

Even his mom didn't message him this early. Of course Emma would. So early that he hadn't even had coffee.

Why are you working so early?

It's quiet and peaceful and I can focus. And my favorite conference room is free so I can use the big monitor.

Oh, and I have your algorithm results.

What? Why didn't she say that first? Ok, be there in 30.

He made it to the office in record time. After seeing his brother yesterday, he was more motivated than ever to find someone who could help him salvage the remnants of his family.

He grabbed a coffee and turned toward her favorite conference room. But paused. The least he could do was get her one too. He pushed the buttons for cappuccino. It was sort of like a cappuccino. Didn't add sugar. Weirdo.

Two cups of coffee. His laptop bag hung on one shoulder, threatening to slip off. His sunglasses fell from his head and teetered on the end of his nose as he approached the room. He tried to use his hip to push the handle down and splashed coffee on his jeans. "Fuck." He looked through the glass door. Emma was sitting there, laughing at him.

"Help, please," he said, a thread of irritation in his voice, through the practically soundproof glass.

She made a big production of sighing and taking off her headphones and rolling her chair back inch by inch, the wheels moving as slowly as bad bandwidth. Yet the whole time, she was still smiling with complete amusement.

She pulled open the door, her arm sliding up the edge and blocking his entrance to the room with her body. "Can I help you? I mean, you look like you need help."

"Uh, yeah. I got you a coffee. Apparently the last time I'll do that. Take it." He thrust it toward her. Now he could slide his sunglasses back on top of his head and save his suffering forearm from his laptop bag, which he was carrying like an old woman with an oversize purse.

"Oh, why, thank you." Her eyes lit up in surprise as she tasted the coffee, just a sip, and looked up at him through her eyelashes. He tried not to notice how cute she looked, her nose hidden inside the cup, inhaling the coffee. But puppy cute. Like a tiny stray he'd found outside his house who needed help.

Rishi shook his head and glanced up at the projected screen. Now it was his turn to laugh. It reminded him of when his professor had once said, "Done code is better than perfect code." This was definitely just done.

"Wait, are these the bugs you're trying to address? What *is* this code?"

"Look, I'm not an app developer, but I've been reading up." She unplugged her monitor, like she could hide the evidence. "I told you I needed help."

"I'll fix the bugs in the log. I think you should leave that to us app devs, honestly. You might break something."

"Oh? Well, hopefully I didn't break your marriage code."

Sometimes she really exasperated him. "Emma, you can't be perfect in every aspect."

She tilted her head and pursed her lips, doing that puppy thing again. Or maybe like her part-android brain couldn't process what he'd said.

He didn't mean perfect in *every* aspect, of course. He shook his head. What was wrong with him? "I just meant you're not an app developer. You're good at web crawls, right? Desktop development? That's more than most people can say."

She straightened up and typed on her laptop. "Well, I guess you'll be the judge of that. Should I put the candidates for the future Mrs. Iyengar on the big screen?" She looked at him before plugging in the HDMI cable.

He looked at the hall, still empty. Still way too early for anyone to be in here. "Sure. I'm ready for the big unveiling." He took a deep breath and crossed his arms, leaning back in his seat. *Was* he ready? What if it hadn't worked? Or what if he felt insta-love just by looking at the screen? Should he pray or something before she showed him what the results had come up with? He'd practically promised his mom he would take care of it. That he could find "the one." And after his conversation with Sudhar, one of these women had to work.

Rishi's feet tapped on the floor. Why was a sudden cocktail of impatience, dread, and curiosity swirling in his stomach? A perfect match could be presented to him in a few short seconds. Because if he knew anything about Emma Delaney, it was that she strove for perfection.

And control.

And with passion.

If they really went on an Indian tour together, outside the confines of Bangalore's best eateries, what would it be like? He'd have to show her the best things about the country he called home. Let her taste the coconut-seeped curries of Kerala. Visit a roadside dhaba in Punjab where the paneer melted on your tongue. Show her the famous Madurai temples in his hometown, but also his favorite Ganesh temple, the tiny one near his apartment.

She'd have to see the flower vendors at Gandhi Bazaar, with their overflowing baskets of marigolds and roses, and eat chaat from his favorite cart in Vijayanagar. She'd take his India, place it in her mouth, and suck the joy of his country like a mango seed.

And end the tour by seeing what other flavors they could search out in the curves of each other's skin.

What the hell was wrong with him? That couldn't happen. Obviously, it couldn't. And yet the thought snaked through him, a depraved viper swallowing his brain whole. He slumped over on the table, his elbow on the cold metal, his palm catching his forehead.

"Are you okay?" Emma had pulled her laptop up and slid it over toward him.

"Yeah, yeah. I'm fine. Just forgot something." *Like my mind.*

"Here you go."

Rishi took a deep breath.

On the screen were two beautiful young women, Lakshmi and Radhika. Both with master's from good schools. Lakshmi was educated in the UK, Radhika at the Indian Institute of Technology—a school he hadn't gotten into. Radhika's family ran a large textile-export company; Lakshmi's family owned a gold store.

Perfection. Just as he'd expected Emma would deliver.

But why did he feel nothing as he looked at their faces?

Of course, it was unlikely there would be a spark, a small fire that churned inside him when he looked at the photos. As his mother always said, you grew into love. It didn't just happen at first sight. That was lust, right?

And family came first, didn't it? He needed to find someone they would embrace. Someone who would understand his family situation and be supportive. Someone his sister's future family would approve of too. He couldn't end up like Sudhar. And he couldn't put his family through that twice.

He had to find a woman who could relate to his world. A woman who would please his mother with her knowledge of prayer and ritual. A woman who would be a partner and challenge him, educate him, make him be a better person. Maybe she was out there, and maybe Lakshmi or Radhika was "the one." They'd grow into their relationship. He hadn't even met them yet, and he was already doubting. Why?

"Thanks for doing this. They seem to be perfect." He slid her laptop back to her. "Will you email that to me when you get a chance?"

Emma looked up. "*Huh.* Did I say that right?"

"What?"

"I'm trying to learn Hindi."

He couldn't believe it. She was trying to pronounce *yes.*

Rishi laughed and shook his head. "Sort of. More like *haah.*"

"*Haah.*" She tried again. "Well, I thought if I'm here in India, I might as well try. Plus, my Indian movie watching is exponentially increasing. It would be cool to understand what they're saying some of the time and not have to rely on the subtitles."

"Have you watched a lot of them?"

"Just a few. A lot of girl hates boy, boy hates girl, and then somehow they're thrown together because of a late train or evil landowner and fall in love."

He didn't usually watch the romances unless his exes dragged him to one. He opted for comedy or action films, plots where a vigilante saved the day and restored justice to the oppressed. They had fewer songs and more realistic plots. In reality, most people were thrown together by carefully constructed family orchestrations. That was reality. Bollywood romances were the fantasy.

"Did you like them?" Rishi asked, curious if she felt the same way about Indian movies as she did about their coffee. Too sweet for her tastes. The memory of watching the film version of the Kama Sutra flashed in his mind. Had she seen that? Not that he would ask.

"They were okay, but like every romantic comedy ever, I don't believe people fall in love like that. It's unbelievable. How can they hate each other, then have a lot of ridiculous arguing, and bam!" She slammed her palm on the table. He jumped in his seat. "With one word or look, they're suddenly in love." Emma locked eyes with him for a moment and then glanced back at her phone. "Or maybe it's a hair swish that does it. There is also a lot of hair swishing."

"Hair swishing?"

"Yes, the slow pan on a girl as she turns around, the focus on her hair like it's a whole other character?"

Rishi could only laugh in response. "The amount of effort my mother puts into my sister's hair, it *is* like another child of hers."

Now it was Emma's turn to laugh. "Well, I'm sure she has very beautiful hair then."

Rishi nodded. He pulled out his phone and found a picture of Dharini, then turned the screen to Emma.

"She looks so young!"

"I know. I still remember helping change her diapers." Rishi sighed, glancing at the picture. "I can't believe she wants to get married already."

"How old is she?"

"Twenty-two."

"Jesus. When I was twenty-two, I didn't know what the hell I was doing with my life. At least she knows what she wants, I guess."

"Yeah, maybe that's how I should look at it," Rishi said. Emma had a point. He should stop obsessing over the shock that his baby sister was all grown up and be happy that she had a vision for her future. Dharini was probably more mature than he was anyway.

"Okay, I guess I should get back to work. And you can start looking at these bugs. And the ladies, of course." She cleared her throat. "Do you think that you'll find true love with one of the women I found?"

What a weird question. It threaded a shiver up his chest. "Who knows? We'll see what happens." Why couldn't they go back to talking about movies?

Silence overwhelmed the space between the two of them. They both sat holding their coffee cups and staring into them like the next move would be obvious. It was like a wall had been erected, a maze of a wall. He was the mouse, and he had to find the small nugget of truth at the end. Emma was his guide, and somehow he wasn't as pleased about the perfect results as he'd hoped.

He got the feeling she wasn't either.

{ /** *. // }

The results of Emma's code had been taking more brain space than he'd anticipated. It had been a few days since he'd sent the profiles to his parents, and he was simultaneously anticipating and dreading the results of them contacting their parents. He had to focus on work and not on his nebulous future.

He stared at his computer, reading through the first iteration of feedback from the team before their check-in meeting with Jas. The game design of the app wasn't meeting Emma's standards. She wanted this color and this interaction. The user's performance moved them backward and forward like a Choose Your Own Adventure game, depending on what they got right and wrong. They'd done at least four iterations already as they tried to achieve her vision. Maybe she was right. Okay, probably right. But it was making Manuj and Rishi work harder to get the correct updates in.

As he tried to fix one bug out of the many, grasping at anything that could help, an instant message from Jas popped up in the corner of his screen.

Rishi, can you stop by my office when you're free?

On my way.

Rishi was glad for an excuse to leave the nitpicky feedback that was making him dream about the project. Well, more like have nightmares. Emma, shunning him for his lack of perfection, or trapping him in the office as punishment, making their relationship like the stupid game in the app. Her green eyes lasering him into submission as he fell over, paralyzed, some pixelated cartoon version of Rishi from the nineties.

He shook his head, dispelling the vision when he got to Jas's office.

"Hi, boss," Rishi said as he stood in the doorframe.

Jas waved Rishi in. "I have something I want to discuss with you. There's a conference in Cochin in a few weeks, the International Computer Science and IT Conference, and I was wondering if you would go and help present on our work with the project?"

Rishi's heart picked up in pace; excitement flooded his veins. He'd never been asked to go to a conference for TechLogic before, but he'd been working his ass off. At least this would be some sort of consolation for not getting the promotion. "Sure. Great! I'd love to go."

"I'll have my assistant make the booking. Emma and Kaushik are also going."

Rishi nodded, but his mouth dried up as he processed what Jas had just said. "I'll start talking with them about the presentation."

"Great." Jas stood up and shook Rishi's hand. "Also, I know this year has been a little disappointing for you with the change of events, but we still consider you one of our most valued employees."

"Thanks." Rishi tried to smile, but "valued employee" didn't have any money tied to it. Didn't come with a relocation and extra pay. He left Jas's office and walked down the hall, imagining all the things he wanted to say to Jas.

"Hey, Rishi, want to go get a coffee before the meeting?" Emma's voice called down the hall behind him.

An invisible string pulled him back. His feet pivoted.

"Yeah, definitely." The words just came out like that. He didn't even think about them. What was happening to him?

"I've been looking for you everywhere," Emma whispered as their feet locked in step together. "Did you look at the profiles and send them to your family? Did my code work?"

They opened the door to the outside patio and started making two cups of coffee. "It did, or at least I think it did. I sent them over to my parents."

Emma carried her coffee to a table, and Rishi followed. "Do they interview them? I remember my grandmother doing that with my dates for high school. I'm sure this doesn't surprise you, but the guys I went out with were as nerdy as me."

"Really?" He didn't consider her a nerd. More like an annihilator of nerds who got in her way. She could star in her own app-based game: *The Nerdinator*. She'd throw calculators at their eyes and capture their heads between her legs. Suffocate them in her—

What was wrong with him?

He cleared his throat. "Wouldn't your dad be the threatening, interviewing type? Although I can see my mom doing that more so than my dad. Maybe not with my sister, though." He imagined how they'd tag team meeting any potential grooms for his sister, the equivalent of a date. But if he was honest with himself, he'd probably overtake both of them. It was his little sister, after all. "Or me. I think I would actually be the hardest on someone for my sister because I can just be real with them."

Emma shifted in her seat and looked out over the patio toward the nearby busy road. "No, my dad wasn't around to do that, so it was my grandmother." She huffed a laugh and looked down at her lap. "And I don't have any big brothers to look out for me. That would have been nice, though."

The smile she gave him when she looked up was not a happy one. It was a sad smile. Rishi was afraid he'd crossed a line. Maybe her parents were divorced, and she didn't like to talk about it.

"Anyway, you don't seem like a nerd." Emma might not be the nerdinator, but nerds didn't have purple streaks in their hair and try to boss everyone around. Nerds didn't have curvy bodies and dress to show it. What had these guys been like?

She laughed. "Oh yeah, total nerd. Like science club, debate team, math club nerd."

"Debate team I can totally see."

"And my grandmother had this shotgun over the couch in the living room, and when these poor guys would show up to take me to a dance or something, she'd pull it out and threaten them. Drill them with twenty questions. Like we ever did anything besides kiss." She wrinkled her face up. "Actually, I don't know if that even happened with them."

She laughed, shaking her head like they were sharing some kind of joke. But all Rishi could do was stare at her lips. How could she not remember victimizing a poor boy with those pink pillows of doom? Or with her smile that stretched across her face? Those agile lips could wrap themselves around anything.

Again? He shook his head like he could shake her lips out of it. She gave him one of her *What's wrong with you?* looks.

"Uh, so what you're saying is that your grandmother threatened to shoot your dates when they came to your house, in case they . . . ?" I mean, what could he even say here? God help him. Hopefully she'd just fill in the blanks.

"Yeah, exactly. So anyway, I'm hoping that your parents are easier on your love interests than my grandma was."

Her eyes were sparkling. Almost like they were on the verge of tears, but in a happy way. This was something new. This sort of joy only got released over the best tomato chutney or the crispy edges of a dosa. She wiped at her eyes. "Sorry. I get emotional over my grandmother sometimes. She was a really amazing, unique woman."

Rishi pictured his grandmother, who had lived with his parents until a few years ago. The white-haired, able-bodied woman who had cooked breakfast and lunch with his mother until the day she'd died. She'd always sneaked extra treats for him, covered up for him when he'd been bad to spare him a smack from his father. "Did you lose her? I lost mine a few years ago. She was pretty amazing too."

"Really? I'm sorry." Emma's hand stretched across the table, like she was reaching for his, and then retracted like a turtle's neck going back into its shell, under the table. He looked up at her face, and she looked like she'd seen a ghost. "Hopefully you got to spend time with her."

"Yeah, she lived with us and was kind of a badass."

Emma laughed. "Yeah? Mine was a badass too."

"Obviously." He could picture exactly where Emma got her guts from.

"Uh . . . so what's the whole process like to determine if a woman is 'the one'? Do these ladies just go up to your parents and say, 'Namaste, I'm applying to marry your son'?"

"Namaste?" Rishi shook his head and let out a weak laugh. Although he wasn't sure if the laugh was at her choice of words or at the bizarre contact that had almost happened between them. Had Emma really just tried to touch his hand? "No."

"But I thought it meant hello in Hindi?"

"We usually say 'hi,' or 'hello,'" Rishi said, trying not to laugh at the face Emma was making, at her eyes squinting at him, her lip curled at the corner. He could see the processing happening in her circuit boards. Like a small punch in his chest, he shamed himself. Okay, maybe *circuit boards* was a tad harsh.

She leaned back in her chair and threw her arms up. "Why am I bothering to learn Hindi then? Everyone speaks English anyway."

"Remember the movies? And so one day you can understand this. *Tumhare aankhen bohut sundar hai.*" She'd never know what he'd said; he'd said it too fast. It felt good, having the upper hand for once.

"Wait, what was that again?"

"I heard you're going to the conference in Cochin too?" He smiled, ignoring her question.

"Rishi, tell me!" She swatted at his arm, but he yanked it away.

"Nothing . . . I was just kidding. I just said 'so you know what they're saying in yoga class.'" He'd never tell her he'd just said she had beautiful eyes. He didn't even know where it had come from. Like her green lasers had transformed into emeralds.

"Yes, I'm going." She exhaled a sigh of defeat.

He glanced at his phone and chugged his coffee. "Okay, meeting time. Let's go."

"Well, keep me posted on your progress with the lucky Radhika or Lakshmi."

Rishi got up from his chair, humming a yes. He didn't know what else to say to her about them. It wasn't that he was hiding anything, but the whole agreement between the two of them had started out so awkwardly. Now it felt even more awkward. He'd just let his parents handle it.

They joined the others in the conference room. Manuj set up the projector and connected it to the tablet they were testing on.

"Okay, team, Kaushik and I have been able to implement fixes for a few of the functional bugs from our initial iteration of the app, so let's show you the results."

Emma leaned back, her arms crossed, watching Manuj demo the app. Halfway through, she asked, "What if we tweaked the code so that there was some kind of hidden Easter egg in the game? So that when you accomplish a level, sometimes you get a surprise reward. Or something cool comes up on the screen?"

"Well, we have the leaderboard in place, as well as the general awards and badges for completing content. So you want something else?" Manuj asked reluctantly. Rishi knew just how many hours Manuj had already put into designing the prototype.

"Yes, we really need to make this app amazing. Like the best app we can imagine. The stakes are really high. We need to have as much motivation as we can for people to continue to use it."

"This is standard across our business apps. We don't have Easter eggs." Kaushik shook his head as if it was the silliest thing he'd ever said. "Maybe you should let us handle this."

Rishi could see the storm brewing inside Emma. Her fingers braced at the table, and her head reared back into her neck as she stared Kaushik down.

"Kaushik, we are not shooting for 'standard.' We are shooting for superior. Five stars. Fun. Creative. Surprising. Life changing." Emma leaned forward. "If you want to be 'standard,' then maybe this isn't the right project for you."

The tension in the room was palpable. Everyone seemed to be waiting to see how Kaushik, whose eyes burned with anger, would respond. If Rishi had to bet, he was sure Emma could take Kaushik down. But if the three of them were to present at the conference, that couldn't happen.

Rishi jumped in. "Kaushik, just because we've been doing app development a certain way doesn't mean we can't change. This isn't a business app. People use business apps because they *have* to. We have to build fun into this one. Look at all the most successful games out there. They're puzzles, and you have to figure out how to unlock them. Sometimes you get bonuses. You want to find what's hidden. But they don't feel planned, or like a series of logical steps; they're more like serendipity." Rishi glanced over at Emma after he'd said this, and something like a half grin was spread across her face, like Rishi was one of her converts, and she'd finally convinced him to come to the dark side.

"I like the idea. It's new, and it sounds fun," Preeti chimed in.

"I'm sure, with the talent on this team, you guys can figure out a way to make it happen," Emma said. "I'll think of some of the Easter eggs we could plant if you figure out how to do it in the code."

Kaushik sighed, shot her a look, then shot one at Rishi that said *traitor* and made a big production of getting up. The most painful team meeting in history.

Emma leaned back in her seat, almost ready to get up, but then she stared at the space above her. Her lips gathered together like she was ready to kiss something, her auburn eyebrows furrowed, deep in thought. And then her smile widened, and she wrote something on her notepad. Envisioning the bonus content? Picturing how a student would use the app? Planning an attack on Kaushik?

Briefly, just briefly, he pictured her with that same daring, told-you-so grin as her hair fanned around her, a riot of red and purple against the white sheets of a bed.

He grabbed his laptop and ran to the door. Wherever that thought had come from, he needed it to recede into the dark corners of his mind and never return.

CHAPTER 18

Kaushik was such an asshole. *Let us handle it.* Who did he think he was? They were all programmers. Maybe Emma didn't know app development like they did, but she knew what made up good design. She'd partnered with the UX team so many times she could practically do their job too. At least she had Preeti and Rishi, who could see her vision. They were her only two allies in this new world.

And Rishi . . . well, with Rishi it was complicated. The photos of the two women were lodged in her subconscious to the point of hallucination. She'd passed a woman in the mall the other day and was convinced she was Radhika. At the grocery store, the cashier had Lakshmi's eyes and shampoo-model hair. Emma had to do the math to figure that the chance she'd casually run into either one of them in a city of twelve million people was less than .0001 percent.

How had Rishi not found someone yet? Those gray eyes, strong shoulders, and full lips. Surely there was a young, beautiful woman who just wanted a good-looking guy with a decent job.

Although that good-looking, smart guy came from a family with money issues. Something she'd never expected.

She couldn't tell him that she felt guilty, but, thinking back to her conversation with Maria about the job, if she hadn't made the argument for leading the app development, Rishi would probably have this position. Emma would have moved on to something else. While she couldn't have kept the job in the US, and it wasn't her fault exactly, a hollowness crept out from her torso into her limbs. Like a chill. But this chill wasn't cold. It was more like an emptiness.

Guilt and sadness and what? She shook her head.

She had to wonder. Had Rishi looked at the two women's profiles and deemed one of them the ideal match?

She shouldn't have cared. But there was something about finding someone for him that made her feel like taking a wrecking ball to one of her office walls. If only she had the strength to knock it down.

She turned her attention back to her monitor. Back to the code.

Emma's eyes were inches away from the screen when an instant message window popped up in the corner.

Tousled auburn hair, the frame of the glasses she had helped select last December, and a clear, sagacious look at the camera. Something fell inside her, barreling down with a low moan of sentimentality and irritation. When Emma had taken that picture, she had felt Jeremy was looking deep inside her.

He was making contact. Like an alien life-form she'd dreamed about from a galaxy far, far away, he had returned. A little burn in her chest, like some ghost embers of their relationship remained. She'd thought of him on and off, but she hadn't reached out. He hadn't made contact. And even though what had happened was only months in the past, it felt like it had happened in another world. Another era.

She clicked on his picture to accept the conversation. He probably just had some kind of logistical question.

Hi there, Jeremy typed. How is life in India?

Emma looked at the time. It was almost three in the afternoon, which meant it was after 2:00 a.m. in Seattle.

Hi, how are you? she asked. She'd wondered about him from time to time, thinking about how broken he'd looked the last time they'd talked. How broken he must have been to act like she was a ghost in the room with him.

It's afternoon here in sunny India, why are you up so late?

I couldn't sleep.

Did you need something? What else could she say? He was notorious for waking up in the middle of the night, doing something for an hour, and then going back to sleep.

A few moments later, Jeremy's photo appeared again in the corner. She couldn't help but click it.

I was thinking about you . . .

Emma sat back, the familiar twisting that had faded over the past few months taking hold again. Her fingers ran through her hair and tugged. Like she could pull him out of her mind. Like she needed to get him out from under her skin. The guilt. The hurt. Just when Jeremy had stopped slinking under it like an angry itch, he was there again, bringing all the confusion with him.

How could she not be confused when she'd given herself over to the relationship for a year, only to have it implode in one moment? One second.

She waited for the little dots to change into the rest of the message, forgetting about the code she had to review. Her body was almost pulsating in anticipation as she stared at the chat window.

We went for dinner at our favorite place down the street tonight, and I was lamenting the last time you and I went there.

Lamenting? So melodramatic. There must be an emptying bottle of Woodford Reserve beside him.

She ran through her head whom he could have gone to dinner with there. It was none of her business anyway. She closed the chat window again and went back to studying the code on her screen instead of Jeremy's chat session in the corner.

The icon blinked again, and she glared at it, hesitating. She could wait five minutes until she was done with her work.

When she clicked it, he was already offline, so he must have typed it and then shut down his computer. We miss you here. I miss you.

He probably just missed their habits. She was almost ten thousand miles away. Jeremy had barely even said goodbye to her. Now that she had been gone for a few months, he missed her? He was probably just lonely or bored. Or sappy with bourbon.

Besides, what would happen when she went back? It would be the same as before. If Emma had learned anything by surviving her parents' deaths and losing her grandmother, it was that work saved her. If she worked hard, she would have success, survival. And that's what was important. She couldn't sacrifice herself for a marriage she wasn't ready for.

CHAPTER 19

Rishi's phone rang, but he hesitated answering. His parents must have had an update after talking to both women's families. Did it seem like either Radhika or Lakshmi were the right match? He'd orchestrated this whole thing, but now it was the last thing he could imagine doing. Because if he picked up that phone, he would have to fake excitement, fake interest, and then he'd dread planning the next steps.

What if he found someone who didn't fit their criteria? How bad would it really be? What if Dharini's ideal husband's family thought that Rishi had chosen poorly?

Not good. Someone had to shine in the family. He was their only hope.

"Ma, hello?" He slunk over to the corner of the patio with his coffee.

"Your appa and I called to tell you we've spoken to Radhika's parents, and they are good. Nice family, good connections. They're involved in the textile business, which is always growing. They came over for coffee."

"And?" Not that he needed to ask. He knew where this was going.

"We want you and Radhika to meet. She's in Bangalore also."

A gurgle of dread and nervousness bubbled up inside him. His heart pounded against his chest. Was it a sign that she was "the one"?

"Oh. Sure. I mean, I can just contact her, if you give me her mobile number."

"I will talk to her parents and send you her number. You can meet her after work one day this week."

This week? So soon? "Okay."

"I think she will work out well. Don't judge her so fast, this one."

"What happened with Lakshmi?" There had been two matches. Emma's algorithm couldn't have pulled up only two women, just to have one of them be a dud.

His father's voice came in on the line. "She is already talking to some other suitor, so it doesn't seem to be fortuitous." So formal sometimes.

The voice on the other end spilled out of the phone, rhapsodizing about all the good things that happened over afternoon coffee. He cradled his forehead in one hand as his fingers worked at the temples and down to the bridge of his nose. A pinched pain slid across his face. "Okay, I need to go. I'll meet her soon."

Rishi hung up the phone and sat on the edge of the balcony's rail. His future flashed before him like a portending slideshow. Coffee with lovely Radhika, who is sweet and good and smart. It's a sunny day and the sun sparkles off her hair. Rishi thinks yes, it's what's good for the family. Then the engagement ceremony. She looks good in the sari his parents bought her. She's curvy, pretty. Surely his mother will think she has a good body for having babies. Then the marriage, a whirlwind. They get to know each other on a honeymoon. Then family pressure is on. *Baby?* Then *Another baby?* They ask every time they see the couple. And they grow older, just raising children and never really knowing each other's dreams and aspirations. And then they forget they have dreams and aspirations, and he's in his sixties, retired. The kids are done with college and have jobs now. He and Radhika sit in silence because they can only talk about their children.

And all he can think about is a redheaded girl he knew thirty years ago.

A quiet filled him. The opposite of the storm that had been brewing inside his chest. The quiet was almost worse.

No. He shook his head. That was impossible. All his married friends were happy. They had amazing relationships. He was just being stubborn. Making excuses at this point. He hadn't even met Radhika yet and was already foreseeing how she wouldn't be a good match. He was using his bizarre relationship with Emma as another excuse to delay marriage. And he didn't have time to delay it. His family was depending on him.

Numbness overtook his body, his mind. A buzz of white noise filled his ears, replacing the recollection of his mother's words, the cars honking on the street. If Radhika wasn't the one, how could he disappoint his parents again? They had done so much for him. But how could he marry someone he didn't love, who didn't ignite the spark he craved? A spark that could explode into flames with the right woman?

Radhika *could* be "the one." After all, she checked all the boxes. He'd meet her soon, and then he could make a calculated decision instead of conjuring up the worst scenario possible. Maybe she was the perfect match, just as Emma's marriage code had promised.

{ /** *. // }

The traffic was twice as bad as it usually was during the evening. His finger found the horn on his bike and pressed it hard, like a finger in an enemy's wound. Pressure filled his lungs, and his heart thumped against his chest. He felt so alone in this mass of cars and autos and bikes. The million people around him. All of them closing in. He just needed to escape. To get out. To calm down before he had to meet Radhika.

He needed to go home to Madurai and see his family. A little over two months he'd been back from Seattle, and still he hadn't gone home. He'd mailed them Seattle-themed presents and promised he'd be there soon. The idea of taking a vacation day had felt wrong at this point, with the app deep in development and him just returning from the US. Or was it that he didn't want to be apart from Emma?

He was a crazy man. Something about her was warping his sense of reality. Here he was, on his way to meet his potential future wife, and all he could do was imagine seeking solace in Emma's arms, his cheek against her breasts, the scent of tangerines and roses wafting from her neck.

He shook his head. He had to stop thinking like this.

The traffic surged ahead, and he had never been more thankful for the brusque dance of vehicles as he wove in and out of the narrow spaces that appeared in the traffic.

By the time he'd found parking near the café, he was fifteen minutes late. He took a quick look at his phone to remind himself what Radhika looked like and sucked in a calming breath. She *was* beautiful.

Surveying the vast patio of umbrella-covered tables, he searched for her. A woman sitting alone, closest to the ferns that lined the patio, was smiling at him. Was that her? Dark, round eyes, auburn highlights in her hair, narrow shoulders.

Rishi walked toward her. "Radhika?"

"Yes, Rishi?" she asked, standing up.

"Yes. Hi. I'm sorry I'm late. I got stuck in traffic."

"No worries, same here. Do you want to get a coffee?"

He glanced at the cappuccino in front of her. Damn, he should have bought her one. He probably should have left thirty minutes earlier. "I'm okay. Can I get you anything?"

"No, I have one." She gestured to the cup.

Rishi sat down. The line was long, and his nerves were already buzzing under his skin. The first conversation was always so awkward. All the thoughts in his head, the appropriate questions to ask, the gracious platitudes he was supposed to offer, they all seemed to fly away. He looked at her; she expected him to say something. He was reduced to a mute, a nervous adolescent who had never spoken to a girl before. His mouth opened, and he stuttered. What was wrong with him?

"So . . . uh . . . you . . . live in Bangalore?" he managed to get out.

"Yes. I grew up here, went to university here, and now I work at a small software company."

"But your parents live in Madurai now?" Rishi asked. He remembered his parents inviting them over.

"They moved after I started working. Wanted to go back to where they were from."

Rishi nodded. "My parents also live in Madurai, but I've been here for seven years. They hate coming to visit because of the traffic." He didn't add that his apartment was so small two people had to sleep on the floor when they did visit.

"The city has changed so much in the last twenty years. But I still love it. I don't know if I want to live anywhere else." She paused, and her face froze as if she'd said something wrong. "I mean, I could. I wouldn't mind living somewhere else if needed." Her eyes flitted to his and then looked away quickly. A faint blush crept into her cheeks.

Item #1: She would move. Possibly adventurous?

As adventurous as Emma? She'd moved to India for work.

Rishi took an inventory of what Radhika was wearing in hopes he could gauge something about her. Did she go to pubs? Did she like expensive clothes? Would she thrive on gold jewelry like his mother? She wore a teal-and-yellow salwar kameez, a single gold chain around her neck, gold bangles, her hair in a braid, and a few rings that an astrologer had clearly suggested. A yellow sapphire, which could be worn to increase prosperity. Or mean she was depressed or had some kind of health problem. She also wore a blue sapphire ring, which his uncle had worn to fight baldness. But that didn't seem to be her problem. In reality, her parents had probably forced them on her fingers, like Rishi's had over the years, at an astrologer's suggestion.

His overall assessment of Radhika: traditional. *But interesting.*

"What do you do for fun?" Rishi asked.

"My friends and I go to the mall sometimes. We also go to coffee shops a lot. I like watching films."

Everyone liked watching films and going to the mall and drinking coffee. Actually, Emma had never mentioned going to the mall. She'd started shopping, though. All those colorful salwars turning her into a bright-haired peacock who strutted through the office. Yammering about her movie watching, trying to speak in Hindi. A small laugh escaped him. Radhika gave him a curious look.

"Yeah, I do those things too." He tried to cover up for it. *Seriously, man, get it together.* This was the time to figure out who this woman was. "What do you hope to do in the next ten years?" He tried to make it not sound like an interview, even though they were really interviewing each other for the role of spouse.

"I want to keep working; that's important to me. I like my job. In ten years, I expect I would have a child, maybe two, but I'd like to travel first. I've never been to North India." She looked into her coffee as she said this, her eyes flickering to his and back to her cup.

Would Radhika be okay with having a relationship with Sudhar and Sona? Even if Rishi's parents disapproved? They could go there on their honeymoon. But he would really love to show Emma North India. They would have so much fun, eating sweet, sticky jaleebis and drinking spicy chai for breakfast out of clay mugs. The giant cups of buttermilk with mustard seeds and curry leaves cooling them down after touring ancient forts all day. She'd probably never been to a desert or ridden a camel.

But he had to focus on Radhika.

Item #2: She wanted to live a little before settling down and having children.

Item #3: Wanted to keep working, not just stay at home.

All the boxes were being checked.

"I've only been to Delhi once. I'd like to go to Rajasthan and see the old forts and palaces, though," Rishi said. He paused. "Tell me about your job."

Radhika shared some of the projects she was working on, but coding was coding. Both of them were in IT, so at least they spoke the same language. She was soft spoken, and her parents had probably coached her not to appear too excitable or overeager. She'd likely endured the same kind of advice his parents had given to him.

"What do you do?" she asked after explaining her job.

He talked about the app and the goals they longed to achieve with literacy. Her eyebrows lifted and her eyes rounded even more when he spoke. At least she showed some reaction, and her eyes focused more on his as he spoke.

"That is amazing. I hope you accomplish your quest for literacy," she said when he was done. A fresh shine appeared in her eyes. Excitement? Validation? Was this a hint of the woman beneath the facade?

"Me too." He leaned toward her, maybe an unconscious gesture showing that he wanted to know more about her. More about her thoughts. "I think the plan is for us to partner with mobile service providers once it's ready. And NGOs." At least this woman shared some alignment with his thoughts around the work he was doing.

"That's great. I volunteer for a local charity here that helps poorer children go to school."

Rishi was amazed. If ever there was a match for him, maybe this was it.

They talked for a few more minutes, and then Radhika said she had to leave and meet some friends for dinner.

This could work. The idea was growing on him. She was beautiful and smart and nice and caring.

"It was really nice to meet you."

"You too." Her smile broadened and her eyes lit up.

Yes, this could work.

He held out his hand. What would happen when they touched? As he took her soft grip in his, he waited for a zap, a surge, a spark— something that would indicate how their bodies would react together. Would they sizzle and smoke like combining ammonia and acid? Let off sparks that flowed into his heart and made it pulse an extra beat? *Touch her and feel something,* he begged of his hand.

He didn't even realize that he was holding in his breath until she'd pulled her hand from his.

Nothing.

He'd felt nothing.

He studied her walk as she strolled down the street. She was interested in his work. She seemed to want to keep her job and not just stay at home. She wanted to travel, and she volunteered.

Would she fit well in his family? Would his parents approve? Would they be able to carry out their lives as any normal couple would? Would it be easy? On all counts—yes.

He looked down at his hand and frowned. Why didn't it know what was best for him? Stupid fucking hand.

CHAPTER 20

Rishi hadn't seemed like himself the past week. Maybe it was taking too long for his parents to go through the process of getting him married. Maybe because he wanted to get married so badly it was tearing him up on the inside.

He might have seemed like he was holding up a sad-face mask over his gray eyes and thick lips because it was taking so long. But when Emma thought about him married to one of those beautiful, appropriate women, it was like someone had wadded up her soul and chucked it in the shredder. She was probably just jealous. Jealous that he could be close to finding his perfect someone.

She also missed the guy who teased her mercilessly and made her eyes roll at every other word. She sneaked behind the partition and popped up beside his desk like a jack-in-the-box. "Hello, Rishi."

He tremored in his chair. "You can be terrifying when you want." But he was smiling. All she wanted was a smile.

"You know, we haven't embarked on any tours lately for lunch. I was thinking you could help me expand my horizons today. Perhaps take another trip of the palate?"

"Sure. What are you thinking?"

"I don't know. Something decadent. But wholesome. Rich, but comforting." Maybe whatever Rishi needed was the equivalent to truffle mac and cheese, her comfort food of choice back home.

"Those are quite the parameters you've set." He squinted at her but then held up his hand. "Actually, I know the perfect place."

"I knew you would." She'd already retrieved some of the light in his face. He just needed a little challenge to get his mind off whatever was bothering him.

"Meet me in the garage at noon? I actually have two helmets now."

She almost said thanks, but then she shook the idea from her head. He must have bought it for his soon-to-be wife, who would need a helmet to ride with him. No more bike rides with Rishi. No more lunch dates. The disappointment slunk inside her, but she swallowed it with a smile. "Perfect. A motorcycle ride and a decadent, wholesome, rich, comforting meal."

She pivoted on her feet but could hear Rishi doing one of his laugh-sighs that she liked to think he did only for her.

{ /** *. // }

At noon, Emma took the elevator down to the garage and stood near the wall of motorcycles, unsure which was his. The one she stood in front of was sleek and black and curvy, and as she studied it, she had to wonder if there was something seductive about riding this voluptuous chunk of metal.

"It's that one!" his voice called out behind her, echoing off the cement walls and ceiling.

Coincidence or fate that she'd found it? Maybe she was making her peace with fate more and more these days.

Rishi jogged over to her, and she couldn't help but notice how the muscles in his arms flexed as he pulled the bike out, his back long as he stretched over the engine, his jeans tight as his thighs straddled the seat.

Just the word *straddled* was putting thoughts in her mind that shouldn't have been there.

"Hop on," he said as he started the engine.

The bike puffed and shuddered to life, and she threw her leg over the seat, the vibrations seeming to shake her entire body. Was it the bike, though, or something else?

She clutched onto the bars under the bike seat as they took off, but as they climbed up the ramp out of the garage, the ridges bounced her inches off her seat, and for fear of bouncing right off and down the ramp, she grabbed onto his waist on impulse. He didn't shudder or throw her hands off him, so she let one hand drift back to the seat and let the other stay gently on his waist.

This was normal, right? To fear for your life on a motorcycle on roads pockmarked with potholes and hold on to a driver who swerved through the traffic like he was playing his own racing game. In fact, she resisted scooting up so her entire chest would be flush with his back. It was simply a matter of physics. The matter of their two bodies would make them stronger as one, rather than two, and this tiny wind tunnel between her chest and his back surely could increase the potential for disaster if they did have an accident. At least for Emma, who had no idea what she was doing on the back of a motorcycle.

Yes, this desire to feel her chest press into his back was all just a matter of physics.

Or maybe just physical.

She slid up, allowing her chest momentary contact with his back, but then abruptly pulled herself a few inches away, shaming herself.

This was Rishi. Whom she'd written a marriage code for. Off limits. Looking for the perfect girl (for which she met none of his requirements). Her coworker. He just happened to be handsome and funny and have a nice, expansive back—perfect for her to cuddle against.

He slowed down as they turned a corner near a huge temple that was unlike any other temple she'd seen on the side of the road. This one was white and bulbous with a gold spire on top. Multiple stairs led to it, and it felt approachable, like it was asking people to come up and have a look.

"Here we are." He pulled into a parking spot. "The restaurant is just over here."

She followed him on the side of the road and paused at the tiny, open-air dugout of a restaurant as she examined the small crowd inside. There were flimsy tables and plastic chairs, all filled with people intent on their lunch. A large man with a turban stood behind a series of burners as fire leaped up around his hands while he practically juggled the pans. "Is this it?"

Rishi cocked his head at her and paused, scrunching up one side of his face. "You know, of course you don't want to eat here. Sorry, I wasn't thinking." He started to walk back toward his bike.

"No, Rishi, wait!" she called after him. "I want to stay."

"It's not too local for you?"

She shook her head. What was the point of coming to India if she wasn't going to experience it fully? "Nope. I set out the parameters, and you picked. You haven't let me down with a meal so far."

He nodded, with that sort of downward smile that she now recognized as amused Rishi. "Okay, you will love it. I can already imagine your face while you're eating."

What a weird thing to tell someone. She must have looked like quite the glutton in front of him. "I hope that doesn't mean you think I'm a pig. I'm just a girl who likes a good meal."

"No, I didn't mean that at all." Rishi looked at her, and for the first time, she saw worry in those eyes of his. "I've just seen how you like good food. My whole family lives for food, so I appreciate it." He led her through the small maze of seats and found one remaining table squeezed in the corner. A naked light bulb was suspended over their heads.

"I've never seen a place like this before." She looked around. "Where's the menu?"

"You just have to ask them what they have. It's not a menu kind of place; it's whatever he decides to make." He nodded toward the man behind the fire, yelling and shouting orders at the other younger men who were flitting about.

"It's so funny because the only kinds of places we have in the US where the chef dictates the meal are super-fine-dining places where you have to pay like a hundred dollars a person."

"We have those, too, but honestly, this food is amazing. It may not have five-star ambience or gold-plated silverware, but it is hands down one of my five favorite restaurants in the city." One of the younger men came over to their table, looking gobsmacked from whatever the chef had just yelled at him. Rishi had a conversation with him in Hindi, and Emma tried to recognize any of the words they were saying. When she heard "paratha," her stomach dipped into itself and made a squeaky gurgling sound, as if it approved of the order too.

The guy walked away, and Rishi's eyes lit up. "I think you're really going to like what they have. Parathas, which I know you like. Butter chicken, a Punjabi special. Dal makhani, another specialty—we have to eat it. And sarson ka saag, for the best vegetable you'll ever eat."

"So this is the Punjabi leg of our tour?"

"Yes. I think it's the most decadent, comforting, whatever else you said, food you can get."

"Awesome. Have you been there?"

Rishi's eyebrows rose, and he shook his head slowly. "I'm thinking about it."

Rishi opened his mouth like he was going to say something, and then the guy brought their food over. He set down a stack of two thick parathas with an entire pat of butter melting on top. Another bowl of greens that smelled like cumin and garlic and overall deliciousness. Then another bowl of lentils, more butter melting into the center, and another dish of chicken swimming in a bright-orange sauce that, yet again, had butter on top.

"Wow, Rishi, I don't think there is enough butter here." She looked up to the empty space beside her and did her best vocal fry whine. "Excuse me, waiter. We asked for extra butter on these dishes!"

The man came back and Emma muttered, "Oh shit." She definitely hadn't meant for anyone to hear her. The laugh Rishi was clearly restraining from his pursed lips came out.

"I think he's just here to serve us the food."

"Oh. Good."

And that he did. After the server was done ladling out the various dishes on her plate, the scents and hues mingled to create a cornucopia of color and spice all around her, and she whipped out her phone.

"I've got to get one for Jordana." She snapped a few pictures of her food, then a few of the restaurant around her. "She's going to die with envy."

"Who's Jordana?" he asked, diving into his paratha.

Emma paused while she watched Rishi lick his fingers. Maybe she was a little envious of those fingers.

"She's my best friend, comrade, and confidante. We also eat out a lot together, and she even has a blog of all her favorite Seattle restaurants, so this trip is just killing her. I'll send it to you if you want to check it out. She's an interior designer, so somehow all her pictures are three times as good as mine."

"I'm sure she won't have any with quite the character this dhaba has, though."

"Nope." Emma looked around as she ate, feeling like she was melting just like the butter. The walls were concrete blocks, the chairs uncomfortable, but everyone around her seemed to be smiling with this joyous feeling from the rich, comforting, decadent food Rishi had completely delivered on. "I can't imagine eating like this every day. I wonder what all this butter does to people's arteries."

"I think the food is so rich because Punjab is a big agriculture area, so the farmers need a lot of energy to work in the fields."

"So we're just gluttons then," Emma said as she took a bite of the mustard greens, which were ten times as delicious from the butter. "I should probably go farm something before I go back to my desk and just sit there typing away."

"Or just do some really vigorous typing."

Emma coughed out a laugh. "So you said you were thinking about going to the state of Punjab?"

He sighed and looked off toward the outside, the light making his pupils almost iridescent. "I have some family up there, but I haven't decided if I want to see them or not."

A deep sigh resonated through Emma's chest. "If I can ever offer you any advice, here is what I would say. Don't take your family for granted. If you have family, and you think you should see them, then you should."

Rishi looked down at the table. "I don't know if it's as simple as that."

"Why not? You have family; you should cherish them. You know, of course, unless they're like an ax murderer or something." She shook her head.

"What?" He looked around and huffed a laugh, but she was pretty sure it was because she'd just said "murderer" not quietly.

"I just mean . . . what is so bad that you wouldn't talk to someone in your family?" Because honestly, Emma couldn't imagine not talking to someone over a petty disagreement or some kind of trivial annoyance. It was family. She knew what those relationships meant, solely because she didn't have them. There was nothing like having someone on your side just because you shared the same blood, because you were part of their genetic makeup, because there was something of you in them. And no matter what had happened, you should cherish that.

"It's my brother."

"Oh." Emma had heard all about Rishi's younger sister, but she had no idea he had a brother. "He lives there?"

"Yep. Well, maybe I should say *he* has family there."

"So now I'm confused. Is he adopted or something?"

"No, he married a Punjabi woman. They technically live in Delhi, but her parents are from Punjab, though I guess they are also temporarily living in Delhi with them, taking care of the baby, so maybe I wouldn't go anyway." Rishi's voice had sped up, as if he was reaching a crescendo, but then he just ran his left hand through his hair and looked down at the table. Obviously frustrated, but Emma didn't know if it was at her for asking or just exasperation over the family drama he was thinking of.

Baby. Punjabi wife. His brother's family. Delhi. Obvious irritation over it. A lot of new information to add to her Rishi file.

He looked back up at her, his eyelashes seeming to cover half his eyes. "Sorry, I don't know why I'm telling you all this." He sighed and scooped up some of the chicken with his paratha.

"Probably because I asked," she hummed. So her little marriage code was all making a little more sense, from what she could piece together. "I'm guessing that your brother marrying a woman from somewhere else was a pretty big deal then."

He huffed. "Uh, you could say that. His is the name you are not allowed to utter in my parents' house."

"Jeez." Maybe she had underestimated Rishi's family. "So that's like someone from Texas marrying someone from New York?" She tried to picture how it could be so taboo that there would only be one pair of cowboy boots at the Manhattan wedding.

"Well, sort of, but not really. I told you my parents were super traditional." He sighed. "It's complicated. The family he married into also seemed like bad people, but now I'm not so sure."

"Well, maybe you *should* reach out. If it's complicated, then maybe that's exactly what it is. It's a lot easier to simplify things and say, 'he's good, she's bad.' But maybe that's not the truth. And if you love your brother, you don't want to lose him. Especially just because of who he married and what your parents think of her. Maybe you just need to get everyone together and talk it out or something."

Rishi looked at her with a gaze she couldn't decipher. Maybe he was pissed and ready to blow up at her. He might even flip the table over for dramatic effect. Or possibly he'd just eaten too much butter, and he was feeling a giant butter pat expanding in his stomach, like Emma was. But the words that came out of his mouth were the last she'd ever expect.

"Emma, you're so right."

"I am?" She almost choked on the last piece of chicken.

"Yeah. I can't have my parents poison my relationship with my brother. Maybe this whole thing has just been a giant misunderstanding, because I know they all love each other." He slapped the table. "I'm going to order a buttermilk. Do you want one too?"

She shook her head and held out her palm as if he were already trying to force-feed it to her. Her jeans seemed to have her waist in a vise grip. "If I consume anything else for the rest of the day, it won't be good. I will have to go plow a field."

"Suit yourself."

As he tried to get the waiter's attention, Emma couldn't help but notice how energized he appeared. It was as if the idea that he could resolve the differences between his brother and the rest of his family had changed something in him. Brightened the melancholy that had draped around him the past week.

And she was happy for him, but it was like a little bit of his melancholy had seeped into her. Like a little nugget had lodged in her chest. His brother had married outside the family, to an Indian woman, from another state, and his parents wouldn't talk to him. Wouldn't even let his name be spoken in the house. So the parameters that Rishi had set out for her marriage code weren't as insane as she'd initially thought. He was trying to keep his family together.

And she, of all people, was the last one who could fault him for that.

CHAPTER 21

Rishi's phone rang, and he picked it up. Almost eleven o'clock. "Shit." He rarely slept this late, even on a Saturday, but he didn't even need to ask himself why. He knew why. Sudhar. Sona. Baby Sejal. Marriage. Work. Emma. Conference. Too much making his sleep restless.

"Hello?" he answered, clearing his throat.

"Why didn't you call us after you met Radhika? Your father ran into her father at a shop this morning, and it was very embarrassing that her father knew and your father was blindsided."

"Oh." He hadn't called them. He'd thought about it, but he just wasn't sure what to say. "Yeah, we had coffee last week."

"Last week? Why didn't you call?" She made a clicking noise in the back of her throat, a pure sign of disappointment if he had ever heard one.

"I've just been busy. Work has been crazy."

"You can't work like that when you're married. When will you have time to give me grandchildren?"

He didn't even bother protesting at this point. It was early, and the flow of the conversation could play on repeat, they'd had it so many times.

"I just work hard for you and Appa."

That always dropped the impending marriage-work-too-hard-I-need-grandchildren-now conversation. And she technically already had a grandchild she was refusing to see. But it was way too early in the morning for that conversation.

He'd done a video call that week with Sudhar and Sona so he could see his new niece. She was small and perfect and far away in Delhi. He wanted to find a time to go visit them, find out if what Sudhar had said about the failed investment was real. If his mom would just give them a chance. Emma's advice had made so much sense, and he just needed to figure out how to bring them all together.

"I know." She sighed, like she was sad and proud of him at the same time. Then Amma 2.0 took over. "So did you like her? What was she like?"

"Yes, she was very nice," Rishi said.

"Her father is a good man!" his father yelled into the phone. "His brother too. They said my experience in accounting could be an asset to their textile business."

Rishi could picture them on the ancient mobile phone they shared, hovering over the tiny device like ostriches, waiting for any morsel of information to escape from the speaker they could gobble up.

A job for his dad, who had retired early because he'd thought they'd had enough set away for old age. Until they didn't. "That's good news for you, Appa." Rishi had said "good," but he started to feel ill, a wave of nausea seeming to creep into his limbs as well as his stomach. A dull ache coasted through his core.

"Yes, very good news!" his mother said, the excitement in her voice evident. Her normally somber tone had somehow lifted into one of a jubilant young woman. The news that Rishi had found someone he'd found "nice" had buoyed their spirits into ecstasy. "Dharini will move out, and I'll need a new daughter. Someone I can share our traditions with, someone who will take care of us. Take care of you. Does she seem like someone who will fit in well with our family?"

Rishi sank into his bed. Radhika would probably be the perfect daughter-in-law for his mother. And her family could get a job for his dad? Unreal.

She seemed sweet and kind; he could feel it radiating off her. She was the kind of girl who would want to help, would want to make her new family happy.

How could he destroy their dreams, just for a bright spot of lust in his life? A feeling he couldn't even trust.

"Yes, I think she'd fit well. She meets all your criteria. You can meet her and see for yourself." Rishi couldn't ignore the hint of snark he'd just given to his parents. He'd also created that criteria, but things just felt different now.

His mother muttered something under her breath. So she had caught his little passive-aggressive undertone.

"We will call her parents and see when we can meet in person," his father said.

He could only imagine how his parents would translate his words to her parents. But he couldn't keep delaying. He couldn't keep bouncing back and forth like some kind of indecisive kid who didn't know what he wanted but still wanted everything at the same time. "Okay." He swallowed hard.

He hung up the phone and sat staring into the emptiness of his tiny apartment, numb. A tsunami of emotions pummeled him until he didn't know how he felt. His father's job. His parents' happiness. The need to get married. Tradition. Religion. Radhika.

Marriage would determine the rest of his life. He and Radhika would likely get along, but would she challenge him, question him, demand more of him as a man? She was beautiful, but beauty faded. Maybe she was too nice. She was a fawn in the jungle, rooting out the best leaves to eat. Rishi was a tiger, low and stealthy in the grass, wanting substance between his teeth. He didn't want a fawn for his mate. Tigers devoured fawns. He wanted another tiger.

A tiger? Maybe he was overthinking it. He just needed to get to know her more. After all, people grew into love after marriage. He couldn't expect the sparks to fly off each other after one meeting, or even a month, could he? Like with his ex—they'd known each other at university for two years before they'd become an item. Before she'd electrified him, set his heart on fire, and then turned it to ash.

He had to rely and trust in the romance of commitment, of binding himself to someone he found attractive, who was good on paper and would fit into his family. He had to do it for his sister and his parents, and in the end, it would be best for him.

He got out of bed and stumbled across the room to make coffee. He didn't mind sacrificing for his family with his tiny apartment. When his roommate, John, had gotten married and moved out of their old place, Rishi technically could have afforded the larger two bedroom they'd shared, but at the same time, his parents needed the extra money. So he'd found the rare studio apartment and moved in. Besides, he was barely here, and he didn't take up that much space. And with the multitude of restaurants and Emma now forcing him to eat out all the time, he didn't have to cook much.

He laughed to himself as he put instant coffee into a mug and boiled some milk on the stove. Emma would have been horrified at him making instant coffee. He could imagine her lecture now. *Your grandmother would roll over in her grave if she knew you were making instant coffee! The woman hand roasted her own beans, and you're basically a traitor to her memory! Hand roasted!*

Then she'd get that far-off look in her eye, huff, and cross her arms like she always did when she was pissed at him. And then he'd say something to try to surprise her.

But Emma, we don't bury our dead. She can't really roll over in her ashes.

Emma would be horrified instead of laugh. She'd give him another one of those looks, one he'd labeled *shock and awe*, and chastise him by saying his name as a whisper. He couldn't deny that the way she said his name like that made him imagine how else she'd say it. In the dark. Moaning it in his bed. Playfully teasing him as she slid under the sheets. Nuzzling him in the morning.

He had to stop it. Although he had to imagine that if his grandmother had been able to meet Emma, they would've gotten along. Two women who didn't take shit from him and gave him the exact same knowing look when he fucked up.

His phone buzzed next to the bed, and he took a big drink of coffee, almost burning his tongue. If it was his mom again, he needed just a few moments of peace before launching back into her matchmaking game.

He slouched on the bed and picked it up. It was Emma.

Rishi, I'm in the need for green. I'm homesick for trees. Lots of them. Preeti suggested I go to the botanical garden, but she has some family thing. Do you want to go? If you're not busy of course?

I'm not busy. I'll come pick you up. Give me 30?

He wrote that fast enough.

Awesome!

He'd been looking at his day full of just sitting around, maybe trying to see one of his friends for a beer, and then Emma sprang into his life again. He chugged his coffee, jumped in the shower, and was off on his bike in record time.

{ /** *. // }

After picking up Emma, Rishi drove to the botanical garden, a place he had only been to once before, when his parents were visiting. It felt like the kind of place you would only go to on a date. Or take your family. Intimate, but still in full public view.

But in what world would it ever be possible that he and Emma and his family could all be together in the same space? Emma had cared so much about his family reconciling, but why? She didn't know them. She didn't know how his parents had treated their own son, his brother. And yes, it was complicated. And yes, Emma was right. They all needed to talk. But even getting them all in the same room would be a challenge.

Why did she care so much, or was she just offering advice because she liked to order him around?

A smirk spread on his face as he waited at a red light. But she didn't really order him around, did she? They were more than that now. How they'd met had put a cloud over them. Well, more like a storm. But it was all blue skies now, like this day. Blue with the occasional hazy cloud, and those clouds were more aligned with his parents' nagging than with anything having to do with Emma.

"Do you think I'm nuts to want to go to a garden?" she asked, her breath on his cheek. It matched the heat from the arm that was wrapped around his waist. He couldn't ignore how natural she felt holding him. He tried not to read too much into it. In the US it was probably completely normal to hold on to the other person's hip on a motorcycle.

He shook his head. "I get it. Seattle is very green. And all the green in the city here is covered in dust. So it's like a brown green."

"Yes! Exactly." She clutched at his shoulder with her other hand, and it made him sigh.

They pulled into the botanical garden gates, and he parked amid the dozens of bikes there.

"I know what it's like to be homesick a little," he said as he took off his helmet and helped hers off as well. "I was only in Seattle for a month, but I had some dark times."

Her left eyebrow rose up, and her lips turned down. "Your parents?"

He laughed. Trying to escape them by moving halfway across the world wasn't really dark; it was more ridiculous desperation. "It was the food, honestly."

A hum buzzed out of her. "Oh yeah, I can totally see that. Well, aren't you lucky I'm forcing you to take me to all these fantastic places to eat?"

"Most definitely." He was lucky, although he'd never say it to her unprompted. He'd somehow developed a new taste for the food he'd missed so much. But now, instead of just missing it because he'd grown up with it, he seemed to be developing new taste buds to detect the flavors she was moaning about at every meal. "Does your friend with the food blog miss you?"

Emma sighed as they walked up the path. "Oh yeah. We talk on occasion, but she's so busy with work and her fiancé and eating without me. It's mostly envy-inspiring comments on Instagram."

"It's hard to keep in touch when you're so far away sometimes. But hopefully our little stops around the city will make up for it. And you get to go to Kerala soon."

"I'm so excited about seeing a new place. I just want to stuff myself with everything in this country before I have to leave."

He swore she looked a little sad as she said this, and he laughed. "You've been here like two months. You can't be sad at what's happening almost a year away!"

She side-eyed him and looked amazed, possibly at herself. "I know, it's crazy, right? It's like I never really got the chance to leave Washington State too much, and now that I'm here, I just want to soak all the newness up."

They walked past more plants than he could've seen in the entire rest of the city. Flowers on a peacock statue, flowers cascading out of pots like waterfalls, flowers shaped into an elephant. A crisp green lawn that you couldn't walk on, with more flowers lined up in manicured rows.

"Is this green enough for you?" he asked.

"Yes, it's pacifying my inner Pacific Northwest nature girl."

"Is that a thing?"

"I think so. I was almost hungry for it, you know? Like I woke up today and looked outside, and there were cars and buildings, and I just needed some plants." They'd reached the point where the trail led them around a lake flanked with trees. "Oh, and this is exactly what I needed." She put her hands on her hips and looked out over the water.

"You can just pretend like you're back in Seattle here," Rishi said as they started on the trail around the lake. The trees overhead blocked out the sun, and while it was crowded with other people strolling around the lake, the sounds of traffic were muffled, barely audible from a distance.

"I guess I don't want to pretend I'm in Seattle; I like being here. I love exploring and discovering new things. Sometimes I think I just get so caught up in working and making a living that I don't stop to just feel and live. Does that make sense?" She shook her head at him.

"Yeah, totally. I think we all do."

"And when you take a minute to just breathe and take in your surroundings, all the stuff that feels like it should matter doesn't really matter as much as we make it out to. Like, I'm always so worried about being good at my job and being successful so I can pay my rent and pay off my student loans. But in reality, if I step back and just remove myself from everything, I realize I'm not going to get fired. I will still pay my bills, have a roof over my head, and all that."

"You worry about that?" Rishi asked. This was a shock to him. Emma had the same money concerns he did, but she'd just come out and admitted it. "So do I."

"And you're so good at your job!" She half laughed and smiled at him. He felt warm, even though the sun was still hidden away behind the branches. "Doesn't it all just make sense now?"

Rishi didn't have to ask what she meant. He knew. She was talking about how they were so much the same, and yet still so different. How they both wanted job security and success and had been willing to fight tooth and nail for it. Even fight each other.

It felt so natural to take her hand at this moment and walk down the path, feeling like they had reached the end of something. But instead of the end, it felt like something new.

CHAPTER 22

Emma hadn't seen Rishi for a few days, other than in their requisite team meetings and a few hallway conversations about the project. In fact, if she hadn't known better, she would've thought he was avoiding her. And that just couldn't happen. They were like comrades in arms now. Friends. And maybe some weird sexual tension had been lurking up inside her, flooding her veins and making her want to do inappropriate things like feel his skin, kiss him, stroke his face, smell his neck, slide her hands up his chest and maybe inside his pants . . .

She blew out a breath. They were still friends. And coworkers. And he was still looking for a wife. But that didn't mean they couldn't hang out. He was standing by the coffee machine when she went to get a cup.

"Hey," she said, oddly feeling like they'd had a fight and she was trying to slink back into his life.

Rishi's eyes looked like they were awake, but something in them was dull. Those shimmering gray gems had a coating of dust on them. Something was going on because his sad-face mask was back on. "Hi."

They both sort of stared at the machine. Emma had to do something. "Hey, we don't have any more meetings today. Let's go get coffee. Like real coffee. At the café down the street. My treat."

He looked like he was thinking over some internal debate in his head, and then, coming to a conclusion, he gave a resigned nod. "Okay."

She wanted to tell him to not sound so excited, but she resisted. She was there to coax his inner Rishi out of this life sack that had once held him. He stretched his arms behind his neck, his biceps small mountains on his arms. A chiseled life sack.

She sighed. "Come on, let's go." She backed away from him, but her hands were outstretched, beckoning him as her fingers fluttered. Yeah, she looked like a goofball, but if that's what it took . . .

"You look nice, by the way."

She froze in the corridor between the cubes and looked down. She was wearing one of her Preeti-approved purchases, a bright-blue salwar with some sequins that made her feel like a fancy peacock. She kept telling herself everyone dressed like this, so it was fine. It was fine that she couldn't find black and gray outfits. Rishi had seemed to like the last one she'd worn, and she couldn't deny that something about his compliments had urged her to wear another one. "Thanks." It would help if she couldn't feel herself blushing.

They walked to the coffee shop down the street, small clouds of exhaust puffing at them from auto-rickshaws, the loud honking from cars, the small beeps from scooters, the roar of the occasional motor-cycle engine as it revved up to squeeze through some narrow passage, all creating the soundtrack for their short journey. Why Emma felt like they should be holding hands on this weird walk was beyond her. It was like the same kind of naive tension she'd felt with a boy in middle school. Naive was exactly how her brain was behaving.

"You know, the noise shocked me the first week I was here," Emma said. "But now, it just feels normal. Like it's always been there."

"It *has* always been there." Rishi laughed.

"I guess I mean in my life. I'm surprised I'm so used to it after a few months."

"Well, it seems like you've acclimated to everything here. I don't think a lot of foreigners do. Last time this guy visited from the Seattle office, he wouldn't go anywhere without a car with air-conditioning, kept the windows rolled up, and only ate at his hotel. I was like, 'Dude, you are missing out!' But he didn't care."

"He *was* missing out. What's the point of even traveling if you don't eat everything you can? Such good food. It's amazing to me how many of the Indian restaurants in Seattle serve the same exact thing. And now, being here, it's like I've never had Indian food before. Like dosas. Poriyal. Pesarattu. Idlis." She'd just had lunch a little over two hours ago. Was it possible she was hungry again?

"What's been your favorite?" Rishi asked.

"I think the most interesting dish I've had was okra, I mean bhindi, cooked in some kind of mustard sauce. Something I never thought I'd like, but it was amazing. I'm like salivating right now." She laughed.

"You should have my mom's. It's so good."

"That would be fun!" The words just came out of her mouth. What would it be like to meet Rishi's family? His sister? Eat his mom's cooking? See the bedroom he grew up in? What kind of posters did he have up? Or did he have a collection of sports trophies? She turned to ask him but saw he had a far-off look in his eye. Maybe she shouldn't have said that. Was it inappropriate to say she would like to visit his family? God knows it wasn't the only inappropriate thought she'd had about Rishi lately.

She cleared her throat and got back on a topic that didn't involve Rishi or his family or the things she'd thought about a few nights ago as she drifted to sleep. Like his chest and the way his shoulders stretched the cotton of his shirts. "Oh, and the parathas, I forgot to even mention those. I mean, I could go on for days just about food."

They'd sat down and had ordered two cappuccinos from the server when Rishi's eyes finally lit up.

"Hey, Emma, what if we continue your tour of India with a hookah?"

She eyed one of the three-foot-high hookahs sitting next to another table. "Hookah. Hmmm." Her eyes narrowed as she watched two guys smoke at the table across the patio. She'd never smoked before, except for a failed attempt during a phase of high school rebellion that had made her cough so hard it hurt. But when would she and Rishi have more moments like this? When would she ever get another opportunity to try it?

"It's good, I swear. I'll order one, and you can try it if you want."

"Okay." That seemed easier than admitting she was nervous about hacking fit #2—not the sexiest event to witness. Although she shouldn't care about that. She wouldn't.

A man set one of the tall hookahs on the floor next to their table. Rishi stuck the pipe in his mouth, and she could have sworn he was teasing her with it as he gently cradled the end of the hose, his tongue curling around the end, a serious look in his eye as he sucked in deep, his cheekbones like razors as he looked at her. The sound of bubbles erupted from the base on the floor, and she looked down at it and realized that her mouth had been hanging open, the drool ready to spill out.

And it was not drool from wanting to smoke.

Jordana had once listed out the things she'd done to impress Charlie—eaten brains of something when they went to Japan, taken surfing lessons at a wave pool in February, and spent a week at his parents' small town in Kansas, population 450. She'd never understood the lengths that Jordana went to, to make Charlie happy, and vice versa. But sitting here, she wondered if maybe when it was the right guy, this was one of those things you sacrificed on your quest to impress him. Even if that quest was futile and buried under an algorithm and a portentous marriage, with a side helping of childhood asthma.

"Do you want to try?" Rishi held out the end of the pipe like a dare.

She took the pipe from his hands. "What is it exactly?"

"Watermelon mint."

"That's the flavor, but what's in *there*?" She pointed at the metal dome resting on top of the pipe that was almost at eye level. She had to get her mind off the eroticized sucking in front of her.

"Molasses. And a little bit of tobacco. It tastes sweet." The words that followed in her mind were *sweet. Naughty. Forbidden. Lips. Suck.* A little shiver crept up her back. "Try it."

She put the tip of the hose to her lips, the same small plastic piece Rishi had put his around, and sucked. She'd once passed a lollipop to a boy she thought was cute. He'd stuck it in his mouth, and she'd cried out in disgust, but when he gave it back to her, like a secret, she put it back in her own mouth when no one was looking, thinking it was like a kiss. She was regressing to her ten-year-old emotional self with this boy in front of her. Maybe inadvertently sharing some saliva. The crush from hell.

She sucked in gently, letting the smoke roll around her mouth, making sure not to inhale to avoid creating a horror movie called *The Hack* in front of Rishi. And yet, she couldn't help it as she felt the smoke tickle the back of her throat and then grip her larynx. "Oh no!" But she didn't get the last word out, just the cough.

He set her water in her hand, and she drank. "Ugh!"

"You inhaled quite a bit. Just keep it in your mouth, like this." Rishi took the pipe. She was staring at his parted lips as the smoke rolled around, he was staring into her eyes, and the intensity between them was strung tight like an invisible force, freezing them both where they were, unable to look away or move. Her breath tightened in her chest, and it wasn't from the smoke or the choking. She blinked, needing to break the spell, and he shifted in his seat. What the hell was going on?

Maybe it would have been better if they'd just sat there, her coughing while he was disgusted, because whatever this was, it wasn't good. It had fired up a little hope that was promptly extinguished as she thought about their reality. Marriage. Coworkers. Wife algorithm.

{ /** *. // }

Rishi was trying really hard not to laugh. At least this was getting his mind off his family and his current predicament. It was comforting to know that Emma wasn't an expert in everything.

"Try again. Less inhaling. Or not inhaling at all."

"Are you sure?" She wrinkled up her face at him, but the smile was still there.

"It's quite pleasant; just don't inhale." He handed the hose back to her, and her fingers tentatively pinched it. Their eyes locked again, and her fingertips slid down the hose until her hand met his.

A wave of nerves zoomed up and down his arm from the heat of her hand. It was like a spark had lit up his entire groin before exploding into needy firecrackers that threatened to disintegrate him. Zigging and zagging around, they played a game of billiards across his lap and thighs, and then the cue ball landed straight in his chest.

Like a bomb had exploded right in front of him, he was speechless. Rishi stared down at her fingers grasping the pipe. Fingers. Emma's fingers.

He took a deep breath and exhaled, his head slowly tilting up to meet her gaze. The one thing he'd been waiting for, searching for, had just hit him. The one reaction he'd been looking for in every woman he'd met over the years, at his parents' request. And now here it was.

With Emma.

Her mouth closed around the pipe, and her cheeks hollowed as she sucked. Those lips parted, and her tongue curled as she released it, and the smoke exited in small billows and ribbons from those perfect pink lips. Her tongue. Her lips. Her hooded eyes. He was almost in a trance, watching as the smoke curled around her tongue.

"Like this?" she asked. Was her voice like two octaves deeper?

He cleared his throat. "Keep doing it just like that." The words had escaped his mouth before his brain could tell it what to say. Yeah, that didn't sound sexual at all.

He was so screwed.

How had it happened? Had they just been spending too much time together?

His entire life had just done a 180-degree turn, while she was looking at something on her phone like nothing had happened. Emma was oblivious as his heart crumbled along the fault line that ran through him.

He was terrified of what he would do. What his body would do. And this was just after touching her hand. What would happen from a kiss? Or more?

He needed to leave, but he couldn't leave. He'd just gotten a hookah. "I'm going to get something to eat. Do you want anything?"

"Sure, surprise me." She smiled like he knew her. It was the kind of smile a girl in a movie would give a guy she was in love with. Who knew her inside and out. His hand ran through his hair, and he wanted to just yank it all out. Instead he walked to the counter.

He needed to put some distance between them. Distance. Kilometers. Not the three meters from here to the counter. He got a veg puff and a samosa, just pointing at the two things nearest him in the bakery case. He didn't care, just needed some excuse to let his body calm down. To reset his mind.

He set the two small plates in the middle of the table. "What's this?" She pointed.

"A veg puff."

"May I? You can have this hookah back. I got a taste, and that's all I needed. Checked it off my list."

Just a taste. He'd had that too. But he wanted to check more off his list. He really had to stop thinking that way.

She moaned a little as she took a bite. "What is this flavor? It's so good!"

"Oh, just some spices." Maybe food would distract him from what had happened. "You know, everything here is just sautéed with some spices. It's essentially all the same technique, with a variation on the spice and amount." So clinical. He just needed to talk in recipe code. If he actually knew any, of course, that would've helped.

"Yes, I'm sure it's that simple. You just sauté vegetables with spices, and that's it?" Her eyes shone like green glass, and her bottom lip curled up, mocking him. He wanted to grab her jaw and show her lips how serious he could be. It didn't help that she was ecstatic about all things food. She was going to get that foodgasm look all over again, and then his mind would just go back to where it shouldn't be.

"Yes, and maybe some coconut." He cleared his throat. What was he going to do?

"That sounds a little too easy."

Nothing about this was easy anymore.

"I'm not a great cook, so I usually make eggs and toast or something." She shrugged.

His mother would be horrified that a woman in her late twenties couldn't make anything but eggs. And his mother was a strict vegetarian who didn't even eat eggs, nor did she know Rishi did. His and Emma's future flashed in his mind: the two of them living off omelets and feeding two little brown-skinned, redheaded children. He laughed darkly, wondering from which part of his subconscious that image had materialized.

But that was the problem. It wasn't his subconscious anymore. It was something real. His body had just proved it to his mind. That question of *What if?* now loomed before him, penetrating his more sensitive organs and drawing them to attention.

And would he ever know the answer to the question he most wanted to ask: Did she feel it too?

CHAPTER 23

Emma ordered tea and samosas while she waited for the flight to be called for boarding to Cochin. She examined the crowd while trying to find Rishi. She hadn't seen him much that week after their hookah outing except for meetings, where he'd given her perfunctory greetings and status updates. As she sat on one of the barstools, she pulled out her guidebook and started reading about Kerala.

Just from reading the first pages about the Indian state on the Arabian Sea where the conference was being held, she'd discovered that Kerala had a tiger preserve as well as houseboat tours down something called "the backwaters"; it was also home to Ayurveda, the traditional Indian medicine of herbs and oils. Kerala was "God's own country," the book proudly exclaimed.

"Staring at a girl in her underpants getting rubbed with oil? For shame, Emma."

She swiveled around on her barstool to find Rishi and Kaushik standing behind her, Rishi with a delicious grin spreading across his face.

Heat crept up from her chest and threatened to take over her face and neck with its particular brand of embarrassing rouge. "I was just reading about the ancient art of Ayurveda," she stammered, which was skewed by her struggle to get the right sounds out. "I'm staying in Kerala until Monday, so I'm trying to figure out what to do."

Rishi nodded, looking into the distance. "That's a good idea. Almost like a free vacation, since you don't have to pay for the flight. What are you going to do?"

"I have no idea." Emma sighed and looked at her guidebook. "Jas said I could get a car and driver from the hotel, who would drive me around. Maybe I'll see a tiger or go on a boat ride . . . I don't know."

She leaned back against the bar, taking in the sight of Rishi, his T-shirt clinging to the curve of his biceps and fitting a little too tightly across the chest, his jeans hugging his thighs like they were in love and never wanted to let go. And his eyes, which somehow she'd once described as concrete, were shining and silver, like labradorite stones. When the sunlight filtered in through the window and his eyes caught the light, they almost glowed like a cat's.

Something had definitely happened when they'd had coffee. Or had she hallucinated it? You couldn't get high off a hookah, could you? If so, it was a high that had carried over for days.

"Excuse me—I'll be back in a minute." Rishi walked off, his head swiveling around, likely searching for the bathroom. Kaushik followed behind him but made a turn for the line at the gate.

Too bad she couldn't be touring the state with Rishi all weekend.

What was she thinking? Somehow all this marriage searching must have plucked a bright jewel of jealousy from her chest. He was soon going to be matched with a perfect woman who'd checked off all the boxes. Not that any of that *should* matter. She and Jeremy had been perfect on paper, but that thing that said *I can see myself discovering you for the rest of my life* just hadn't been there. But Rishi had goals. He had a sister. He had a plan to get married, and soon. He didn't have time to date, and even if he had, Emma would not have been the type of woman he'd consider casually dating. What would be the point?

She jumped off her stool and swallowed the rest of her tea and headed toward the growing line for her flight.

{ /** *. // }

It was after ten, and the three had checked in and had dinner and were still sitting in the hotel's restaurant, Kaushik talking and talking while Emma and Rishi split dessert—gulab jamun, round, syrupy balls lightly scented with rose. Every time their spoons clanked in the bowl, her heart seemed to ridiculously reply with an elevated beat.

"It's almost ten thirty," Kaushik said, looking at his watch. "We'd better get to bed. Our presentation is at nine."

Emma looked across the table at Rishi, who nodded and downed the rest of the beer in his glass. Sighing, Emma did the same, and they all went upstairs together, Emma falling behind the two as they had some kind of heated conversation in half English, half Hindi. Hinglish, Rishi called it. Everyone in India seemed to speak at least three languages. The small amount of time she'd devoted to learning Hindi had only let her ask if someone wanted something to eat or what their name was. She tried to catch what they were saying, but they were too fast.

"Good night!" Emma called out at her door. She knew she sounded annoyed but couldn't bring herself to care. Rishi waved from outside his room but was still talking to Kaushik. About cricket? Was that what she'd heard? She shut the door behind her, shaking her head. Ignored. Whatever.

She'd made a pact with herself when starting college that she wouldn't be the odd man out anymore. The wallflower. The nerd with hand-me-downs and crazed hair that wound itself into frizzy knots. And yet here she was again, the outsider. All because she wasn't learning Hindi fast enough.

What was that phrase Rishi had said to her in Hindi a few weeks ago? She looked at her phone, where she'd noted it down right after they'd talked. It had slipped from her mind, only to resurface now. Maybe she hadn't spelled it right, but she could trust in the internet to correct her mistakes. She copied the words she'd transcribed and pasted them into the browser.

Tum harai ankhen bohoot sunder hai.

The top result shot a bolt into her abdomen. A bolt that zapped below her navel and then sank lower. She collapsed onto the bed, heart racing, stomach swimming. That couldn't have been right, could it?

She swiped her thumb across the phone. All the results were the same. While she didn't know what a few of the words were, she knew *tum* was *you*.

And the key words were *bohut sundar hai*. Very beautiful.

Rishi had said she was beautiful. Correction: *very* beautiful.

A ridiculous smile ached at her cheeks, and she fell on the bed, delirious. She burned inside to tell him what she'd discovered. Her cheeks hurt from smiling so wide.

But did it matter, when he was trying to find a wife?

She lay still, but confusion swam around her, creating the kind of ache she had when she couldn't solve a challenging coding problem, her stomach sinking after she'd stared at the computer all day and forgotten about lunch. And pondering the puzzle of this man was causing clenching and twitching between her thighs. It wasn't math. It wasn't being engaged in her work. It was lust and longing and want.

She hypothesized what Rishi would do if she knocked on his door. If P, then Q. What were the potential outcomes? What did the consequents look like?

If Emma knocked on Rishi's door and he was asleep, he would be upset and ask her to leave. And remind her that no matter the attraction, he had to find an Indian wife with shampoo-model hair, even if he once thought she was pretty.

If Emma knocked on Rishi's door and Kaushik was there, still arguing with him, Emma would make up a lame excuse about borrowing sugar or something.

If Emma knocked on Rishi's door and he was awake and alone, he would either (a) tell her to leave because he was going to bed; (b) engage her in polite conversation (and remind her that he had to find an Indian wife with shampoo-model hair, even though at one point he thought she was a lovely specimen); or (c) engage her in the Congress of the Cow position, whatever that was, because he needed to live in the moment, and damn his search for an appropriate wife.

She pressed her hands to her eyes and kicked her feet. She told herself to focus on her vacation, which she had not planned, and their presentation in the morning. Besides, it wasn't like she would have the guts to tell him how she felt anyway.

How ridiculous would it sound? *Oh, Rishi, I know if it had been up to you, I wouldn't even be here in India, but I think you're hot and can't stop thinking about how you'd be in bed. And that whole thing about me finding you a wife because you need to get married—can we just push that aside temporarily so I can get this out of my system? Just exorcise these erotic demons that keep thinking about your eyes and biceps and thighs and chest and hands? And snake?*

It sounded absolutely ridiculous.

Though she *was* planning on going to a tiger preserve. What was more dangerous? Encountering a tiger, or letting her guard down for Rishi?

CHAPTER 24

Rishi tapped his foot, waiting for the host to finish his introduction. He'd never presented at a conference, although Emma had assured him it was easy. She'd told him to look over their heads at the wall in the back of the room. At the time it seemed like a good strategy, but now all he could do was stare at all the faces staring back at him.

After TechLogic was introduced, Emma took the microphone.

"Hi, everyone, I'm Emma Delaney, and I'm going to start by telling you how this app idea was conceptualized based off our work on a similar desktop project, Project Helix, in the US branch of the company." Emma pressed the small buttons on the remote to move her slides forward. She didn't show a single hint of nervousness as she discussed the work they had done and how success had come about, and she even dived into some of the code iterations for the true geeks in the room.

Why couldn't Rishi be as calm and confident as her? And why hadn't he realized the first few times they'd talked how sexy confidence looked on Emma?

As the timekeeper at the bottom of the stage held up ten fingers, she wrapped up her section and handed it over to Rishi, who took the mic from her, his hand wrapping around half of hers during the handoff. As the velvet touch of her hand slid beneath his, something tugged deep within. For a moment, he froze in front of all the little heads in the audience. They looked like a coating of barnacles on the bottom of a boat, eyes all waiting expectantly for him. He remembered Emma's advice, and his eyes shifted to the blank wall behind them. With a deep breath, he was able to walk through the slides, his gaze shifting from the wall to the projection screen behind him, and able to ignore the sea of faces in between the two.

When Rishi was finished, he joined Emma at the side of the stage. It was then Kaushik's turn to demo the app. A cameraman edged toward him to shoot a close-up of the phone to project on the monitors so the audience could see it better. Instead of showing off the app, Kaushik bent down so that his face was even with the camera lens, as if he were what the videographer was aiming for, not the phone.

The cameraman stumbled backward and fell off the stage, with him and his equipment tumbling the three-foot drop to the floor. Rishi sucked in his breath and started toward him. Before he reached the edge of the stage to see if he was okay, the cameraman had gotten back up on his knees, waving that he was all right, and Kaushik apologized, stuttering as he tried to start the presentation. Rishi kept a straight face, but he wondered if this incident had completely damaged the company's reputation. How could Kaushik be so foolish?

"God, he is such an egomaniac," Emma said under her breath, her hand covering her mouth.

"Mm-hmm," Rishi hummed, eyes still focused on the demo.

He tried to watch Kaushik, but instead his mind went to the trickle of Emma's breath that had seeped out warmly with her whisper. How would that breath feel on his ear while she whispered what she wanted him to do to her? He envisioned her hotel room, Emma beckoning him in. When he got inside, she pushed him onto the bed, her hair tickling the bridge of his nose and her lips teasing his. At this point, he didn't know how much longer he could stand the fantasy without finding out if the reality was possible.

Once the presentation was finished, the audience applauded, and the three of them walked down the stairs, heading to the side of the room to find new seats. Kaushik told them he was going to leave.

"Aren't you going to stay for at least a few of the presentations? Jas had us come all the way here," Emma said.

"No, I can't," Kaushik said, looking around the room. "It's too embarrassing. I don't want anyone to remember me."

Before either of them could protest, Kaushik had walked out of the room. Rishi shrugged, but inside his chest, it felt like every bit of him was leaping in applause and congratulations, high-fiving this glorious fate: alone with Emma for the rest of the day.

"Let's grab a seat," he said, unable to hide the immense smile pulling at his lips.

{ /** *. // }

At five, the day was done. Emma stretched in her chair and looked at Rishi. "I'm starving. Do you want to go to somewhere in the city? I feel like I haven't seen it. And I could use some fresh air."

As they walked toward the door, at least twelve people stopped them to compliment them on the presentation. It was an hour later by the time they reached the doors to go outside.

"Someone is popular," Rishi said. Every man they'd walked past had wanted to shake Emma's hand and congratulate her on the project.

"They were talking to both of us." She gave him a sideways look, but a smile raised one side of her mouth.

"Yes, I'm sure the fact that everyone stopped us and talked to mostly you had nothing to do with your excellent presentation, your name gracing renowned papers, or . . ." He had almost said *being the most beautiful woman in the room* but had caught himself. "Uh . . . or wanting to ask you questions about Helix," he said, staring off toward the coastline.

Emma hummed in response, as if she was thinking his words over. "It's never this hot in Bangalore, is it?"

"No. This is Kerala. God's own country and God's own sauna. If you can wait to eat a few minutes, we should go see the fishing nets before sunset." Rishi had only been to Cochin once as a child, but he remembered the giant fishing nets that hung over the water. Back then they had reminded him of a huge slingshot. But instead of slinging rocks at schoolmates, they flung nets out to catch fish and prawns from the ocean.

This was his chance. His chance to sweep up Emma into a moment she wouldn't forget. Whatever happened after this trip, whatever his parents needed him to do, he had to get her out of his system. He had to undo the Emma that was coating every inch of his mind. He couldn't think straight; he couldn't focus on the right priorities; he couldn't even escape thinking about what she would think about what he thought. Hopeless.

He had to know what was between them before he could move on.

How could he do this? In front of the romantic backdrop, with the sun setting in the background, the fishing nets stretched out over the ocean? Thrusting her up against the elevator on the way to their rooms? Confessing his feelings after too many Haywards and, if she laughed in his face, being able to blame it on a loose tongue controlled by a 50 percent functioning brain?

"Fishing nets?" She looked at him as if he'd spoken in another language.

Maybe that wasn't the best idea. But she should at least see them. Tonight was his chance to scoop up the best of his world and gift it to her. "They're really cool. I promise."

As they strolled in the humidity, Emma stopped as they walked, reading the menus at the restaurants, with the smell of cardamom, cumin, and fried seafood wafting about, trying to decide what to have for dinner. "Let's come here on the way back," she said at one café and then another.

"That's the seventh restaurant we have to come back to. I've been counting." Rishi laughed, again the urge to throw his arms around her coming over him. Her excitement about the food was contagious. Even he was about to give up the quest to see the fishing nets.

"They all smell so good! I'm starving. Where are those nets?" She glanced around, hand shielding her eyes.

A few minutes later they approached the beach, where a group of people had gathered at the docks. Farther down the coast were long poles, tied together and swept up and over the ocean, hoisting wide nets suspended horizontally over the water. From a distance, they looked like sinking ships, the posts holding the nets as they stretched down toward the water without falling into it. And there weren't just a few: there were six, eight, twelve—they couldn't see them all. The way the sun lit them, like a naked light bulb hanging over the waves, was more than just a postcard moment.

"Cool, huh?" Rishi said beside her, wondering what she would do if his arm sneaked up around her shoulder.

"Very. How do they work?"

"I have no idea." He laughed and turned to the left at the noise gurgling up and down the road. "Hey, there's a fish auction going on." Rishi grabbed her bicep, trying to uncurl her arms, which were crossed over her chest. He was aware of his fingers against her torso. He let go once they were walking, but when they reached the auction, Rishi pulled her again so they could get up front. He tugged a little too hard, and she shot forward, her chest landing against the side of his.

"Oops! Total accident," he said, but Emma didn't seem to mind that her chest had collided with his. In fact, she hadn't moved. Her eyes were focused on the display in front of them. It felt so natural for their bodies to fit together like this.

On a makeshift wooden platform smeared over with sand, buckets and trays cradled miniature gray octopuses, thin shimmering fish, and prawns ranging from two inches long to almost a foot. Flanking the buckets were long thin fish and smaller fatter fish, all of them dry, with flies buzzing about. A few of the prawns were trying to crawl around in the buckets. They weren't all dead, just slowly suffocating.

Emma walked away, her hands folded over her stomach.

Rishi jogged over. "Dinner?"

"Yes, but I think I'll have to skip the fish."

"Okay, but you're missing out!" Rishi said, rubbing his hands together and practically drooling. He could taste the coconut and curry leaves the fish would be swimming in. The salty-sweet tang of the prawns sprinkled with chili powder and jaggery. The mussels cooked with shallots, garlic, and garam masala. Coconut milk dousing it all.

On one of the quaint cobblestone streets they had walked up earlier, Rishi and Emma stopped at a sidewalk café and took a seat at one of the tables. A large round mosaic lamp hung from a black-and-white-striped awning, illuminating the space.

When the waiter came, Rishi couldn't decide and ordered three different seafood items while Emma decided on a paneer dish and mixed vegetables. As the waiter walked away, Rishi called out, "Oh, and two Haywards 5000s!" He smiled at Emma.

"Feeling dangerous?" she asked.

"Maybe just a little." He raised his eyebrows. "By the way, we need to continue on with our Indian food tour. You have to try some fish. We're in Kerala."

"We'll see. I feel like that auction might have turned me off fish for a while."

"You just need to be turned on again." Rishi realized what he said, then noticed the color spreading through Emma's cheeks as the waiter delivered the beer to their table.

"What do you think happened to Kaushik? Still sulking in his room?" she asked.

"He's called me twice," Rishi said, pouring half the beer into a glass for Emma. "But I thought maybe we would just go out. Even though I know you adore him so."

"I kind of feel bad for him. There's a first for everything." She laughed.

The waiter came back, filling their table with too many plates of food. Fragrant spices encased a fried fish garnished with halves of miniature limes and sliced green chilies. Another fish was unwrapped from a banana leaf, coated with spices, and steamed from within. Rishi's fleshy prawns swam in a fiery-red curry. Butter melted onto flaky parathas. The whole table smelled like coconut, roasted tomatoes, a million spices, and the freshness of the tropical coast. He cut a piece of the fish and held it out to her.

She took a bite and her eyes closed. This must have been a hint of what she looked like in the throes of ecstasy. Head tilted back, throat pulsing, eyelashes fluttering against her cheeks. A hum vibrating her lips.

Could Rishi do that to her with his hands and mouth?

"Okay, maybe I made a mistake in my order," Emma said, her sultry smile spiking up his jeans.

He cleared his throat and told his body to behave. "Don't worry: I got enough for both of us."

"You know you want some delicious vegetables." She held up a bowl.

"Oh no, I don't. I had enough vegetables growing up to last me a lifetime."

"So when did you stop being vegetarian?" she asked, taking some of the fish from his plate.

"College. My family is from the priest caste, so we don't eat meat. Or drink. Or smoke. Or gamble. You know, anything that is unpriestly."

"The only one of those I haven't seen you do is gamble, so I'm guessing there may still be one-fourth of you that's priestly," she teased.

"Well, there are casinos at most of the hotels here, so we could go, and you can see that I am only priestly by birth. After I left home, all the priest flew out of me." He punctuated his proclamation by placing a prawn in his mouth.

"What do your parents think about that?" she asked, tilting her head.

"They don't." Rishi shook his head. "They have no idea."

"You hide it from them?"

"It's not hiding if you neither admit to it nor deny it, right? It just never comes up." Another innocent lie meant to protect them. Emma reached over and grabbed another bite of his fish curry. "I see you are not sticking to your recent decree to not eat the fish. The priest in me is really judging you right now."

"I had to sacrifice for the tour. Tell your inner priest to be more understanding. As you are clearly sacrificing for the tour as well. You just happen to be on tour every day." She leaned back in her chair, stuffing some paratha in her mouth and grinning. "So your parents don't know you live a double life?"

"No." He shook his head. It was better that way. Spared them needless heartburn. "You never hid anything from your parents?" Rishi asked. Emma knew everything about his life, it seemed, and all he knew of hers was that she had high school dates whom she may or may not have kissed and a grandmother who threatened to shoot them.

She shifted in her seat and looked off toward the ocean. The red vines of her hair blew across her face as a wind from the coast swept over them. Rishi's hand lifted up to brush them out of her face before he realized how absolutely inappropriate that was and settled it back in his lap before smacking it into compliance with his other.

"My parents died when I was eight." She swallowed, but she wasn't chewing anything.

A shock reverberated through him. That was the last thing he'd expected. "I'm sorry, I didn't know." That was so long ago. What was Emma like when she was eight? How could losing both your parents that young affect you? Her face didn't reveal anything, but now he wondered what else she was hiding. His cousin had been sixteen when his dad died of cancer. Old enough to understand what was happening, but it had been hard and had definitely changed him. What did it do to you if you were a little kid?

"It's okay. I just don't like to bring it up."

"But why? It's a part of you. You've obviously made an amazing life for yourself despite the circumstances. Do you mind if I ask what happened?"

She shook her head and blew out a breath that was more of a grunt. "Some asshole drunk driver hit them. On a bridge. They were flung over the side, and . . . well, that's what happened." She looked over to the side again. Her eyes had soured. He hoped she wasn't going to cry. He didn't want to be the reason.

"So that's why your badass grandmother was the one pointing the shotgun at your dates instead of your dad?" He smiled at her and hoped that would get maybe half a laugh out of her.

It did, thankfully. Emma laughed and sniffed at the same time. "Yeah." She nodded at him, her lips curled up in a sad sort of smile.

"Thanks for sharing that with me."

She took a bite of paratha. "I guess that's why I like food so much too. My grandmother was *not* a cook." She shook her head and laughed. "Based on what you've said about your mom's cooking, I'm pretty sure her worst nightmare would be walking into my grandmother's kitchen. We didn't have money, so we ate some pretty weird, kind of gross old-school stuff."

"Like what?" Now Rishi was intrigued. What food did Emma think was gross and weird?

"Well, do you know what Spam is?"

"No."

"Count yourself blessed. It's like, I don't know, pureed meat parts? And they smoosh them into this can, and then you cook it." She shivered. "And cheese that didn't actually contain dairy. And lots of pickled things. There was once a jar of pickled pigs' feet in our kitchen." She held up her hands like she was surrendering. "Although I swear I never touched those. That's where I drew the line."

"Pigs' feet? Pickled?" Rishi was trying to conjure up how you would even do that.

"Yeah, I hope I'm not ruining your meal."

"No way. This is the best." And he wasn't talking about the food.

After a few beats of silence where they both ate a few bites of food and smiled at each other, Emma said, "Rishi. There's something I want to say to you." She took a drink of beer and leaned forward. "I just wanted to say I'm sorry for how things happened. With the transfer to the US not working out, and you not leading the project. I know it was disappointing for you, and you must have resented me, but I'm really glad you're on the team and that we've gotten to know each other."

Something seemed to crack inside Rishi's chest. Or maybe *soften* was a better word. "I don't think it was your fault, though. You don't need to apologize."

She nodded. "I know. It just really sucked for you. And you're so great at your job. If you weren't on the project, I don't know what I would do."

"Suffer with Kaushik as your lead dev?"

She rolled her eyes. "Oh my God, can you imagine?"

"Actually, no, I can't. I mean, I can imagine the bodies that you'd leave behind in the wake of the Kaushik-Emma Armageddon, but . . ."

Emma laughed. "That's totally what it would be. Rishi, what would I do without you?" Her hand crawled over to his and gave it a squeeze. He looked down at it and squeezed it back. A perilous squeeze. The most dangerous squeeze in history. Did she think that too? Because her fingers crumpled up and retracted, slinking back into her lap.

He wanted to say, *Nothing. Don't do anything without me. Let's find out what this is. Let's see where this goes. Who cares if it's wrong or impossible or stupid?* But he couldn't. He couldn't risk it. What if Emma was just joking? What if this was just how she was with everyone once they broke down her frosty exoskeleton? What if this wasn't special, and he said or did something that would ruin the project or their relationship or his job?

Instead, he just downed the rest of his beer.

After dinner, they walked through the lamplit streets on the way back to their hotel. Rishi was acutely aware of his proximity to her. Their hands would accidentally graze as he leaned over to point out a church or some other architecture, and he craved the feel of her hand in his again. Trouble. That's all this was.

Rishi held the door open for her when they arrived at the hotel. They stepped into the elevator and both stood against the wall, staring at the door. Was it hot in here? Had they turned off the AC in the elevator? Sweat broke out on his brow. The vision he'd had earlier of thrusting her up against the elevator wall and confessing his attraction sneaked up.

Or what would happen if he pulled her into his room and kissed her, his hands exploring what his eyes had imagined? What would she do if he pushed her against the corridor wall and let his mouth roam the expanse of her throat? He stared straight at the elevator door, not knowing what to do.

Time was running out. He'd never have this chance again.

His body was radiating heat like the sun to Mercury. Nine thousand watts per square meter. He needed her to rid his body of the excruciating warmth.

The tiny ding announced they had arrived at their floor. Rishi stood aside so Emma could get past. His thoughts fumbled as she walked toward her hotel door. He only had thirty seconds to plot his seduction, thirty seconds to concoct a plan. Or thirty seconds to do absolutely nothing and relieve himself in his room. And wonder. For the rest of his life: *What if?*

They reached Emma's door, his heart pumping wildly. His head told him to wish her a good night. Every other part of his body told him it would not be appeased until he knew what she felt like in his arms.

That zing between them kept flashing in his mind. How satisfying it had been to finally know it existed. That he hadn't fabricated its existence. That the zing was real.

And that satisfaction led to something unsatisfied within him. He needed more. He needed to feel it with his whole body.

The door to her room was already cracked open when Emma turned around. Rishi's mind was still anxious with its decision.

"Rishi," she said, gazing up at him. "I have to tell you something. Remember a few weeks ago when you told me something in Hindi?"

The sudden change in subject had his brain topsy-turvy. Hindi? What had he said?

"Something something *bohut sundar hai?*" Her hand came to rest on his chest. A tentative touch, her fingertips exercising the lightest pressure on his shirt buttons.

But the energy shot through him again. Lightning that sizzled into his chest and slid down his abdomen. He glanced down at her fingers planted on his sternum, and then back to her eyes. Her eyes, which now shone with the same need he felt inside. Light and dark at the same time, glowing with a catlike heat. Could this be real?

What had he said? That her eyes were beautiful. How did she remember that? Because she was Emma, that was why. He exhaled deeply. "I might recall that."

"Well, I looked it up," she said, her gaze flashing from her hand to his eyes. "You've been found out." Her palm lifted, and one finger pierced him in the chest and then slid down to where his shirt met his belt and then disappeared from his body.

His breath seized. Looking into those eyes, those deep pools of sea green, he couldn't stop himself.

Fuck it.

"And I meant every word." He leaned down, and her mouth met his halfway. His lips fit perfectly onto hers, sucking on them, hungry and curious. Emma's body caved as she fell against the door from Rishi's weight, stumbling back until it slammed against the wall of her room. Rishi threw it shut. Before he put his mouth onto hers again, he paused, studying her reaction. Emma pinched the collar of his shirt and pulled him to her. Heat surged through his veins. The sizzle and ache in his body seemed to be melding into one sensation, rendering him weightless.

Emma sank against the wall, her arms around Rishi's broad shoulders as she dug her fingers in.

The skin on her neck tasted like the spray from the ocean. Her tongue felt like silk in his mouth. Under his hands, her skin radiated fire and velvety softness. The back of her neck was like a peach he'd tasted only once before.

Rishi breathed into her hair. He couldn't make up his mind what to do next because he wanted everything, and now. But he had to be patient. He should be savoring this woman like she savored a meal.

She grasped his neck, running her hands through the thick hair at the back of his head. "What are you going to do to me?"

"I'll show you," Rishi said into her ear, taking it in his mouth before he released her. He bent down and with one arm grabbed her behind the knees, and with the other across her back, he lifted her up.

Emma sucked in her breath as he picked her up, then laughed when he threw her on the bed. "You're insane."

Maybe he was. No, he definitely was. But he couldn't think about any reality right now other than the reality in this room. Get her out of his system? Was that what he had thought earlier? The innocent idea that once could be enough?

She'd fully invaded him. Taken over. Stormed the castle of his body and set up camp. Implanted pleasure at every guard station that should have been protecting his best interests.

When he'd rearranged his travel for the weekend at the airport, had he subconsciously planned on her unleashing that uncaring beast who forgot about his family and pressure and the right thing to do in their eyes? Because now, all that felt *right* was spending three days in Kerala, exploring the uncharted territory of Emma Delaney.

CHAPTER 25

The morning light seeped under Emma's eyelids. She blinked them open to find Rishi, his chin on her breast like it was a pillow and his left hand extended over her, trying to wind the one purple lock of her hair around his index finger.

Her body tensed, every nerve inside her ready to push up off the bed and run out the door. Last night . . . had she made a mistake? It was so ruthlessly unexpected. The pleasure unanticipated. The urge to still squeeze him against her, wrap her legs around his thighs, and feel their bodies become one unwanted. But it was there, and she couldn't get rid of it—this strange mix of being completely terrified and excited at once. Her stomach was swirling with apprehension as she tried to figure out what all these feelings meant. Whatever happened—was happening—was completely devoid of logic. Maybe for once in her life, she'd just have to go with it.

And what did Rishi expect? A onetime fling before he settled down with Miss Doctor-Actress-Chef-Maid with Perfect Hair? She couldn't deny that she'd had a Rishi itch to scratch. Maybe he'd had it too. But that itch was still there, and the idea that they wouldn't be able to explore more of what had happened last night made a little hole in her chest. A dark, smoking bullet wound. He was getting on a plane today, while she would be going on her solo Kerala adventure. And then what?

"Hi," she said, dislodging her arm from under his back. He looked up at her, his eyes deep in thought. What thoughts? Suddenly she was frozen with shyness. And shy was the last thing she should be feeling after what they'd done last night.

Maybe she was being shy because of the startling, frightening truth she faced while looking into those eyes: That she didn't want him to leave. That she didn't want this to end.

"Good morning." Rishi smiled, although it looked almost sad. He extracted his hand from her hair and leaned forward to kiss her.

She wondered what to say, what to do. She had never been intimate with someone who was so off limits, with whom she worked, and who was searching for a wife. But this odd easiness that was coursing through her body was offsetting the anxiety of all the unknowns.

Maybe there was hope.

It felt right and good and perfect. Like they could collapse into a puddle of laughter and sighs. How their bodies could intuit one another's needs. How even their minds seemed to be wandering down the same random thought paths sometimes.

She shivered, but in a good way, and his hand trailed down her arm, causing more goose bumps, but of a very different variety. She sighed and shook her head. She didn't know what to do with him. He bit his lip and raised his eyebrows in response. *I don't know either,* they said.

Had it ever been like this for her? With Jeremy? She tried to remember the first time with him after too much drinking and a really good night out with their friends. Jeremy's textbook moves did the job, but she couldn't remember ever feeling like *this*.

This was a wave of emotions—euphoria, lust, happiness, contentment—that she couldn't quite put into words. It reminded her of all the times when Jordana would gush over Charlie. How she once compared her heart to a nest that could explode tiny songbirds out of her chest. Emma had thought she was crazy, but now she understood what she'd meant. Was this what being in love felt like?

"What's going on in that head of yours?" Rishi asked, his lips tugged up in amusement.

She sighed and slapped her hand on her forehead. She'd just keep it there to hide from reality. The one lying directly on her. "I think I'm losing my mind. It was probably only a matter of time."

"Why exactly are you losing your mind?"

She glanced down at his chest and arms, her mouth dry. Her hand drifted to the valley between the swells of his pecs and stroked a finger down his chest. After all, this might be the last time she could touch him like this. "Well, I have you lying on me, all gorgeous and naked. I have three days off work. I have no clue what I'm doing or where I'm going today. And I have no idea what to do with any of it—you, my days off, nothing." She leaned back into the pillow. What had she done? So unprepared. So blindsided by last night.

"I totally understand because I'm lying on you, and you're also all gorgeous and naked." And then his hands began their slow, torturous search for Emma's pleasure zones.

God, could this be real? Could this thrumming inside her, this sweet ache, play on repeat?

"And I also have three days off work, in Kerala, and have no clue what I'm doing."

Emma's head jerked up. "You do?" Her earlier moment of panic and worry disappeared. Maybe they could just stay in this bed all three days while Rishi sweetly continued to torture her.

His hand traced her torso. "Yes, after you mentioned it at the airport, it seemed like a good idea, so I ran over and changed my tickets."

She hummed, processing what he had said. He had changed his ticket and hadn't told her until now. She punched him on the chest. It was so hard that she almost said ouch. "Wait, did you plan this whole thing? Last night? The fish and the nets and the sunset? The checkered tablecloths?"

"You mean making you nauseous by watching some fish suffocate, then smelling it, and putting you off eating my favorite food in the entire country? I thought it would be super hot. All totally planned."

"No, I mean it was just so . . ." Romantic? Was that the word Emma was looking for? Perfect but imperfect? Just like her and Rishi. "It was just fun and surprising." *And made me have to find out what would happen between us.*

"If you would like your own personal tour guide, we can explore Kerala together. And maybe we can have more of this . . ." Rishi slid down the length of the bed. She tried not to think about if he would do this to Radhika or Lakshmi. That cavernous hole in her growing deeper. Dreadful thoughts would be spelunking in it soon.

One more chance to be with him before it was all over? Could she just not think about the consequences for once? Her mouth had opened to say yes when someone knocked on the door.

"Emma?" a loud voice called through the thick wood. It was Kaushik.

Her eyes rose to meet Rishi, and they both froze, still as statues. Emma surveyed the room and saw her clothes in a discarded, haphazard pile with Rishi's clothes, her bra flung toward the door (had Rishi used it as a slingshot?) and their underwear in a puddle at the base of the bed.

Emma ran through the possibilities of what Kaushik might possibly need in her room. "Just a minute!" she called to the door and then whispered to Rishi, "You go in there." She pointed at the closet door and kicked all their clothing toward it.

"Good morning," she said, opening the door and hoping she didn't smell like a sexpot. He'd be suspicious, if only because she was way more cheerful than she'd ever been with Kaushik. She tried to look pissed off.

"Emma, I'm just leaving for the airport. Do you know where Rishi is? He didn't call me back yesterday, and I thought we had the same flight."

Emma tried to look thoughtful, as if she were recollecting something. "You know, I didn't see him after the conference last night, but I remember him saying something about having a really early morning flight. I bet he's already gone."

"Oh, okay." Kaushik's eyes roamed the room behind her, and Emma panicked.

"Well, bye, I am going back to bed." Emma started to shut the door.

"It's almost ten. Checkout is in an hour."

"Mm-hmm. Okay, thanks. Bye." She gave him a little wave as she shut the door. She stayed still, listening as his heavy steps trod down the hall.

She opened the closet. "Rishi, checkout is in an hour. As my tour guide, did you happen to already make an itinerary?"

"So that's a yes?" He grinned as he clutched his clothes around him.

Was he going to make her beg for it? Was it not absolutely and painfully obvious that she would go with him? "Yes, it's a yes. What should we do?"

"Don't worry, Emma. You can get anything you need in India. You want a car and driver to escort you around the entire state? One call and they'll be here in ten minutes. It's just one of the many conveniences of living in a country with a billion people. There is always someone available."

"Let's take a shower then." She smiled at him. "We can get clean and dirty at the same time."

CHAPTER 26

The lush trees outside were so different from the seaside city of Cochin. A green backdrop for their drive. Green like Emma's eyes. Green like the color his mother would turn if she knew what he'd done last night.

Oh, last night. His skin itched thinking about it again. How good it felt, how freeing.

He didn't know how it made sense or why it had happened, but when he woke this morning, his future stretched out before him like a blank slate waiting to be etched, rather than a game board where he needed to move ahead in the proper order to win.

The grand prize in the game: making his family happy.

Then his mind flashed to Radhika. Was that real? Could he be engaged soon without talking to her further? He'd have to bring his parents' quest to a halt.

Yesterday, he'd convinced himself that being with Emma was something he had to shake off his skin, a fix that he needed. But now, all he could do was think about her more. Where he could get her alone again, preferably with a bed. What their lives would look like together in Bangalore. Could they really be something together?

And how he would deal with his parents.

His stomach rolled on itself as he thought about it. It would be fine. Wouldn't it? What had they said about Radhika's uncle having a job for his dad? He shook his head. Of course it would be fine. Rishi would keep sending them money, even if that meant he'd keep living in a closet for an apartment. Maybe he could get Dharini a new job at TechLogic so she'd wait to get married.

He had three glorious days of freedom ahead of him. With Emma. They had a tiger preserve to explore and a houseboat to ride. There was no sense in spoiling their holiday with worrying about his parents' reaction when he told them no to yet another bride-to-be.

Or was he getting ahead of himself? What if Emma thought this was a check to make on her India bucket list? Or she just wanted someone to hang out with on the long weekend? What if they drove each other crazy and weren't even on speaking terms by Monday?

But even as these thoughts popped up, like foolish, hopeful excuses for avoiding confrontation with his family, something inside him vehemently disagreed. And Rishi knew it was right, this tiny but potent voice. Something was happening here. Something he hadn't even felt with Sapna. How was it that the love he'd felt after two years of friendship was still dwarfed by his feelings for someone he'd known for only a few months? How could he be feeling such an ache just imagining her absence?

"Have you ever seen one?" Emma's voice woke him from his tiresome train of thought.

"Seen a what?" Rishi asked.

"A tiger. I just can't believe I might see one outside of a zoo."

They were halfway to the town of Thekkady, which Emma had suggested should be first on their agenda since the tiger preserve was there. Rishi didn't want to spoil her fun, but it was called a tiger preserve, and that might mean there was just one tiger they were preserving.

"I've never gone to a tiger preserve, so I'm not sure how many are actually there," Rishi said. "The British killed most of them during colonial times. If you don't see one, you'll know who to blame."

Rolling down the window, he let the breeze rush over his face. There were so many trees. The green canopy of the forest arched over them, the air slightly misty in the higher elevations, cool enough you could wear a jacket.

The driver slowed the car. "Boss," he said in the local language, Malayalam. "Elephants ahead."

"Emma," Rishi whispered, and his hand met hers with clandestine creeping on the seat. The immediate comfort from just touching her took him aback. He looked at her, dread coming over him, but the look on Emma's face at seeing the three elephants marching, tails swishing side to side, taking up both lanes of the road, dismissed any worries and just let him enjoy her pleasure.

Emma gripped Rishi's hand, frozen. "It's like *National Geographic*."

"Good thing they are going the other way," Rishi said as they watched the herd exit off the road into a cluster of trees. "Angry elephants are a lot less cute."

"Well, that was amazing. I can die happy now." Emma sighed, her head falling against the seat.

"Because of a few elephants?"

"Well, that and other things," Emma said, gliding the edge of her hand along his thigh.

That was it. Rishi was just going to have to forget about his family for a few days. Forget about his worry and just focus on the moment. All the moments they'd have together.

{ /** *. // }

They pulled into the driveway to a Dutch-styled brick-and-stone hotel. As they checked in and got their keys, the man at reception shifted his eyes back and forth between the two of them.

He was attempting to diagnose their situation: Lovers? Illicit affair?

Emma wasn't wearing a mangalsutra around her neck to signify she was married to him. He waited for the guy to slip into Malayalam and ask Rishi. If they were a real couple, those suspicious looks would happen all the time.

They dropped their bags off in the room and decided to explore Thekkady. The town itself was mostly filled with tourist shops, shelves lined with oils and spices, small tiger statues and T-shirts. Emma spotted a sign for a midnight trek through the tiger preserve.

Rishi sighed as he looked at the sign, a thousand rupees, which was a ridiculous price for a trek where they wouldn't see any animals. Plus it was pitch black at night in the forest. If there were actual tigers lurking around the preserve, they wouldn't allow people to walk around during the tigers' prime hunting time. But that spark of Emma's eyes, like a little kid going *Please! Please!* got him. They decided to go after dinner.

At ten, they walked toward a small shack next to a rusty gate marking the entrance to the preserve. The gate was covered in barbed wire, top and bottom. Six other tourists stood waiting for the midnight trek to start. Without a word, the two guides, dressed in jeans and button-up shirts, handed out stirruped canvas tubes.

"What are these?" Emma asked.

"Leech guards."

Rishi squinted at the canvas leggings in his hand, wondering what kind of superleeches were in the jungle that could creep up to your knees.

After they'd started, Emma, who seemed a little shaky, grabbed Rishi's arm and dragged him to walk right behind the man with the gun. Thirty minutes into the two-hour trek, and with no wildlife in sight, Rishi had given up any small expectations he'd had.

The guard stopped, holding out his arms to bar anyone from moving. Emma clutched Rishi's hand. The guide shone his flashlight into the brush and illuminated two wild pigs. Emma laughed beside him, and her grip loosened on his hand.

Ninety minutes later, the guides had shown the group a shadow that was supposed to be a bear across a river, and a tree limb that was apparently a snake. The gate they'd entered shone ahead, reflecting the guide's flashlight.

Emma leaned over to Rishi, disappointment making her voice a whine. "No tigers!"

Rishi laughed. "There is no way a tiger is going to come near eight people walking with flashlights and being way too loud. They're secretive creatures."

"So you knew?" She stopped walking, her mouth open as she waited for an answer.

"You seemed like you wanted another *National Geographic* moment, so I was willing." He shrugged, smiling at her as they exited the sanctuary.

One of the girls screamed and stomped her feet. "Get them off me! Get them off!"

Emma grabbed on to Rishi and gasped, looking at the howling woman. The leeches were everywhere on her leech guards, squirming around like tiny black worms trying to find a gateway through the canvas.

Rishi and Emma examined their own leech guards, which also had a few wormy leeches curling themselves on the tan canvas. Emma looked a little paler than usual, her fists tightened into balls, her body stiff. He gingerly removed the leechy leg warmers from Emma's legs and threw them in a pile with the others.

"There's your *National Geographic* moment." He laughed. "All better?"

Emma nodded, but Rishi wasn't convinced. It was two o'clock in the morning, and they hadn't slept much the night before. She must have been tired. And disappointed. Maybe he should have protested going on this jungle trek.

Emma was silent as they walked to their hotel. After Rishi opened the door to the room, she sprinted into the bathroom.

After a few minutes of hearing nothing in the bathroom, Rishi stood outside the door, worried. Was it something he'd done? Something he'd said? "Emma?" The door pushed open as he knocked, and he could see Emma's reflection in the mirror, twisting her body around, writhing in front of the sink, her hands searching her skin. Then they sank into her hair, trying to separate the thick chunks of curls as she looked at her scalp.

She was completely naked.

His voice got caught in his throat, and he had to clear it. "What are you doing?" he whispered in a shallow, husky voice.

Emma pushed her hands on the edge of the sink, blushing. "I . . . was looking for blood-sucking parasites that are out in the jungle. Like leeches. And ticks."

Rishi normally would have laughed, except when a naked woman stood in front of him, he made it a rule to be very, very serious.

"Let me continue searching for you then," Rishi said, spinning her around, his hands on her hips. Emma kept her hands folded in front of her, clasped together at the V of her thighs.

"I didn't want to ask you."

"Nonsense. It's part of my job as your tour guide." Rishi bent down to the floor, stroking her calf and foot. "Looks like we're all clear here," he said softly, moving his hands up to her knees. One finger caressed the back of her knee, and Emma's body sank a little.

"You're very thorough for a guide." Her voice was soft, but a hint of mirth ran through it. At least she wasn't freaking out anymore.

"Looks like you are spotless here too," Rishi said, bending his head behind her other knee, teasing it with the tip of his tongue.

Her body shuddered against him. This was definitely one way to get her mind off leeches.

Rishi's hands slid up her thighs. "These look very, very good. Flawless, in fact," he whispered, sliding his hands up and down the fronts and backs of her thighs. "But I feel I could better conduct my investigation in the adjoining room." He turned her around and backed her into the bedroom.

"You are going to destroy me," she sighed, hands tangled in his hair. "Or give me a concussion. I almost fell over."

Rishi started to laugh, and then Emma pushed him on the bed. "You know, I always believe in paybacks," she said as she slid down the length of his body, unbuttoning his jeans.

"What kind of payback are we talking about here?"

She pulled out a condom and ripped it with her teeth. "The best kind."

CHAPTER 27

It was the first weekend Emma hadn't thought about work since she could remember. The thought came to her as she and Rishi sat at the helm of a thatch-roofed houseboat, floating along the narrow backwaters of Kerala. Leaning into the wooden chair embedded into the floor, she watched a flock of green parrots squawk through the leaves of the palms. The words *Easter egg!* sparked in her mind. Like a little unexpected prize on this journey she was on.

Although maybe Rishi was really the unexpected prize.

She looked over at him, sitting next to her as he stuffed a piece of pineapple in his mouth. Rishi ate it as he steered the boat behind a spindly steering wheel. They'd been on the boat for a few hours, with nothing to do except lie in the full sun, gaze at the forest of coconut trees that lined the backwaters, and sneak off to the onboard bedroom. He'd even convinced the captain of the boat that he could steer it himself through the wide expanse of the clear teal water. So they could be alone.

Emma shoved a piece of pineapple in her mouth as well. The bright acidity made the sides of her tongue jump alive. Was it her imagination, or was it the sweetest, best-tasting pineapple she'd ever had? The past few days had been some of the most fantastic in her life. She looked at the man sitting next to her, the one she had resisted for weeks, the one she'd confided in, and the one who now architected pleasure in her body with exacting precision.

She was sure she looked like a fool with little love hearts in her eyes.

She should remember they were working together for a reason. They spent so much time together for a reason.

Because she had given him something in return. A textbook algorithm to find his perfect wife.

She'd somehow managed to ignore this fact for two days. And now they had to go back tomorrow. Back to reality and work and wifely searches. This was all going to be over, like a dream. A dream she'd remember every time she and Rishi met to discuss the app. Maybe when she watched him get married. Surely the whole team would be invited.

Panic lurched up inside her, sticking inside her esophagus, burning at her breastbone. She had been a fool. And what was worse was that she didn't even want to bring it up with him. Like the longer she could ignore this unspoken truth of their lives, the longer she could push it down, suppress the realness of it. Why should she spoil the moment by polluting this utopian scene with a barrage of questions about why he had to get married, if he had to get married, and what would happen to them after tomorrow?

Or maybe she'd resisted because she didn't want to know.

Rishi's hand tangled with hers. He raised their joined hands and kissed the back of hers.

Her worry fluttered away as she glanced over to him, his eyes aglow in the sunlight reflecting off the water. Was it too soon to go back into the bedroom? Every time they'd scampered in the room, she couldn't help but wonder if the captain and the cook could hear the two of them.

Whatever could or couldn't happen between them, she didn't want to give up at least the pleasure she'd unearthed this weekend.

It was too much to look into those eyes. To ask what they were thinking. To not know what they thought about the future or what was happening in Rishi's brain.

She pulled him tight against her and kissed him in the middle of this river, with the palms and sky as their only witnesses. The sun shone down on them, filling her up. This feeling, this fullness, had been missing from her life. And now she needed it more than anything she had needed before.

It was easy to swallow the pinhole of doubt in her mind.

But she didn't want this to happen. How could she? She was catapulting herself into a place where hearts were broken and promises shed, and she was willingly going there because of this. And what was this? Pleasure? Infatuation? Lust? Insanity? Whatever it was, it was all Rishi.

Maybe he was avoiding thinking about tomorrow too. Tomorrow, they would have to go back to Bangalore. Back to reality. Back to the project. Not losing themselves in each other. Not sailing around in clear waters beside a palm-dotted coast.

She could barely put it into words, but something had changed. Something had bloomed between them, and Emma felt like a garden bursting forth with life.

She could only hope that she hadn't killed it with one touch of her finger.

One keystroke.

One painfully perfect textbook algorithm.

CHAPTER 28

The bubbly ring of Skype was somehow in direct contrast with how Emma was feeling, and also a mirror of it. She'd been waiting four days to talk to Jordana after her trip with Rishi, unable to find a time outside of work when Jordana was available. She'd told Rishi he couldn't stay the night due to the basic fact that if she couldn't talk to her best friend today, she might just melt into a puddle of confusion.

And then she finally appeared on the screen. "Emma!"

Jordana looked the exact opposite of her right now. She was standing in her door, a polished, fantastic blouse on, with that somehow dewy glow she kept even after work, when Emma usually felt her own makeup had sort of melted off as she'd stared into the radiation of the computer monitor.

"Finally! It is so good to see you!" Emma sighed. "You just have no idea."

"How are you?" Jordana cocked her head a little. "You must have just woken up. Isn't it like seven in the morning there?"

"Oh yeah." Emma held up her coffee cup and examined her face in the tiny square at the bottom of her laptop. Her hair was wiry and electrified and in need of taming. "And I swear no one is at work until ten, so that is how desperately I wanted to talk to you."

Jordana sat down on her couch. A couch that she and Emma had slouched on too many nights watching movies and eating takeout. "What's going on?"

"Remember that guy Rishi from Seattle, the one who—"

Jordana leaned forward and rolled her eyes. "Oh no. What did he do this time?"

Emma laughed. Clearly she'd regaled Jordana with too many woeful tales of Rishi right after she'd moved. "Well, it's more like what didn't he do . . ."

"Oh my God. You two hooked up!" Her mouth hung open, but the glee was apparent. "I shouldn't be surprised. You bitched about him way too much for it to be just an annoying coworker. So is he like a rebound from Jeremy?"

Emma hadn't considered the idea that Rishi might just be a rebound. "Aren't rebounds supposed to be, like, you walk into a bar, and there's some hot guy you normally wouldn't go out with, like a hockey player or a tattoo artist . . ."

"I've dated a tattoo artist—remember Jack? And Charlie used to play hockey."

"The point is, we work together, and we have a lot in common and . . ." Emma stared off at the corner of the room because she couldn't bring herself to say all the things that mattered. That created this internal push-pull she was feeling, like her emotions were walking a tightrope, and with one misstep it could mean disaster.

"I thought you basically hated each other." Jordana pulled the phone closer to her face and whispered, "Is it, like, hate sex?"

"What? No. Wait, what's hate sex? Have you had hate sex?" Emma laughed.

Jordana shook her head. "Never mind. This call isn't about me! How do you feel about him?"

Emma put her head in her hands. "I don't know."

"Oh, we're going to figure this out." Jordana paused, and Emma looked back at the laptop. "Like if he were a food, what would he be?"

The first thought that popped into her head made her realize how dire this situation was. She pulled her knees up to her chest and looked over them at her laptop. "Truffle mac and cheese."

Jordana's eyes got wide, and she sat back. "Whoa, girl, you've got it bad."

Emma nodded. Her worst fear. Of course Jordana would be able to pull it out of her in a way that only the two of them would understand. "We went to this conference and had such a good time. But before that, really the past month, we've spent a lot of time together, and now that we're back, he's been staying the night every night—I mean, I had to basically kick him out last night so I could call you. And honestly, I was sad about it." She sighed. "I know I'm rambling, but I just don't know what to do."

"What's the big deal? Because you're like his team lead or whatever? People hide their relationships from people at work all the time. I'm glad you found someone. It sounds like he makes you happy."

Emma moaned. "I know." The past week had been possibly the happiest she'd ever been. It made the sinking feeling in her chest sink that much lower. Like it was a sinkhole that was waiting to swallow her heart up. Every day, they'd gone to work together, Rishi dropping her off at the corner so their coworkers wouldn't suspect anything. They'd timed their coffee breaks together while sneaking gropy little touches under the table. At lunch, she usually sat with Preeti and her friends, but she and Rishi would give little knowing glances to each other a few tables over. Then, after work, they'd drop their stuff off at Emma's, hop in bed, and then go grab dinner. Back at home, they'd sometimes cuddle on her couch and watch a movie.

Then wake up and do it all over again.

It was romantic and sexy and sweet and perfect.

And possibly doomed.

Jordana squinted at the screen. "Emmie, what is it?" she sang softly, like she was trying to coax a kitten out of a tree. But then her eyes got big, and she made a clicking sound in her mouth. "Wait, oh shit. I remember now. Weren't you helping him find a wife with all those silly requirements?"

Emma nodded, slower this time. "Yep."

"Well, is he still looking for one?"

"I don't know. I found two women that fit his 'criteria,'" she said with air quotes. "And he sent them to his parents. And the weirdest thing is that I hallucinate seeing them everywhere. Like at the store or walking down the street."

"Hmm . . . well, it's not like he's getting married next week, right? You all just hooked up this weekend? It feels too soon for the conversation, so see where it goes. Maybe it's just a fling, or maybe it's true wuv," she said, mimicking *The Princess Bride*.

Jordana was right. Why was she panicking in the quiet moments she was away from Rishi? While it might have felt like a stronger bond than she'd had before, it had only been days; in a few weeks they could call it a fling, and maybe then he'd be on his way, and she'd be on hers.

She breathed deep, her lungs feeling heavy. The idea that it could have just been a fling seemed to make something ache inside her. Like she already missed him. But that was ridiculous. She'd had to force him out of her house last night, making excuses about needing to get some work done. Because in the past few days since they'd been back, it had been bliss. Days that had blinded her to what had come before. To the complexities of Rishi's life and his marriage code.

"You're right, Jordy. I don't know why I'm freaking out. Who knows what the future holds?"

"Just take your time with it. God knows you did with Jeremy!"

238

She and Jeremy had taken their time, staying the night together on Saturdays and usually having methodical dates planned out during the week. It was nothing like this. The frantic desire to always have Rishi around. To make coffee with him in the mornings with his jokes and her hip bumping him. Hell, she didn't even care when he teased her about her hair sprouting its own personality before she could put product in it.

"Yeah, you're right. Maybe we just take it slow." But as she said the words, something inside her knew it was too late for that.

"I mean, don't get me wrong. If you want him around all the time, do it. That's what Charlie and I did, and look where we're at now. Just follow your heart." As if on cue, Jordana's front door opened behind her, and Charlie came into their living room. Jordana turned around and leaned up on her knees to kiss him. "Hey, babe, say hi to Emma!"

"Hi, Charlie!" Emma said. "Don't make fun of my hair."

He laughed. "Hey, how is India?"

"It's good. Really good. I'll let you go. But thanks for the pep talk."

"Is that what that was? I thought you were just dishing out some gossip on your love life. Keep me posted!" She smiled big and looked off to the side. "OMG. Now Charlie wants in on your gossip. He's like, 'What love life?' Bye, sweetie." She blew an air kiss into the phone, and Emma waved back.

"Bye!"

She ended the call on her laptop and sank back into the couch. Maybe she was overthinking things. Per usual. If Jordana didn't seem to think that Rishi's need to get married was a huge deal, why should she? After all, you didn't hook up with someone and then demand they devote themselves to you, right? That was a bit extreme. She'd just take her time and see where things went.

Her phone buzzed.

I missed you last night : (Hope you got your work done.

I missed you too. See you soon.

And she meant it, even as she asked herself how it was possible to miss someone for a mere ten hours when she saw him literally all the rest of her time.

CHAPTER 29

Rishi hummed his favorite song and then sang the chorus out loud as he turned a corner, heading toward Emma's house. The words bellowed from his lips. *This world around us is unreal. The people around us are unreal. You and I are the only things that matter.*

He didn't care who heard him. Now he fully understood why movie heroes broke out into song for 100 percent legit reasons.

His heart was beating in his stomach again. If only the world around him were unreal. If only the world he and Emma created with their bodies, with their minds, were the real one. It felt the most real. But it was also the world where families didn't exist, pressure was absent, and tradition didn't matter.

His parents had called at least five times in the past week, and the last thing he was going to do was answer his phone when he was attempting to explore what was happening with Emma. He'd texted his mother today so she wouldn't worry, telling her he was busy. He just needed some time to figure out what to do. And what was happening to him.

He'd never felt this constant need to be with someone. He'd tried to tell himself it was because he and Emma had spent so much time at work together already. They were practically joined at the hip anyway, so why not be physically joined at the hip? He could joke himself to death over it, try to rationalize it in a hundred different ways, but in the end, he'd never felt this way. He'd never met someone who, with one look, could know there was something rolling in the undercurrent under his skin. He'd be thinking about a problem with the code or with his parents, and she'd look at him. "Hey, what is it? Just tell me." Like she just knew.

And she knew other things too. Like how to carefully trace patterns of desire on his skin. To carve out longing like a craving he never knew he could have. Or how, when they touched, their lips had entire conversations about the complex feelings between them. Push and pull. Fight or flight. Need and want.

When she'd asked him to stay at his own place the other night, he'd panicked. They'd moved too fast. She was sick of him. It was completely irrational. She'd held him tight, pushed him up against the wall, and as her hands slid down his chest, she'd whispered in his ear, almost with sorrow in her voice, "I'll miss you."

After that, he'd marched her over to the sofa, and they'd made up for being apart for mere hours. Hours!

He swerved into Emma's driveway, trying to find comfort in the fact that they'd made up for it more times than he could count since then as well. Was this how addicts felt? Or was it something else? He used to call it lust, but now . . .

Emma appeared at the door before he'd even gotten his helmet off, bouncing on her bare feet in the entryway. "Hurry!"

Either she had something she needed to talk to him about with work, since he'd vowed to stay away from her all afternoon, or she was as impatient as he was. All he wanted to do was clutch her to his chest and join his mouth with hers. And other parts of their bodies as well. He dislodged the helmet from his head as he walked toward her door.

She pulled him in, ran her fingers through his hair, slammed the door, and pushed him against it. Her mouth searched his, exploring with her tongue. She pulled on his hair, slid her hands down his chest, pulled his shirt over his head, and buried her head below his breastbone. Rishi couldn't help but laugh. "You've had a rough day, I take it?"

"Don't laugh at me. I feel like an addict." She looked up at him, eyes glistening with want and mirth. "You're my fix. You'll just have to take it while I satiate my need." She lunged into his neck, her tongue tracing the tendons under his skin.

Rishi put his arms against the door in surrender. She could have whatever she wanted. "I'm yours."

He wasn't the only person who apparently felt like he was addicted. He laughed.

"What is it?" she asked.

"I was also just contemplating whether I was addicted to you. It's comforting to know the feeling is mutual."

She hummed into his neck. "Why do you always smell so good? Maybe that's what I'm addicted to."

"Maybe I'm addicted to having women boss me around. You were very assertive in our team meeting today." Her eyes narrowed as he paused. "I liked it. And of course you were right. I think even Kaushik agreed."

"Then the world very well may be on the verge of collapse," she scoffed as she headed into the kitchen. "Do you want some tea?"

"Sure." Rishi's phone buzzed, and he pulled it out of his pocket.

We met Radhika's parents today and bragged on you so much. When can you meet them?

His mother. Maybe the world *was* on the verge of collapse. He sighed and put the phone back in his pocket. He would deal with her later. They'd waited this long; they could keep waiting a little longer for him to get married. He had to understand what was happening with Emma first.

He walked into the kitchen and eyed Emma's chai-making skills. "So you conquered South Indian coffee and figured you'd take over her sister, masala chai?"

"Oh yeah. Actually, I went over to Preeti's house after work today, and she and her mom taught me. So I got all the things, and you're my guinea pig." She held a cup out to him. "If it sucks, you know, just tell me."

He took a sip. "It's actually pretty good."

She held up her phone. "Well, I might have recorded step-by-step instructions so I wouldn't mess it up."

"Of course you did." That was such an Emma thing to do. "So how was her family?"

"So nice. Her mom even gave me a hug when I left! And told me she'd gladly teach me how to cook anything I want to learn. Isn't that sweet? Their family is vegetarian too."

Rishi's parents had never even hugged *him*. He had to wonder, if he brought Emma home, what would happen. His mom possibly wouldn't even allow her in the kitchen, but if she did and somehow helped Emma cook something, would she eat it? His sister of course wouldn't care and would likely give Emma a big hug goodbye, because he knew they'd get along. His dad, maybe, wouldn't care. But his mother. With all her hopes and dreams and visions for the future, she would view any woman Rishi brought home with a critical eye, and with one look she'd know that Emma was not the daughter-in-law she'd hoped for.

But was it crazy to even start thinking like that? It had been two weeks since they'd gotten together.

"Rishi, I've been thinking . . ."

"Uh-oh." Rishi smiled at her. Sometimes he just said these things to watch her do the cute thing where half her face seemed to squint at him.

"Can we go somewhere next weekend? Like continue our real tour of India, just not with food. Kerala was so fun, and there's a lot of country to explore."

As much as Rishi wanted to go jetting around the country with Emma, they just had the weekend, really, if they didn't want to raise any suspicions at work. He could already hear Kaushik starting some rumors. *Well, they both were off the Monday after the Kerala conference. And now they're both off again?*

"What about going to Mysore? It's a few hours away, and there's a famous temple and a palace and, oh, a famous dosa named after the place."

"You know the way to a girl's heart, Rishi." Emma put her arms around his neck. "Through a dosa."

He laughed and kissed her, the sweet spice of the tea on her lips.

A trip away was exactly what he needed too. A place where he and Emma could explore more of who they were together.

CHAPTER 30

Emma flipped through the tourist book she hadn't opened since the first day she'd landed in Bangalore and researched Mysore. A place where she could be free with Rishi and not worry that her coworkers would see them having coffee or dinner. "Mysore has a famous temple, a palace, and what else can we do there?"

"I'm sure we'll find lots of things to do." Rishi half smiled at her, the things in his mind obviously involving a hotel bed, and reached for her hand on the seat between them.

Working side by side with someone you constantly imagined straddling on their desk chair was hard. Even though it had been a few weeks, her mind volleyed between Rishi's body, code iterations, Rishi's hands, tweaks to the app, and the upcoming alpha version launching soon. An actual working version with her bugs fixed and new shiny additions.

But her personal life bugs weren't fixed. Her feelings for him had not crumpled up into something she could sweep under a rug. Emma knew from his search, his talk of his family, and her Indian friends back in Seattle that marriage was a complex thing here. There were traditions and family and hierarchies. Everyone expected children, and dating was something that was only done for short bursts of time before marriage was inevitable.

All this was coming down on a woman who had just refused her boyfriend in Seattle on the same terms. Could she accept them now, from Rishi? And would he even want her to?

Perhaps there was a reason she'd imagined what their children would look like. She rolled her eyes. Thinking way too much about something, as usual.

Jordana was right about "the talk" a few weeks ago, but now it was staring Emma down. It was likely one of the items on her Mysore itinerary.

As they entered Mysore, the city reminded her of the older areas in Bangalore she had driven through. The buildings were stained auburn from years of industrial growth and pollution, and the shop signs bore fading paint and water stains. Men announcing their wares pushed carts filled with vegetables, fruits, or plastic jugs and toys. The ever-present billboards for diamonds and gold and silk presided over the scene. Emma wondered if the models in these advertisements had some kind of super upper-body strength from the sheer weight of the jewelry on their heads and necks.

First on their itinerary was to visit Chamundi Temple. The driver they'd hired parked the car, and Emma and Rishi walked up a huge staircase to the top of the temple complex. The entrance to the temple was guarded by a mustachioed statue, twenty feet tall, wielding a curved sword.

"Who's this pirate guy?" Emma asked, staring up at the statue.

"Oh, Emma, that is not a pirate but a buffalo demon. A shape-shifter."

"Shape-shifter? I'm intrigued."

"I'm not. You shift in as many shapes as I'll ever need."

She shook her head at him, even though she could feel the grin stretching across her face.

They wove through the crowds of humans, ice cream carts, toy shops, and piles of sour green mango with chili powder and salt. Rishi stopped at one of the stalls to buy flowers and fruit for the temple to give as an offering.

As they rounded the corner and the temple came into view, Emma stopped midstep. People talked about the Pyramids of Egypt as being spectacular, but this was amazing. The temple was a pyramid of carvings upon carvings that rose a hundred feet toward the sky. Each row of stones had elaborate sculpted gods and goddesses lining the center. The top of the temple was painted a dusky gold. Someone must have climbed the temple and cleaned the spaces between the carvings with a tiny broom to clear the dust from the countless deep grooves.

"Did someone make all those carvings by hand?" she asked as Rishi pulled at her elbow to get in line, joining the hundreds of other tourists in a maze of rails.

"Yes. As my mother would say, doing anything unless it is for God is not worth doing."

Emma looked up at his face, which was set in a sneer as he examined the temple. She followed his gaze. Around twenty monkeys climbed around its sloping tiled roof, eyeing the food people held tight as offerings.

All those things Rishi had said about his family, how traditional they were, how religious, his priestly background—it all came back to her.

"Are you religious, Rishi?" Religion seemed to be embedded in life here, and they'd never even discussed it.

"Yes. I mean, I pray and follow our customs. For the most part. I believe in God, but I'm not a zealot. More of a practical follower who enjoys a good drink and a good chicken kebab." The corner of his lip tugged up. "What about you?"

For some reason the question hit Emma in her chest. It was a topic she rarely discussed, but when she saw a monument like this, it made her question everything. "I've never gone to church or anything. After my parents died, my grandmother stopped going."

Rishi nodded slowly. "I can see that. Some people lose faith when traumatic things happen."

"And other people cling to it like it's all they've got." Emma wasn't wired that way. Apparently neither was her grandmother. She remembered sitting down at dinner with her grandmother a few years after her parents had died. Emma had asked then why she'd stopped going to church. Her grandma had said, "When a freak accident like that takes away your daughter, praying to the God that makes the universe function like clockwork just doesn't make sense. And fate doesn't make sense. And the world doesn't make sense."

And here Emma was now, fifteen years later, questioning God, fate, and the world. All over again.

Once they'd entered the temple, Emma studied the stained grayish-brown brick walls, so plain compared to the extravagance of the temple's outward appearance. It was like a sacred cave, the darkness lit only by tiny oil lamps and the cool dampness calming her hot skin. The smell was waxy and moist, edged with musky incense. Emma hesitated at the entrance, not knowing what to do inside.

"Rishi, what am I supposed to do in here? Pray?"

"Yeah. Pray for what you wish for." They walked toward a crowd of people who stood outside a roped-off pathway and squeezed their way to the rope. Rishi pressed his hands together in front of his chest and closed his eyes.

She was following his gesture, placing her palms together, when a priest approached the rail they were standing behind. As the priest walked in front of the line of people, he carried a small tray with a lamp, and the crowd placed flowers or money on it in exchange for him saying a prayer and hovering a brass dome over their heads.

World peace. Her family's happiness in the afterlife. Jordana's success. Rishi's family. Rishi. The app's success. Poverty vanquished. All the things she could pray for. But who would listen to her? A woman who hadn't prayed since she was a child. Sure, she'd thrown her hopes out to the universe in times of stress and hoped they'd stick somewhere, but this was something completely different.

The monotone cadence of the priest's chanting soothed Emma and made her feel completely out of her element. As the priest approached them, Rishi moved his hands from the points of prayer and over the flame of the lamp and then put them up over his head like he was smoothing down his hair while the priest chanted and held the domed instrument over Rishi's head.

Emma's head was still turned to Rishi when the priest stopped in front of her. Fumbling, she laid a hundred rupees on the tray. She put her hands over the fire as Rishi had done, bowing slightly. The prayer. The prayer! *Please, God, let us all be happy one day together.* The brass dome grazed the backs of her hands as the priest shuffled away.

That they could all be happy one day? That's what had come out of her in the moment? Where had that come from?

She gazed at the statue of Durga, the goddess she'd just prayed to. There were multiple statues, carved in a dark stone with the age of centuries imprinted into them. This larger one had an eroded nose and chin, filed down from moisture, a green silk sari wrapped around her. Thick garlands of roses, tulsi leaves, and jasmine weighed it down.

A man lay down in front of the statue, his face touching the floor. Emma questioned her recent overuse of hand sanitizer, trying to keep a host of germs away, while this man fully embraced them, kissing the temple floor where millions of people had walked in their bare feet.

Maybe he believed that fate would keep him from getting toe fungus on his lip. All these people believed in fate, and she had eschewed it for so many years. Fate was the antithesis of her life—this idea that how you made yourself meant nothing in the face of the things that just happened to you, that your life was sorted and predestined. That she and Rishi were always going to have these feelings between them. No matter what had happened in her past, or his, or what course their lives took, they would find themselves drawn to each other, unable to reconcile the reality of their different worlds. But not able to stop themselves, and for her, not able to stop thinking about him.

And there was the fact that he was always going to get married to please his family. Maybe he'd stalled it, but could he really not follow through with his family's wishes?

Maybe with her prayer she had just been caught up in the moment, like this no-fear-of-the-foot-fungus guy.

"Rishi, how old are these statues?"

"The gods? Almost a thousand years old, I think."

A thousand years old? Emma's brain searched for what else in the world was a thousand years old. A push from behind made her stumble as a wave of people came toward the priest's area. Her eyes searched for Rishi as she felt a tug on her arm. They squeezed through the mass of moving bodies toward the faint light that came through the exit door.

"That was intense," Emma said, catching the breath she hadn't realized she'd been holding. If Rishi hadn't guided her out of there, she could imagine being pulled under a human tide.

"It's a famous temple, so it can get kind of crazy."

As they walked farther down the hill, they found themselves before a giant black cement cow statue.

"This is Nandi," Rishi said.

"And who is Nandi?"

"Nandi is Shiva's bull, and how he travels throughout the world."

"What's this?" Emma asked, pointing to something that looked like a stone birdbath with a narrow dome on top of it.

"That's a Shiva lingam. It's the male part of Shiva. It gave birth to the world."

"I love that there are monuments to godly penises at temples, and buffalo demons."

"Hinduism is complex. That's why you can't convert to it. It would take too long to catch up with all the nuances." He winked at her.

Emma laughed, but then it quickly fell apart. His religion. His culture. His family. Her prayer that they could all be one.

She swallowed as she leaned against a nearby brick wall, staring at the Shiva lingam. "Rishi, I know it's been like three weeks or something, but I just need to come out and ask what's going on. With us, with your marriage plans, with your family and the results I found for you. I like you, and the last few weeks have been amazing, but I just don't know what we're doing, and I need to ask you about it. I thought I'd wait and see if maybe this feeling was just going to go away, or maybe you'd declare you were marriage-free or something, but I just have to ask because I think about it, and, well . . . it's bugging me. Big-time. More like haunting me. And/or torturing me." And now she was rambling.

She looked back at the giant stone penis and waited for the fallout.

{ /** *. // }

Rishi took a deep breath. So Emma felt the same way after all. It shouldn't have surprised him, as their thoughts and movements seemed to mirror one another's constantly.

"I know that was a big rambling mess, I just . . ." She shook her head.

"No." He grabbed her hand. "It wasn't. I feel the same way too."

"So, what do we do?" She sat down on the nearby bench.

"I need to talk to them. My parents. Tell them to stop trying to fix me up. I've been thinking about it." He smiled, hoping that would ease some of the difficulty for her. It couldn't have been easy to be interested in someone with familial expectations like his.

"But what about your brother and what happened to him?"

"That needs to get resolved too. Like you said, the whole thing is ridiculous."

"You know, I told you about my parents passing away when I was a kid. Not having a family is hard. Luckily, I had my grandmother, but when she died a few years ago, I had nothing." She looked away, at the town below the temple grounds. "I *have* nothing."

Rishi pictured giving Emma a family she deserved. His mom showing her how to cook something in the kitchen as Emma balanced a toddler on her hip. Rishi swooping in to grab their child, to join Dharini and Sudhar bickering in the living room. His dad telling him how happy he was that they had so much joy in the house.

But how much of a fantasy was that?

"You have me, and that friend you're always talking about," Rishi said, wanting to put his arms around her, choking back the desire to touch her in public like this.

"Thanks." She smiled up at him. "But I'm telling you this for a reason. Family is important, and I don't ever want to upset your relationship with your parents. It's hard not having people that will love you just because you're you. Just because you share the same genes."

That hit him, hard. Family in India was the most important thing you had. People said it all the time. It was a core of their culture. Except when family disobeyed your wishes and then never spoke to you again. Except when family meant his brother.

It was why Rishi was compelled to do the right thing in his parents' eyes.

Why he blindly followed some of their practices—at least when he was home.

Why he had tried to accept the fact that he'd marry someone his parents would approve of.

"I think I need to go to Madurai next weekend to meet with them. I'd ask you to come, too, but I don't think it's going to be a fun trip."

He imagined confronting them as they sat in the tiny room where they entertained guests.

His mother erupting in sobs, pounding the sofa.

His father stalking off to the local liquor store and sneaking two shots of brandy. A harmless gesture for Rishi, but for his father to violate his belief system and imbibe a forbidden beverage would be the worst it could get.

He wanted to make his parents happy and help his sister find the husband she deserved, but he had to think about himself too. It was his life they were holding in their hands. And he couldn't be with Emma while they were orchestrating something in the background. And he couldn't have them string Radhika and her family along either. He couldn't find himself engaged in a month and still wondering if what he and Emma had experienced was something permanent and real.

"Emma, my family will always have a place in my heart." He swallowed hard. "But they'll need to make room for you too."

Hopefully they would. The split inside him warmed as it fused together. He had to find some way to make this right.

CHAPTER 31

Rishi stepped off the train in Madurai, squeezing himself and his bag out the door, surrounded by crowds of people. The heat was immense, and the force of the sun doubled it. He brought his sunglasses out of his bag and looked around at the crowd. There was not a single pair of sunglasses in sight; everyone here was used to the sun. He put them back in the bag as he walked outside to find an auto to take him home. No reason to get charged double just for a pair of sunglasses.

Standing outside the pastel-painted brick of the Madurai train station, he stopped at the line of yellow-topped auto-rickshaws. Some of the drivers stood around, bored, spitting chewed-up betel leaves on the ground, while others jerked their heads toward Rishi and asked, *"Enga?"* Where? His parents' home was almost ten kilometers from the station.

"Ellis Nagar," Rishi said to the driver nearest him. The driver eased his head side to side and spit a stream of bright-red betel nut on the sidewalk. He jerked the handle on the floorboard and started the three-wheeled vehicle, not looking before pulling out onto the road.

Now that the meter was on, Rishi put on his sunglasses to keep the black exhaust billowing around him out of his eyes, and he sent a text to his father saying he was on his way. The driver looked in the rearview mirror and asked in Tamil, "Where are you from?" Rishi probably looked like a tourist to him, with his too-long hair and dark jeans.

"Here. *Inga.*"

"You don't live here now," the driver said, half question, half observation.

"I live in Bangalore now, but family is all here."

"Long journey."

"*Amam.*" Yes. Fortunately there were night trains to and from Bangalore and Madurai, and he could sleep through anything. The rumbling on the tracks, the snoring of the old man beneath him on the bunk, the clack of the toilet door flying open in the hall. It was only when the old man had hacked up something ferocious in his throat that morning that Rishi had opened his eyes, reality slapping him in the face, far away from his dream starring Emma.

The driver dropped him off, and Rishi approached the open door to his family home, the smell of toasted cumin seeds, ghee, and cardamom begging him to enter. He rubbed at the chipping yellow paint on the doorframe. Things seemed to have been in an ever-increasing state of disrepair in his childhood home, but his mother would never spend money on something like chipping paint. She would, however, spend money on gold bangles and necklaces that would be squirreled away in a metal cabinet. Locked up, only to be retrieved for weddings and holidays. *That* was an investment, she said.

"Hello?" he called out, and his mother hurried toward the door.

"Rishi, so good to see you!" she said as Rishi bent down to the ground and touched her feet. Folding his hands in front of him, he rocked back and forth on the ground three times. His father and sister also joined them in the hall, and Rishi went through the ritual with his dad and then patted his sister on her head like she was four instead of twenty-two.

"Ha ha, very funny." Dharini reached her hand up to do the same to him, but she was a foot shorter, and he lunged out of her way.

"How was your journey?" his dad asked as they walked inside.

"Long." Rishi smiled. "But I slept most of the night."

"Coffee?" His mother brought Rishi a cylindrical steel cup. It was her way of greeting him in the most welcoming way possible.

"Thanks, Ma," he said. He drank the sweet, milky coffee by pouring it in his mouth, the metal cup not touching his lips.

"Rishi, it has been four months since we saw you last. We thought you were going to come home when you returned from Seattle. You need to come back more. Your hair is so long." His mother pulled at the shaggy hair Rishi had tried to smooth out of the way. "And you look so thin! You need to eat!" She shook her head and clicked her tongue against the back of her teeth.

Rishi glanced down at himself.

He had been lifting weights at the gym for the past year, trying to bulk up, not to seem thin. His mother always told him he looked thin, though, even when he had come home pudgy and swollen from college after eating too much fried food from the roadside stalls. It was her ritual every time he came home, one she'd likely instituted to give him permission to eat as much as he wanted of her cooking—food that couldn't be replicated at even the best restaurant in Bangalore.

"I was going to, but we've been very busy with this new project, so it's hard to take a day off. Then I went to Cochin for the conference, but . . . I'm here now." He smiled weakly.

"Yes, brother, thank you for gracing us with your presence," Dharini said, her palms pressed together in front of her. Definitely sealed together with irony.

"Where's your coffee, sis?"

"I only need coffee in the morning. And at work when I'm bored." Her head flopped dramatically toward her chest, and she let out a few fake snores.

Rishi's mother went to finish cooking lunch, and his father went out for an errand, so he and Dharini went outside and sat down.

"Wow, so your job is that exciting. What are you doing?" Rishi asked.

Dharini explained her work, consulting on code updates for banking websites, which Rishi had to admit was not as exciting as developing an app to help people read.

"That really is boring. So we can blame the banking industry for your search for a husband?"

Dharini laughed. "I mean, I want a family and a husband, and I want someone good, so might as well start looking now."

"Are you sure you're my sister?" Rishi squinted at her and laughed.

She leaned forward, and her finger went back and forth between their faces. "Look at these eyes, brother. They're the same." Then she retreated back to her chair, looking proud.

Their eyes. Rishi opened his mouth to tell her about Sudha's baby. But she was definitely being kept in the dark. They all protected her like she was still a little kid.

"I saw the pictures of Radhika. She's very pretty."

Ugh. Already this conversation? "A girl needs to be more than pretty to marry, you know. Remember that when you're looking for your ideal guy."

"But didn't you customize your search or something to find her? Like she is perfect? That's what Amma told me."

"I'm sorry you didn't get to come to Seattle and visit me." He was just going to change the subject instead of entertaining her.

"I know. Maybe next time." She shrugged.

"Don't you want to take some time and travel or something before you get married?" Rishi asked. She was so young. How was it possible she was ready to settle down? "Like, if you stay in your job long enough, maybe you can travel for work. I got to go to a conference in Cochin and represent the company. That was great." What was really great was the by-product of the conference, though.

"Look at your smile!" She laughed. "Bragging suits you. Did you present all by yourself?"

If she only knew what he was smiling about. "Uh, no, there was another colleague with me, Kaushik." The last thing he needed to do was mention Emma and have an inquisition about a foreign girl who'd traveled with him to Cochin. His face would turn into a billboard advertising all the ways he felt about her. Then the questions would build until he gave in and confessed everything, and then his family would dissolve into a puddle of tears.

He'd felt so strongly when he was back in Bangalore, crafting the perfect argument in his head about why he should wait to get married until he was sure he'd found "the one"; how times had changed, and his parents needed to realize it; how Sudha's marriage wasn't all bad for them, but they were twisting it around to suit them. Now that he was here, seeing his parents and his sister and hearing about how she actually did want to get married, all those arguments twisted in his mind, their perfect endings scattering away from him.

His mother called from inside the house. "Rishi! Dharini! Lunch is ready! *Saapda vaanga!*"

They both walked inside. The smell of his favorite food had a direct line of communication with his stomach. *Thank you for bringing me home,* it called out.

Rishi sat at the table while his mother dished a small mountain of rice on his steel plate and dripped ghee on top of it. She topped it with a cup of spicy sambar, roasted eggplant, and green beans poriyal. He wished he could cook this for Emma. Maybe he could try. Was he really ready to try cooking something for this woman? He did have it bad.

Rishi dug in with his right hand, mixing everything up and stuffing pinched fingers of rice in his mouth. After finishing a cup of peppery rasam and curd with his rice, Rishi sat back on the chair, patting his stomach. His mother brought a steel tin from the kitchen.

"Now I have to go to the gym two more times next week to make up for all this food." Rishi smiled at her. "Do you think you could write down the recipe for me?"

"Recipe?" His mother's mouth hung open. "Dharini, did you hear what your brother said?"

"Rishi, you're going to cook?" Dharini squinted at him in complete disbelief.

"Yeah, why not? I should try, right?"

"I can tell you. It will make a good impression on Radhika."

He ransacked his brain, hoping for any start to this vital conversation. Being here, in their house, was a reminder of just how desperate his family's situation had become. How much they were hoping the joining of another family would help strengthen their own.

The cushions on the sofa were faded and worn; chipped and broken tiles lined the floor. One bathroom faucet still leaked, so they'd turned off the water source to it rather than pay for repairs. The plastic chairs on the front porch were cracked and had been put back together with duct tape. And the TV looked like it was from the 1990s.

Soon he would hear how his father needed just a few more years of work. But no one wanted to hire him. No one wanted to hire a man approaching sixty when they could hire a twenty-five-year-old. How much could his promotion have helped anyway? What would a few thousand extra rupees a month do?

"I made your favorite." His mother reappeared beside him, holding out a tin stuffed with cardamom- and saffron-laced laddoos.

"What's the special occasion? Just me?" Rishi's eyes lit up as he took one and then reached for another as his mother almost snapped the lid on his hand.

"You'll get a stomachache! We'll have more this afternoon."

"Awesome," Rishi said, his mouth half-full. More this afternoon? "What's this afternoon?"

"Radhika's parents are coming today to meet you. Your father didn't tell you?"

"What?" He couldn't have heard her right.

"Your father didn't tell you—"

"Wait, they're coming to the *house?*" He spoke slowly, clarifying what she was saying. Why wouldn't his parents have said something? Anything?

"Coming for tea," his mom said in the next room as she put the dishes on the shelf.

Rishi scrambled to his feet and followed her into the kitchen. A newly made fried snack mix of spiced lentils and rice sat in a bowl, draining on newspaper. Making snacks from scratch? Laddoos? Sure signs that someone special was coming to the house.

Rishi felt like he'd been crushed by one of the cement blocks his mother had fashioned for shelving with planks. How had he not noticed those before?

He turned his attention back to her. "Why did you invite them?"

"What do you mean? I didn't know when you were coming next, and you need to meet them. If you and Radhika are going to get married, they have to approve. But they'll like you." She paused and examined his face. "What's wrong? I thought that's why you were coming so suddenly this weekend. I sent you an SMS saying they want to meet you. It's been weeks since you met Radhika, and she's the only one you liked out of all the girls; I thought you had finally decided to progress with the marriage."

"What?" Rishi's heart pounded in his chest. What was he going to do? Make up a story to them about how he didn't want children or was planning on quitting his job? Could he act like a madman or espouse outrageous ideologies about women so they would think he was crazy?

All that left a bad taste in his mouth. It would make his parents look equally as bad. There was nothing he could do that wouldn't tarnish his parents' reputation, and in their community, word could get around.

"You said you liked her." His mother stared at him hard. Her eyes said a lot more words than her mouth: *Do not disappoint me. Do not embarrass me. Do not change your mind about this. It's too late.*

When Rishi didn't respond, she resumed washing dishes. "And they were going to try and have Radhika come too."

Fuck. Rishi leaned against the doorjamb, his body feeling lifeless, numb.

"We've already gone to the astrologer, and your horoscopes match perfectly. That's what I was calling about last week when you were too busy to pick up. We've already discussed dates." His mother let out a small giggle. Nothing could have made her happier than planning his wedding.

How had this happened? He'd come to put a stop to his parents' wife search, and all the while, they'd been exploring dates for his wedding.

"You have to stop them from coming over!" Rishi blurted out. What could he say? "Tell them to cancel it. Tell them whatever you like. I can't get married. I think it's the start of my *elara sani*! Ask the astrologer. Bad luck has been happening for the past four months." Anything to stall. But even as he said the words, he knew they weren't true. Emma had seemed like the start of his bad seven and a half years, but in reality, her appearance in his life had all been for the good.

His mother turned off the faucet. "What are you doing? What is this all about, Rishi? You had your elara sani in your teenage years; it started when you were seventeen. Don't you remember how difficult university was?"

Rishi vaguely remembered the gold ring he'd had to wear with a gemstone that the family astrologer had given him. Until he lost it one night after he and his bunkmates had split a bottle of whiskey. What was the purpose of that gemstone? Elara sani, of course.

"Maybe you should get a second opinion." He was ready to launch into how he'd met someone. How she seemed perfect, but he needed some time. Because perfect to him may not have been perfect for them.

"The astrologer said this is the year. That you've had a long journey to come here." She shook her head. "You've had so many girls interested in you. Now here is one that you like, and she likes you. And what is this? You're trying to destroy your father and me? Now here is another one you don't want? What is wrong with you? Don't you think about your sister?" His mother started sobbing as her words speared Rishi's chest. She was probably upset, thinking about Sudhar as much as this situation he himself had put her in.

He didn't know what to do. Stay strong or embrace his mother? The argument was stuck in his mouth. His sister. How could he do something to make his mother cry and keep his sister from the life she wanted? "Mom, I'm not ready."

His mom sniffed hard and wiped her eyes with the edge of her sari. "All we tried to do was raise our sons to be good boys. To help us, to take care of us and your little sister. Now we have a perfect match. A girl who you like, horoscopes that line up perfectly, someone you can have a good family with. I want grandchildren!" she wailed. "And you"—she pointed at him—"you're like your brother. You want to throw us in the dustbin like some trash. You forgot we brought you in this world, we gave you a home, we paid for your schooling, and this is the thanks we get. Embarrassment, poverty, ungrateful boy."

She rushed past him into the bedroom and slammed the door behind her. Her sobs seeped through the wood.

Rishi was left alone, feeling nothing but an aching hollowness, like his mother had taken a scalpel and carved out his organs, leaving an empty cavity behind. What had he been thinking? He could just waltz into his parents' world and disrupt it, and after all the calls, the talk of Radhika, his mother's desire for grandchildren, his sister wanting to get married?

He'd had Emma write up that stupid algorithm that had brought Radhika into his life. And now he had to pay for it.

His father came home and looked at Rishi and then toward the bedroom door. "What happened?"

Rishi opened his mouth to explain, but all that came out was a sigh. His father knocked on the door and opened it, and his soft voice volleyed with the sharp acrimony of his mother's.

When his parents' room grew quieter, he pushed the door, and it creaked open.

His parents were sitting on their bed, side by side, hunched over. His father looked over his shoulder, shooting him a glassy-eyed stare of accusation that stung his very soul. He'd never seen his father cry, had never seen that look of utter disappointment and blame.

"I'm sorry," Rishi said. He walked over to the bed and sat beside his mother.

"You're killing your mother," his father said in a low voice.

"I need to lie down," she said and then leaned back on the bed, clutching her chest.

His father got out the blood pressure monitor. "Let me check your BP." As he wrapped the fabric around her arm, Rishi examined the care he gave to his mother. They were just two people, thrown together on their wedding day, sight unseen. Here they were, thirty-one years later, still married, still helping one another. They'd made it work, and they'd had no algorithm, nothing except for the stars aligning in their favor.

Except he doubted either of their hearts had been captured by someone else before the marriage.

"Your mother's BP is too high," his father said. "She needs to rest."

Now Rishi had upset his mother so much she'd had to take to her bed.

Killing your mother.

What could he do? His mother gave him a vacant look, still rubbing at her eyes. He'd have to think of some excuse, one that wouldn't give away what was really going on with Emma but would still keep him from marrying Radhika. There had to be some carefully worded reasoning that could keep his parents from this despair while still protecting them from the truth. The truth would surely be worse than this.

His mother's high blood pressure had plagued the family since before Rishi had known what blood pressure was. Was he truly the cause of such an attack? He could suck it up and hide the truth from her a little longer. He'd been doing it his entire adult life.

As Rishi walked away from his parents, he thumbed through his brain to figure out how he could get out of meeting Radhika's family without upsetting his mother. Or some reason Radhika and her family wouldn't want him.

Through ridiculous scenario after ridiculous scenario, he came up with nothing. Nothing that would be a calm, rational explanation his parents would understand. And the truth certainly wouldn't help.

But what was the truth?

That he had feelings for a woman his parents would never approve of. That they would disown him if he married her. Would it come to that? Could he end up like his brother, without family members who would speak to him?

Rishi sat on the back stoop and stared at the pepper plant vine that climbed up their garden's banana tree. The leaves had dried up, the pepper berries ignored. Instead of bright green, they were blackening, withering on the vine.

Rishi had to ask himself whom he was doing all of this for.

CHAPTER 32

Rishi sat quietly in his parents' living room chair, feeling like an imprisoned man preparing to be judged. The cushion was flat, like all the stuffing had dripped out of it. Around him, his mother and sister scuttled around the house, as if he weren't there, getting ready for their guests. His dad read the paper for what seemed like the fifth time that day. His body was still except for his right leg, which wouldn't stop shaking with its endless nervy tapping on the floor. What was Rishi's story? How could he not embarrass his family and still come off as the kind of man who was not husband material?

Brakes squealed to a halt in front of the house. A man's deep voice carried over the small garden, quieting the birds that always gathered and squawked at this time before dusk. His own father walked straight and slow to the front porch to greet the guests, while his mother, now recovered, fussed with her sari and seemed to float an inch over the floor, her feet invisible, hidden by the gold threading that embroidered the silk at the hem.

As he heard the needlessly flattering greetings outside, the weight of this event fell on his chest like a rock. His heart pounded against it, this invisible pressure. He wanted to shout at the guests outside.

You know the house is not lovely. It's falling apart.

My mother does not look well. She was just on the verge of a heart attack.

Instead he sat quietly, staring at the currently empty room. His sister brought a tray of sweets to the table and then a bowl of snacks, shooting him a look out of the corner of her eyes. Rishi straightened up at her request and tried to look normal. Not like his organs were crumbling on the inside. The robust father—Radhika's father—entered the room, taking up more space with the aura that seemed to surround him. "You must be Rishi!"

"Hello, uncle," Rishi said, standing and shaking the man's outstretched hand. Behind him peeked a delicate woman, his mother's size. The first thought Rishi had upon seeing the two of them was if he ever suffocated her when they had sex. "Hello, auntie." He bowed slightly, his hands pressed together, staying formal.

Radhika entered in a peacock-blue sari with gold trim. His voice caught in his throat. She looked beautiful. Her makeup was done, the sari fitted around her slim but curvy body. Her nose was slightly pointed. Would his actions make these kajal-lined eyes shed tears today? He swallowed the guilt that stuck hard in his throat. "Hi, Radhika."

"Hey, Rishi," she said, her eyes reflecting the beadwork on her sari. A light of hope for a future with him was so apparent that Rishi had to look away.

"Please, sit down." He gestured to the daybed and the sofa.

His parents talked with Radhika's parents while he and Radhika sat there like store dummies, sipping tea and smiling whenever either of their names was mentioned. Their parents volleyed strengths about their children back and forth, using keywords like they had developed their own search engine optimization to maximize their results.

Rishi wanted to contradict his parents each time they blurted out some hyperbole about his job, but it was impossible to contradict his mother. He might as well have called an ambulance.

His heart slowly sank to meet his stomach, eclipsing his will, fraught by his family on one side and his desire for a happy future on the other.

The rest of their short visit went much the same, and by the time they'd left, Rishi felt wrung out and exhausted. Like the Rishi he knew on a day-to-day basis had been squeezed out, and a lifeless sack was all that was left.

"Rishi, you were well behaved. Thank you for not embarrassing us with these notions of yours," his mother said, cheery and bright. No one would have thought that four hours ago she was lying in bed, clutching her chest.

"Amma," Rishi said, warning her in a tone used only when they were alone. She was testing his patience. "Nothing's changed."

"You like her. She's a pretty girl. I can tell."

He narrowed his eyes at her, but she turned into the kitchen, oblivious.

If his mother knew who Rishi truly liked, they *would* be rushing her to the hospital.

Rishi went to sit on the veranda. It was quiet in this area of Madurai. Too quiet. Rishi had become accustomed to the constant soundtrack of honking, rickshaw engines rattling, and lorry horns announcing their too-wide path down his narrow Bangalore street.

His father and mother came out and settled into the sofa.

"This neighborhood used to be more active when I was a kid. We used to play cricket in the street and run around. Now there's nothing. No one," Rishi said.

Everything seemed to be empty: these streets, his parents' gazes as they looked into the darkness. His mind was empty too—of ideas about how to get out of this marriage—and his heart because all meaning had been poured out of it, and it was left with nothing more than wanting Emma. He pulled out his phone and texted Emma. **What are you doing?**

"Most of your school chums now have families of their own. But the children stay inside, watching television," Rishi's mother said. "You will see soon. You and Radhika will have children. I hope you let them breathe fresh air, not spend all their time inside."

Rishi sat back, sighing. Emma's message appeared. I told you I was catching up on my movies. Trying to see if my Hindi lessons are working.

Anything good?

I just watched Veer Zaara. So depressing.

We should continue the tour of India—the film version when I get back. :)

I miss you.

Rishi smiled at the phone. He texted the same message back.

"What is making you so happy? Radhika?" his father asked, halting his conversation with Rishi's mother about the neighbors' families.

How's everything going? Emma wrote.

"Nothing." Rishi shook his head. His mother seemed fine now, but would one more confrontation today be the turning point in her health? She seemed so happy. His father pleased. And Rishi felt like he was dying inside.

His fingers paused. What could he say that wouldn't wreck her with worry? He'd find a way to fix this. No sense in her getting worked up over it.

Everything is okay so far. I'll tell you about it when I get back.

And what would he tell her? He could either destroy himself or destroy his family.

The truth was that he'd been hiding who he was and what he wanted for so long that his own parents didn't even know him. He loved them, he took care of them, and he wanted a wife who would be everything to them. But when he wasn't around them, he lived a life they didn't approve of, and there was no reason not to continue hiding it from them. He'd seen what a hint of the truth could do to his mother today. His ex-girlfriend, his lifestyle, Emma, the duality of what they wanted and what he wanted were like a crack that split him up and down. And that crack was splitting wider and wider with each of the lies he'd told to protect them.

CHAPTER 33

While Rishi always enjoyed the night train to Madurai—the visits from the tea wallahs and the somehow soothing clank and whir of the train—when he went back to Bangalore, he took a plane. He wanted to be back in his world as soon as he could. A city where he felt like he could be himself, he could be with Emma, that felt like his chosen home.

He texted Emma as he got in the auto-rickshaw and told her he was on his way to her house. Damn the traffic—he couldn't get there fast enough.

It was good to see his family, even if the conversation hadn't gone as he'd planned. It was like something in him got swallowed up whenever he was home. In Bangalore, he was his own person, with a career and friends and Emma. But back in Madurai, his parents and his house and the town seemed to suck the independence out of him. He reverted to his inner child, and not in a fun way. He had to work on this. Regardless, he'd call his parents tomorrow and tell them to put a stop to their planning.

Maybe face to face hadn't been the best idea. If he'd just done it over the phone, then his mother would have cried to his father and ripped Rishi to shreds. She could have said all she'd wanted out loud, and neither of them would have had to feel guilty and apologize later.

Dharini, the sole logical person in the house, would ease his mother's worries, and somehow Rishi would make it up to her. Surely, she could wait a little while longer. She loved Rishi and would understand. He was the older brother, after all.

When the rumbling auto paused outside Emma's house, she opened the door and waved. She looked so happy. Her smile was broad, her teeth standing out white in the darkness outside. As he walked toward her, she seemed to be doing a little dancing shuffle. She was so excited that he had cleared the wedding slate with his parents; how could he disappoint her? He was calling them tomorrow anyway. He'd find a quiet spot, a time in the afternoon so his mother could rail against him before Dharini got home from work, and it would give him time to talk to his sister too. It was a plan.

"I missed you!" she said, shutting the door behind them and wrapping her arms around him.

"Me too." His voice was muffled in her crazy hair. He loved her crazy hair. It could vine around his face, his head, and swallow him whole, and he wouldn't mind.

"How was your trip home? Are your parents okay? How did the conversation go? Do you need a drink? Do you want me to ask more questions?" She laughed.

"You know, I could use a drink." He sighed and sat down on the couch.

Emma returned with a glass of wine. "I hope this is okay."

"Thanks. And the trip could have definitely been better. My family is crazy. I know you said that you shouldn't do anything to upset my family, but I feel like when you meet them, you'll question that statement." He laughed.

"*When* I meet them?" She smiled up at him, snug against him on the couch.

"Yeah, we'll have to figure out a time. More like I need some time before I can go back again." He wondered how much time he would need after tomorrow's call before he could go back home and then take Emma with him.

"But they're still talking to you, though?" she asked, her eyebrows raised in worry.

He drank half the glass down. "We'll see what happens when I call them tomorrow." Tomorrow he would put all his parents' meddling to a stop. He'd just have to explain how unreasonable they were being. How he felt. It was his life, and they would have to accept it.

"And this is what you want to do?" she asked. "I'm worried that I'm interfering in your family."

"No. Don't. This is what I want. And honestly, I should have just done it in the first place." In fact, he probably should have just left his parents' house when they'd said Radhika's parents were coming. He kissed her, and the way she melted into the sofa under his touch, with a little gasp into his mouth, made him need her touch all the more. Her arms clutched around him, pulling him tight as she hummed against him.

He didn't need a drink. He didn't need the escape that Emma provided for him. "I just need you," he whispered.

{ /** *. // }

He rolled over and let his hand roam over Emma's bare skin. Over the silken, barely present fine hairs on her arm, the galaxy of freckles painted on her shoulder, and the gentle nudge of her shoulder blades on her back. He squeezed her tight against him.

Rishi never knew it was possible to have this. A woman who could be his partner at work, in the bedroom, and at all times. The app was looking good, and everything had gone over well at their first real demo of its functionality. Even Emma was impressed.

His phone buzzed with a call on the table beside him. He looked at the screen. Mom. When would she ever realize he liked to sleep in?

But nothing could spoil his morning now, not with Emma beside him. He could be strong now that she was with him. He'd tried calling the day before, but she hadn't answered.

He grabbed the phone and walked into the kitchen so he wouldn't disturb Emma.

"Good morning, Amma," he said, rubbing his eyes from the sunlight that blazed through the living room windows.

"Rishi, sorry I didn't see your call yesterday. I went to the doctor, and he gave me some new medicine for my blood pressure," his mother said.

Worry struck him in the chest. Had he been the cause of this new decline in his mother's health? The other day, he half suspected it was falsified, a tool to guilt him into marriage. The other half agonized over whether it was real and if his decisions could tip her enough to be hospitalized. "What new medicine? Is everything okay?"

"It's fine," she said.

His father jumped in on speakerphone, talking over her. "Now she's on twice the dosage. And no salt at all. No salt in the food. I have to add my own salt."

Of course, that would be his father's concern. Not enough salt in the food.

"Well, I'm glad you called back. And I'm glad you're okay. There's something I wanted to discuss with you." He resisted saying, *Again and for the last time.*

"We also wanted to talk to you. September tenth," his mother said, as if that should have some significance.

Rishi racked his brain. Not a birthday, not an anniversary. "Is it Diwali?" he asked, thinking maybe they would do something for the holiday.

"No," his mother said with a teasing sort of tone he hadn't heard in a long time. Rishi's heart joined his stomach in that pool of dread.

When his mother's voice teased and sounded so joyful, it was only about one thing. "Your engagement ceremony."

She'd said it like it was the most exciting news of the century. Like she had planned an elaborate surprise party for him and had just jumped out of a cake. How could this be happening? He was just there.

"Amma," he said and then sighed. The conversation he'd been planning out in his head became much more complicated now that they'd planned a date. His mouth opened in rebuttal, but what could he say?

Think of what happened last time, he told himself. *Your mother clutched at her chest because you wanted to cancel a simple family visit.* He took a deep breath, a calming breath. His heart beat against his chest like it wanted to get out and punch something. "Amma, what did you do?"

"Both families went to our astrologers yesterday, and when both astrologers said the same date, we knew it must be fate."

"Fate?" Rishi asked dryly.

Fate was Emma coming to India. Fate was her finding Rishi to be on the team. Fate was throwing the both of them in Cochin together.

Fate was not two astrologers matching dates. It couldn't be.

"Now, I know you are not excited about getting married now. But that will change. You and Radhika can keep talking and meeting and getting to know each other. It's so convenient you're in the same town. You know, just getting coffee together, not visiting each other's homes," she said, cautioning him, as if that was her biggest concern.

"I told you I wasn't ready—"

"Her family offered your father a job, and he starts work on Monday! This is also the good news! Now you don't need to send us money anymore. You can save it for you and Radhika and your family. Then we'll find a good match for Dharini. You'll both have lovely weddings, and we'll finally have our children settled."

This was crazy. Was his mother's desire for her children's marriage making her blind to what her son wanted? What he needed?

Rishi's body sagged against the counter. The milk boiled, and his body, on autopilot, combined it with the coffee. He put in an extra spoonful of sugar, stirring, watching the vortex created by his spoon as it spun around the mug.

"Rishi, are you still there?" His father's voice echoed through the phone.

But Rishi couldn't feel anything. He was already working through how to get out of this. His mouth opened to say, *No,* to say, *Cancel it,* to say, *Tell them I refuse,* and each time he pictured his mother clutching her chest on the bed. What could he do? Talk to Radhika himself? Would his father lose his job then? His mother sounded happy for the first time in years. And all at Rishi's expense.

He had to sort it out. Emma had found him Radhika; maybe she could help him find a way to rid himself of Radhika. He shook his head at the irony. He'd have to talk to her. Explain what had happened. She'd seen the solution to reconciling his parents with his brother. They'd do that. Then, together they'd work out a plan. Everything they'd done together had been successful. Ending this engagement would be successful too.

"I have to go," he said and then hung up the phone.

"Who was that?" the sleepy, half-moaning voice behind him asked.

Rishi's stomach tumbled on itself. "Let me make you coffee first." He poured some coffee into a new mug and added the rest of the milk. He had no idea how the hell he was supposed to start this conversation.

CHAPTER 34

Something was going on. She could feel it.

Emma rubbed her eyes as she stepped into the kitchen. The humidity in the air wasn't just from the steam wafting off the milk; it came from Rishi too. Like energy was pulsing off him.

His gestures were jittery as he searched around the counter for the sugar, which was right in front of him. His hands shook as he handed her a mug of coffee.

"Why do you have to make me coffee first?" she asked. She took a sip, then spat it out, dribbling it back into the cup. "Rishi, the milk's curdled." The slightly putrid taste made her recoil.

"Sorry, I . . . uh . . . I hadn't actually drunk mine yet." His mug clattered on the countertop, and he took the cup from her hands.

Emma shook her head, her brain as jumpy as Rishi's incessant movements as she got a new carton of milk from the cupboard. "Reserves," she said, rinsing out the pot.

Rishi got quiet, and a fizziness bubbled up in Emma's stomach. "Are you going to tell me what's going on?"

She'd felt this intensity before. Like a spark of genius before a code fix materialized in her mind, or the day when her phone had buzzed and she didn't want to answer it, knowing, just knowing, her grandmother had died. She couldn't handle the palpable energy in her tiny kitchen for much longer. And the way Rishi was acting didn't portend the best of news.

"Yes, but I'm just not sure how to begin."

She looked over her shoulder. He leaned against the counter, arms folded, thumbing his lip, staring into space.

Like chemicals deciding what to do when they were mixed together, she thought the particles between them were ready to explode. "I think it's always best to just say it," she said, although she wasn't sure she meant it. It seemed like something you were supposed to believe, supposed to say in this kind of phony calm.

"You remember Radhika?" he asked.

Radhika. A photo, a résumé. A sinking feeling in her stomach. "The unfortunate result of an even more unfortunate algorithm?" she asked with a weak laugh.

"Yes," he answered, and he ran his hand through his hair. "My parents . . . before you and I ever got together, I had sent them . . . I mean, they had contacted her parents . . ."

"You don't have to recap what happened." Rishi was stumbling, and she didn't like the idea of why he might have been. "What's going on? You just went home and spoke to your parents, and they were stopping your marriage-search stuff."

He looked up at the ceiling. "Yes." He paused. "But then my mom had to go on bed rest, and Radhika's family came over, and I told her I wasn't interested, but they won't listen to me."

"Radhika's family came over?" Could she have heard that right? Emma's heart was sure to explode as it pounded against her chest. Rage funneled through her body. "Wow, you somehow forgot that small detail." How much else had Rishi left out?

Apparently everything that was important.

"I didn't want to upset you. I was hoping to spare you some of the drama."

How could Rishi want to spare her the drama? They shared everything—work, food, their bodies, a bed. How could she have been so foolish? She could see the beautiful Radhika, waltzing into Rishi's parents' house, their minds blown by her credentials, her good looks. Radhika, overjoyed that she'd found a man like Rishi—handsome, qualified, smart, hilarious. Emma was going to be sick. "Spare me? You *lied* to me." She shook her head.

"I didn't lie to you. I just left out some details so our time together wouldn't be ruined." He took a step toward her, as if he would hug her.

As if she would let him. Emma raised an arm, blocking him. She froze. *Our time together.* Did he really just say that? As in, *limited time together before I leave you to get married.* Her worst fear had come true. How could someone who was supposed to be so smart, such a good coder, be a complete idiot in matters of the heart?

Something seized in her chest. Maybe karma was a real thing. She'd broken Jeremy's heart, and now Rishi was breaking hers. Crumbling it into tiny pieces with each word. Each word that said, *You should have known better, Emma. You should have expected this. In fact, you did, didn't you? You just wanted to ignore the reality of your situation.*

"What are you trying to tell me exactly?" She was trying not to cry because she didn't even need him to answer the question, really, did she? Now it all made sense. He was just biding his time.

"I don't know. I'm not sure how to explain it."

"Let me try. You're getting married to Radhika. Is that what you want to say?" Emma tried to stay strong, but the weight of what she'd just said had her leaning over the counter, clutching her face in her hands.

"Sort of, but I don't want it to happen. I want you."

"Why, so you can just prolong our affair before you get married to her?"

"I had no idea they were going to call me this morning and tell me that they'd set a date for the engagement ceremony. I didn't expect them to just arrange this marriage with the other family without talking with me first. In one day!"

Emma froze. That couldn't be real, could it? An engagement ceremony? Rishi took a step closer to her and leaned in, trying to look her in the eye. The milk pot boiled over, thick white foam spilling over the edges.

"Fuck!" Emma jumped up and switched off the gas. She grabbed the pot, and the pain shot through her hand. She jerked her hand off the handle, and Rishi grabbed it.

"Be careful," he said, examining the red streak across her palm.

She shook her hand out of his grasp. "I'm fine." Her hand pulsed with the burn, but it was nothing compared to the rest of her.

She had to stop relying on him for help. Or for anything. She should have known better. The only thing she could rely on was work. Her job. She knew this. She knew it better than anything.

Pain pulsed in her hand, under the burn, matching the pulse of an impending headache at her temples. She took a deep breath and looked at Rishi, whose glassy eyes searched hers. What were the words he'd used?

The family. A marriage with the family.

She could feel her eyes narrowing at him even as they began to burn too. *Don't cry. Don't cry, Emma, not here. Not for him.* She rubbed at them, her anger mixing with the hurt. Rishi was getting a new family. One that did not include her.

"I can't believe this." She said it more to herself than to him. She should have seen this coming, but her brain had been won over by her emotions. "You told me you were going to tell your parents. That you wanted to explore what was happening between us. And I believed you!"

"Emma, I don't want to marry her."

This had been going on for weeks, and she'd shared a bed with him every night since—his arms wrapped around her, their legs entangled.

And he'd whispered lies to her with every word and every kiss. The word *love* had been on the tip of her tongue so many times that the soft muscle was now charred into a frostbitten wound.

And the worst part of it all was that she was shattered inside. Now the tears were coming, aching at her throat, scratching at her nose, and there was no way she could stop them.

She turned around and cradled her face in her hands, elbows propped up on the counter. Her right elbow was in the gooey milk spill, and she didn't care.

"You expect me to believe that, when just a few months ago I wrote you code to find your perfect woman? And now you have her. And you have a fucking engagement planned!"

"Yes!" He slapped the counter, breathing hard, staring at Emma with insistent eyes. "I do want you to believe it. You should know me better than that."

She wasn't going to fall for those eyes again.

If only she could go back in time and not come to Bangalore so none of this would have happened. She wouldn't have left Seattle, wouldn't have asked Maria for this job. Wouldn't have this rock inside her chest that made her heart feel heavier than every other organ.

"Yeah, we know each other so well you've been lying to me. Who knows what you want and who you are."

"I want you," he said, walking over to her side, his hand tentatively rubbing at her back. "I'm so sorry. My mother was unwell, and she got upset when I said I didn't want to meet Radhika's parents, and . . ."

"Oh, really? That sounds better? Your mom is sick, so you are going to marry someone that meets your criteria perfectly?"

"No, that's not it. I know it's hard to understand, but finding her son's wife is what she lives for. All she can think about is finding this perfect woman who understands her, who she can pass her traditions down to."

It was all worse than she'd imagined. It wasn't like someone could convert to Hinduism and just pick up on centuries of tradition, ritual, and language. The shard of a family she didn't have elbowed its way into her chest. She would never be considered good enough to be an acceptable wife in Rishi's world. "Well, I think we both know that can never be me."

"It doesn't matter. I want to be with you."

"Yet you're getting married. Oh, let me guess, is this something you think can happen on the side?" Emma pointed back and forth between the two of them. "Is that what happens when you 'have to' get married?" She put air quotes around the words *have to* and leaned back against the counter, studying him. He hadn't even tried to defend himself.

"You know what, Rishi, I don't need to hear any more. Get out of my house." This was done. Rishi was done making excuses for his excuses, and Emma was done trying to hide her blotchy face from him. She didn't want him to see how much he'd hurt her.

"You don't understand. I need to explain. I'm not leaving until we talk this through."

A sick laugh bubbled out of her. What did he want to talk about exactly? "Just go. There's nothing to talk about. As far as work goes, I'll talk to Jas so we can minimize our face time together. Maybe Manuj can be promoted. He's a superior coder anyway."

It wasn't true, but Emma didn't care. She wanted a barb under his skin so he could feel a tenth of the pain he was inflicting on her.

He narrowed his eyes at her. "What?"

"I said. Go."

He disappeared into the bedroom and emerged a few minutes later wearing his clothes from the day before, slinging his bag over his shoulder. "Emma, this is not done. I don't want to leave you. I don't want to stop working with you. I want you."

"Unless you are *not* getting married and you actually tell your parents, who then accept it, there is nothing between us to discuss. And after this and what you've just done, I don't see any universe where that is going to work out." She took a deep breath. "Now please leave. I want to be alone."

"Emma," his voice practically begged. He came toward her.

"Nope. Go." She turned around and started cleaning up the mess on the counter.

His footsteps clicked on the marble, the locks scraped, and the door opened and shut. Then he was gone.

"And you *are* a mama's boy!" she yelled to the closed door.

Emma hunched over the mess on the stove, her head hanging, a dead weight. A ruthless sob echoed out of her mouth. Little clear splotches appeared in the creamy mess she'd made on the countertop. Tears. Much like the mess she'd started months ago. A mess that had begun with writing a fateful algorithm and falling for her gray-eyed coworker.

CHAPTER 35

Jordana's hair and half her body filled Emma's laptop screen. Jordana was sitting at her kitchen table, her knee propped up, and a teacup practically dangled from her hand. Her other hand sank in her hair as she sighed into her chest. Emma almost laughed, except nothing could make her laugh today.

"Jordy, I can't see your face."

"Sorry," she said like it hurt her to say the words. "I'm a bit off my game today. Mostly because I surpassed all my game last night, if you know what I mean." Jordana rubbed at her eyes with the palms of her hands and blinked at the screen. "Okay, I know I look like shit because it's early and I'm hungover, but what's going on with you? You look terrible. Did you finally catch the plague?"

"Please, stop sugarcoating it." Emma was trying to be brave, confident, and all the things that she'd told herself a thousand times in the face of adversity, assholes at work, and loan bills that felt like an avalanche more than a flurry.

"Sorry, but seriously, are you okay? You look like I do. Did something happen?"

Emma nodded, pressing her lips tight so she wouldn't cry. For herself. Jordana had seen her cry more than anyone else, but it was not a normal thing. And this was just a breakup. People had them all the time.

But her lips couldn't press together hard enough. One of those terrible, silent, shaking sobs that hurt her back and her chest at the same time lurched up from the abyss of sorrow inside her and shook her to the core.

"Emma, sweetie. Oh my God, I'm sorry; I was just joking. Tell me. Let it out, whatever you need."

She blew out a big breath, trying to exhale anything Rishi related out of her. "I'm okay."

"The hell you are. What is it?"

"Rishi. He's getting married. He lied to me. I'm an idiot. It was never going to work, and I . . ." She looked anywhere but at the laptop, because she knew the truth would be staring back at her in Jordana's eyes.

But instead of Jordana stating the obvious—*Wasn't he always going to get married to his perfect wife?*—like the good friend she was, she just said, "Tell me what happened."

So Emma told her everything that had happened, in painstaking detail, but let fury at herself surface so she wouldn't cry again. She'd need an electrolyte IV if she lost any more tears.

"I told Jas I had food poisoning yesterday so I wouldn't have to see Rishi. I couldn't function. And today everyone stayed clear of me. I'm sure because they think I have terrible diarrhea instead of . . ." She shook her head.

"A broken heart?" Jordana asked.

"How can it be broken already? It's been a few months."

"Emma, some people know on day one. But how did he leave it? You kicked him out, and then he said he was still getting married?"

"I don't think he needed to say it explicitly. We've all known this was coming, and I was in complete denial." He'd sent some apology texts and the regular cadence of status emails he sent to everyone. Obviously he was fine. Maybe feeling guilty, but functioning. Like a functioning heartbreaker. While she was a nonfunctioning broken hearter.

"So what are you going to do? You have like eight months left on your agreement, right? You can come back here; we'll take care of you," Jordana crooned.

Curling up on Jordana's couch watching movies while splitting a bottle of wine sounded divine. Perfect even. But she'd also just started an adventure and wasn't quite sure she was ready to end it.

"I don't know. Maybe I will be able to talk to him at some point in the future, but not yet. If you get a text later this week saying I'm on my way, though, you know what it means."

A few days had done nothing to ease the pain he'd caused her. While she wanted to see the project finished, she didn't know how she'd be able to endure the coming months. Just sitting in the same room as him had invaded her with a sadness she didn't want to acknowledge. Today, she'd felt his eyes on her the entire time in their team meeting. She'd had to resist turning her gaze toward him with all the energy she could muster. One sorrowful look and she might have been able to ignore the fact he was getting married, that he'd lied to her, that in no way possible could he destroy his family for her.

What would the next few months be like? Watching him make wedding plans. Thinking about him while he was away on his honeymoon. Or after, when he'd bring Radhika in to meet the team, all glowing and happy and shit. He'd introduce her to Emma like she was just another coworker. She couldn't even think about it.

"I'm here for you. I'll get you a puppy and find a new apartment if you need it. I'll screen any guys who tempt you and ensure they are worthy of you. Because from whatever you said, the only thing standing in between you and Rishi is his parents, and that just doesn't make sense to me."

Emma shrugged. "It's complicated for him. I'd never want him to break with his family because of me."

"Well, I don't get it. And I know you have a way different perspective on it than I do, but you are amazing, and if he can't work his shit out with his family to at least see what is happening with you, then fuck him." Jordana's eyes were on fire.

"Whoa." In that moment, Emma was glad Jordana wasn't in Bangalore, or else Rishi might have been missing some crucial body parts. "I appreciate your intensity, Jordy. I feel like tomorrow I can go into work and know that at least if I feel like shit now, if you ever met Rishi in person, he would feel shittier because of whatever you'd do to him."

"Damn straight." Jordana rubbed at her eyes again, the fire zapped out of her.

"Okay, I'm going to go to bed, but you should go take some ibuprofen or something." Emma smiled, trying to reassure Jordana, and possibly herself, that she was fine.

"I will. Take care, and I'll check up on you later this week." She blew a kiss to Emma, who did the same and then closed her laptop.

{ /** *. // }

Emma wasn't feeling great, but she felt better. Better meaning that she wasn't going to cry in the office. She'd been thinking about Jordana's call and trying to reconcile the Rishi she knew with the Rishi who'd lied to her and wouldn't stand up to his parents. It just didn't compute. But she also needed some time before she could talk to him and tell him what a fucking louse he was. She'd gone from sad Emma to angry Emma, fortified by Jordana's hungover ire.

She walked to the patio to refill her coffee. But when she opened the door, she stalled. Rishi was sitting at a table, his back to her, talking on the phone. He wouldn't notice her. And why should she care? *He* was the one who should have been slinking away from her.

She strode to the coffee maker and pressed the buttons for cappuccino. She stared at the machine, willing it to hurry. Why did it always need to warm up when she was in the biggest rush?

"No, I have to go home this week. The engagement is set for next month."

She choked on her breath. He was getting engaged in mere weeks? He'd excluded that little detail. The hurt stinging at her chest from the conversation at her house was back in full force.

Somehow, deep inside, she'd hoped it was all just a misunderstanding, that Rishi would stand up to his parents and surprise her on her doorstep one night, begging her forgiveness. Because of her. Because he thought what they had was special.

She'd gotten caught up in a frenzy of lust and love and had forgotten the world she was in. But reality had proved she was nothing more than a statistic. A number. A typical fool for love. The bumper stickers were right. Karma was indeed a bitch.

The machine in front of her buzzed, and while she was tempted to linger a bit longer to hear what other hidden information she might uncover, she resolved not to care. She couldn't care. Not anymore. No matter how much it burned away at her chest.

She returned to her desk and hoped the rest of the day would be as Rishi-free as possible. Back at her desk, an email from Jeremy dinged into her inbox.

> Emma, I've been trying to reach you on Instant Message but you must be busy these days. You'll never believe it but I'm in Bangalore for a work trip. I'd love to see you, at least for dinner or something, and catch up. I've missed you and want to hear about all the incredible work you're doing. Maybe we could meet tomorrow night?

Emma's stomach rolled at the thought of Jeremy here in her new town, where she was dealing with heartache from her new boyfriend. Well, ex-boyfriend. When she thought about her life with Jeremy, it was like watching a reality TV show starring two other people. She was the bad girlfriend who constantly missed the chance to see him, or even touch him, with their conflicting busy schedules. She'd send a text that she was at work late. A message that she was going out with Jordana. Or she'd fall asleep with her laptop in bed even as he waited on her.

Her eyes closed, an internal wince pinching her. Somehow those things had never been a problem with her and Rishi.

It would be good to see Jeremy. They'd broken up, but it wasn't like they despised each other. They'd shared too much for that. Now, knowing what it was like to be heartbroken, she owed him that much.

She wrote back to him.

> What a coincidence! Sounds good. I will clear my night for you.

{ /** *. // }

The next day her stomach was still tied up in knots. She'd almost called in sick but couldn't show how hurt she still was. She had to stay strong at work. Collapsing into her desk chair, she looked at her calendar.

When she'd agreed to see Jeremy yesterday, she'd thought it was a good idea. But now it didn't seem like it anymore. She grumbled at her monitor. She didn't want to have a breakdown over her new boyfriend with her ex. That would be horrible. Maybe seeing Jeremy would be a reminder of how quickly she could recover from a relationship.

She sat at her desk, counting down until 6:00 p.m., and when it came, she took the elevator down. Before getting off, she took a deep breath and pushed her shoulders back. She blocked Rishi from her thoughts. She brushed off the past glorious weeks and tried to forget the one horrific moment when her heart had been trampled to bits.

Jeremy was outside her office, sitting in one of his company's cars, a driver at the wheel. Emma walked over and knocked on his window.

The way his face lit up upon seeing her made her involuntarily smile. He jumped out of the car, and she stepped back. Jeremy was wearing a plaid button-up shirt and his usual tight jeans. She'd bought him that shirt for Christmas last year. A reminder of how well she knew him. And how she hadn't known Rishi at all.

"Emma." He smiled, taking her in his arms with a longer embrace than she expected.

She inhaled deeply, smelling the scent of cedar and moss she knew so well. It took her back to getting ready in the morning, fighting over the sink they shared. To leaning in and kissing his lips when she got home from work. To making dinner together in their miniscule apartment kitchen, where Jeremy always insisted she taste whatever he'd made to see if it needed salt or spice.

The length of his arms wrapped around her tight. Jeremy was a foot taller than her. She remembered this, and the way his arms felt on her back. Familiar. Like home.

All those emotions flooded over her, trying to squeeze into the cracks that Rishi had just left in her heart.

"How are you?" He stood back and placed his hands on her shoulders, studying her. "You look amazing."

"I'm not sure I deserve that, but thanks." How could he be so kind to her after all she'd put him through? "How is your trip?"

"Good. And now wonderful since I'm seeing you. Ready to go?"

Emma had to admit that it was comforting to see him. Like being wrapped in a blanket that smelled like home. They might have broken up, there might not have been anything between them now, but Jeremy still knew her. She knew him and his family. There were no added complications because of his family. They'd adored her, and there had always been something deeply comforting in that.

She got into the car.

"Can you believe the company gave me a car to take around?" he asked, sliding in beside her and shaking his head, that goofy, nerdy laugh of his filling the back seat.

It was like old times. "I know. I feel completely spoiled. My place is so nice. Like, soooo nice."

"This is Raj." Jeremy patted the seat in front of him. "I was telling him how I usually ride my bicycle everywhere. He thinks I'm crazy."

"No, no sir." Raj smiled politely in the rearview mirror.

Emma laughed at how proper the driver tried to stay, knowing that he must think the tall, lumbering man behind him was out-of-his-mind crazy. Jeremy just talked to everyone about everything. She'd forgotten this about him.

"I wanted to eat at my hotel, if that's okay. It's supposed to be amazing," Jeremy said.

"Sure." But Emma wondered why he'd picked his hotel, her thoughts veering off into his room. Was that what he expected?

They pulled up to one of Bangalore's five-star hotels that looked like a palace and walked down a dark hallway that led to a restaurant, situated outside on a stone patio. The walkway to the restaurant's terrace was lit with torches, highlighting the stone pillars that lined the sidewalk. A drummer sat on a platform tapping on a drum.

The host showed them to a table. Flames flickered around the perimeter of the patio, and tiny fires reflected in Jeremy's horn-rimmed glasses.

"You look so different," he said, shaking his head in disbelief, his voice a little breathy, like he was trying to suck in all the air around him.

"Really?" she asked, looking down.

"You have jewelry on, and your shirt, the color is so . . . bright! And your face seems to have this glow about it. Just very different for you."

She was glowing? He must have been hallucinating, since the best description for her current state of being was that she was rotting on the inside. "Well, I guess I do wear actual colors here. There aren't too many clothes in gray and black." Her nerves sizzled all over her body. She was lit up. Nervous being around him. But why? Was she nervous about what his intentions were for the evening? It was just Jeremy. But something about this made her remember what it felt like to be fawned over—and forget what it felt like to be rejected.

"How is everything?" Jeremy leaned over the table. "How is life in India? It seems to be treating you well."

Emma had no idea where to start. Although she knew exactly who she'd leave out. "It's good. It was a bit hard at first."

"Are you glad you decided to take the job?" He shifted in his chair, and she caught an almost imperceptible frown. She couldn't help but feel like he was evaluating her, gauging her current situation.

But how could they just pick up in the present without addressing the past? "Jeremy, I have to just start out by saying I am so sorry for the way we left things." He just looked at her. "I really hope you're doing well."

"Yeah, you know, I'm okay . . . doing my best to get over you." But he laughed. He was smiling.

She wasn't sure what to say, but she was glad he wasn't falling apart on the inside, and they could do something normal like have dinner together without him yelling at her. "Work's been pretty good. I'm glad I decided to stay with the organization, and India's super cool. The toughest parts were just figuring out a new way of living. A new system, you know? Like how to get around and where to eat and all that kind of stuff that comes with moving to another country, I guess. But the app is progressing well."

"Your company is doing some great work," Jeremy said.

A giant gurgling sound leaped up from her stomach, and she realized that she hadn't eaten lunch today or much over the past few days because of Rishi. At lunchtime, she'd thought about how easily duped she'd been, and her head had sunk onto her desk, and she'd sobbed there for a moment before remembering she was at work. At least a few times a day the vision of Rishi and Radhika would bubble up and send a direct line of nausea to her stomach. But she wasn't going to think about him now. "Speaking of work, I didn't have lunch today. Can we order?" She looked over the menu, the prices quadrupled over a normal Indian restaurant she'd go to. "It's so expensive here."

"It's like ten or twelve dollars for a dish, Emma," Jeremy said, squinting at her.

"I guess that's true." Emma slowed her speech, recognizing for the first time that she was so used to prices being in rupees now that she didn't bother converting to dollars anymore.

"And don't worry; this is my treat. What looks good?"

Emma suggested they order the chicken tikka, shahi paneer, and the bhindi masala.

"Bhindi masala? It says 'ladyfingers cooked in a spicy tomato-and-onion sauce.'"

"That's what they call okra here, but I have no idea why." She always imagined green witchy fingers crusted in a thin coating of fuzz when she saw the description. "It's really good; don't worry."

They ordered more drinks, and Emma asked how work and life were back in Seattle. Summer was ending, the two whole months of it. She laughed as he recalled how they'd braved the wind and rain together on their bikes, their friends shocked at their steadfast bicycle riding despite the weather.

"I do miss riding my bike. Riding on the roads here would be a death wish," Emma said.

"Well, you're almost halfway through the project, right? You'll be back in Seattle in no time. Emma, I meant what I wrote you. I miss you." Jeremy looked at her over his glasses. "When you come back, I'd like to see if we could put the past behind us and start over. I was ridiculous with the proposal. I've had some time to think about it. There were a couple people at work who were getting married, and I got excited. I kept thinking about you and me. I mean, I know we hadn't even discussed it." He let out a sigh. "When I told my mom what happened, she said it was the most romantic but stupidest thing I'd ever done." He grinned, reaching out to take her hand where it sat on the table.

Emma looked at his hand on hers, feeling overwhelmed by the suggestion. His mom was right. His mom, a round, smiling woman with glasses like his, who had eagerly asked Emma to make cookies with her last Christmas. Who enjoyed spending time with her. Who had hugged Emma when she'd found out her parents and grandmother had died and had let Emma cry on her shoulder.

It was exactly how Rishi's parents probably felt about a potential, acceptable bride. She looked off into the fire on the patio and exhaled deeply, trying to keep the threat of tears at bay.

A series of memories rushed through her: she and Jeremy, reading through the Science section of the *New York Times*, drinking lattes at their favorite coffee shop, strolling along the waterfront arm in arm.

If an equivalent of arranged marriages existed for them, she and Jeremy would have been perfect on paper. The kind of couple people would fawn over. He was smart, funny, handsome, and fit into her life in Seattle so well. They shared the same friends, the same interests, and their life together would be much of the same.

What would happen in eight months, when she left Bangalore and was transplanted back into the same life she'd left? Clearly nothing here was going to work out, at least not romantically.

Her lips parted as she searched for the words to reply. The only word in her head was *Rishi*. She blinked and shook her head. She took a drink.

"Say something, Emma," he pleaded.

Emma smiled. "I don't know. We'll see." Was it just her busy work schedule that had made them drift apart? Was it her determination to be successful? Maybe that would all change. Or was that the rum in her cocktail talking? Coaxing her into avoiding loneliness. To know someone was there for her. To warm the cold that was the night desert of her heart.

They finished eating and split a gulab jamun for dessert. As the warm, syrupy dessert slid down her throat, the sweetness was so overwhelming that tears threatened to prick her eyes. She'd had this same dessert that first night in Cochin with Rishi.

Rishi, lifting her against the wall, their breath mingling through savage kisses. Kisses she didn't even know she could have. The touch of his hands searing her skin. His mouth melting every nook of her into a pool of want. Their bodies practically laughing together, overjoyed in the sensation as they became one. Like they could speak their own language, a new language. One that she thought she might even speak forever.

Little wet needles burned at the corners of her eyes. A biting sensation at her nose. She had to stop this. She couldn't think about Rishi anymore. He'd left her.

"Excuse me, I'll be right back." She scooted her chair back in a rush and headed toward the restroom. She had to rid herself of this pain. She couldn't let Jeremy see it. See how she'd been destroyed just days ago. He'd probably think she'd deserved it, after what she'd done to him. Maybe she did.

After splashing some water on her face and taking a few deep breaths, she smiled big and bright at herself in the mirror. "You're fine. Just fine." Maybe if she convinced herself, she could convince him.

She returned to the table, and Jeremy started talking about some new technology his company was working on and why he was in Bangalore. Emma couldn't focus on what he was saying. Her hands were fidgety. A restlessness burned in her chest. She needed a distraction. She needed everything to stop reminding her of Rishi.

She looked up at Jeremy from under her eyelashes. Selfish shame pushed at her chest. "What are the hotel rooms like here?" she asked, the words blurting out as he took a breath. She wasn't even sure his sentence was finished.

"They're nice. Crazy fancy. I feel like everything in India is just over-the-top five stars, you know?" A sly smile widened his lips. "Remember that time we went to the Oregon coast and stayed in that super-shitty room, and it rained like the entire time?"

Emma laughed. There were burn holes from cigarettes in the comforter and a ceiling light that buzzed when it was on, and the room smelled like insect spray. "How could I forget? I refused to walk barefoot in it."

"Well, it's much nicer than that. A thousand times. You could definitely take off your shoes in this one." He took a drink and looked over his glasses at her again, a look that Emma had always jokingly called his "Business Time" look. His eyes burned into hers. "Why don't you come see mine?"

Why not? What did she have to lose now? That's why she'd asked about his room, right? A swirling nervousness plunged into Emma's stomach. "Sure." She swallowed hard and smiled as Jeremy's fingers stroked the top of her hand. She resisted jerking her hand back. The slight tickle made her stomach feel a little queasy. What was she doing?

Jeremy paid the bill, and she followed him back down the romantic, candlelit pathway to the hotel entrance.

As they walked, their hands swayed with their steps, his right with her left. Was he going to hold it? She hoped not. They hadn't held hands in a long time.

He was talking about work when the elevator opened, and they stepped inside. He hit the button for his floor, and Emma nodded at him as he talked. It all felt so . . . familiar, just like old times. They were two people who knew each other, steeped in the comfortable fabric of their lives, stitched together in a snug history.

Jeremy's family would be thrilled if they got back together. Jordana might roll her eyes, but she'd get over it. And Emma would go back to relying on work, because making a difference in the world had always fulfilled her. That's all she needed. Maybe she would join his company. That way she'd resist looking up Rishi in the company directory every other day.

The elevator opened. "After you," Jeremy said, holding the door open.

Her arms shook with indecision as they walked to his door. Was this right? Was she just trying to get back at Rishi? Was this what she wanted?

They were at his room door.

"I'm so excited you came up," Jeremy said, opening the door for her.

Inside was a luxurious room—cushy pillows, clean white walls, gold-tinged decorations. What sounded like spa music was being funneled in from somewhere.

Like a honeymoon suite.

She closed her eyes. She'd be so happy to stay in this room with Rishi for hours, days, months, ordering room service, feeding each other mango and pineapple, searching for the other's body in the sheets.

But instead he would be sharing his honeymoon with Radhika, practically a stranger. Though they would know each other by the time his honeymoon was done. Inside and out. The threat of tears returned, burning behind her nose.

"Your room is amazing," she said, but she could hear her voice tremble even as her legs carried her to the bed. She rubbed her hands along the comforter. "What is this, like a thousand thread count?"

"I have no idea." Jeremy walked over to her and kneeled on the ground, his hands on her thighs. "Emma, I miss you so much when you're not around. We can take our time with things. We don't have to rush anything when you come back. You could even get your own place. I'll keep Steve the renter around a little longer."

Sweet, kind Jeremy. Her hand came out to cradle his face, the stubble starting to grow already, pricking at her fingertips. His eyes were searching, hopeful. He clutched her hand, pressing it into his face, sliding kisses along her palm.

But this wasn't the person she wanted to say these words. She didn't want it to be Jeremy asking for another chance. She wanted it to be Rishi.

She almost sobbed right there on the bed. Rishi had ruined her in mere months. She couldn't get over what had happened between them, and the thought of doing again to Jeremy what had been done to her was just wrong. She wouldn't want to inflict that kind of pain upon anyone else.

She jerked her hand away at the last minute, and Jeremy sat back on the carpet, confusion sweeping over his eyes.

"I'm sorry." Tears spilled down her cheeks, and she buried her face in her hands. This was not what she wanted to do in front of him. This was not the plan at all. But she couldn't be that way with him. Not again. Not after being with Rishi and knowing what it could be between two people. She'd never had that with Jeremy. She might have been comfortable, and it might have been easy, but she didn't want to go there again. She couldn't.

She wiped at her eyes, eyeliner smearing the backs of her hands. Jeremy looked at her as he sat on the floor, his face a mask of confusion, obviously wondering what the hell had just happened.

"Jeremy, I just can't."

CHAPTER 36

Rishi had searched the entire floor for Emma when he'd gotten off the phone. She'd been in her office the whole day but was no longer there. Her laptop was gone. Her purse, gone. He'd stuck his head into various conference rooms, searching for her, and then he'd seen her slip into the elevator. He'd run down the hall and pressed at the buttons, but he'd just missed her.

He'd missed her in so many ways since she'd kicked him out of her apartment. The past few days she hadn't answered his calls or texts. He'd gone to her house and knocked on the door so long the people upstairs had come outside and stared at him over the balcony. When they found themselves in the hall together, she'd abruptly turned around, and he'd caught just a whiff of her shampoo in her place.

When the next elevator came, he got off on the ground floor and searched the lobby for her, his heart racing. He had to tell her. He had to give her the news. But what he saw shocked him.

Some asshole was hugging her outside their office building. The way that guy was looking at her told Rishi that he wasn't just a friend. Friends didn't undress other friends with their eyes. Friends didn't let their fingers linger on one another's arms. She got in the car with him. They drove off together. Who was he?

Sickness pooled in his stomach as his gaze followed the car out to the main road. The thought of her even having dinner with another guy ignited a blazing jealousy inside him. A fire that leaped up, burning into his arms, his hands, and forming fists and making him want to hit something.

Maybe that guy. If only he knew where they were going.

But who was he kidding?

He'd seriously fucked up. Keeping Emma out of his family drama had not been the right thing to do. Hiding his intentions from his parents had not been the right thing to do. He should have known that. Rishi couldn't hide his real life from his parents forever, and doing so had potentially ruined the one thing he'd ever had that was real. That moment when she'd kicked him out of her house, and each time since when she'd refused his calls or didn't reply to his texts, he'd felt it inside. Each rejection felt like a shot, piercing the skin and lodging itself in the wound. Now he'd been pummeled with them, and he knew what absolute pain felt like.

She could have been helping him this entire time to think of a better solution, coming up with a plan that would save him from the feeling of falling apart. Like he'd lost it all. Everything.

Was she feeling it too?

He knew what was between them. He'd have to trust his gut on this. He'd never be able to just forget her. His parents could throw a thousand beautiful, appropriate women at him, and he'd still be comparing each one to Emma.

Maybe it had looked bad when he'd tried to tell her his family had arranged a marriage, but he'd never gotten out the most important words: *Help me stop it.*

His palms pushed at his eyes. This was all his fault because he'd believed he needed to shield her from the truth. He'd been shielding everyone from the truth, and the end result was now the worst fate he could imagine. His life, built up like walls of lies around him, was a total mockery. He'd been trying to be someone he wasn't, all in the name of protecting the people closest to him. Protecting his parents from knowing the truth about what he wanted. Protecting them from the reality of Sudhar and his family. Protecting Emma from the reality of his life. Just because he didn't want them to suffer. And now he was the one who was truly suffering. After all, it was his life to live. Not theirs.

And now it might be too late. But he couldn't let her fall for some other guy.

She'd said that his parents had to stop the marriage, and that they had to stop looking for someone before they could be together. And he needed to prove it to her.

He had to hurry. He had to go back home.

{ /** *. // }

Rishi took the first train to Madurai that night. As soon as he'd collapsed on the seat, he emailed Jas to tell him he couldn't be in on Friday because of a family emergency.

He texted Emma. Maybe at least a few words from him would make her remember what they had. And if she felt even a hundredth of what he did, maybe it would be some kind of consolation. Even if she didn't respond, he hoped that it would at least make an impact until he could truly make things right.

It was early morning when the train arrived in Madurai. The auto pulled up to his house, which still looked shut up from the night before. He paid the driver before walking up the stairs to the porch and pressing gently on the front door. It didn't move; no one had come out yet. He'd have to wake his sister up on his own. She was the only one who could help him.

Rishi didn't even need the coffee he'd grabbed at the station. Energy fueled his system. Nervousness prickled his skin. So many thoughts blew through his mind. His mother's heart. His father's job. Radhika's pride. His parents' dreams for him and his sister.

But did he really need to worry about Radhika? She was beautiful, smart, had a good job—she would find someone perfect for her. Rishi just had to let her know. He had to be honest with her too.

He walked around the side of the house to his sister's bedroom window. Luckily his parents' room was on the other side. He knocked and loudly whispered, "Dharini, wake up. It's Rishi." Nothing. He tapped at the glass again. Then the iron of the locks rattled.

An eye appeared through a slat in the shutters, his sister's narrowed eye. She undid the lock and opened the window. "What are you doing here?"

"I need to talk to you."

"We have a front door," she said, her hand on her hip. "I thought you were a ghost or a burglar."

"It's six a.m. A little late for ghosts and burglars."

She rolled her eyes. "I'll let you in."

"Don't wake Mom and Dad."

Dharini waved behind her, and he tiptoed to the front porch, where she was already holding the door open. "Can we sit out here?" he asked.

"What's happening?" Her voice was still stuck in the fog of sleep as she collapsed on the bench. "You didn't even bring me coffee?"

"I'll make you coffee, but first hear me out." He sat down beside her and took a deep breath. "I need help with Mom and Dad. I don't think I should marry Radhika. In fact, I want them to stop looking for some time. But a lot of this has to do with you, so I want to explain myself and get your opinion."

"What?" She rubbed at her eyes.

"You're old enough now; you know that not everything works the way it's supposed to. Shit happens all the time. In fact, I'm not even a vegetarian." It was like admitting he ran over puppies for sport—that's how guilty he felt.

"Really? You eat meat?" That seemed to have woken her up.

"I also think I'm in love with an American girl. Who is not Indian. She's white and has red hair and green eyes."

Dharini shook her head and held out her arm.

"What?" he asked, looking at it.

"Pinch me. I feel like I'm in a dream, and they say you need to get pinched to know if you're sleeping or awake."

"Seriously?" He pinched her, and she jerked her arm back. "Ow!"

"You said to pinch you, sis. Anyway, this is not a dream. This is my life. And I've been hiding it from all of you because you want to get married, and Mom and Dad are afraid that if I'm not married, you won't be able to find a good husband. I mean, I'm also afraid of this."

Dharini leaned into the bench and stared out into the street. "Okay. So you don't want to marry Radhika. Maybe you want to marry an American. But you're almost engaged because of me?"

"Yes. Pretty much. Also, something else I've been hiding from you. The whole family has actually been hiding from you. I've been talking to Sudhar. He has a daughter. Her name is Sejal."

"What?" This seemed to have gotten the biggest reaction from her. "I have a niece?"

"Yes." He pulled out his phone and showed her the pictures Sudhar had texted him. "Look, she has our eyes."

"Oh, she does. Sejal," Dharini cooed as she tested out the name. "How are they?"

"Well, the thing is, Sona's family lost money in that bad investment too. So it wasn't just Amma and Appa, like everyone seemed to think."

Dharini looked toward the front door. "No one told me."

"I think we've all been a little guarded with our truths, and it's time to stop. But I have to know. Is it so important that you get engaged in the next year, or can it wait for some time? Can it wait until I have things figured out?" If Dharini could just agree to wait a year, then he could figure out if he and Emma were the real thing, or if he needed to go back to the drawing board. At least he had an algorithm that worked now.

"Rishi, I know I'm the youngest. I know I'm the little sister. But why didn't anyone ask me what I think until now?" She shook her head, like he was a misbehaving toddler who should have known better. "I don't want to marry anybody who doesn't accept my family for who they are. I don't care if my oldest brother married the wrong woman. I don't care if my other older brother marries some American with red hair. All I care about is that you are happy, and that I can find someone who will be happy with me. For who I am. For who my family is. I wouldn't want in-laws who judge my family. I'm old enough to know how the world works. And I'm also old enough to decide what's right and what's wrong."

Rishi was stunned into silence. His little sister was so grown up now. Maybe she wasn't as traditional as he'd thought. She'd always had opinions, but what she'd said was unexpected to say the least.

"But you should have told me about Sudhar. He's my brother too." She looked so hurt, so lost beside him.

Rishi bit at his lip. "You're right. I should have told you about Sudhar. But maybe you and I can get the family back together. You should at least hear what he has to say."

She stared out into the street like an accident victim in shock and then nodded. "I can't believe he had a baby and didn't reach out to me."

"He's terrified of Mom and Dad. Probably didn't want to put you in a bad position."

"Yeah. Amma can be a little scary when you cross her."

"No shit. Considering that, are you sure you can settle for a husband whose family doesn't care about Sudhar marrying outside the community and losing our family's money? And then maybe even with me marrying *way* outside?" God, had he really just said that out loud? Emma wasn't even speaking to him.

"It wouldn't be settling. I would never want to be with someone who wasn't interested in joining our family because of one mistake. I mean, if what you say is true, then Sona's family isn't even that bad. Maybe just stupid."

Rishi laughed. "Maybe not the whole family. I think it was just one shady uncle."

The milkman's scooter hummed up to the front gate. Rishi ran down and grabbed a packet of milk. "Coffee?" He returned to the bench and dangled it in front of his sister.

"Yes. And you can tell me all about this American girl."

"Emma?"

"Yes, Emma. Emma and Sejal. So maybe two new ladies in our lives."

Rishi could only dream that his parents would be so welcoming of these two new additions.

CHAPTER 37

After a brief period of chaos when his mom walked into the kitchen and saw him and his sister making morning coffee, things settled down. His mother kept mentioning preparations for the engagement ceremony, assuming that was why Rishi was there, and Rishi couldn't keep ignoring her comments.

He excused himself to take a bath and, with the bedroom door closed, pulled out his phone and searched for Radhika's number. It was almost nine. Was that too early to call? She would probably be getting ready to go to the office.

If she was upset over what he had to say, then she could find some sympathy with her friends at work. If she was seriously upset, she could call in sick. Morning was fine. And Rishi was desperate. But hopefully his new "truth conquers all" approach would work.

He pressed the call button, sealing his fate for good.

{ /** *. // }

When Rishi exited the shower, his father's voice was booming from the living room. After throwing on some jeans and a T-shirt, he glanced at the message on his phone. Everything would be okay. Maybe.

He tiptoed down the hall and listened to their conversation.

"Not ready? Every man is ready for marriage!" his father huffed.

"What is this about? No marriage at all or just not now?" his mother cried out, panic welling up inside her.

"He wants to do the right thing, and I think we should allow him to. He wants to be ready for his wife, and now is not the right time," his sister said. Oh no, what had happened when he was in the bath?

"He's not been ready for years. When will the day come? All of the good ones will be gone by then. He'll be like that old uncle down the street with his twenty-three-year-old wife. I don't like that." His mother shook her head.

"And Radhika? And her family? What will they say?"

At this, Rishi had to step in; it was now or never. He walked around the corner.

"I already told Radhika," he said. "I called her and told her I wasn't going to marry her. She knows." His parents stared at him, their mouths open, faces twisted in confusion. He wouldn't add that she'd cried. That she'd already told her friends she was getting married. That people would think something was wrong with her.

But Rishi had tried to use his charm and talked her down. "You are so beautiful and smart and amazing," he'd said. "Any man will be lucky to have you. I mean, how many have you turned down already?"

"Seven," she'd said between her sniffles.

That was more than he'd expected. "Radhika, you know it's not you. I think you're great. It's just not right. I'm in love with someone else."

The words had just come out. And they hadn't felt wrong or shameful or false. He'd smiled. How simple it was, just to be open about it.

"Bastard!" Then she'd hung up on him. And his smile had disintegrated. He hadn't necessarily expected her to be happy or anything, but no one had ever called him a bastard before.

He called back, but she didn't answer, so he texted her five apologies. When he'd gotten out of the shower, though, he had a response.

OK.

She'd said okay. Which was better than anything he'd hoped for.

And then, shortly after that came another one. There was another one for me too.

She'd had someone else in mind this whole time as well? He'd shaken his head at the ridiculousness of it.

His parents both started with their questions at the same time. "Why didn't you say anything earlier? What will her parents say? When will we get grandchildren?"

"Look, this isn't the right time. I'm not going to get married now, and if you keep pushing it, I'll never get married and you'll *never* get grandchildren from me." His voice got louder than he'd intended. Maybe he was pushing it. He glanced at his mother; her face looked pale. "I want all these things as much as you do, but you need to let me do it my way. Dharini is okay with it, and that's what is important."

He looked back and forth between them. "You need to think about me. It's my life. The rest of my life. We'll all be happy if you just let things happen naturally."

"Rishi's happiness is important," his sister agreed, breaking the tense silence that had settled over the room. "I'm not marrying anyone who won't accept us for who we are and what we have."

His mother stood up and walked with shaky steps past him. She paused outside her bedroom door. "You don't know how people are. It's not the same for us."

"I suppose I have to call the parents," his father said, sighing. He swung his head around to look at Rishi. "I assume you apologized to Radhika and she's okay."

"Yes. I apologized many times."

His father nodded. "Maybe I can appeal to them and still keep the job offer."

"Sure, Appa, you should try that." He had to at least sound reassuring. "But if it doesn't work, we'll be okay."

Rishi walked over to his sister, who was finishing up her coffee. "Thanks, sis. I owe you one."

She smiled. "You owe me some sleep. You'd better be nice to her."

Rishi didn't need to ask who she was referring to. And he would. He would be very, very nice. If she would have him.

CHAPTER 38

Emma had made it to Friday. She just had to get through one day of work, and then she'd have the weekend to figure out what to do. She could evaluate if staying in Bangalore for countless more months would be possible, or if she should just contact Maria and see if she could come back to Seattle early.

She was still in bed, even though she should already have been at work by now, and curled her knees to her chest, the sick feeling in her stomach swelling if she didn't. Her eyes burned from tears that had welled up and made her eyelashes sticky. Why hadn't it felt this bad when Jeremy had stopped talking to her? She and Rishi had known each other for less time, and logically this should have been easier to get over, right? But maybe logic wasn't at play here. Maybe it was the murmur in the back of her head that she'd been ignoring. Fearing.

Love.

And now he was gone. She stared at the text he'd sent earlier.

Emma, don't give up on me. I'm going to make it right.

What could that mean, when his engagement was days away? She hugged her arms tight around her belly.

It had been so easy to tell Jeremy the truth about how she felt. That it was over between them.

The phone vibrated on her table. Rishi's name appeared on the screen. And that picture she'd taken of him in Cochin, propped up on the bed. She wished she'd deleted it and replaced it with a poo emoji or something. Now she had to look at it every time he called and she didn't answer. Another seething reminder.

She pressed her lips together. What was he calling for? And should she answer now, after that text? After all the hurt and all the worry and all the heartache? No. She'd let it ring.

It took all she had to get up and walk into the bathroom, then pack up her laptop. She needed to leave for work. Telling people she had food poisoning could only work so many times.

She glanced at her phone before putting it in her purse. A text from Rishi.

Please pick up. Or call me. It's urgent.

What if someone had died? What if it was about the project? Urgent? What did that mean?

She took a deep breath and had resigned herself to calling him when her phone rang again.

"Rishi? Is everything okay? I mean, with work." She tried to sound calm, like she hadn't been fretting over him every day this past week.

"Oh my God, thank you for answering. I was worried you wouldn't."

She took a deep breath and remembered her pride. Reminded herself that she couldn't let him hear her heart breaking over the phone. He couldn't have that power. "Nonsense, I can be professional. We still work together."

"Emma, there is nothing professional about this call. What are you doing this weekend? Please say nothing."

"Um . . ." She racked her brain for something, anything, that would sound like she was back on her feet and not totally destroyed. Before she could think of something, he'd started talking again.

"Come to Madurai. I'm here. I bought you a ticket. I want you to come here, meet me, see where I'm from. Meet my parents. Everything. All of it." He sounded so happy, hopeful. Could this be real?

The twisting in Emma's stomach untangled and turned to confusion. *Everything. All of it.* All of him—that's what he'd meant. "Your parents?" she said to clarify.

"Yes. It's all over. The wedding's off. I want to prove it to you. I love you, and I—I mean, does that freak you out?"

Love? Emma's heart soared in her chest, but her brain told it to stay put. Tears of joy threatened to prick at her eyes. Not yet. She couldn't let her emotions get the best of her again. What was happening? "Rishi, I don't know. We need to talk. Your family . . . the lies . . ."

"Yes, I know. God, I was such an idiot. I want to make it up to you. We can talk here. I want to show you around. But we can talk before too. Okay, how about if I come back to Bangalore tonight, and then we take the bus to Madurai in the morning? Or I'm sure there's a flight. I'll look. Give me a sec." Rishi was speaking a hundred miles an hour, blazing through his words like a bullet train.

He was crazy. Losing his mind. "Rishi, I can travel by myself. I'm a big girl."

"So you'll come? Thank God! I was worried I'd lost you. That you'd found someone else."

His words ripped a hole in her chest. If he only knew just how much she *didn't* want to be anyone else's. "Seriously?"

"I'm not kidding. I had a 'life flash before my eyes' kind of moment." He paused. "Okay, you're going to come? It's going to be good, and this is all going to work out."

Work out? Had he done it? "The wedding is off for real this time? There's no engagement ceremony?"

"No. Nothing. I'm a free man with extremely pissed-off parents. Look, I felt terrible about keeping information from you. I thought I was protecting you, and instead I was digging a hole for myself. More like a grave. You said you didn't want to have anything to do with me until all that was taken care of. And it's taken care of. I called Radhika, told my parents. It's done. I'm yours. If you'll have me."

She still couldn't get the words *I love you* out of her head. But there were other things to consider. "Your parents . . . do they know about me? About why you called off the wedding?"

"Well, my sister knows. We'll get there. Baby steps. They're fragile creatures, and I've just destroyed their future plans for me."

"Is it too soon for me to come?"

"No. I want them to meet you. I want you to meet them. I think it's important to both of us. And I need to make this right with you."

It *was* important to her, and she wanted to make it right too. That she couldn't deny. Hope had been blooming in her chest since his text message had come in yesterday. She'd tried to see the situation with his family from his perspective, although it didn't make sense to her. But maybe she was missing something. Maybe it was harder for him than she'd assumed. Maybe seeing his world would unlock something.

"Okay, I'll come." She sighed. Was this really the best thing to do? "Anyway, I've wanted to see those cool temples you're always bragging about."

She heard a noise in the background that sounded like a thud. Had he just jumped up and down? "Yes. Perfect. We'll go. We'll do it all."

Rishi sounded so excited. But was she being beyond hopeful? Was she so lovesick that it was making her crazy? After all, he'd lied to her. Could they reconcile their differences? Could he finally stand up to his parents?

As Emma hung up the phone, she had to wonder if Rishi's "all of it" included shattering his parents' dreams forever.

{ /** *. // }

Emma sat on the eight-hour bus ride to Madurai, traveling through city traffic jams; through small towns where cows, goats, and turkeys braved crossing the road; and along highways that were coated in shiny black asphalt, where the bus driver drove much too fast for comfort, zooming past the countryside. In the distance, women wearing bright saris were colorfully sprinkled throughout the rice fields, like the surprise of confetti across the green landscape.

What was going to happen when she got to Madurai? They'd talk, Rishi would apologize, and then . . . ? And what were his intentions? Was he just postponing the inevitable? Or did he think he and Emma would get married?

A small panic lit Emma's skin on fire. But if she was being honest with herself, it wasn't like she hadn't thought about a future with him. She'd envisioned what their children would look like. She'd imagined how they could work together. Whether they'd live in Seattle or Bangalore. It wasn't like you could date someone endlessly when you had two different passports.

But what did she want?

She'd always imagined that her husband's family would be her new family. Really, that had been the best part of being with Jeremy. Christmases and Thanksgivings with a bunch of people who treated her like she was one of them. And was that possible with Rishi's family?

Something inside her said, *I hope so.*

When she arrived, Emma stood with her bag outside the station, looking for Rishi. Around her, hundreds of people shouted and moved about in such a tightly packed area that from above, the whole scene must have looked like cells dancing around in the small hole of a microscope.

The old Emma would have stayed put. Insisted that he come back to Bangalore so they could talk it out. And now she was alone, where no one was speaking English, and the idea of even finding Rishi seemed impossible.

A hand on her shoulder made her jump. She whipped around.

Rishi.

Just seeing the tentative smile on his face made her entire body melt. All of her relaxed. She wanted to collapse onto him, hold his chest to hers, and sink her head into his shoulder. But no. They hadn't talked. It wasn't right. Yet.

"I'm so glad to see you," he said, grabbing her bag.

"Sure," she said, a tight smile hiding all the emotions sifting through her mind.

"I booked you a room at a hotel nearby. Let's go there and talk, and then we can go to my parents' house. If that's okay?" His eyes searched hers.

"That's fine." She wasn't quite ready to let go of everything she'd been holding in.

They left the train station and made their way toward the hotel. Emma glanced around; to the left was a giant temple, a rainbow of carvings stretching toward the sky.

Her head swung around. To the right was another temple, colorful and just as tall, set farther in the distance. The buildings were all so low, and these colossal monuments to God were the only thing you could even pay attention to.

"These temples are incredible," she said.

"I know, they're huge. The amount of time and effort and money people put into them is also incredible. I'm just so glad you came, Emma. I wanted you to see where I'm from."

"Thanks for taking care of it. The hotel, the ticket." Emma felt so formal with him all of a sudden, her body tense. They needed to talk this out, and soon.

"Are you kidding? It's the least I can do. I was so afraid I'd lost you."

Rishi reached out and squeezed her hand, and with that small contact, Emma felt the formality evaporate from her body, warmth replacing the cold that had filled her bones the past week. She squeezed his hand back.

Rishi got the key, and they took the elevator up to their room. She'd felt so nervous with him, that first time in the hotel elevator in Cochin, as the tension mounted between their bodies. Heat generated from so much anticipation, so much longing. The zig and zag of nerve endings volleying in her body. And now that nervousness was back. Different, but back.

He smiled at her. "Do you want me to order some coffee for us?"

"That sounds good." They walked to the door. Each step Emma took was heavy and thick. The room. Their talk. Their future.

Rishi unlocked the door. The room was simple and clean, with two queen beds. He dialed room service and ordered coffee. Emma sat on one bed and Rishi sat on the opposite bed, facing her.

"Okay, coffee ordered. Step one." He put his hands on his knees, and a shiver seemed to coast up his body. "God, I'm just so nervous, it's crazy." He shook his head.

"Me too," Emma said, relieved it wasn't just her. "Why? Why are we nervous?" She punctuated it with a nervous little laugh, as if to say, *See?*

"I know why I'm nervous. I have some explaining to do, and I'm afraid you won't forgive me, and I'll pine over you for the rest of my life."

Pining for the rest of his life? Over her? Emma wanted to smile but reined it in. "Why don't you just start from the top, before we were yelling at each other, and explain what happened."

"I guess it started when I came back here after Cochin, to tell my parents to stop looking for someone. But they thought that since I was visiting, it was an opportune time to invite Radhika's family over. I told my mom no, but then she had heart palpitations and had to go lie down. So I didn't push it. I was really afraid what would happen to her."

"So, then they came over, and you met her parents?" Emma asked.

"Yes, they came over for a few hours and had tea. I wanted to do something, offend them or show that I wasn't a good fit for their daughter, but then my mom would just look at me, and I'd feel bad and answer their questions. She's always had these blood pressure problems, and recently they've worsened, but now she's on some medicine that seems to have helped it." He shook his head. "Anyway, I still told them I wasn't interested. My mother somehow thought that I was just nervous or something. And when she got a green light from the astrologer, she went ahead and planned the engagement, without asking me."

"And that's all that happened?"

"Yes. Then, when they called me at your house and dropped this bomb on me, I was going to ask you for help. I wanted you to help me plan how to stop it for good, but then we just got into a fight. And now, they're all pissed off at me. Well, except Dharini. She's okay with it."

A shard of hurt bit at Emma's chest. He was going to ask her for help, but then she'd just yelled at him.

There was a knock at the door, and Rishi went to get the coffee from room service. She watched him, marveling at how familiar his movements had become over the past months, how familiar all of him had become. She should have known he wouldn't just get married so suddenly.

Rishi brought her a cup of coffee, and she took a sip. God help her, she'd even started to crave the sugary-sweet South Indian coffee.

Emma was speechless. If that had been too much for his parents, then what would she be to them?

"When my brother, Sudhar, got married, and my parents weren't happy about it, he had this idea of how to bring the family together, to sort of make it up to them. His wife's uncle had found this guaranteed investment, and my dad gave him most of his savings. But it was actually bad, and my parents lost . . ." He swallowed and looked at the ceiling.

"What is it?"

"All of their money. This is why I was scared to tell you. Most women would have an issue with it."

"I hope you know that I don't care about the money thing. But I do care about what I'm walking into. After all this, how are your parents going to react to me?"

"We'll take it slow. I'll introduce you as my colleague, which is not a lie, by the way. And they'll learn to love you."

Emma fell back on the bed and moaned, still clutching her coffee. This was his plan?

He moved over to her bed and stretched out beside her. "I know it's a lot."

"Uh, yeah, you think? They're going to hate me. No matter what. I'm like the slayer of weddings. The destroyer of dreams." But as she looked into his eyes, the ones she'd missed waking up to for days, she knew there was no way she wouldn't try.

"They just need time. You're a wild card, but I happen to love drawing the wild card from the deck." He kissed her nose. "I've also been thinking about how to get my family all in a room, like you suggested months ago. I think we need to all just talk it out, and that should help. With everything."

"Okay," she said, but it was more like a question. There were a lot of wild cards involved.

"I'm sorry I put you through all this crap because I couldn't stand up to my parents."

"I'm sorry too, Rishi," she said. "For jumping to conclusions. You had this list that I didn't fit. I don't have family. I'm not from your culture. I just assumed the worst."

"We're a team. The best team I can imagine. Will you help me reunite my family?"

She nodded. How could she not?

He cupped her face and drew her close, sinking his lips onto hers. Emma felt it in her body, twisting at her toes, coasting warmth up through her thighs, tickling her abdomen until her arms needed to hold him. She fumbled with her coffee cup as she tried to feel for the table and then heard it fall on the floor. But she didn't care. It all felt so absolutely right.

Well, except for one thing. Or maybe a few things. Actually, it could have been many things.

CHAPTER 39

They caught an auto to take them to Rishi's parents' house.

What was Emma getting herself into? "Do I need to do anything special or different?"

"No. Just be normal," Rishi said.

Emma held on to his hand and squeezed. Normal. Normal. Normal. What was normal? Work Emma normal? Girlfriend Emma normal? Emma living in India and having no cultural context for what to do normal? She was probably overthinking things. Maybe it would be fine, and they'd be so freaked out about everything else that they wouldn't even notice her.

But she did want them to notice her, right? She wanted to charm them so they'd forget about the ideal fiancée and would be pleased to have a woman like Emma in their lives.

Right.

They drove down a highway lined with small shops, people selling vegetables along the side of the road or grinding sugarcane for juice. The road was dotted with small markets and the occasional cow or goat munching on the dry grass. After some instructions from Rishi, the driver turned off the main road into a neighborhood. All the buildings were various shades of yellow or beige, with small balconies and busy neighbors outside chatting, hanging up laundry to dry, or tending to their gardens.

They pulled in front of one of these homes. A small woman, her graying hair tied in a thin braid, stepped outside.

A man Emma assumed was Rishi's father appeared on the porch, wearing a button-down and a white sarong. He was thin, with thick salt-and-pepper hair that stood atop his head. A young woman peeked out from inside. It was like they were all waiting to see what he was bringing home. Well, so much for not being noticed. Already she felt like a wild specimen ready to be studied under a microscope.

Emma stepped out of the auto and stood on the sidewalk, silent. Panic flooded her senses. What should she do? What would she say? She hadn't thought about this scenario. She needed more time. Like a course on How to Behave in Front of Your Indian Boyfriend's Parents 101. Or at least the CliffsNotes version.

His parents' faces were twisted up, their eyes narrowed. His sister looked like she was about to burst with laughter. All of them were staring at her.

"Come on, colleague," Rishi said, nodding toward the house.

Could he not see that his family was less than pleased to see her? She swallowed hard.

Rishi met his parents' eyes and gestured toward Emma. "This is my friend Emma. We work together at TechLogic."

"Nice to meet you," Emma said with a smile, trying to hide her surprise at the crumbling corners of the house and his family's stony, unchanged expressions.

But then his mother spoke in a shaky voice. "Hello."

"Welcome," his father said, and they turned to go in.

At least that was something. Emma followed Rishi, mimicking the way he shook the shoes off his feet and left them on the porch.

"I'm Dharini." His sister held out her hand to formally shake it, and Emma took it.

"Nice to meet you, Dharini. I've heard a lot about you."

"Me too," she said quietly, like they were coconspirators.

As they walked inside, Emma paused at the doorway.

The front room was small, with a concrete floor. Small ceramic figurines and stuffed animals sat in a glassed curio cabinet. Plastic-wrapped posters depicting gods hung from every wall in the room, beads and garlands of plastic flowers cascading from the corners of the pictures.

Emma sat on the sofa, the springs trying to reach up through the cushions, while Rishi and his family volleyed some kind of tense conversation back and forth in Tamil, but it was quiet and restrained, like a wild horse with some reins on it.

His mother handed Rishi a cup of coffee in a tiny steel cup with a deep steel saucer under it. She handed Emma a small ceramic coffee cup, briefly making eye contact before whisking her eyes away quickly. Maybe Emma had smiled a little too much. Rishi poured the coffee back and forth in between the saucer and the cup. After he had mixed it, he held the steel cup by the rim with his fingertips and poured it into his mouth without allowing the cup to touch his lips.

Emma remembered Rishi saying that in his family, they didn't touch their mouths to anything when they drank and didn't take bites out of anything; they instead broke off pieces to eat. They didn't use silverware, either, and washed their plates outside the house. Saliva had some kind of unclean quality, and Emma had wondered on more than one occasion how these rules applied to kissing.

She held the rich coffee-and-milk mixture in her hand, curious why she'd gotten a different cup, the saucer chipped in two places, when everyone else got shiny steel cups like in the restaurants.

If Rishi wasn't marrying Radhika and his father was out of work, would that mean that Rishi would keep supporting them? She remembered Preeti saying something once about how many parents moved in with their children once they were married. Would that happen to Rishi?

The woman in front of her who couldn't even look her in the eye—would she want to share a house with Emma if she and Rishi got serious?

And would Emma want to share a house with her? Could she be the mother Emma had always imagined?

She swallowed and tried to smile at everyone perched on the various chairs in the room. They stopped talking, and all of a sudden the room fell strangely quiet. No horns or traffic noise outside, only the chirping of the birds. It was perhaps the first time Emma had been surrounded by quiet since she'd moved to India. But rather than being peaceful, it was more like the greenish cloudy sky and wispy eeriness that she'd witnessed as a teenager right before a tornado had swept through a nearby town.

"You work with Rishi, is it?" his father asked.

"Yes, sir." Emma tried to be on her best behavior, unsure what to say or how to say it. Now she felt like her prom date who'd had to stare at the shotgun over her grandmother's head as she grilled him. *Oh, karma, how you mock me.*

"You have business in Madurai?" he asked.

Emma opened her mouth and gave Rishi a sideways glance. What should she say?

"Emma was here to see the temples and remembered that I was home and called," Rishi jumped in.

His father nodded. "Ah, I see." But the way he'd said it made Emma think he saw the truth, and not the feeble excuse of temple touring.

His father looked back and forth between Emma and Rishi. Emma swallowed hard and looked at her phone. Maybe she should leave. The last thing she wanted to do was cause another argument between Rishi and his parents.

His mother brought out a tray of snacks, crunchy bits of fried lentils and peanuts. A plateful of round laddoos and sliced burfi, rich with cashews and saffron and cardamom. The spicy aroma wafted toward her.

Emma practically drooled at the display on the table in front of her. His mother glanced at Emma, obviously not sure what to make of her. She said something to Rishi in Tamil. His father jumped in, the three of them whispering together, shooting a few looks her way. She didn't know what else to do but smile. If only she'd tried to study their language instead of Hindi . . .

Evidently satisfied with whatever the conversation had been about, his mother left the room. His father gestured to the bowl on the table. "Please, have some."

She pulled out her phone to take a photo first.

"What are you doing?" his dad asked.

"Oh, I just take pictures of all my food."

He laughed like she was a crazy person. "Really?"

"Do you post them on Instagram?" his sister asked.

"I do."

"Okay, I'm going to follow you."

"Oh, thank you." She smiled at his sister. Maybe she and Rishi did have an ally in the family.

Rishi disappeared into the kitchen and then came back out. "I told my mom that you would stay for dinner."

"Is that all right?" she asked, looking at Rishi and his father.

"You're our guest." More like a declaration than an invitation. His father got up and walked into the back of the house.

Emma's eyes followed him. Was he trying to escape her?

"Want to see the neighborhood?" Rishi asked.

"Sure."

"Let's go on a walk." Rishi jogged off to the front porch, and she followed. He tapped his shoes together and held them upside down.

"What are you doing?" Emma asked,

"Checking for scorpions."

Rishi might have been checking for scorpions, but Emma had the feeling she might have already been stung.

CHAPTER 40

There was nothing like a home-cooked meal. Even though his parents were borderline raging at him, they couldn't deny him food. And Emma's presence had diffused the situation. They couldn't continue arguing with him in front of a guest.

Emma clutched her stomach as they pushed away from the dining table. "I never thought I could eat that many dosas. But they were so good. Thank you so much, auntie!" Emma shouted toward the kitchen door.

Rishi called to his mother, who was still cooking her own food. "Ma, Emma loves your food. She says you're an amazing cook."

His mother mumbled something about how her cooking wasn't that good, but he could hear self-satisfied laughter. She'd never had her food photographed or had strangers fawn over it. Maybe in time it would all be fine. He'd ease Emma into their lives, and they'd see she wasn't so different from a traditional pick they would have normally selected. Especially over food. If anything could make his mom happy, it was being complimented on her food.

"Well, I guess it's getting late. I'll take you back to your hotel." They walked outside, and Rishi started his father's scooter up. It wheezed to life, nothing like his bike in Bangalore.

"It was nice eating with your family. I haven't done that in so long. And the food was amazing!" Emma climbed on the back behind him.

"I can tell my mom is happy you think so. It's not often she gets to cook for a foreigner who takes photos of her meals." She laughed and he started down the road, and the night air whipped around them, cool and musky. Emma's arms wrapped around him, and her head rested on his shoulder. He couldn't wait until they were back in Bangalore and could reclaim their life together.

When they reached her hotel, he asked, "Hey, do you have your return travel booked yet? I was thinking we could take the train that leaves tomorrow night at seven—it's an overnight train."

"Let's do it. Maybe I can see the temples tomorrow. Then I won't be a total liar." Emma jabbed him in the side with her elbow.

After they'd said goodbye, Rishi pushed his father's scooter motor hard to get home. Eventually, *eventually*, his parents would get to know her and understand why she was the woman for him.

He walked in the door to find his parents cornering Dharini, who was sitting on the daybed, frozen stiff. They wheeled around when he entered, fire in their eyes.

"What's going on with you and this Emma girl?" his mother asked.

And so began the Emma Inquisition.

"Is she why you broke off your engagement?" his mother went on. "She is why we're in this situation!" She threw her hands up, gesturing toward the ceiling, the walls, he didn't know.

Rishi had to clear all of this up. There was no way his parents could think badly about Emma. "This has nothing to do with her. The match with Radhika was a mistake. You need to know that. Things have changed. I want who I want. Dharini is okay with it."

"Dharini is a child. She doesn't know how the world works," his father said.

Dharini made a squeak of protest.

"How could you do this to us?" His mother looked at him and started crying.

Rishi had had enough. Enough of his parents forcing his guilt. Enough of this crying for no reason. "Ma! I'm not doing anything to you. This is what I'm telling you. Besides, you would like Emma. She's brilliant and kind. She loves your food. She's everything you would want in a daughter-in-law." The words had fallen out of Rishi's mouth before he could grab them and shove each one back in.

It was way, way too early for that. He closed his eyes, soaking in the depth of what he'd just said. He'd resolved to be more truthful and not protect his family, so what could he say now? That they didn't need to worry about her as a daughter-in-law? He couldn't, because maybe they would.

"I told you," his mother said, pointing at his father. "You said there was nothing, but I could tell. You said she's a colleague only."

Maybe it was too soon to have invited her home. But what was done was done.

"Look, I hadn't planned for all this to happen this weekend. You would like her, too, if you gave her a chance. If you saw past tradition and religion and looked at her for the person she is."

"She can't be my daughter!" his mother cried out, burying her face in her hands. "Dharini will go to some other family, and Sona is no daughter to me. We'll be alone and poor with no one to take care of us."

"Mom, how could you think that?" Sometimes his mother jumped from A to Z instead of A to B.

"Listen, we need to think about Rishi's happiness," his sister said. "Isn't this all because of me? And what Sudhar did? Don't punish Rishi."

Their parents stared at her like she'd officially gone crazy.

"Thank you, Dharini. You're right. She might be from a different place and a different culture, but you should look at this as an opportunity to learn from her. You can learn new traditions. And make new rituals. So can she. She can learn our ways too."

"I've seen exactly what someone from outside our culture does to my sons. I don't need to see it again. I won't!" His mother shook her head and walked out to the porch. His dad followed. Rishi could hear his father's whispered consolation through the open door in between his mother's sobs.

He got up to follow them, but his sister pulled at his arm. "You need to give them time."

One thing that his mother needed to see was that Sona was not a source of evil. That her family had been affected, too, by her uncle. Yes, it had been a big mistake to trust him, but his parents couldn't keep living without Sudhar in their lives. They needed to see that while one bad thing had happened, Sudhar was living a good life; he was happy and had a baby. Surely this had to help them all.

And if Rishi was going to stop covering up reality for his parents, they needed to embrace reality too. And that meant finally bringing the family together.

CHAPTER 41

One week. Emma had been back in the office a week. And had tried to get her mind back into work mode, a mode that wasn't coming easily. Even though they'd launched the first iteration of the app for pilot testing, and it had been really successful, nothing seemed that exciting, not even the app with all the cool features she'd been advocating for—a game, hidden Easter eggs, the works.

How could anything be exciting when she felt like she was destroying Rishi's relationship with his family?

Preeti stood in the conference room they were using to test the code, the door open, her face in a faint blue glow from the computer monitors.

"Emma!" Preeti shouted when she saw her, and she waved her over. "I've been waiting to get you alone. You'll never believe it!"

"What? What is it?" Emma hurried inside the conference room.

A shy smile danced across Preeti's lips. She looked around and leaned toward Emma, grabbing onto her arm. "I found someone. I'm engaged."

"Congratulations!" Emma hugged her friend and couldn't help but think that, thank God, Preeti would finally get to kiss a boy. "Tell me about him."

"He lives in Bangalore, and he's also a programmer. But he's very nice and very smart."

"And handsome?" Emma said with a wink.

"Yes, and *also* good looking." Preeti gave her a sly grin. "I hope you'll come to our engagement ceremony. It's in a few weeks."

Now there was an engagement ceremony she could get on board with. "I would be honored!" Emma headed toward her desk and was on the verge of tears. Happiness for her friend mixed with her thoughts about Rishi.

If Rishi and Emma were together, would he constantly miss his family? Would he always wish he'd had a traditional marriage? He hadn't spoken to his parents since they'd been back in Bangalore.

Back in her office, Emma tried to focus on her work, but the code on the screen turned and swirled around like constellations dancing in the night sky. She'd start down one path of code, and her thoughts would migrate from work to Rishi. Distracted again and again.

Her feelings were half fit together, and the rest a mess. Rishi. Love. Marriage. His parents.

Life without Rishi. Rishi's life without his parents. She didn't want a life without him.

Her head sagged in her hands over the keyboard. She wasn't getting anything done. The twisting, sick feeling inside her overtook all thought, consumed her with its weighty pull.

An idea jutted its way through the mess of emotions. If his parents were that worried about Dharini getting married and being able to find the perfect husband, then maybe Emma could help. She had a perfect algorithm that could find a man who matched not only Dharini's criteria, but also his parents'. And it could find someone who not only was perfect but wouldn't judge the family by an older brother's mistake or by whomever Rishi might marry.

She just needed to plot with Rishi to find out what to include, and they could have some potential matches custom made for his sister.

Surely that would show his parents that she could help their family and wasn't completely foreign to their traditions just because she was a foreigner.

She rushed over to Rishi's desk and tapped him on the shoulder. He spun around, a curious look on his face. "Yes?"

"I have an idea," she said.

"Okay, about . . . ?"

"I'm going to revamp the marriage code. But this time for Dharini. I feel like it could help your parents, you know, like me." Maybe that was a stretch this early on. "Or maybe, at least tolerate me?"

Like a light had switched on behind Rishi's eyes, they seemed to glow. "Hey, that's not a bad idea. It could help lessen the stress of finding someone for Dharini."

"That's what I was thinking. We'll just address each roadblock as it pops up." She got out her notebook. "Okay, I need some information from you, and Dharini, of course. I know we'll use the same cultural attributes as yours, but her guy will also have to love animals, from what you've told me. And be open minded. What did you say before? Traditional yet modern?"

He shook his head and got out his phone, searching for Dharini's name. "Who knows what my little sister wants. We can call her."

"Great. Let's do it." Emma was ready to do anything to get into his parents' good graces. Or at least out of their bad ones.

"When the web crawl is done, what do you think about another weekend visit to Madurai?"

Emma stared into space, considering. It meant another weekend of his parents staring at her suspiciously, making her feel like an evil temptress from some alien planet. And every word they spoke in Tamil seemed like it was about her. But that's what she'd signed up for, wasn't it? "I guess that's the only way this is going to work."

"I just want them to see how hardworking you are and how you've done all this just for them. To show them you care about their happiness, and Dharini's."

"You think the marriage code 2.0 is going to do that?"

"I have a few other ideas as well. Consider this phase one. We have a little more prepping to do."

CHAPTER 42

Rishi knocked on the door of his family home for the second time in a month. His mother couldn't say that Emma wasn't bringing them together more often, at least. Dharini answered the door, and even though it was almost eleven, he could tell she'd just woken up by that half-lidded, cloudy gaze he knew so well.

"Haven't had your coffee yet, sis?" He patted her on the head. It was so easy to do when she was so much shorter. But she'd always be his little sister, even if he was finding her a husband.

She shook her head, an annoyed look on her face. The smell drifting out from inside the house, cumin and chili and turmeric, wafted toward Rishi; his stomach growled. He'd only eaten a few idlis this morning, saving space in his stomach for his mom's cooking.

Dharini peeked around him and said hello to Emma, who was at the far end of the patio, as if she were afraid a tiger was going to leap out of the room and get her. If the situation weren't so serious, he'd laugh that Emma was intimidated by his parents, while he was certain his parents were terrified of her.

Emma smiled and waved at his sister.

His mother came into the hall. "Hello, Rishi." Well, at least his name was still allowed to be spoken in the house. The first time he'd texted to say he and Emma would be coming this weekend, she hadn't replied. Then he'd called her, strategically arranging with Dharini beforehand to make sure his mother actually picked up the phone. They couldn't refuse a guest. They couldn't refuse their son.

Yet, at least.

"Hi, Amma." He bent down and touched her feet, showing the respect he still had for her. Showing that her rituals were not dead.

"Emma, she's not going to bite you," he whispered. "Come on." He waved for her to join him. She came to his mom as well and bent down on the floor, following Rishi's gestures. His mother stood shell shocked, her mouth open, looking from Rishi to Dharini and then back to Emma. Because she had to, she uttered a blessing in Emma's direction. He tried not to smile. His plan was coming together perfectly. Well, so far.

His mom turned around and walked toward the kitchen. "See, it's working!" Dharini whispered.

Emma's eyes were wide in question as she looked at his sister. Even though Rishi had explained how they showed respect to their elders and answered Emma's hundred questions about the custom, even practiced it, pretending her sofa was his parents, he could tell she was still overwhelmed.

"Relax." He squeezed her hand. "It's going to be fine."

"I hope so. Otherwise . . ." She swallowed and released his hand as his mother came out of the kitchen. What was the "otherwise"? He didn't have a chance to ask her because his mother was coming toward them with a tray of four coffees.

She set them on the table in the middle of the room. "Your father is out at the store."

They all sat down and drank their coffee, staring at one another in silence. Rishi, stunned that his mother hadn't yet pulled him aside and reprimanded him. Dharini, silently giggling to herself about what she was witnessing. His mother, confused at what to do about this foreign girl who was acting like Rishi's cousin or, dare he say, like a potential bride.

"The coffee is delicious," Emma said in Tamil. The handful of words that Rishi had taught her. *Kaapi romba nalla irruka.* And "The food tastes good." *Saapad romba nalla irruka.*

Even though she'd only learned a total of five words in his native tongue, his mother faltered with her coffee, looking at Emma like she was some kind of creature. A polite creature, but strange nonetheless. His mother's glance volleyed back to Rishi like he was the Dr. Frankenstein who'd created her.

"See, Ma, she's learning Tamil."

"And she found me those matches," Dharini added.

His mother had never been stunned speechless like this before. He hoped this wasn't the moment before she clutched her chest and fell on the floor. Or reached for a bottle of aspirin. Or said a prayer before passing out.

"Ma, say something." Rishi shook his head at her.

She blinked more than a few times, like she was considering what to say. She didn't look at Emma, but to Rishi she said, "It's very nice."

He didn't want to ask what "it" was, for fear that she was referring to Emma, but probably it was the searching or the learning Tamil or the showing of respect. Maybe all three. Rishi smiled at Emma to let her know everything was okay, and she took a sip of her coffee, the look of worry fading from her face.

"So, how did the matches turn out?" he asked Dharini.

"One is very good. Another also good." She tilted her head in approval, a knowing smile on her face. "One boy, Rohin, his family has a golden retriever."

"Nice. So you found a dog lover."

"The other one says he's always wanted a dog."

"Either way, it looks like a puppy could be in your future," Emma said.

"Yes, thank you. I can't imagine two better guys."

"I'm hurt. Deeply," Rishi said, his hand over his heart.

"You are the best guy. I'm sure Emma agrees."

"Emma agrees with what?" His father's voice came from the door.

They all turned to look at the same time. "Emma agrees that Rishi is a good guy, Appa," Dharini said, staying strong. He was proud of his sister. Those years he'd been forced to help change her diapers were all worth it today.

"Everyone is sitting around having coffee together?" His dad studied the scene, his eyes settling on his mother, obviously wanting an explanation.

"They came, Emma showed her respect, is speaking Tamil . . ." His mother stood and threw up her arms, like she was helpless in the face of so much respect. She walked into the kitchen, muttering to herself.

Rishi's father eyed him with a look that Rishi could only shoot back at him. In Tamil, Rishi said, "Emma's here to talk with you. So you can get to know her. She found the matches for Dharini. It's important you know that she's supportive of our cultures and traditions."

His father exhaled through his nose and, likely remembering Emma was still a guest, nodded toward her. "Hello, Emma."

"Hi, uncle."

"Excuse me." His dad walked into the kitchen, and Rishi followed him.

"Mom, Dad, there's something you need to understand." Both looked at him. "Emma is here because she wants to get to know you. She found matches for Dharini because she cares about this family. We knew there would be some good families with a modern outlook who would understand what happened with Sudhar was not our fault, so we found them. I want her in my life, and more importantly, she wants you in her life too. She doesn't have parents, and it's important that you are kind to her."

His parents both studied him, their faces inscrutable. "The matches were good," his mother said, nodding.

"What happened to her parents?" his dad asked.

"Traffic accident. When she was eight."

His father made a sympathetic noise with his tongue. "So young."

"Poor thing," his mother added.

"See? This is why it is important that you are kind to her. And she is trying to be *very* kind to you."

Rishi didn't know if it was because his parents were tired of being upset or worried they'd lose another son, or if the potential matches for Dharini had placated them, but they dropped the subject. "Dharini, Emma, *saapda vaanga*!" his mother called out. Just like that. Like it was a normal lunch on a Saturday. And then they all came together to eat.

Emma searched Rishi's face, and as he handed her a plate, she whispered, "What the hell is happening?"

He smiled and shook his head. "Don't worry, you're doing great."

His mother came around as they sat at the table and dished out a mountain of rice, sambar, gently spiced and crispy cauliflower and potatoes, and his favorite eggplant sautéed to the point of melting. Emma took a photo, and his dad stared at her, but he could have sworn there was a hint of an amused smile creeping into that frown.

His mother laughed in the doorway and walked back to the kitchen to finish frying the popadams. "I'm sure she thinks it's like food paparazzi. You've elevated her food to celebrity status."

Then, as she took a bite, of course Emma moaned. "It's just so good!" she said to his dad; he looked back at her, dumbfounded, then at Rishi, who just shrugged back. Between bites, Emma leaned toward the kitchen and shouted, "Auntie, *saapad romba nalla irruku*."

His mother just laughed. She wasn't used to having her food fawned over. Maybe their family took her cooking skills for granted. "It is really good, Mom." He wanted to add, *even moan-worthy*, but that would have been pushing it.

What was important was that they weren't attacking him for bringing Emma to the house. They seemed amused by her, if anything. Maybe they thought this was all a temporary thing that would fade in the future, but for now, it was as good as he could hope for.

Now that phase one of Rishi's plan for his family to accept Emma had been put into action, it was time to start on phase two: bringing his family back together. It had been too long. Senselessly long, and for no reason.

CHAPTER 43

Emma couldn't believe that Rishi's parents had seemed okay with her. Like, actually tolerated her. She had no idea what a future would look like with them or what would happen, but at least she had eaten some good food, supported Rishi, and really, she'd enjoyed herself. Yes, it was painful not understanding 75 percent of what was said. And yes, she had to smile and act like she wasn't dying to know if they were talking about her, but walking through the town with his family and feeling part of something bigger than just herself—well, that was comforting. And something she'd missed.

And it was Rishi's something—his family, his home. Dharini was adorable and had pulled out baby photos of him at one point. It just felt so normal. So normal for them to sit around and laugh at pudgy baby Rishi and for his dad to tell stories about his childhood. Maybe her fears about not being accepted or not fitting in with his family had been completely unfounded.

It was fortunate that at work they were now in a testing phase for the app, and things had slowed down, because studying Tamil and figuring out how to cook at least one of these recipes his mom had given her were going to take some serious time.

Her phone rang. She looked down at the name. Maria? She'd pinged Emma a few times through instant messages and had forwarded her a few funny emails, but she hadn't called her in the five months she'd been here.

"Awww, did you miss me?"

"Emma, of course! How's my favorite globe-trotting programmer?" Maria's voice was from another world and flooded her with memories: late coffees in the office as they tried to solve bugs, coffees that turned into wine and then turned into Emma making fun of her crazy statement necklaces. If only she'd called her on video so she could check out what she was wearing.

"I'm good. I miss you guys!"

"Yeah? I hear the project is amazing and that the app is getting rave reviews from our testers."

"It is. I'm really excited about it, and the team has done an absolutely amazing job."

"Well, I'm sure you pushed them to excellence, as always."

Maria always knew how to make Emma happy. It was like her whole body melted into a smile at her praise. "It's been a great experience, truly." And she meant that in more ways than one, but she wasn't going to release a full, no-holds-barred disclosure of her new relationship with Rishi quite yet.

"Good! International experience always looks great on a résumé, which brings me to why I've called. Since everything's been shaken up at the company, I've accepted a new role, and I'm building a team. And I need a new director."

Maria whispered *director* like it was a bomb about to go off. Director? And just like that, it went off in Emma's head. Director equaled promotion. Leadership. Cool projects. All the things that came with being a leader at a company. All the things she and Maria had dreamed up when things got tough. Everything she'd ever wanted.

She was actually drooling. Like someone had set down a fresh, unshaven truffle in front of her instead of a job title. Her dream job with her favorite manager. She swallowed. "Oh, really?"

Maria laughed. "Yes, really. And I think you'd love it. It's in the AI group, so you don't have to go back to developing products for the sales team. It would be super fun, and you'd get to work on simultaneous translation for our cloud solutions."

"Wow." The ability to give people the gift of comprehension was almost as good as literacy. In fact, she could totally use simultaneous translation right now.

"I thought you'd be excited."

"I am! So excited. Thrilled. Ecstatic. All the words!" But Rishi? Her project? Her team? Bangalore? Her life as she knew it? "But what about the app? Could the job start when I move back in a few months?" It was seven months, but who was counting?

"I'm pretty sure I could get Jas to let you go. Sounds like everything is running smoothly, and it sounds like . . . Rishi, I think? . . . he could take it from there."

"Uh-huh . . ." How had this happened? Everything she'd ever wanted in work had just intersected with the peak of her happiness in a head-on collision. "And if I wanted to see it through?" she asked weakly, because she was pretty sure she knew the answer.

"Emma, you know how fast things move around here. We're building the team in the next month, so I would definitely need you back here by then." She paused. "Am I missing something? I thought this would be an automatic yes from you. It's everything we've talked about."

"I know. It is." Although she didn't sound like herself, and Maria knew it. She normally would have been thrilled, but things in Bangalore had taken a very unexpected turn. "I just love this project, you know? I don't want the team to think I'm abandoning them. Let me think about it. When do you need to know?"

"Probably in the next two weeks? If you're not interested, I'll need to post the job and find someone else."

Could she really give up an opportunity like this? "Okay, sounds good. I'll let you know. I really appreciate it."

They said their goodbyes. One month. Only one more month with Rishi. One more month in Bangalore. There were many things they hadn't done. And she'd just started making headway with his parents. They didn't hate her anymore. She tried to envision her life without him back in Seattle. A little hollow formed in her chest at just the thought. Was it a life she would want to live?

But on the other hand, she wondered what would happen in the seven months she was here. Whether his parents would ever accept her, or whether she and Rishi would be reliving the same series of events over and over.

CHAPTER 44

Emma opened her door, and Rishi presented her with the gift in his hand. "Okay, so it's not potato-artisan-cheddar-whatever pizza you said you liked in Seattle, but a friend of mine said this was the best pizza in town." He hoped it tasted as good as it smelled.

"Thanks. That was sweet of you. And I splurged on the one hundred percent taxed imported wine." She held up a bottle, rolling her eyes. "You know, back in the US this costs half of what I paid for it here. I don't miss many things, but finding wine that is not ridiculously priced is definitely one of them . . ." Her eyes took on a far-off look. She must have really missed the wine. What else did she miss?

An idea lit up in his brain. "Maybe we can take a trip to Singapore or something next month? Or Thailand? Go through duty-free, and you can get two bottles per person. That will help, right? Four bottles of wine. We'll just savor what we get and take a short international trip once in a while." He wanted her to love Bangalore as much as he did. Not that they had to live here forever, but . . .

"Like an international trip every month to keep up with my wine drinking?" She laughed. "That would be fun." Her hand ran through his hair, and she smiled into his eyes. But something was different. Was there some sadness in there? Melancholy? What was going on?

Maybe this was the time when he should have been asking her the other thing on his mind. Was this crazy? They were still basically hiding their relationship at work. "There's something else I wanted to ask you about."

"What is it?"

"Well, we spend so much time together; I'm practically staying here every night . . . what do you think about moving in together?"

"Really? Are you ready for that?" Her eyes welled up, and tears shimmered on the surface.

Hopefully those were tears of joy and not terror. "Yes. If you are."

"But what about your parents?"

"We don't have to tell them." Like he was going to tell his parents he was living in sin? That would not get Emma on their good list.

She leaned her head against his chest with a groan. "Oh, Rishi." She sniffed and shook against him. Okay, definitely not tears of joy. And not the response he had been hoping for.

"Uh . . . I mean, we don't have to. It just seemed more practical, and we could test out how things are—"

Her voice muffled in his shirt. "It's not that. My old boss called me today. She's got this amazing opportunity for me. I don't even have to apply for it. She's just handing it to me."

Rishi could already sense where this was going. "Let me guess. She wants you to move back to the States."

Her hair bobbed up and down on his chest as she nodded. He clutched her tightly, feeling like he'd just been hit by a car. At some point they'd have to make an India versus US decision, but when that time came, months from now, they'd figure out what their future would look like. Although Rishi already thought he knew what their future looked like. It was him and Emma. Somewhere. That's why he had been pushing her on his family. That's why they were making all this effort. "So, what are you going to do?"

"I just don't know. It's everything I've ever wanted. A promotion. I'd be a director."

He closed his mouth because the words that wanted to come out were, *You can't leave. Don't go. You can't take it. Stay here.* But her ambition and passion were what had attracted him to her; could he ask her to pass that up? "But do you *have* to go back? Could you take the new job and stay here?"

She shook her head. "I'd have to go back. In a month."

"But what about us?"

She joined him on the sofa, where he'd slunk down to think this through. "Of course I'm thinking about us; that's why I told her I needed time to think about it. I wanted to talk to you, but I'm still not any closer to my answer. It may sound ridiculous, but I don't have any real support network, you know? Like, what if I lost my job? I'd be screwed. I'd have to sleep on a friend's couch. Whereas you have a home and family to return to. I always promised myself, and vowed to my grandmother, that I would do whatever I could to get ahead. So I wouldn't have to live like I used to." She shook, like a little shiver had crawled over her.

"But you have me."

"Okay, true, but I can't stay here forever, and you can't just come to the US whenever you want. I don't know if I'll get another opportunity like this after the app is done. What am I going to work on next? They're phasing out of desktop development, and you know I am not an app developer. I don't think you have to worry because you're here, in high demand. But me? I don't know . . ."

"You're in high demand too. Hell, they basically imported you to lead this project."

"That was all Maria. And now she's moved on." She threw up her hands and sighed. "At first I thought I could take it, and we could do long distance, but then the reality of that just seemed impossible. And how would you get a job in the US? You already tried to do that."

"Yeah, not that easy to just move there." Unless they were married. Rishi wasn't even going to broach the topic. Emma wasn't yet comfortable enough with his parents, and that was an important first step.

"Then I thought maybe it would be easier for you. If I just leave. Then you wouldn't have all this family drama to worry about." She rubbed at her eyes.

He turned to her with all the force he could muster. "Emma, don't ever think that. Any drama that happens, it's fine. It's you who I care about. Besides, it was definitely time for me to have that talk with my parents." He took her hands. "I don't want to keep you from your dreams, but I would be destroyed if you left. I love you, and if there is any doubt in your head about how I feel, I want you to know that."

She looked up at him, suddenly so fragile looking in the dim light, like one of those porcelain statues his mom had locked up in the curio cabinet. "I love you too." She kissed him delicately, her eyes open, and something about that kiss was filled with wonder and sadness and joy, all at the same time.

He wanted to give her a life that she was happy with. He'd do whatever he could so that she wouldn't leave. "I promise we can take a trip, and I'll get you some wine. Fancy imported shit. Whatever you need to feel at home here."

She laughed through her sniffles. That was a good sign, wasn't it?

"Maybe next month?" That's probably when he would have enough money for it. "My brother is coming to Bangalore in a few weeks, so after that."

"Really? Your brother?" She squinted at him. "So is this just a casual 'let's get our brotherly love back on track' kind of visit, or something else?"

"Well, you know we've been talking, but I want to get the family back together like you suggested. It's something I've been chatting with him and Sona about. I'm going to invite my parents, too, and show them that we're all just people who care about one another and that their wedding wasn't a total disaster. I'm convinced that once my mom sees her grandchild, all anger will be forgotten."

"So that's your plan? All pinned on a niece you haven't met?"

"Yeah, but she's really cute. Everyone likes cute babies."

"Uh-huh." Emma eyed him suspiciously and laughed.

"She looks like me, you know?"

"Yeah, you already said she was cute." Her elbow jutted into his side.

If only that would be enough to keep her from taking the promotion and leaving him. It wasn't as if he could ask her to stay. It was a great offer, and it would be selfish to keep her from pursuing an amazing career opportunity like this one.

"Well, I'm hoping she's cute enough that my mom will at least allow Sudhar's name to be spoken in the house again. It might take time, but . . ." He swallowed up what he really wanted to say.

Hopefully it wouldn't take longer than it would take for Emma to decide to stay here and give them all a chance.

They'd allowed Emma in the house after they'd found out how Rishi felt about her. They'd acknowledged her presence, even if his mom still pestered him about marriage. His parents just needed to see that even through adversity, Sudhar, Sona, and Sejal were happy. Was he trying to convince Emma or himself?

CHAPTER 45

This plan seemed crazy to her, but Rishi was a little crazy himself, and his family was like a book whose pages she'd only thumbed through. There was a lot more to learn. No matter how many newspapers she scanned, no matter how many times Rishi had regaled her with stories about their customs, his family life still felt like the kind of experience you had to live through to understand. And she'd only been living a sliver of it.

In the auto on the way to Rishi's, the driver's eyes flashed in the rearview mirror a few times as they drove through the packed, winding streets, Emma's dupatta stretched over her mouth as if it could keep the particles of dust and exhaust from entering her lungs. She was used to the stares now, the curious eyes. Jordana had sent her a small tub of Manic Panic, and her purple strand was freshly violet. She'd even dyed another strand on the left side of her head, which she never did. Maybe she should have waited until after meeting Rishi's parents again. Oh well, too late now!

"Left, *maadi*," she said at the intersection, using what little of the local language she knew. Auto Kannada, as Preeti had called it. The driver's eyes filled the mirror again, but this time it was a mix of surprise and amusement she saw in them.

"Local, ah?" he asked.

"I live here."

He made a little grunting noise. Well, maybe if she could fool him, she could play the part for Rishi's parents too.

Because, depending on how today played out, she might get the answers she needed. She needed to respond to Maria's request soon. She'd already sent her one reminder email, asking if she'd made up her mind. Something inside her questioned why she hadn't answered her yet. And why she hadn't told Rishi they could move in together.

She jumped out of the auto and took a breath before knocking on his door. There were voices inside. The brother and sister-in-law were there. A baby's cries filtered through the open window. Rishi's parents would be there soon as well. She knocked, and Rishi flung open the door with a big smile on his face, holding a baby.

"Emma! Meet Sejal." Rishi grinned at her like he'd never been so happy. The baby was tiny, pudgy in all the right places, a dark mark smeared on her cheek—something Rishi had said they did to block out the evil eye. And she could see why: this baby was pretty perfect. Her eyes were lit up, silver as a sizzling cloudy day, just like Rishi's.

"She has your eyes. And she's adorable." Something about seeing this baby, like a tiny Rishi, made her wonder again what their baby would look like. If they ever got that far. She sighed and smiled. Behind Rishi were two figures taking up his entire tiny kitchen. "How is everything going?" she whispered.

"Good, good. Come in." Rishi stood back, and Emma entered his apartment, which she'd only done a handful of times. Her place was closer to the office and closer to town. And twice the size of his.

She shook off her shoes at the door and walked toward the kitchen area. "Hi." She waved tentatively at Rishi's guests. She'd never met them, although she felt a sort of silent kinship with them. Outsiders from the Iyengar clan. Lovesick fools. Tradition breakers. Or perhaps self-saboteurs; she wasn't sure which. "I'm Emma."

"Emma, hi!" Rishi's brother came toward her. "It's so nice to meet you. This is my wife, Sona."

Sona took a tentative step forward, and Emma almost took a step back. The woman was stunning. Her hair shimmered, her eyes were big and brown and shone with warmth, but she seemed shy. Well, here they were, a pair of evil temptresses.

"Hi, Emma."

"So nice to meet you both!" Emma said. "I hope you had a good trip."

"Oh yes. It was long with the baby, but she slept most of the way."

As if on cue, Sejal made a cute cooing noise. Maybe Rishi was right. There was no way his parents could stay mad with a face like that thrust in front of them.

They had coffee and chatted about their jobs and travel, although there was this odd undercurrent of tension. All Emma wanted to do was ask them if they were worried, or what their plan was when Rishi's parents came, but other than the sense of heightened nerves in the room, no one said anything about it.

Emma took their coffee cups in the kitchen and called for Rishi.

"What's up?" he asked and then gave her a kiss.

"Hey, so does your brother know your parents are coming?"

"Yeah, why?"

"Okay . . . it's just that everyone is so calm."

Rishi turned and examined them. "I mean, what are they going to do? Should we all sit here and talk about how worried we all are? Why not enjoy the moment?"

Emma opened her mouth to protest. She was so used to everything being talked about. She'd therapized the loss of her family for years with countless shrinks, and with Jordana she'd hashed out everything until they couldn't even remember what had started the conversation in the first place. Maybe that was the whole reason Rishi had been keeping things quiet. Just one of those fundamental differences between their worlds. Why bother getting all worked up for no reason, instead of just seeing what happened? Maybe that was better than Emma feeling like she needed to know every little detail, dissect it, and then stress over it.

She could definitely have less of that.

Rishi's phone buzzed. "Well, things will get a lot less calm in a few minutes. My parents' train got into town, and they just got an auto to bring them here."

"What do we do?"

"Make them coffee?" Rishi shrugged.

"Right, coffee." Coffee was pretty miraculous, but she wasn't sure it was the poultice that would solve all their problems.

Rishi was talking to Sona and Sudhar in the main room of the apartment, and Emma had heated the milk until it was bubbling up into a boil, just as a knock sounded at the door. In that moment it was like everyone in the apartment held their breath. Only the sizzle of the milk could be heard as it leaped up the sides of the pan.

Rishi greeted his parents at the door. Emma joined him, and his parents looked surprised to see her. "Hello, uncle and auntie. Did you have a good journey?" Emma asked.

"It was good," his dad said. His mom nodded, that sort of side-to-side nod that acknowledged you.

Rishi grabbed the coffee from the kitchen and brought it out for his parents. "So, I have a surprise for you."

"Oh?" His parents both looked at him.

Rishi leaned over to Emma. "Can you go get Sejal?"

Panic leaped up in Emma's chest. She was supposed to carry the baby in? What the hell were his parents going to think? "Are you sure that's a good—"

"It's fine," he said before he started talking in Tamil to his parents.

"Oh-kaaaaay." She walked into the bedroom and picked up Sejal carefully. She'd really only held a handful of babies before. A cousin when she was ten, a niece and a nephew, and her coworker's baby who had been thrust in her arms. But looking down at Sejal, who stared up at her with big round Rishi eyes, she simply melted. Sona and Sudhar just smiled at her. Apparently they knew all about this plan, with Operation Baby Sejal as the cornerstone of the family win-over.

Emma walked back in, smiling as she savored Sejal's weight against her—until his parents jumped off the couch and started yelling at Rishi in words she didn't understand. Sejal started crying, and Emma froze as his parents scowled at her. "Uh? What's going on?"

"It's not our baby!" Rishi yelled back at his parents, shaking his head. "This is Sejal."

Emma tried to rock back and forth to calm the baby down while also holding her so his parents could see her face. "See? No red hair." She smiled. What else was she supposed to say? His mother's scowl returned. Okay, maybe that wasn't the best thing to have said.

"She's Sudhar's baby."

"He's just left her with you? Why?" His mother pushed herself off the couch and came to Emma.

"Do you want to hold her?" Emma held Sejal out. Rishi's mom's face had that dewy, melting quality like Emma's had probably had a few moments before. She took Sejal from Emma's arms, and the baby looked up at her grandmother. "She has eyes like Rishi."

His dad came up and stood next to his wife, smiling at the baby, but then he glanced back at Rishi. "What is this all about?"

"Well, I thought it was time we put the past in the past. Sudhar has a baby now, and Sona's family didn't intentionally try to ruin you. You should be grandparents to Sejal, and she needs to know the other side of her family. It's been too long, and I want us all to be happy together."

His mother's mouth hung open. "So you're talking with Sudhar? You are in contact with him?"

"Mom, I'm here."

Sudhar and Sona emerged from the bedroom, and suddenly it was like a cannon had been set off. Sejal was in Emma's arms again, and his parents were spouting off in Tamil, and even though Emma couldn't understand most of what they were saying, she could tell it was not good.

Sona came up to his mother and tried to touch her feet, her hands in front of her chest as if in prayer, and his mom actually stepped back so she couldn't touch her. She turned her attention to Sudhar and started railing at him, while Rishi and his father argued. Sejal started crying in Emma's arms again, and she was at a loss for what to do. Her eyes searched for Sona, who was crying as well, and Emma tried her best to keep the baby happy while Rishi's family sorted out this mess.

"How can you think that you can just have us meet, and all will be fine?" Rishi's dad asked.

"Appa, I didn't. I want you to talk!"

"We're done talking. Last time we talked, we lost everything. Everything!"

"Rishi, don't be a fool. I hope you didn't give them any money!" his mom said.

"Mom, please. Let's just all sit down and *talk*."

His mother shook her head like talking was the craziest thing ever suggested. "Rishi, who are you? What has happened to you? You cancel your engagement, you start talking to Sudhar, you think you want to be with this American woman! You've lost it!"

As they kept talking, all the warmth and joy that had briefly filled Emma from meeting the rest of his family started trickling out of her, along with the hope that Rishi's parents would one day accept her. The brief daydream of having a cute baby of their own with eyes like Rishi's vanished. She'd been trying so hard. She'd been trying to learn the language, cook his mother's recipes, wear the right clothes, and say the right things. And for what?

They'd switched back to Tamil and were still arguing. This was between them. It was a family issue, and clearly, Emma was not family.

She walked to Sona and gave Sejal to her. "I'm sorry, but I think I should go," Emma said. She didn't belong here with his family. They had enough to deal with, and apparently she was a component of why Rishi had "lost it."

"That's how they were to me too," Sona whispered back. And although Emma smiled and nodded, that was all she needed to hear. That's how they were to *her*? Sona, who was from the same country and the same religion? They hadn't gone to the wedding, and they didn't talk to her. Emma's fate was standing before her.

While his parents might have been tolerating Emma, that was really all it was. Tolerating. She was essentially waging another war within his family. Did she want to do that again to them? They were still fighting a battle from two years ago. Why was she doing this to Rishi? His parents would never get over this, or them.

She walked toward the door and put her shoes on. "Emma, what are you doing?" Rishi asked, coming over to her as his parents argued with Sudhar.

"I need to go. I don't belong here, and your parents clearly don't want me in your life. I'm just an added complication. You should just focus on your family." She opened the door, begging herself not to cry, although she could feel the tears resting on the surface, ready to cascade down.

"No, wait. Let's talk about this. My mom was just upset; she didn't mean what she said."

"Yes, she did." Emma shook her head and walked outside as his parents continued their rant. At least this time it wouldn't be about her.

"Just give me a minute," Rishi said, and he walked back to his parents, but an auto drove by. She flagged it down and hopped in before he could come back outside.

She felt increasingly deflated as the auto neared her home. Somehow, as she'd gone to Rishi's today, she'd been hopeful. Dressed the part of helpful girlfriend who tried to fit in with her boyfriend's family. She'd toted the baby around, trying to play parental reconciler. Who was she kidding? If they'd never accepted Sona, how would they ever accept her? And she was not going to be the one to keep Rishi from his family. If Rishi wasn't going to stop them from being together and wrecking what remained of his family, then maybe she was the one who would have to take the first step.

When she got home, she poured a glass of wine and sat down at her laptop. She looked at Maria's email again. The offer to go home. A promotion. A new life. A life where she wouldn't tear up the family of the man she loved. Maybe she'd start fresh and meet someone new. Someone whose family would accept her for who she was.

Because Rishi needed his family, and Emma wanted a family too.

CHAPTER 46

His parents were insane. That was the only way Rishi could rationalize why the two caring people who had raised three successful children could lose their minds and not listen to reason.

"Just stop it!" Rishi had never yelled at his parents so loudly, but he couldn't take it anymore. Yes, he was supposed to respect them, but he was doing all this because he respected them. Because he wanted to put back together the broken pieces of his family. Now Emma was upset and had left, and that was the end of any leftover facade he was still trying to maintain. "What is wrong with you? Don't you see that you're destroying your family?" That might not have been how he was supposed to talk to elders, but he'd had enough.

"He destroyed it first!" His mother pointed at his brother, like he was a toddler. "He married her and abandoned the family."

"No, he did not. He married the woman he loved. Just like I want to marry the woman I love. I know it was hard when you were younger to do that. Life was different. I get that. You learned to love each other. My friends, who also had arranged marriages, love their wives. Dharini, who will have a traditional marriage, will also love her spouse. But there are different ways to go about who you want to spend your life with. You need to understand that."

"Her family has taken our money," his dad said.

"My family also lost their money. Didn't you get our letters and emails?" Sona asked, her eyes still teary.

"Oh, we got them, but we tore them up and threw them in the dustbin." His mother, defiant, crossed her arms and sat back against the couch. He'd never seen her so determined to not listen to reason.

"Mom, maybe you should hear what they have to say, since you tore up all their letters." He was really trying to not roll his eyes.

Sona and Sudhar told their side of the story, both of them crying at different points, about how hard Sona's family had struggled, how terrible they all felt. How her uncle had disappeared, and when the family contacted the police to find him, he seemed to have just vanished. Rishi's parents seemed to calm down at that.

Rishi walked into the kitchen and tried calling Emma again. But she didn't answer. Again. She wasn't replying to his texts. Where was she? She'd just disappeared outside, and he didn't know what had happened to her. Had she just gone home, or had something happened?

He walked back into the hall and was shocked to see his mother crying and holding Sejal again. Sudhar had come to her side and had his arm around her, and his dad was leaning over, his finger in Sejal's pudgy fist.

Like a family portrait. But someone was missing.

"This is really great, but I need to go to Emma's house. She's not answering the phone or my messages, and I'm worried. She left here upset," he said, shooting his mom a look. "And I don't know what's going on."

"You really care for her, is it?" his father asked.

"Yeah, Dad, I love her."

His mom looked up. "I should apologize to her. I shouldn't have said those things in front of her."

Rishi thought only one of those things had been in English, but that had been enough. "You mean just saying those things in general, right, Ma? Not just in front of her? You know she's been trying so hard to fit in for you. She's taking Tamil from a tutor after work twice a week, she's trying to cook your recipes, and she's making every attempt to understand your world. You've done nothing to try and understand hers."

She nodded. "You're right. I should apologize to her. For thinking those things too."

"Well, maybe just apologize to her and say you appreciate her effort. You know she doesn't have her own family. It's really important that you accept her."

They nodded.

"Why don't we all go to her place?" Sudhar said. "I have a car, and if something happened, you won't be alone."

"Okay." Rishi tried not to overthink the implications of his entire family journeying to Emma's house. "Let's go."

They all piled into the small five-seater, with Sona clutching Sejal in the back, and drove to Emma's house.

{ /** *. // }

Rishi knocked on the door, his heart thumping in his chest. If something happened to her because of his parents' words, he'd never forgive himself. Car wreck, auto accident—whatever could have happened to her, he didn't want to think about it. But then the lock on the door clicked.

"Emma? Are you in there?" He pounded on the door.

She opened the door. "Hi. Why are you here?"

"What do you mean, why am I here? You scared the hell out of me."

"Rishi, I just couldn't. You're like my Achilles' heel. My weak spot. My . . ."

"What? Look, I'm sorry about my parents. They're crazy, but it's getting better, I swear."

"You always say that, but I realized today that no matter what I do, they're never going to accept me. I can dress, act, speak however I should, but they'll never just like me, for me." She shook her head.

"Yes, they will. They already do. My mom was just upset, and she's going through a lot."

"I can't do this to you. I don't want a life like your brother and his wife have, where their child is cut off from half their family, because I don't have family to give them. Or you. Don't you see, if I stick around and we're together, you'll regret it, and you won't talk to your parents, and even if you're pissed at them, I don't want any resentment between us, and . . ."

She rubbed at her eyes. Was she crying? "Emma . . ." Rishi took her hand. "I know you've been through a lot. I come with a lot of baggage, I guess . . ." He leaned in and wrapped his arms around her. "But I swear, it's better. It's going to be better. They've had a . . . what do you call it? A 'come to Jesus' moment." He inhaled the scent of her hair.

"How is that possible?" She stepped out of his embrace. "It's been, like, an hour. And maybe they'll be nice today or tomorrow, but when it comes down to it, would they ever accept me? No. Not in a million years."

"Just give them a chance."

"I did. I gave us a chance; I gave myself a chance. And nothing's changed. Why are we going to torture ourselves for the next seven months? If I leave now, you can pick right back up where you left off. Your normal life."

"Emma, this is my normal life. You are part of it."

"Rishi, is she there? Is she okay? I want to apologize." His mother's voice was almost at the door, and Rishi practically jumped away from Emma, but it was almost worth it to see the absolute shock on her face.

"What's going on? Is that your *mom*?" She wiped at her eyes, which were now betraying how completely freaked out she was.

360

His mother walked up to her doorstep from around the corner. "Emma! You are here. Listen, I am so sorry for what I said, and I appreciate all the effort you're putting into language and everything." And then his mom did an odd thing; she held her hand out to shake Emma's. Rishi tried not to laugh.

Emma took her hand and shook it limply in hers. "Thank you, auntie."

The noise of activity behind them grew as the sounds of Sejal crying and Sudhar moaning something echoed toward the house.

"What's happening? Is everyone here?" Emma asked. From around the corner, the rest of the family emerged in a great bustle, his dad trying to help Sudhar. Sudhar and Sona fussing over Sejal. Sejal crying as Sona held a bottle and tried to test it. His mother turned to try to also interject into the conversation.

"Oh, yeah, we all came," Rishi said. "Uh, can they come in, or is your place . . . ?" He didn't want to ask if she had bras hanging from the doorknob or if she had picked up all the condom wrappers off the floor.

"Uh, yeah, come in." Emma held the door open as the flood of people came inside, asking her if she was okay, Sona asking if she could change Sejal's diaper, his dad asking for the toilet. It didn't get more family than that. "I'll make coffee," Emma said. "Rishi, can you help me?"

He joined her in the kitchen.

"So, what's happening? A few hours ago everyone was about to kill each other, and now everyone's all happy and your mom is talking to Sona, and I just really don't understand."

"Oh, Emma, that's how family is. You know, it's always the worst before it's the best."

She opened her mouth to say something and then stopped.

"Are we good?" he asked. "You didn't answer my calls or anything, and I was really worried."

She wiped at her eyes again. "It's nothing. I was on my laptop and was about to do something stupid about work. You saved me just in time. Maybe life is like your family. Like you said, it always feels really bad right before it gets really good."

"It's true but totally unfair," he whispered and then kissed her.

The sizzle from the boiling milk caught them off guard, but Emma just laughed and turned the stove off. She said, "That was the last of the milk. Now who's saved the day?"

CHAPTER 47

The firecrackers had started going off at dawn. Actually before dawn. Emma was sleeping on the daybed at Rishi's parents' house when she woke up, and only the faintest hint of light was outside. The room was swathed in that predawn blue, and it would have been peaceful with the sound of birds in the trees, like the morning before, except then—BANG! Bang bang bang bang bang bang! Ten times over. Again and again. Like she was stuck in some machine-gun battle at the front.

The children of Madurai's war of Diwali. That's at least what she'd call it in her head.

"So you're up?" Rishi stood at the door, a cup of coffee in hand. He'd slept in his parents' room on the floor.

"How could I not be? So many firecrackers. What is it, five a.m.?"

"Oh, it's practically six." He sat down on the bed next to her. "When I was a kid, we used to have contests in this neighborhood to see who could get up earliest to light the first cracker. One year I was convinced that I needed to be it, so I woke up at three, snuck out the door, and lit like ten strands of them."

"What?"

"Needless to say, my parents were not pleased. I got no less than ten lectures on blasting my fingers off and how they needed to help me with the crackers."

"Wait, how old were you?"

"Eight maybe?"

Emma shook her head. "You were clearly crazy then, and you're crazy now." When they were at his parents' house, with all of them stuffed into just a few rooms, she missed this shared intimacy and these quiet moments. There was no privacy, no alone time, except before everyone woke up, or after they went to bed. Otherwise they had to take a walk or go to the store to catch some alone time.

Not that Emma minded the hustle and bustle of a family house. She'd grown up in a small house, then a trailer with her grandmother. There wasn't much room of your own, and somehow that forced intimacy created more intimacy. You had to know about each other's business. In fact, Rishi's mom had forced some kind of medicine down her throat that tasted like chalk and cumin so that she wouldn't get sick from eating all the food on Diwali; she'd literally made Emma open her mouth and had thrown it down her throat.

But she couldn't deny that somehow, it had made her happy. If Rishi's mom would stuff preventative medicine down Emma's throat, that must mean she liked her, right?

"What time are Sudhar and Sona coming over?" They had stayed the night in a hotel down the road. While there was no room for them in the house, Emma also wondered if they wanted to ease themselves back into the family. It had only been a few months since Rishi had gotten them all back together.

"Well, probably in a few hours. Do you want coffee? We can sit on the porch and watch the sun come up."

"Do I want coffee? Yes, what kind of question is that?"

He went into the kitchen and brought her one of the steel cups with a matching saucer. She always looked at it a little sadly. She might have grown used to everything else here, for the most part, but she still missed her twelve ounces of caffeinated bliss in the morning. This was like three or four at the most. At least she'd been indoctrinated into the steel-cup gang. No more of that chipped beige ceramic for her.

"I'm going to introduce your family to the American Big Gulp. I feel like if they saw that, then they wouldn't judge me for wanting a proper-size coffee to wake up."

"Well, if you hurry, you can have two before my mom wakes up and catches you breaking her coffee protocol."

"I have a feeling I'll need a few to get through today."

When Sona came over, she and Emma were relegated to vegetable chopping on the dining table while they were fed an endless supply of sweets and snacks. Dharini helped her mom cook, and in the small kitchen it was a tight fit with the both of them anyway. Neighbors kept bringing over small boxes of sweets and bags of savory snacks, and now Emma understood why her stomach had needed to be prepped for today. It was all about food. Cardamom-laced laddoos, big and orange and round. Squishy yellow and white sweets sitting in rose-scented syrup. Fried snacks that smelled like cumin and chili, coiled round like a snake. More snacks with peanuts and fried lentils that were a little too easy to stuff in her mouth.

"These would be so good with coffee!" Emma exclaimed to his mom as she sat in the kitchen cutting green beans into the tiniest pieces possible.

"Emma, you always want coffee." His mom shook her head and smiled.

"She's totally onto you." Dharini laughed.

Sona leaned over to her and whispered, "If you want my advice, compliment her. That's the best way to get more of what you want."

Emma smiled conspiratorially at her new friend. "Auntie, it's only because you make the best coffee. It's so delicious I can't stop myself."

Rishi's mom giggled like a schoolgirl. "Okay, okay."

Emma held up her hand to Sona in a high five. "It's true, anyway. She does make damn good coffee."

Sona shook her head and laughed. Emma was just glad they could all find this amusement in one another.

{ /** *. // }

After their feasting and naps, everyone put on the new clothes they'd bought for Diwali. Rishi had told Emma to get a sari, and they'd gone shopping the week before in Bangalore. He'd said the sari was a gift from his parents. They'd asked him to get her something since she was coming home. With Dharini's help, she had it pinned and tucked into place. It was turquoise with purple edging. A chiffon silk with embroidered peacocks on the pallu that hung down the back.

"There!" Dharini stepped back and admired her work. "You look very nice." But the way she had her hands clasped together, she looked like a proud mother on her daughter's wedding day. Speaking of which . . .

"Dharini, how's it going with you and the guy you've been talking to? The one the code pulled up? Um, Rohin, I think?"

Dharini's eyes turned a little fluttery. She had on a new silk salwar kameez that was purple and yellow and made her eyes sparkle and her skin glow. "Oh, Rohin? He is nice. I think I'm going to ask Amma and Appa to talk to his parents. I'm not in a rush, but I like this guy."

"Good. Rishi said he seemed like a nice guy too." He'd interviewed him for the role of husband to his sister, like it was a job. Although it was a job. A very important job. Dharini was a sweetheart.

"Yes, and he has the cutest dog." She held out her phone and showed Emma a picture of a golden retriever and a young man.

"Is that him?"

"Yes, but don't tell my parents."

Emma smiled. She had to wonder in this family if having a photo of a potential husband and his dog on your phone was that illicit. "My lips are sealed. But that is a very cute dog. I'm sure you'd make a great dog mother." That made Dharini laugh.

Emma made her way to the mirror that was propped behind the door and studied herself. She almost took her own breath away—was that even possible? While the sari had been a pain to get on, and she still didn't understand how six yards of fabric was the magic number for this garment, she felt more like a princess than she ever had. There was something magical about the sparkling sequins and the sheer extravagance of covering yourself in so much silk. She turned to check out the fanning peacocks on the back.

"Thank you, Dharini, for helping me. Really for everything." Because she had to wonder, if it hadn't been for her willingness to postpone her search for a husband, would she even be here today?

"Wait! One more thing." Dharini rushed over to the chest of drawers and pulled out a small box. She grabbed one of the small jewel bindis inside and stuck it on Emma's forehead. "Okay, now you're ready." She opened the door and Emma exited, nervousness pooling in her stomach. Would Rishi think she was trying too hard? Would his parents approve of the sari she'd picked out?

But as she walked through the kitchen, his mother stopped what she was doing and stared at her. "Hmm. Very nice." She nodded.

"Thank you. You look very nice as well." His mother wore a burnt-orange silk sari with maroon accents. Gold thread all over the place.

"Sudhar bought it for me."

This made Emma smile. But not as much as when Rishi came around the corner, wearing the dark-blue silk kurta she'd made him get and a pair of tan salwar pants. He never wore traditional clothes, and she'd begged him to get the shirt because his eyes practically glowed when he'd stood in front of it. She had to swallow. Was that drool? Was she drooling in front of his mom? So inappropriate! "You look nice." Although the word *nice* didn't cut it.

"So do you," he said. But his eyes looked thirsty. Like he was drinking all of her in. Apparently *nice* was the theme of the day. "Let's go outside."

Dusk had just settled, and fireworks lit up the neighborhood with bursts of sparkling light. More firecrackers popped in the distance, along with the occasional giant rocket that shot into the sky and exploded in crackling light-up glitter.

"Emma, you look just . . . damn. I don't even know what to say."

"I could say the same thing about you. Just damn." She laughed.

He circled around her slowly. "I want to just take the edge of your sari and spin you like a top until you unravel. It looks good on, but it's making me realize it's been four days since I've seen what's under it."

"Rishi, don't you think your parents would think stripping me naked in the middle of your street might be a tad inappropriate? I've been on my best behavior." They couldn't even touch one another for fear his parents would see, or the neighbors would see, and start some kind of crazy rumor.

The way he sighed and clenched his fists made Emma laugh. "I'll wait. But you're putting that back on when we get to Bangalore, and then I'm taking it right off."

"I'll have to take Dharini with me to put it back on me."

"Shhh." He closed his eyes. "Don't mention my little sister while I'm still living out the fantasy in my mind."

Sparks shot up into the sky. "These are so cool. When are we going to let off the ones we got?"

"Soon. I just wanted to do something first. With you. Alone."

Her attention came back to him. "Oh?"

He sighed, took her hands in his, and got down on one knee. "Emma, here, in my home, where you've been so patient and understanding about everything in my crazy family, I just wanted to thank you and say that the only thing that's missing from this crazy family is you. I love you. I think I always loved you but was so pissed off at you that I couldn't see it. But I've learned and I've grown with you, and I want to keep learning and growing with you for the rest of our lives. Will you marry me?"

Emma was speechless. The air sucked out of her lungs, seemed to shoot off into the sky. Tears came immediately to her eyes, and she started sobbing. All she could do was grip his hands tighter.

Rishi gently extracted his left hand and fumbled in his pocket. "Oh, shit. I forgot the part with the ring."

Emma laughed and wiped at her nose, and she was shaking so hard she almost fell forward, but he caught her. How could she be so happy that she couldn't even talk? Tears and laughter and an absolute unbelief that this was happening under this sparkling sky.

"Here it is," he said, holding it in front of his face. It was a simple ring, a cluster of diamonds set in bright twenty-two-karat gold. "It was my grandmother's nose ring. I had it set in a ring. For you."

Emma laughed. "It's perfect." He took her hand and slid the ring on. "I'm proud to wear something from your family on my hand. I know they've come a long way. Are they okay with this?" She didn't want to ask the question but had to.

"No. Actually, I drugged my mom, raided her jewelry box, and stole it so we could run away together." His squinted eyes told her exactly what he thought about her asking that question after all they'd been through. "What do you think?"

"I think that I can't believe this is happening." Her laughter caught in her throat. She was still shaking a little with joy. Could you shake with joy?

He stole a quick kiss in the street. "Now, who cares what the neighbors say? You're going to be my wife."

The word settled on her. Rishi's wife. Part of his family. She hugged him, dizzy with disbelief that this day had actually come. "Now we have a whole new reason to set off fireworks."

He took her hand. "Come on, let's go tell the family the news."

The family. Sister, parents, brother, sister-in-law—all of it hers now. They'd given her a chance. They'd accepted her. They'd trusted her love for Rishi.

And now they were her family too.

ACKNOWLEDGMENTS

Having the book in your heart published is a literal dream come true, and like many others have said, it takes a village. I feel blessed that my village is populated by the most amazing people I could imagine and want to thank them all—for supporting, inspiring, and guiding me along the way.

First, I need to thank my husband. You have been so patient when every weekend, I hide myself in my office and write, write, and write some more. Not to mention the encouragement you've shown me over the years as I tried to piece the right story together. At least next time we tell the story of how we met—the boy who grew up in the steel-factory town and the girl who grew up next to the oil refinery somehow meeting by luck in Bangalore—we'll have a new way to end the story!

I don't know if this book would have seen the light of day if it weren't for my awesome agent, Kimberly Brower. Thank you for taking a chance on me and *The Marriage Code* and believing in both of us! And thank you to the amazing team at Montlake, which has been phenomenal to work with. Lauren Plude, I'm so happy this story resonated with you and you decided to bring it to life! Selina McLemore, thank you for having a sixth sense for story and being a great editing partner. And to the copyediting team—Lauren Grange, Bill Siever, and Riam Griswold—thanks for having such a great eye for detail. And Micaela

Alcaino and Kris Beecroft, I'm so happy you captured Emma and Rishi's story in such a beautiful cover!

To help this story get to where it is today, I have a lot of my fellow writers-in-arms to thank. Melissa Marino, a million thanks to you, my mommy dearest, for plucking me out of the Pitch Wars pile and helping me get this book on its way! Julia Lee, #BestCritiquePartnerEver, thank you for reading this like a million times and giving me feedback when I most needed it. Sarah Schoenfelder Harrison, Carla Taylor, Gina Panza Woodruff, Kate Ramirez, Sofie Darling, and the Austin RWA critique group and crew—thank you for your input in the early stages of this; I cherish the writing community we have in Austin! And to my dear friends who love to read and adore India, thank you for sharing your perspectives on this story, especially Shandra Koehler and Leslie Ennis, who helped me see the direction this story should take from the beginning. And Frankie Ashok, I owe you margaritas for the rest of time for reading my manuscript and sharing your thoughts. But don't worry, we'll drink them together! Sudharsanan Sridharan and Dhivya VK, thank you for always responding to my random requests for programming clarity and last-minute emails about culture! Katie Webb Kneisley, you are always my model for any best friend character because you are just the best!

Thank you to my parents and family, who always encouraged me to write, even from a very young age—you always believed in me and fostered my creativity through every outlet you could think of! I still think of that "Being a Floor" poem you framed and hung in my room and my Snoopy journal I had as a little kid. If those didn't pave the way, I don't know what did!

And finally, this book would have never been possible if it weren't for my husband's amazing family, who opened up their arms to me and welcomed me into their world. I know it wasn't easy for them, but I have never stopped appreciating the warmth they've shown me, even when we're half a world away, whether they were being patient as I stumbled through understanding their customs or trying to wrap their heads around the concept of a girl from a small Kentucky town entering their lives. I'll never forget when we met on that first Tamil New Year and their son oh so cleverly left us alone for hours to force us to talk. Well, it worked. And is still working thirteen years later. Cheers!

ABOUT THE AUTHOR

Brooke Burroughs has worked in the IT industry for over ten years and lived in India—where she met her husband—for three. Burroughs has experience navigating the feeling of being an outsider in a traditional, orthodox family. Luckily, she and her in-laws get along well now, but maybe it's because she agreed to a small South Indian wedding (with almost a thousand people in attendance) and already happened to be a vegetarian with an Indian food–takeout obsession.